I T was Pauline's idea. When Jim told her he was going to Miami for a meeting of management personnel consultants, she'd said, "Let me meet you there. Do you realize that we've never spent the night together?"

"You're right," he said, feeling uneasy in spite of his pleasure with her.

He rolled over, wrapped arms and legs around her body and buried his face in her long hair. "Pauline, if I didn't have you . . ."

Responding to his embrace, she said, "Maybe I shouldn't argue with a professional word merchant, but you're using the wrong one here. I don't like that word 'have.' People ought to stop trying to *have* people."

"Now *you're* trying to tell *me* it's over . . ."

Pauline turned, pressed his face and lips against her small stiffening breasts. "Oh, no, I'd just like another word, Jim. What about *enjoy?* You can *enjoy* me—"

Pleasant Places

a novel by

SAMUEL A. SCHREINER, JR.

FAWCETT CREST • NEW YORK

PLEASANT PLACES

THIS BOOK CONTAINS THE COMPLETE TEXT OF THE
ORIGINAL HARDCOVER EDITION.

Published by Fawcett Crest Books, a unit of CBS Publications,
the Consumer Publishing Division of CBS Inc., by arrangement with Arbor House Publishing Company.

ISBN: 0-449-23769-9

Printed in the United States of America

10 9 8 7 6 5 4 3 2 1

To my daughters, Beverly Schreiner Carroll and
Carolyn Cort Schreiner, and my wife,
Doris Moon Schreiner,
who have made wherever we lived a pleasant place for me.

The lines have fallen for me in pleasant places;
yea, I have a goodly heritage.
—PSALMS 16:6

Chapter I

There are few sounds more frightening than the ringing of a telephone in the night. Jim and Susan Horner, struggling up out of a party-drugged sleep, each hoped the other would answer first. Since the instrument was on her side of the bed, Susan finally fumbled it out of its cradle. Her voice modulated instantly from a husky hello to a piercing, anxious, "Are you all right? Are you all right?"

Jim knew it had to be Betsy. Hand held over the mouthpiece, Susan said, "There's been some kind of an accident, Jim—she's at the police station." Then back into the phone, "Oh, no! Oh, my God! He'll be right down."

Already sitting up and wishing mightily that he hadn't had so much to drink, Jim was prepared for almost anything but what his wife said when she put the receiver back, "Sissy Stanton's been killed."

As the first wave of relief at knowing it wasn't Betsy subsided, another of shock tumbled over Jim's mind. Killed. Dead. At seventeen. Not two hours before Jim had been watching this girl dance with a less than fatherly interest that shamed him now. The Sissy Stantons of this world didn't die.

Nothing of his first reaction could be articulated. "How's Betsy mixed up in this?" he asked Susan.

"I don't know. She sounded hysterical. Oh, isn't it awful?"

"Yes, awful," Jim agreed, putting on the first pair of pants he could find which were somewhat inappropriately the bright red ones he had worn to the party. Summer heat still lingered at what the clock told him was 2 a.m., so he grabbed a blue sailing shirt with the club monogram on the pocket. He was out of the house and on his way within minutes.

During the dozen years he had lived there, Jim Horner had seldom experienced deep night in his hometown of

Worton. Like most everybody else, he was in bed storing up energy for weekdays in the city and weekends spent on the golf course, the tennis courts, the Sound. When the men of Worton gathered, glasses in hand, to denounce the rat race, Jim often wondered which part of their split level existences they were talking about. Their pulsating lives, his own included, were daily denials of death; the few obituaries in the weekly Worton *Record* tended to record the passing of some well seasoned parent who had the misfortune to be living with the children. As for the children's children, all of them in Worton had bright futures as a matter of course—and none more so than Sissy Stanton.

Now, however, as his headlights, feeble against the night, led him down the lonely, leafy tunnel of Bramble Road, Jim Horner found it necessary to realize that a death darker than the little death of sleep could come to Worton. It was more of a feeling than a thought. The snake of dread slithered up his back. Passing houses slumbering snug against his knowledge of disaster, he wished for light and sound. The small echoes of life—a forgotten garage light here, a left out dog barking there, the single bright eye in the black brow of a house beyond—seemed only to make matters worse. Yes, death could come even here in the night. And if it came to Sissy Stanton, it could come to anyone.

The party had been at Brookehaven, the estate of Sissy's grandparents, Judge and Mrs. Amos Hartwell Brooke. Some considered it one of the most spectacular pieces of real estate in America. Certainly, it was close to being the most expensive. As land alone, each of the twenty acres lying along the Connecticut shore of Long Island Sound were worth $50,000 and going up. God knows what they would bring, though the house, anywhere else, would be regarded as a monstrous reminder of a national failure in taste around the turn of the century.

The main attraction of the place was, of course, its seascape. From the house's deep porch, which had been designed in the days when corseted women and flanneled men believed in taking the sea air in rockers, or the tower that rose above the building's high, ivy-shawled shoulders, the eye could sweep the whole southern arc of the compass. Where the Sound widened to the east, there was a curve of horizon; across the way lay the long blue cloud of Long Island, and, to the west, on a clear day, the towers of Manhattan rose in silhouette like a mirage lying on the water. In the middle of the property, a tidal inundation, creeping around a rocky, pine-haired arm of land, shimmered like a jewel at high water and became a marshy showcase of wild fowl when the sea ran out. To the north, a century's stand of trees screened the land from any prying eye and provided a refuge for deer and raccoon and muskrat. Only on nights when a north wind brought the sounds of the New England Thruway over the trees like a reverse sigh of surf would a dweller in Brookehaven be reminded that he was living in the twentieth century and virtually in the midst of the world's largest concentration of human beings.

Finding the place was hard, even for invited guests. Along Soundview Road, little more than a macadam snake twisting through the forests of Worton's waterfront area, Brookehaven was marked only by two crumbling brick pillars through which a gravel lane, rutted by a thousand passages, vanished into the woods. Among the ragweed across the road stood an ancient mail box on which the weathered letters spelled BR OKE. It was believed that the judge left it unrepaired as a joke, for broke was the very last adjective any of his fellow citizens of Worton would ever have thought of applying to him.

Scarcely a week went by without a mention and usually a picture of Judge Amos Hartwell Brooke in the pages of the Worton *Record*. He was without question the town's first citizen. Although the judge part of his name was mostly honorary, stemming from very brief service on a minor court in his youth, the rest of his fame was clearly deserved. At the time of the party in his seventieth year, Judge Brooke was, among other things, senior partner in the legal firm of Brooke, Hilsman, Stanton and Seabury with offices in New York, president of the aptly named

Sound Realty Company, a director of County Bank & Trust Co., elder in the Worton Presbyterian Church, chairman of the Worton Fund Drive, past commodore and director of the Worton Yacht Club, charter member and director of Golden Hills (so named for the flaming fall maples) Country Club, a director of the Worton Library, chairman of the Town Republican Committee, member of the Harvard and New York Yacht Clubs. Such was the aura around the judge's name that Susan Horner sometimes tried to borrow reflected light by telling people they had bought their Bramble Road ranch house from the judge himself, even though they had seen only a saleslady in his office.

Brookehaven had been built by the judge's father, G. Hartwell Brooke, as a summer escape from the sweltering floor of the New York Stock Exchange. Thus the Brookes, who were into their second Worton generation, their family and most of their friends, stood serene above the tide of executive types swept in and out of Worton by modern business practices. Only the Italians, mostly huddled into an area of small lots north of the tracks, could claim as long a heritage; their fathers and grandfathers had been imported to build the railway. It was, in fact, a curious coalition of these two groups that resulted in closing Worton's gates to the suburban flood of the Eisenhower years. For different reasons, both groups disliked strangers and higher taxes. By strict zoning and winking at the unethical, if not illegal, practices of realtors, as the sellers of land liked to call themselves, they kept Worton a happily buzzing WASP's nest, tended carefully by Italian hands. A measure of how well this worked was what had happened to Worton's one experiment in veterans' housing—a couple of streets of Cape Cods built to sell at around $10,000 to take advantage of the G.I. loans after World War II. With attics expanded and cellars converted to play rooms, they turned over at $26,000 and again at $40,000 plus and the end was not in sight. Even the Horner's $52,000 ranch on Bramble Road would now go for eighty or more with the new wing. Jim almost had to laugh remembering how a fellow in the office whistled when he said he was moving to Worton and told him, "Worton? Boy, when you get there, you've got it made. There's nowhere to go but down." On the contrary, everything—and everybody—in Worton seemed always to be going up.

For the Horners, the unexpected invitation to Brooke-haven had to be considered a move in the right direction. Though the Brookes were the kind of people you nodded to in church or at the club, their secret and stately lives moved in an orbit far above the Horners'. But a clue as to why they had been included lay in the invitation itself. The envelope was addressed in a finishing school hand to Mr. and Mrs. James Gilbert Horner and Miss Betsy Horner. Inside a simple but elegantly engraved card said: "For Sissy. Cocktails and buffet 7 p.m. Friday, July 17. RSVP Brookehaven."

"Well, obviously, the Brookes want Sissy to get to know some of the young people around here," Susan said with a pleased smile. "I think you should be flattered, Betsy."

"Why me? It's grotesque. Sissy Stanton doesn't even know I *exist*," Betsy said.

"How can you say that? You knew her in junior high before she started going away to school, didn't you?" her mother said. "I think it's nice that you were included—that we were included. I've always wanted to see what Brookehaven looks like. Haven't you, Jim?"

Jim Horner wasn't so sure. Judge Brooke and the people around him, like Sissy's father, Bill Stanton, had a way of looking right through him on the club dock or the station platform. To be noticed now on account of his daughter wasn't especially flattering. He rather agreed with his daughter's reaction, but he had more sense than to say so. Fortunately, Betsy saved him from answering the question at all.

"You go ahead, but I just *can't* go," she said. "I have a date with Ron."

"Ron who?"

"Ron Dominick."

"I don't think I've ever heard of him," Susan said.

"Oh, mother, he's just *the* quarterback on the team. This is the first time he's really noticed me . . ."

"But who are his parents, I mean—"

"His father's the police captain. He . . ."

Susan's face took on a stubborn look. "Well, you are going to this party with us, Betsy, whether you like it or not. We couldn't afford to send you away to school, but I think it's time you got to know Sissy and her friends. After all, you did meet most of them at the club when . . ."

"Unfortunately . . ."

Jim winced. It hurt him more deeply than he liked to admit that Betsy, and now her younger sister, Julie, refused to get involved in the club's sailing program where both he and Susan thought they could take renewed advantage of living in a place like Worton and acquire the friends the cost of living there afforded them. Whatever his own reservations, and he had them, he knew that Susan saw in the Brookehaven invitation a chance to justify some of that cost, and perhaps she was right. Certainly, Betsy was getting her own way far too much these days. Jim decided to back Susan this time: "Get this straight, Betsy—we are all going to that party, and that's the end of it."

Susan gave him an appreciative smile, but Betsy said, "Oh, Daddy . . ." and ran out of the room to hide the shame of tears.

As it turned out, Betsy had managed to get her way anyhow. Halfway along the rutted road through the Brookehaven woods, a dark, muscular young man in jeans and a T-shirt stenciled "Win with Worton" stepped in front of the Horner car. He gestured toward a little field off to the right, then stuck his head in Jim's side of the car. "Would you mind parking over there, next to the Cadillac, sir? A station wagon will pick you up. . . . Oh, hi Bets! See you later, huh?"

"What's that all about?" Susan wanted to know as they pulled off into the parking lot.

"That was Ron," Betsy said. "When he heard I was going to be here, he took a job . . ."

"Well, you're not going to run away from this party . . ."

"Oh, no, Ron wants to stay as long as he can. They're paying him a dollar an hour, and he figures there'll be tips."

The station wagon bumping down the lane to pick them up was an old "woodie" from the thirties. Jim Horner could remember admiring it at the last antique car parade when the judge himself had sat proudly behind the wheel, nodding his magnificent mane of white hair at the little knots of spectators lining the way. Driving now was a retired policeman whose face the Horners had often seen at school crossings in recent years. "Evenin'," he said when the Horners got in. "Nice evenin'. Like I said to the missus, the weather's always nice for the judge's parties. I said to the missus Judge Brooke must have some influence up there."

The Horners laughed politely then, but the remark now lingered in Jim's mind as a terrible irony. Certainly, everything about Brookehaven as they came upon it spoke of an "influence up there," a long and continuing blessing upon the Brooke family from a kindly divinity. They were let out of the wagon under a *porte cochere* with arching brick columns that looked as if they had been scuffed by the hooves of nervous horses. The door stood open on a wide central hall in which the twilight lingered like an echo on polished dark panels and beams. As they passed through toward a bank of French doors leading to the porch and lawn where the party was in progress, Jim noted the stiff-collared portrait of what must have been G. Hartwell Brooke above the fireplace on one wall and more hull models of sail boats than he had seen in the New York Yacht Club on another. Doors stood casually ajar to vistas of mellow antique furniture, warm Oriental rugs, crystal chandeliers, long gold mirrors, great Chinese temple jars.

On the porch, they paused in a kind of wonder. Brookehaven's view was at its most magnificent. The westing sun, reflecting itself from the mirror of the pool at high tide, tinted everything, even the people gathering under a large tent set up on the lawn, with soft gold. "My, how lovely!" Susan said.

"Yes, wouldn't you know—pure gold. Only Judge Brooke could afford it," Jim said.

"Hush, Jim, somebody might hear you. This *is* a big party. You'd better stick with me; I don't think I'll know a soul."

"That will make two of us," Jim said.

"Three," Betsy added.

"Oh, you'll be all right," Susan said. "I think I can see some of your friends now. Isn't that Jane Atkins over there . . . and Francy Adams?"

The girls she was pointing out were part of stiff, little knots of young people gathering around a bandstand at one end of the tent where a small combo was testing the sound system with squeaks and squawks from their electronic instruments. At the other end, the older people were assembled by a long bar made of planks thrown across sawhorses and converted to a kind of elegance by a white banquet cloth and silver vased flowers of the season. At the corner nearest the house, a group of Brookes and Stantons stood in an informal receiving line. As soon as he saw the Horners, Judge Brooke detached himself and came forward, both hands outstretched, as if he were greeting his oldest friends.

A large man, the judge moved with more vigor at seventy than most men achieve at forty. Under his wavy white crown, his flesh glowed in the golden light with the residue of a lifetime of good living. He fixed them with an unguarded gaze from wide blue eyes that were accustomed to pleasant scenes, and his voice rang with the comfortable note of unquestioned authority.

"Well, Jim Horner—and you must be the Susan Mrs. Brooke has been telling me about," he said. "She said you were the cleverest young woman in the church guild, but she's been holding out on me—she didn't tell me you were the prettiest. And this is Betsy? Like mother, like daughter. Well, you know everybody I'm sure. The bar's over there—plenty of coke and punch, Betsy, and there will be music soon . . ."

Spying another arriving group behind the Horners, the judge deftly handed them on to his wife, Helen, and the Stantons. Like a tree that had always been shadowed by a great oak, Helen Brooke seemed small and delicate, almost withered. Not so their daughter, Marion Stanton, who had inherited her father's frame and voice but had unfortunately grown to resemble the horses she kept at Golden Hills Hunt Club. Shaking hands with Marion and her husband, Bill, whose prematurely gray hair contrasted oddly with a face that still had the look of a spoiled choir boy, Jim Horner wondered how they had managed to produce Sissy. Perhaps she was a throwback to her grandmother, Helen Brooke, who had clearly been petitely pretty as a young girl. In any case, he would never forget the vivid beauty of this girl, the kind of girl who seemed only to grow in the rich soil of a place like Worton.

Thinking back on it, Jim had a hard time deciding just what it was that so impressed him about Sissy Stanton. It was more than looks, though the blue black of her very long hair and straight brows, perhaps like the judge's before he went white, was dramatic. It had something to do with her bearing; she displayed her pride of position with that unconscious grace you see in well-bred animals. Jim could remember looking at pictures of Sissy at various ages jumping horses at the Hunt Club, and, as he held her firm hand and almost stammered under the level appraisal of her dark eyes, he had the feeling that already at seventeen she had her life as expertly controlled as her horses. At that moment, no known hurdles would seem too tricky for this girl who, obviously, had everything.

Like everybody else, Jim and Susan Horner headed straight for the bar, leaving Betsy to drift alone toward the forming and reforming eddies of young people. Jim felt sorry for her, because even adults seemed to find social life in Worton intolerable without the universal lubricant of liquor. At every gathering arriving guests appeared to have the sands of the Sahara in their throats; nothing but the most strangled conversation was possible before these dry passages were damped with drink. The party at Brookehaven was no exception. Women stood nervously along the fringes, trying out smiles, while their husbands pressed up to the bar behind which two sweating black men splashed liquor into glasses as fast as they could. The man pushing in beside Jim was easily recognizable as the newly installed president of one of the world's great oil companies; the Worton *Record* pictured the arrivals and promotions of the town's executives even more faithfully than the engagements and marriages of their daughters. Jim stuck his hand out. "Mr. Avery, I'm Jim Horner."

"Horner? Oh, you must be the fellow who cleaned up in the Lightnings last Sunday?"

Foolishly pleased, Jim grinned and said modestly, "Just lucked out, I guess . . ."

"Not at all. Not at all. I was on the committee boat with the commodore, and we were all saying how smart you were to take that tack inshore."

Suddenly Jim's pleasure was replaced with an even more foolish resentment, a reprise of the feeling he had had when he learned that the Averys were admitted to the club within months of arriving in Worton. He had been passed over two years running—despite his expertise—before he forced himself to ask for the votes of, at best, casual acquaintances on the membership committee. Yet here was Avery, not six months in town, riding on the committee boat with the commodore and dining at Brookehaven. Of course, he was a neighbor of the Brookes, having bought the old Atkins place on Soundview. Still, Jim looked closely at Avery to see if he could detect what it was that lifted such a man above the ordinary struggles and obligations of his fellow citizens.

Nothing apparent. Short, apple-cheeked, sixtyish, with neatly trimmed white hair spread thinly across an expanse of scalp and eyes owlish behind thick glasses, Avery could have passed for a department store Santa Claus on leave. He wore only the protective feathers of his fellows—brass buttoned blazer and flannels—another matter of unease to Jim who had noticed that the Madras jacket that went well on Bramble Road seemed out of

16

place in Brookehaven; besides himself, only the youngsters gathering at the other end of the tent were so gaudily adorned. It wrenched him back to those first few days at Harvard when, walking the Yard in the double-breasted suit that had looked so good in the Emporium, he wanted only to run and hide. And, like those casually dressed upper classmen, the properly suited Avery had managed in a sentence or two to establish his position as a man at the top, patting a promising struggler on the head.

When he got back to Susan and handed her a drink, Jim said, "Well, I knew we shouldn't feel so flattered. Even the Averys are here. They haven't been in town six months . . ."

"I think they have a son the age of Sissy," Susan offered.

Smiling at faces they recognized from the papers or the platforms of important meetings in town, Jim and Susan drifted aimlessly, amusing themselves with whispered comments about the other guests. "Oh, look over there—that must be Charles Church's newest wife. I think it's disgusting," Susan said.

"Why? She looks pretty good to me."

"You would say that. She was a model, you know. But she can't be more than twenty-five, and he's sixty if he's a day . . ."

A model. Jim took another look. Pauline Church was tall, half a head taller than her shaggy gray husband, and made to look more so by the mass of mahogany hair she had twisted and piled and pinned with a kind of turban that matched the flaming pink of her shirt. The shirt itself was slashed daringly close to the waist . . . partly because a girl so thin had little to hide? She wore a long white skirt which turned out to be pants when she moved. Her face with its high cheek bones and sharp chin seemed a practiced mask until you noticed the eyes—lights danced in them like the warm reflections from a Christmas tree ornament. Altogether a different kind of creature than Worton was used to, but then Charles Church, a many-wived painter who actually voted Democratic was an eccentric who owed his invitation to Brookehaven to the

17

fact that his family had preceded the Brookes in Worton by ten generations.

Susan took Jim's arm. "For heaven's sake, stop staring," she said. "There's Dr. Wolfe sitting all alone over there. Let's go talk to him."

It was a relief to see a really familiar face. The Rev. Dr. Wolfe, their pastor, was nursing his phlebitis by sitting on one of the row of funeral chairs set out along the edge of the tent. When they joined him, Wolfe held out an empty glass and asked, "Mind getting me another, Jim? My leg, you know."

"Not at all, Andy; I'm almost dry myself," Jim said.

Pushing into the bar again, Jim noticed more wild jackets like his own around him. They were covering pink-cheeked boys who were carrying away rum and cokes and gin and tonics. Even though one of them conceivably might have been going to his own daughter, Betsy, Jim thought little of it just then; he was, in fact, thinking how nice it was to have a regular fellow like Andy, a fellow who kept his glass full along with everybody else, for a minister. Andy's actual first name was William, but he preferred W. Anderson Wolfe, perhaps considering it more theological. His sense of the community had enabled Wolfe to quadruple his Presbyterian congregation until they outnumbered the Episcopalians and Catholics. When the wife he brought with him from Pittsburgh died, Wolfe had the good sense to marry a homely but enthusiastic member of the choir named Audrey Atkins, thereby securing for himself a share in a fortune such as few ministers enjoy. As an Atkins by marriage, Andy Wolfe was as comfortably at home in Worton as his most distinguished elder, Judge Brooke. Thin, tall, patrician, his hair silvering nicely with wealth, Andy just by his presence could make parishoners feel they were in the right church. Too bad about the phlebitis, though it did seem an honorable result of standing so long in the pulpit.

When Jim got back with the drinks, he found a group around the minister. One of them, Howard Hilsman, a handsome, fortyish man with the build and grace of a tennis player, a law partner of the judge, was holding forth. "I'll tell you it's going to ruin the party. I've advised Sibel to go it alone. If he does, he'll be the only Republican elected in Connecticut, and then he can call the shots."

"Howard, you're sounding like the Eastern Establishment Goldwater's always talking about," Wolfe said. "You know I think the people out there have an instinct. I think they want Goldwater because they feel it is time to have a firm hand to put down all these riots and . . ."

"My God, you can't be serious, Andy. What if this fellow drops the bomb? Or do you think it is our Christian duty to cook the gooks?" The man challenging the minister was Dr. Floyd Shepherd, an internist who had made a name for himself in town more for his politics than his medicine. By the simple strategy of being one of the few declared Democrats, he had managed to be elected to boards where minority representation was required by law and was now a selectman. A small, cheerful, chubby man who spent more time on the course at Golden Hills than in the office, Dr. Shepherd teased the Republican establishment often for the sheer fun of it, and everybody knew it.

"If you'd spend some time in church instead of on the golf course, Floyd, you'd never ask such a thing," Andy said.

"*Touché,*" the doctor said. "Let's talk about something more cheerful. Did you see what Tony Lema did at St. Andrews? You've played that course, haven't you, Andy?"

"Yes, a long time ago when I was studying in Scotland . . ."

"I thought so. Well, I was over there last summer, and you know that gully in front of the eighteenth green they call 'the valley of sin'—well, Lema was smart enough to drive just short of it . . ."

Taking Susan by the hand, Jim moved away; golf bored him mightily. In any case, conversation was becoming a strain against the electronic vibrations issuing from speakers fixed at each corner of the tent. The song was one Jim had come to recognize and hate from constant repetition in his own house ever since the Beatles had been set loose like a plague upon the land by Ed Sullivan—a wail called "I Want to Hold Your Hand." Still, it was stimulating to watch the kids dance. They were doing something Betsy called the swim because of the way they moved their arms, and, feeling his own body want to respond to the rhythm, Jim resented for a moment their youth and freedom. Dancing was something he'd never had time to learn, growing up in Starkville, and on the occasions since when the experience had been thrust upon him as a social price he had to pay he was awkward and miserable. But he suspected he at least could have gotten away with what these kids were doing—jiggling and bumping without fear of grinding a partner's toes.

"There's Betsy," Susan said. "See, she *is* having a good time."

It certainly appeared that way, and Jim was prompted to dwell once more on the perversity of children, or was it just girls, or was it just Betsy. Down one minute, up the next. In that way, as well as in her fresh clean looks, she took after Susan. At least she didn't suffer from the sick shyness that had tormented his own youth and now apparently that of his other daughter Julie. She was, in fact, jerking, twisting, swimming with such enthusiasm that she and the bobbing skeleton of a boy opposite her were driving the other young people into a ring of admirers around them. "Who's the boy?" Jim asked.

"Tim Hilsman—Howard Hilsman's son. You had him in your Sunday School class, didn't you?"

"Well, I wouldn't recognize him now—he's grown a foot."

"He's been away to Lawrenceville . . ."

Soon the dancing had resolved itself into a kind of contest between Betsy and her partner, and Sissy and a boy named Ben Adams, grandson of the famous Dr. Adams, whose father had fallen on such hard times—through his drinking, everybody agreed—that Ben had to go to the local high school. Sleeker and more finely coordinated than Betsy, Sissy in Jim's eyes turned the dance into a sexual invitation rather than a dance exhibition. It was this vision of a sinuous Sissy, so alive in her tempting movements, that haunted the dark as he now drove. And it was this dance, Jim remembered, that had caused Betsy and Sissy Stanton to team up later to persuade their parents to let them go off with the boys when the party broke up.

Though he knew where it was, Jim Horner had never been near the Worton Police Station. In fact, the only time he had ever exchanged words with a Worton policeman was when he would engage one or another of them to drive the family to the airport. Then they seemed nice enough, jovial fellows. In uniform, however, they were known for their efficiency. After dark especially, people who by the look of their car, the color of their skin, the cut of their clothes, the length of their hair, obviously didn't belong in Worton were picked up or sped on their way. Except for an occasional break-in on or near the Post Road or a moving traffic offense, the Worton police blotter was almost free of crime, and Jim, along with his fellow citizens, found this comforting at a time when large sections of American cities were beginning literally to burn in the fires of hate.

Stepping into the bright light of the station, Jim found himself momentarily confused by the scene. People were milling around under a high, railed desk behind which a sergeant sat with his ear clamped to a phone. The first face Jim recognized belonged to Howard Hilsman. A look at the usually polished lawyer made Jim realize how he, too, must appear. Hilsman's hair was tousled, his eyes red, his chin stubbled, and a gap in his open white shirt revealed that he had hastily pulled clothes over his pajamas. "What happened?" Jim asked him.

"We're not quite sure yet," Hilsman said. "The sergeant's still on the phone to the hospital. We know Sissy's dead, and the Dominick boy she was with is in a coma. They hit a stone wall on that curve in River Road. In one of the Stanton cars."

"What are the other kids here for?"

"The police rounded them up on the beach at Adams

Point," Hilsman explained. "Seems they all went there after the party with six packs they stole from Brookehaven. Sissy and Ron went off alone and . . ."

Hilsman shrugged helplessly. Betsy, who had spotted Jim near the door, came running over. One look at her told him it was no time for fatherly talk, or any talk. Instead, he just put his arms around her and held her close in a way he hadn't since she was a small baby whose shattered world could only be mended by touch. Her body against his felt reassuringly warm against the chill shock of the night's news. He found himself offering a silent prayer of gratitude that *she* was alive and vowing to protect her against all those threatening forces that had seemed to crowd the dark he'd just driven through.

"Are there any charges?" Jim asked Hilsman.

"Not yet. Of course, the possession of alcohol by anyone under twenty-one is an offense, but I think all the police want is information. They're not even sure who was driving," Hilsman said. "Look, the sergeant's off the phone."

Putting the receiver down, the sergeant passed a beefy hand over his bald head and red face in a gesture of bewilderment. "That was Lou—Captain Dominick," he said. "His kid's still out cold. Look, I'm gonna send you all home with your parents, but don't go anywhere because we're gonna want to talk to you tomorrow."

As they moved toward the door, two young men, one with cameras draped from his neck, pushed through them. Jim could hear one of them saying to the sergeant, "C'mon, Grimes, give. This is a big story. Who are all these kids?"

"None of your business," the sergeant said. "You'll have to wait to talk to the chief."

"Have a heart, Grimes," the young man said. "The New York papers will be all over this in an hour. Give us a break."

Impelled more by instinct than conscious thought, Jim shielded his daughter's body with his own and hustled her out the door. Hilsman met them in the parking lot. "I'm afraid that young fellow's right," he said. "The press, especially the New York types, have always resented us for what we have here. They'll blow this thing out of all proportion. But I guess you ought to know that. You're in the business, aren't you?"

"In a way, but a magazine's different. . . . You may be right, though," Jim said.

He realized with somewhat of a shock that he hadn't once thought of the events going on around him as a story. The stuff he put through his typewriter in the antiseptic offices of *News* magazine high above Manhattan happened to somebody else. Jim had been considered lucky, had considered himself lucky, to be tapped right out of Harvard by recruiters from *News* on the strength of his Phi Beta Kappa key and his record on the *Crimson*. He had skipped the usual apprenticeship of the police beat. A highly paid verbal technician, Jim spent five days of every week turning the raw reports that poured into *News* into polished and palatable paragraphs. It didn't matter very much whether he was dealing with a hideous crime or a natural catastrophe or an illicit romance or a political summit meeting, the technique was the same, and so was the result—as coolly artful a reproduction of life as could be seen on any film. Real life—well, life—for Jim Horner began when he boarded the train for Worton and he did not think of the corporation chiefs and celebrities who lived there so much as newsmakers as neighbors of whom he was still in awe.

With this additional worry on his mind he turned to Betsy in the car and asked, "What happened? Do you know?"

"I don't want to talk about it, like, it was too terrible . . ."

Jim reacted with automatic and, he realized, idiotic parental irritation. "I wish you'd stop saying *like* . . ."

As soon as the words were out, he regretted them. It was the sort of thing that always seemed to come up between him and Betsy, to make communication difficult. It was a kind of natural habit that had started with "Get your fingers out of the butter" and "Stop picking your nose" and broadened to the more subtle lapses in language and behavior as the girls grew. Much better just to hold them, as he'd done with Betsy back there in the station. Now their fragile bond seemed broken again.

"I'm sorry, I didn't mean that," he went on. "You've just got to tell me what you know so I can help you, Betsy."

"You can't help. Nobody can. Like, it was all my fault . . ."

"Your fault? How do you mean? I thought they were alone . . ."

"They were. Like, it's . . . oh, you wouldn't understand . . ."

"Why not? I can't if you don't tell me . . ."

"Oh, it's no *use* . . ."

They were pulling into the driveway. Maybe Susan would have more luck, though Jim wasn't too hopeful. Lately, Susan's dialogues with Betsy had been even more difficult than his own. They often hinged on things beyond Jim's awareness, such as the state of Betsy's hair or nails (which she chewed) or her relationship with some other youngster Jim didn't know.

Susan met them at the door and took Betsy in her arms. "Oh, Mom . . ." Betsy said, and they both began to cry. Not for the first time, Jim Horner envied women their tears.

Chapter II

When people asked James Gilbert Horner what brought him to Worton in the first place he tried to sound what he hoped might pass for casual, even sophisticated, about it. It was watching old movies on TV, he'd say. In those flicks, Christmas in Connecticut was depicted as the ultimate good life. As to the selection of Worton from among the many communities stretched out along the tracks of the New York, New Haven and Hartford Railroad, it was just a matter of where they found the house, he'd explain. But it was a good deal more, and he knew it. Worton was surely where America was going, and James Gilbert Horner was determined to go with it.

Jim Horner was, without apology, a dreamer of the American dream, confident that he would awaken one day in that state of ultimate grace prepared for all good men who did the right thing. He had little reason to be otherwise.

On the top of the upright piano in the living room of the little clapboard house in Starkville, N.Y., where Jim Horner had grown up, there sat the silver-framed photograph of a smiling man in uniform around which the whole household moved in reverence. Hardly a day passed without Jim's mother pausing before it, dusting it, rearranging it to catch a better light. Hardly a sentence passed her lips without some invocation of its subject—"As your father would have said. . . . Your father would never have done a thing like that. . . . If your father had lived . . ." And Jim's mother did not worship alone; to nearly everyone in Starkville, Second Lieutenant Frank Gilbert Horner shone in memory as a hero whose untimely death when his plane disappeared in the jungles of Burma cut short the town's most promising career.

This somewhat mythological view of Frank Horner was not without a fair amount of founding in fact. Jim

himself, fourteen at the time, could remember his un-
alloyed pride when his father, though overage and bur-
dened with three children, insisted upon enlisting even
before war actually broke out. Nobody could question
his motives. Frank Horner's pro-Allied editorials in the
Starkville *Times* were so eloquent that many had been
reprinted around the country and were now gently yellowing in a scrapbook on the other end of the piano top—
positive proof that, had he lived, he would have realized
his manifest destiny to become a famous writer. Whenever
Jim's ambition wavered, his mother would flick her eyes
toward the scrapbook and say, "You have it in you to
finish what your father began, if you only try."

Jim and his two younger sisters and perhaps even his
mother never knew the man behind the myth that was
Frank Horner. Frantically busy as a small town editor-
publisher with literary aspirations, Frank Horner had been
more of a presence than a person in his own home; to his
wife, who believed in him, he was all promise. As in the
case of most myths, he was cut off before either the
person or the promise matured. She never learned the real
facts surrounding his death, for in its infinite wisdom the
War Department did not release details of the accident in
which Second Lieutenant Frank Horner, co-pilot of a
DC-3, was involved. After consuming an untold quantity
of Scotch, he and his buddies had been taking a group of
Army nurses joy riding out of Chabua in an effort literally
to scare the pants off them. Frank Horner's death was not
the stuff of legends, and legends were needed in 1944 to
inspire the people back home; accordingly, the War Department sent through a posthumous Bronze Star award
to Starkville, prompting a civic rally in the hero's honor.

From then on, of course, much was expected of young
Jim Horner. Fortunately the boy was up to it, and he had
every kind of assistance from a mother to whom people
generally referred as "a saint." Frank Horner's sacrifice in
going off to war was matched by her own in getting an
emergency job teaching English in Starkville High School
and journeying to Albany nights to earn her certificate. To
help, Jim peddled papers mornings, worked in a drug

store afternoons, looked after the younger girls and generally became "man of the house." If he missed the fun of being young, Jim was scarcely aware of it, because with her rather humorless faith in the promise of life, Emily Horner kept the boy's eyes fixed on the future. Aside from drawing inspiration from his father's heroism, Emily used everything she came across in her work—aphorisms from the *Reader's Digest,* uplifting lines from the Bible, appropriate stanzas from the poets—to instill into Jim, and to a lesser extent the girls, her absolute faith in the reward, both spiritual and material, of work, thrift, sobriety, chastity, faith in God and country. Her favorite quotation was: "Lives of great men all remind us/We can make our lives sublime/And, departing, leave behind us/Footprints in the sands of time."

To get the footprints into the sands of time, it was necessary to have them going in the right direction. In Jim's case, this meant through Harvard. Although the little Finger Lake college, where Frank and Emily Horner had met, might do for the girls, it would not be adequate for Jim. "Your father always used to say that he would never have been stuck in a backwater like Starkville if he had gone to Harvard, and now I am sure he was right," Emily said. Jim didn't question the wisdom of his mother's ambition for him; indeed, he plastered his bedroom walls with Harvard banners, followed the misfortunes of the Crimson on the gridiron every Saturday and hungrily pored over the course catalogues and other literature he got by writing away to Cambridge. The practical problems in the way of reaching this goal were formidable: Jim would be the first Starkville High School graduate ever to aspire to Harvard, and he didn't have a cent. Lacking the size and time to become an athlete, Jim, with his mother's coaching, took the route of scholarship. Working together, they entered every available essay contest inside and outside Starkville; one emotionally patriotic manuscript issuing from the Horner house, entitled "Death of a Father," brought in a $500 prize from the American Legion and national recognition. By the time Jim Horner stood up in that awful suit that cost his mother more than any clothes she'd ever bought for herself and delivered the valedictory at Starkville High School on, in truth, "How to Win in Life," he had a scholarship to Harvard in his pocket.

It worked out that there was quite a step between getting from Starkville to Cambridge and becoming a Harvard man. A scholarship did not provide enough spring to make that step, and Jim Horner soon found himself involved in waiting on tables at the Student Union, clerking in the library, writing for the *Crimson* and later stringing for the metropolitan papers—anything within his power to stay alive. To most of his classmates he remained one of those nice enough, grim-faced young fellows who seemed always to be taking the paths through the Yard at a worried trot. To himself, Jim Horner was hero in all the fables and fictions he had absorbed—the young man making it against all odds, a close approximation to a latter, late-in-the-day, Horatio Alger, and though there were dark nights when he agonized over not being invited to join any social organization, spring afternoons when, running from one job to another, he envied the lucky ones sailing on the sparkling Charles, Saturdays when he had to slam his door and mind against the tantalizing tinkle of ice and girlish laughter coming from other rooms, he was on the whole not unhappy. He expected there would come a time when all those privileges the other students had inherited would become his by right of hard and good work—a more honorable, indeed American, route. In this conviction he was supported not only by all that Emily Horner had built into him but by the assurances of a girl he had met at a Wellesley mixer by the name of Susan Smith.

Jim and Susan were brought together when they were almost forced to start talking to each other because they were both haunting the punch bowl for the same reason: to avoid the embarrassment of dancing. Within minutes, they were on a kind of common ground. He had been too busy making his way, and too shy besides, to learn to dance, and she had been too involved, ironically, with music. Her ambition seemed as vaulting as his: she was going to become a concert pianist; she had come to Wellesley to get a "well rounded" education before launching on her career.

That ground covered, they were soon off into other territory. Unlike Jim, Susan had no economic prod nor any shining ideal to follow to account for her drive. Her mother was a plain housewife—not homemaker, housewife—her father a prosperous pharmacist on Long Island. It was flattering that Jim claimed he wouldn't believe her now, but it was the honest truth that she had taken up music in compensation for being an unlovely child; it was one way in which she could please. By the time some curves appeared and her skin cleared up, she was already committed to it, as her father never tired of pointing out, for countless thousands of depression dollars had been invested and no sensible person would throw such a beginning away. As long as she continued to please, her father spared nothing to open doors for her, even the one at Wellesley to which she, like Jim, was the first student from her high school to be admitted after her father pledged the funds for a small musical scholarship. The only thing she really deplored was her name: Susan Smith seemed too common for a very special person.

Once they started going steadily together, Jim and Susan made what everybody called a "good team." More gregarious, she dragged him to parties; more studious, he forced her to work. She made him stay awake through long sessions of Bach and Bartok, and he read to her out of the poets. Each felt complemented by what the other didn't have. To her, Jim's incisiveness, his drive were all male; to him her vacillations and vanities and sometimes silly fears were all female. Used to the shield of a strong, stern father, Susan positioned herself behind Jim in the same way; nearly unmanned by a strong, stern mother, Jim felt new juices rise and stir in the trusting warmth emanating from this pliant girl. He'd see that her life would be as good as, no better than, it had always been, and she would reward him with adoration. As long as they had each other, what else could ever matter?

By senior year, they were so close that, in the words of

29

the apostle, they had to marry or to burn. No other arrangement occurred to them since Emily Horner had made clear by example and Biblical quotation that sex was to be confined to marriage, and Susan was quite simply a "good girl," the product of a home where her doting and pious parents weighed their gifts of love carefully against her small offerings of goodness. Ironically, both families objected; each thought that marriage would jeopardize the careers for which they were preparing the children.

In Susan's case, the families were right. When Betsy arrived, Susan found little time for the piano. Julie's advent so crowded their small New York apartment that they actually had to sell the instrument to make room for another crib. It was then that the Horners began thinking about a house in the suburbs, though it was the dog that sent them actually looking.

Having a dog was one of the several pleasures of boyhood that Jim Horner had to forgo to make things easier for his working mother, so he knew nothing about them, and cared less. Not so Susan. A series of poodles had taken the place of brothers and sisters in her home; they even slept in her bed until she was old enough to worry about the smell. Though Susan conceded that an apartment was no place for a dog, she'd always stop and pat them in the street and sometimes talk wistfully about having one again. "When I was ugly, only my dogs loved me," she'd say. Jim simply ignored such talk until one day when he was searching the streets of Manhattan almost desperately for a present that might do something for what the doctor called a common case of post partum depression.

Common or not, Susan's fits of anger, weeping and withdrawal were causing the first real tension in their marriage. Among other things, she refused to sleep with Jim. Being patient through the last months of her pregnancy with Julie, as he had been before with Betsy, had its own reward, he kept telling himself, in contributing to the bringing of new life into the world. But when *after* Julie's birth, Susan kept putting him off, he grew irritable and properly lustful. More than once he thought of patronizing the call girls he was always hearing about around the office, especially when he was staring into the empty night after losing another argument in bed to Susan's "How can you ask this soon, so soon after all I've gone through to have your child . . .?" If she didn't want to get pregnant again she could use a contraceptive, couldn't she? The doctor who came up with the diagnosis wasn't much help. "Time will take care of it," he said, "but you might speed it along with a little courting—you know, presents, things like that."

Jim couldn't afford jewelry. Window-shopping his way home one night, he paused in front of a lighted pet shop window. In the midst of a tangle of puppies rolling on a mat of shredded newspaper was a red and white basset hound. It looked exactly the way Jim felt. Slow on its stubby legs, awkwardly falling over its long ears, the basset was obviously a fellow in need. It was also, Jim thought, exactly what Susan needed. He bought it on impulse and carried it home in a swath of towel.

It worked. The evening was the first joyous one in months in the Horner apartment. Since it was close to Christmas, the dog, a female, was promptly christened Noel. Betsy rolled with it on the floor like another puppy, and they could hardly get her to bed. Susan kept saying, "She's darling, Jim. Oh, I just love her!" When finally the children were asleep and the puppy locked away in the kitchen, Susan came over and sat on Jim's lap and kissed him and said, "You know, you really are a sweet guy to think of a thing like that after I've been so mean to you." With a restraint he found difficult to muster, Jim caressed the almost unfamiliar contours of his wife's body lightly until she finally said, "What are we waiting for? Let's go to bed."

When things were right, as they were obviously going to be right this night, Jim often felt that God had rewarded him too soon by giving him Susan. She was what people called "damn nice looking." She had sandy hair that curled just enough that she never had to do much with it, wide-set clear blue eyes, round cheeks, a dimpled chin.

Even after Julie, her figure was so regular in every way that she could step into a size nine right off the rack. If one adjective would suffice to describe the effect of Susan Horner, it might be *clean*. In bed she was warm and soft and yielding, seeming to delight in his exploration of the curves and hidden places of her body. At such times Jim found he couldn't get enough of her, and they would often spend hours in sweet and lazy play before coming together in mutual explosion. With the hunger of long months of fasting to satisfy, Jim was especially anxious to prolong this night, and he wanted, too, to reawaken Susan so that she would get over her depression. Susan was whispering, "Jim, oh Jim, it's so wonderful. . . . I'd almost forgotten," when suddenly she stiffened and shoved him away.

"What's the matter?" he asked.

"She's crying; can't you hear her?"

"Who's crying?"

"The dog . . ."

Jim, who had been deafened by the pulse of passion in his ears, could hear now a low moaning sound. "Well, let her cry—"

"We can't, she'll wake the children. The poor thing's lonely, she misses the other puppies. Go get her and we'll keep her in bed with us."

"Now?"

"The dog was your idea," she said, suddenly cold. "Either you get her, or I do."

Susan was slipping back into her peevish mood, and reluctantly Jim got up and brought the dog to her. Jesus, women. . . . With the beast cuddled against her, where Jim so badly wanted to be, Susan soon slipped off to sleep, leaving him to struggle alone with the ache of frustrated desire. He was a long time falling asleep himself. Soon after he finally did, Susan was shaking him awake again. "She's got to go out. She's down there on the floor running around."

"How the hell can I go down to the street in my pajamas?" Jim grumbled. Nonetheless he grudgingly started to get up, only to say, "Shit," appropriately, as it turned out, as, putting a bare foot on the floor he slid and landed with a crash against the wall. Susan sat up and turned on the light. The place was a mess and the dog, standing on her ears, had the contrite look of a fool who had painted himself into a corner. Susan started to laugh.

"What's so goddamned funny?"

"You. You and that dog. If you could only see your face; you look just like her now." Contrite, Susan went on, "I'm not laughing at you, Jim. But I'm glad I can laugh again. I'm sorry, I . . ."

"Well, thank God for something . . ."

"Maybe we can thank him for something else, too," Susan said. "I think he's telling us it's time to move out to the country where we can find a place that's good for dogs and kids. . . ."

Method in her madness . . . ?

Worton, of course, was more than a place for dogs and kids. Jim had been hearing about it ever since he'd come to New York. It was the sort of place where the men in corner offices lived—exclusive and expensive. Nobody on the editorial floor of *News* would ever think of living in Worton, but they spoke of it with a kind of envious awe, and when some of the young advertising salesmen moved there it was taken as proof positive that they made a hell of a lot more money than editors. All of this talk intrigued Jim, the more so when, almost coincidental with their own decision to move to the suburbs, he was assigned the job of writing a series for *News* on the great suburban boom.

To get a literal overview of his subject, Jim hired a small plane at Westchester Airport and had himself flown in a series of circles ever widening from a midtown Manhattan core. "A great way to look at real estate," he told Susan.

Mostly, though, he found it depressing. Below him for endless miles around lay communities of houses as similar as upturned boxes, each centered in its own green square with only here and there the shining mirror of a backyard plastic pool to vary the pattern. Then out over Connecticut the trees began to thicken so that only the major arteries —the railway, the Post Road, the Thruway, could be seen.

Jim thought they'd overrun the suburban circle and suggested to the pilot that they turn back.

"Hell, that's the best of the lot down there," the pilot said.

"What's that?"

"Worton."

"Really? But there aren't any houses," Jim said.

"Oh, they're there all right—under those trees," the pilot said. "You see, the kind of people who live in Worton are smart. They don't even want God to see what they're up to."

Jim remembered that back in the office. He took a chance and put the pilot's quote into his story, and Harry Margolis, his managing editor who didn't live in Worton, thought it was so great that he promoted Jim to senior editor on the spot. The little raise the promotion brought him together with a loan from Susan's father who was even prouder of having grandchildren than a pianist for a daughter and wanted only the best for them made it just barely possible to swing the $52,000 house on Bramble Road. Though he perfected the self-conscious comeback about watching old movies to turn away office envy, Jim was secretly damn pleased to have shoehorned himself into "the best of the lot." Susan was ecstatic.

Why not? Worton was far enough out the line to have what the real estate agent who showed them around called "the feel of New England." A number of the stores on the Post Road and quite a few houses were actually pre-colonial; even new houses like their own sat on property marked off by stone fences centuries old. Sociologically, except for a very small area inhabited by service and trades people, Worton was distinguished by wealth. Solid wealth. Perhaps naturally through friendship and shared interests, bankers, brokers, corporation executives, lawyers, doctors, engineers, accountants found their way to the place. If there were men from the communications industry or show business they tended, like the other few from *News,* to be account executives, advertising salesmen, producers. The kind of people whose names were in the papers or faces on the TV screen were more likely to gravitate to Westport, which liked to think of itself as "the Athens of Fairfield County." In addition to being a haven for the people who were making it, Worton was a shelter for those who had it made, the nameless clippers of coupons on second and third generation wealth who, wherever their origins, preferred to live in a state without income tax. The result was a community singularly devoted to the protection of property and privacy. A place where it was possible to feel safe.

Although there were times when Jim wondered whether a news magazine writer who was never likely to make that kind of money really belonged in Worton, he never doubted that it was surely right for his wife and children. The schools were good, the nights were safe. That sort of thing was worth a passing fair amount of sacrifice. Besides in those placid years of The Fifties, when the future looked so certain, it seemed almost unpatriotic not to mortgage it, and cheerfully, to give your loved ones the certified good life. He would never forget his first Saturday morning in Worton, standing at the open front door watching Betsy with Noel shuffling behind her set out on an excited exploration of the acre of swampy woodland they could now call their own. Susan had come up behind him, squeezed his waist. "Oh, Jim, this *is* what you've really been working for, isn't it?"

"Yes, sure, I guess so—it's what you want—"

"Oh, it is. Everybody says the schools are so good and . . . well, just wait till we get to know people, it'll be perfect."

Getting to know people turned out to be a little more difficult than getting to Worton. Though they didn't seem to be unfriendly, the people of Worton were uncommonly *busy*. During the week when the men were away twelve hours a day the women were off with their children to various activities; weekends they all seemed to labor together like peasants on their acreage or play furiously at some club or other. The one time they seemed to gather was on Saturday nights, and in those early months Jim and Susan Horner sometimes piled the kids into the car and while out for a drive couldn't help noting the beckoning lights of houses surrounded by a shoal of cars. Actually Jim didn't mind not knowing anybody. A loner by nature, he was quite content after the kaleidoscopic experiences of going daily to the city to spend weekends hacking the woods away from his door and, hopefully, making love to his wife. But after the first flurry of feathering her new nest, Susan's spirits began to sag during long days of seeing only small children and an aging hound whose idea of excitement was dragging her heavy body from one patch of warmth to another as the sun moved around the house.

Finally one Sunday morning Susan shook Jim awake with the exciting pronouncement, "Let's get up and go to church."

It was a startling suggestion. Until then, religion was a subject the Horners never discussed and seldom practiced; they took what they had of it for granted. They were not unbelievers. They were solemnly married in the big Methodist church where Susan had sung in the choir and acted as substitute organist her senior year in high school, mostly to get a chance to learn the instrument. Somewhere on one of their shelves was the gold-starred Bible Jim had been given for immaculate attendance in Presbyterian Sunday School. They usually went to services Christmas and Easter; like as not, they would be visiting one or the other of their parents' homes where church-going was a ritual as regularly observed—and about as meaningless in their view—as teeth brushing. In view of all this, Jim asked, "Why?"

"Oh, I want to see some adults for a change. Maybe we'd get to meet some of them."

Jim wasn't anxious to give over the lazy Sundays he had come to appreciate to more scheduled activity. "Let's compromise," he said. "Let's just drive around and take a look. We don't even know which one we want to go to."

Susan was smart enough to accept what was offered, and it turned out to be rather fun. There were, as Jim observed, "almost as many churches as liquor stores" in Worton, and it took them most of the morning to get around to each of them either before or after a service since they were more interested in observing the people coming and going than the buildings. They paid little attention to the Catholic Church; its rites were alien to both of them. Fittingly for New England, the two oldest churches were the Congregational and Episcopal. The former was housed in a stark colonial building; the latter in a squat, ivy-covered Gothic edifice that might have been transported stone by stone from the English countryside. The Methodists, who operated what amounted to a cathedral in Susan's old town, held forth in what looked like a storefront in Worton; the Presbyterians were in the process of erecting one of those modern structures that could pass for a skating rink or a bowling alley except for the cross on top. But buildings don't make a church, and the Horners were most impressed with the sense of movement around the Presbyterian church a-building. The faces in the congregation seemed younger, and there were so many of them that, the day being pleasant, they spilled over onto the steps of the old building they were using temporarily and listened through the open door. Susan thought the young women, casually hatless and wearing lumpy Peck and Peek tweeds and good shoes, were her sort, and she felt Jim with his crew cut and black horn-rimmed glasses—what she called his "sincere" glasses—would fit too. "If you had your dark suit on, you could walk right in and take up the collection there," she kidded.

Within weeks, the Horners became part of what was considered to be a heartening national statistic of Eisenhower's America, an almost phenomenal rise in church membership. Even secular magazines like *News* were beginning to speculate that Americans were returning to the God of their fathers. Some felt that much credit for this movement should go, like the credit for making peace, to the old general in the White House. Although his religion had been vague as his politics until 1952, Eisenhower was now as openly Presbyterian as he was Republican. Others credited men like the Reverend Doctor Norman Vincent Peale whose message of positive thinking harmonized so beautifully with the tonic chord of prosperity or the Reverend Doctor Billy Graham whose flashing good looks and massed choirs outdrew professional football in stadia around the country. Whatever the reason, going to church was as much the right thing to do in Worton as in Keokuk, and the Horners soon had a sense of moving among good people, particularly when they were invited to somebody's house for a drink after a meeting of the church's young married group. That night they knew they were on their way to becoming a part of the community too.

It was better that way, Jim finally agreed. Parties gave Susan something to look forward to and talk about afterward. He usually ended up drinking too much at them in an attempt to loosen his tongue, since he found he had little to say to his fellow Wortonites, male or female, once they'd exhausted the state of the crab grass. Susan was luckier; she always had the inexhaustible subject of children. Once when he was complaining about this to her, Susan had suggested, "Why don't you take up a sport or something, like sailing?"

Increasingly Jim was sensing that the bond between the people they were meeting was less work than play. Indeed, for the men at least, the daily ordeal of having their bodies hurtled back and forth to the city was made endurable only by the fact that they could shuck their gray flannel suits for shorts and T-shirts and the sport of their fancy as soon as they reached Worton. Most of them seemed almost to change personalities along with their clothes, and it was very hard often to recognize the man you met in the hardware store on the station platform. In Worton gatherings, men seldom mentioned what they did for a living, as if it were almost shameful, but talked incessantly about how they played. It was, Jim guessed, what was meant by the good life and came naturally to gentlemen who had spent the long golden afternoons of youth in sports they took as seriously as their studies. Bringing only a Phi Beta Kappa key to Worton, Jim decided, was almost as bad as wearing the wrong suit to Harvard.

Susan had been more intuitive than she knew, too, in

mentioning sailing. Raised on *Kidnapped* and *Moby Dick* and *Captains Courageous,* in a landscape unrelieved by any body of water larger than a farm pond, Jim had incurably romantic feelings about the sea. Almost from the day they moved to Worton, Jim had developed a yearning to get out on the water. When he was out alone on Saturday errands, he would often drive down to the boat yards and docks in Stamford or Norwalk and just wander around, listening to the great yachts creaking restlessly in the confinement of their slips and daydreaming like an adolescent, as he admitted to himself, about making a "voyage." He never shared this yearning with Susan—after all, what with the mortgage payments he could barely meet and the pediatricians', dentists', veterinarians', hardware, liquor and utility bills he had to juggle and defer, he knew he couldn't afford to do anything about it.

As the early Worton years wore away, Jim Horner had begun to doubt that he would become a hero after his father's fashion after all. The children had come along to exempt him from war service, and, although he had made a few passes at the great novel he was supposed to write, he was really too tired at night and, once their social life resulted in community involvement—he was pressed into teaching Sunday school, calling on neighbors for the community fund, acting as block captain for the Chamber of Commerce's dogwood planting program—too busy weekends. There were some, of course, who would say that he wasn't doing badly by half. His name up near the top of the masthead could be seen by millions of *News* readers every week if their eyes were good enough to unscramble very small type. It earned him an invitation to address the graduating class of Starkville High School as a distinguished alumnus and thereby go a long way toward repaying his mother's devotion. It was enough, too, to bring an income of about $12,000, give or take a little depending on bonuses—good by the standards of his profession and promising to get better if, as seemed likely, he would one day succeed Harry Margolis. Still, nearly everyone in Worton just had to be making more. "They can't all have inherited it," he told Susan, who said, "Why not? Remember when Daddy passes away even we are sure to get something." So there was that too.

Except there wasn't any challenge. . . . he often felt as benumbed as he did driving down the middle of a superhighway, just waiting for his destination to arrive. A man against the sea. . . . well, that was a dream of a different color. But first you needed a boat to get there.

Not long after Susan put his dream into words, Jim Horner got a break. He had been assigned to write the lead story in *News* about one of those messy and menacing things that kept happening out there in the world beyond the snug boundaries of Worton—the trouble in Little Rock. Summoning all the right perceptions he'd learned at his mother's knee, Jim viewed Little Rock not so much as the first act of a dark drama but as a triumph for democracy. "Nowhere but in America would the President use troops to secure the rights of the nation's most down-trodden minority," he wrote. He knew he was doing, in terms of *News*'s policy of comforting its readers, a good professional job, and, more than that, he wanted to believe that he was right. So he wasn't too surprised when Harry Margolis called him in just before train time and said, "Himself Upstairs thinks your thing on Little Rock is the best writing since the Sermon on the Mount. So he wants to break all tradition and give you a byline. I told him it ought to be the reporters out there dodging bayonets who get the credit, but that's not the way he sees it, so you're in luck. Oh, and yes, he told me to give you a five grand raise. Now, take off. Go out and get drunk, get laid, get . . ."

Though he had no intention of getting drunk, or laid, Jim did think the occasion at least called for riding the bar car home. He was excited enough that he wanted to talk, and the bar car was the only one in which he was sure he wouldn't interrupt somebody's evening nap or concentration on the newspaper. Luckily the first face he saw was a faintly familiar one. It belonged to Kevin White, a man with whom he had occasionally ushered in church. White's passion, as he knew, was sailing. When they'd stand around out on the church steps killing time before the services started, White would always be speculating about wind and weather for the afternoon races.

Whether White would know him was a real question. Probably he'd recognize Jim's face but wouldn't remember the name. The vice-president of a large New York bank who had married in his sophomore year at Princeton a girl on the outer fringes of the Rockefeller family, and was required to leave college as a result, White lived in a house near Golden Hills that looked like a set for *Gone With the Wind*. Except for dutiful visits to church, he moved exclusively in yacht club circles, and the names of men who didn't sail were very likely to escape him. Usually Jim felt diffident about thrusting himself upon the Whites of Worton, but the fame and increased fortune he was about to receive gave him courage. Getting a paper cup of bourbon, he sat down beside White. "Evening. James Horner. How goes it?"

"Can't complain," White said. "Except about this goddamned air conditioning. It only works in the dead of winter."

"True. . . . how's the sailing going?"

"Great. . . . do you sail?"

"Well, I've been thinking about it now that I've got the place in shape, and my wife will let me out of the house."

White laughed in appreciative acknowledgment of the Worton man's common bondage to property and wife. "Well—uh, is it Jim?"

"Jim."

"Sure, Jim. . . . Well, Jim, I'm always looking for crew members. Maybe I could give you a call?"

"Well, I'm not very experienced. I'm afraid I'd be . . ."

"Gotta learn some time. It's just a Lightning . . ."

"I'm not a club member. I . . ."

"Makes no difference for crewing. If you get into it, maybe you'd like to join sometime."

Like a lucky gambler, Jim felt the elation of having hit a true winning streak. First the good news at the office, and then this. He couldn't imagine a better way to start realizing his dream of sailing than to learn from White.

As the train screeched into Worton, it took considerable effort for Jim to summon the Ivy League casualness he had finally only learned to manage *after* Harvard, and even then with unease. "If you can stand a rank beginner, please call me," he said.

"I will," White promised.

A measure of the double life Jim was leading by then was what he said to Susan when he got into the old Chevrolet beside her. Almost gone from his mind was the byline and raise he had planned to crow about. "Guess what?" he said. "Kevin White's going to ask me to sail with him."

"Not *the* Kevin White?"

"The very damn same . . ."

"Jim, that's wonderful. Remember I told you that you ought to take up sailing, but I never thought with Kevin White . . ."

"Listen, when I learn how to do it, we might get a boat of our own—oh, I almost forgot, I got a raise today—"

Jim knew it was going to be a night to remember when his wife rewarded him with an affectionate pat on the inside of his thigh. "Oh, it does sound like fun," she said. "Aren't you glad, Jim, that we came out here?"

That night Jim was indeed glad. Through eyes lensed with euphoria, he saw Worton's charms anew. Hidden under its trees, Worton was in a different country altogether from the Little Rocks of the world and far more than a couple of train stops away from the clattering confusion of New York. The people who had planned and protected it had known what they were about, by God, and he was grateful to them for it. Hell, admired them. . . . And one day he and Susan would really be one of them, be part of them. One day, if he worked hard enough and kept on his toes, they too might get one of those places with nothing but the challenging sea for their front yard and a yacht large enough to go out on it. And that day their children would bless them for bringing them up in beauty and tranquillity. Damn right. Believe it.

As Jim stepped into the house that night, Noel greeted

him at the door. He patted her graying head and said, "You like it here, too, don't you, old girl?" She responded with the resonant moan by which bassets seem to remind all within hearing that life is really a trial. Jim Horner was in no mood to listen.

Chapter III

In households all over Worton, ranging from Brookehaven's brick castle to the funeral parlor on the Post
Road to the narrow clapboard home of Captain Louis C.
Dominick north of the tracks, lights burned through what
was left of the dark on the early morning of July 18.
Anxious parents were questioning the children they had
brought home from the police station groggy and dis-
oriented from drink and shock. A young mortician sadly
prepared the body of Sissy Stanton for burial. But in the
wood and leather confines of the study at Brookehaven, a
council of war was taking place. Gathered there were
Judge Amos Hartwell Brooke, his son-in-law William
Chesney Stanton, the dead girl's father, his fellow attorney Howard Morton Hilsman, and Worton's chief of
police, Nicholas J. "Nick" Santori.

Judge Brooke had called the meeting almost as soon
as he learned of his granddaughter's death. Perhaps nobody, not even her parents, was as shocked and saddened
by the news as the judge. Because of her beauty and
spirit, Sissy was the only one of his grandchildren in whom
he had any faith. Whenever he thought of the future, of
the care and keeping of Brookehaven and of Worton
itself, he didn't think of Marion—or his son about whom
he rarely spoke—he thought of her. The party had been
his idea, a way of reintroducing this sparkling grandchild
to the community after so many years away at school.
And lately he had begun to think about rewriting his will
to leave everything in trust to Sissy. In fact, he was thinking about that in bed after the party when the phone had
rung.

At first the judge couldn't, wouldn't, believe what he
had heard. His son-in-law Bill, on the other end of the
line, was drunk as usual and had probably got the whole
story mixed up. But when Howard Hilsman called from

the police station, he had to accept the facts, or what facts were then known. Judge Brooke was not a hand wringer; even in the face of such shattering news, his instinctive reaction was to act. After instructing Howard to round up the people he considered immediately important, he got out of bed, dressed carefully and walked across the hall to Helen's bedroom to tell her as gently as possible. But she was sleeping so soundly, he decided to wait until morning. Maybe, just maybe—but no. In addition to being a man of action, the judge was a realist. It had happened all right, and the problem now was how to deal with it.

In his study, the judge turned on the lights, rang the butler awake on the intercom and told him to bring whiskey and coffee and sat down behind his desk to stare at his favorite picture of Sissy. Hair flying, slim body tensely erect, she was clearing a high hurdle on her favorite jumper. How in God's name could a girl like that get mixed up with some common Italian kid? And how could she be drunk, as the reports had it? He was so sure that Sissy, despite her worthless father, was all Brooke. He himself had had hair and brows like that when he was young—and the same total disregard for physical danger. The whole thing was a dreadful nightmare. Well, there was no bringing Sissy back, and the judge felt that no amount of time left to him would be enough to cure the ache of personal loss. Still, he'd have to try. As a beginning, he took the picture and hid it at the bottom of a drawer, then tried to force his mind to concentrate on what could be salvaged out of this misery.

Judge Brooke was particularly disturbed about what Howard had said about the newspaper men. If they blew this thing up into a scandal, there was no telling what might happen. Practicing law, like sitting on the bench, was for Judge Brooke little more than a cover for the means by which he had doubled and tripled the considerable fortune he inherited. The Brooke money came from trading in land and the money loaned on land in the town of Worton, and the judge knew more than most that the values of anywhere from ten to twenty thousand a property above similar places all over the United States came from Worton's carefully nurtured reputation for serenity and security. It was the deliberate doing of the judge and his father before him, and, as his father was fond of saying, "Amos, no place is better than the people who live in it. A place is like a barrel of apples. If you don't cull out the rotten ones, the whole thing will go bad. So you've got to do that with people too." Over the years, the judge had learned to do that, even to the extent of banishing his own son. The cornerstone of the community's reputation was the reputation of its first family—the Brookes. The only reason he hadn't done anything about his son-in-law Bill Stanton was that, up to now, he had found the fellow useful to him, but tonight he was beginning to think it might have been the mistake of his life.

When the men gathered, Bill Stanton was out of his mind not only with drink but with grief. "That son of a bitch wop kid, I could kill him—go right down there and kill him—"

"Bill, watch your language," the judge said. "You're forgetting that Chief Santori's our guest here, our friend."

"Oh, that's all right, judge. I guess I'd say some crazy things too if—"

"Bet your ass you would," Bill Stanton said. "He killed her, killed my Sissy . . ."

"Now, Mr. Stanton, I've just been to the hospital," the chief said. "The boy's still in a coma, but Lou—that's his father, Captain Dominick—is sure the girl—I mean, Miss Stanton—was driving . . ."

"How can he know that?" Hilsman interrupted. "My son Tim tells me they were all sitting around drinking beer at Adams Point and Sissy and this fellow Ron just disappeared into the dark. Nobody knows who was driving."

"Well, Lou's pretty sure from what the officer responding to the call told him about where the bodies were found. Miss Stanton seemed to have been thrown out the left side, and besides young Dominick had a beer can crushed in his hand . . ."

"Jesus, Santori, what kind of evidence is that?" Bill

Stanton said. "You've got to know anybody can drive with a beer can in his hand. I've done it thousands of times . . . you have, too . . . You won't get away with this, goddamn it . . . I'll . . . I'll . . ."

"Bill!" The judge's voice still rang with the note of command even though his features sagged from weariness and his gold-hued skin had ivoried with shock. "Stay out of this, I'll handle it. Now, Nick, I'm sure you can appreciate what it would do to all of us if Sissy were falsely accused of causing this accident and of . . . of intoxication . . ."

"Sure, judge, but Lou Dominick's sorer than a boil. You know his son, because of his football and all, stands a chance of a full scholarship to college, and a thing like this . . ."

"Well, if that's the problem, Nick, I'm sure it can be arranged," the judge said. "As a matter of fact, I'll personally see that the boy gets to college. It's a promise you can take to Captain Dominick. You have witnesses here, and I'll have Mr. Hilsman draw up papers tomorrow."

"Are you out of your *mind*, Dad?" Bill Stanton said. "You can't—"

"Bill, I told you to let me handle this," the judge said. "Now, Nick, what do you say?"

Chief Santori scratched his stubbled chin and ran a nervous hand through his white, crinkled hair. It seemed an injustice of life to be faced with something like this just months short of retirement from a perfect, thirty-year career. "I don't know, judge. Lou's really wild. He's talking about charges of serving liquor to minors . . ."

Judge Brooke was truly startled; such an affront had never occurred to him. "Against me?" he asked.

"Well . . ."

"It's absurd, Nick, and you know it," the judge said. He picked up the phone and held it out toward Santori. "Here, call the caterer now. He'll tell you how many cases of coke and soft drinks those kids drank. Oh, I gather they did make off with some beer but . . ."

"Now, it's not me I'm talking about, judge, but Lou. He isn't thinking straight right now."

"Well, he'd better start thinking straight. He does want to replace you as chief, doesn't he?"

Santori, a practical man, stood up and started moving wearily toward the door. "I'll do what I can, judge."

"Wait a minute. What are you going to tell those reporter fellows, Nick?"

"Well, judge, I hadn't thought much about it. Just answer their questions, I guess."

"That won't do," Howard Hilsman said. "You've got to have a story and it has to be convincing. As a matter of fact, chief, maybe you could use some help on this. You're not used to those sharks from New York. Why don't we get that fellow Horner over here?"

"Jim Horner? Why him?" the judge asked.

"Well, he's in the business, has some sort of job on *News*."

"Oh, I didn't know. I thought he . . . Kevin White told me he's been cleaning up in Lightnings and . . ."

A very strange sound, somewhere between a laugh and a sob, came from Bill Stanton. "Oh, my God, I don't believe it. Sissy's dead and you sit there being surprised just because a man's a sailor he can't be in the magazine business . . ."

"You know damn well what I mean," the judge said, "but maybe he can help. Give him a call, Howard. Why don't you have some coffee or a drink while we're waiting, Nick?"

When Hilsman finished his call and reported that Horner was on the way over, Stanton asked, "What if this Horner wants to get the story himself?"

"Oh, I'm sure he wouldn't do that," Hilsman said. "His own kid's mixed up in this. Anyway, I agree with what the judge was saying. Horner is in the club now, he seems to be okay—went to Harvard, I believe . . ."

This was reassuring to Judge Brooke who, despite his show of friendliness earlier in the evening, really didn't know Horner at all. In making up the list for Sissy's party, they had pretty much gone by the club rosters, picking people who listed children Sissy's age. The judge guessed he'd seen Horner around the church some, and, as a sailor himself, he was impressed with what he'd heard of the man's racing record. And then, of course, a fellow Harvard man. Probably Horner worked on the business side of the magazine. The writing kind, the kind who made a living from telling other people's secrets, couldn't afford to live in Worton, thank God, except for Fielding Small, the novelist, whose father had been in oil with old John D. and had left him half a million or more. You couldn't call Dan Parker who owned the *Record* any kind of a newspaperman or writer since he was, sensibly, interested in running the thing at a loss to promote his politics.

"Well, let's work out our story and see what Horner thinks of it," the judge said.

The second call in the night reaching into Bramble Road was not as frightening, because the Horners were still wide awake. Jim and Susan were sitting at the kitchen table pouring black coffee into Betsy and trying to be patient with her rather disjointed account of the evening. Between crying jags, Betsy kept blaming herself for what had happened. As they pieced it together, Ben Adams had been taking drinks from the bar down to Ron in the parking lot. By the time the party was over, Ron was already drunk, but he wanted to drive Betsy and Sissy in the Stanton car over to Adams Point, where all the kids were going to meet. Betsy was scared, told Ron he was drunk and insisted that Sissy drive. She didn't realize Sissy was drunk too. This made Ron furious with Betsy, and he sulked all the way. At the beach he started drinking beer and playing up to Sissy.

"He did it just to get even with me, I know," Betsy said. "Then when he took her away . . ."

"How drunk was Sissy?"

"She was bombed out of her mind. I didn't know it or I would have driven myself," Betsy said. "I only realized it later at the beach. She was staggering all over the place. I thought it was pretty funny and that's when Ron really got mad at me and took her away . . ."

"Why didn't anybody try to stop them?"

"Well, I guess we were all, you know, like . . ."

Now Susan was upset. "You were drunk too?"

"Well, not as . . ."

"My God . . . ! What will people say . . . my daughter . . ."

"You should talk . . ."

"Betsy, hold your tongue!" Jim said. "Your mother and I are not seventeen. . . . Now I wonder who the hell that could be, calling?"

Driving again through the dark of this endless night, Jim's sense of dread was replaced by puzzlement. Why had he been asked to Brookehaven? Hilsman had been guarded and curt over the phone—something about needing help. Help with what? Those men ran the town. The only clue he had was Hilsman's reference out there in the parking lot of the police station to his being in the newspaper business. God, how he hoped they weren't going to ask him to do anything with the press. He had a nagging concern that he might be missing something he ought to take to *News,* but for the life of him he couldn't see any *national* interest in what had happened. And as they said in the office, *News* was a national magazine.

In fact, hearing the story from Betsy made him realize what a pitiful and almost sordid little affair it was. The vision of a drunken little Sissy dispelled all of his murky, romantic notions of her as some kind of privileged princess who could not be touched by life. Certainly not by death. She was every bit as human and innocent and vulnerable as his own daughter. They were, in fact, a bunch of kids who'd gotten themselves in trouble because they couldn't handle booze, and Betsy was right if impudent in suggesting that her mother and he and all the hundreds of other adults who'd gathered there at Brookehaven were liable for the example they'd set. What he was afraid of was that Betsy was going to go on being silly about assuming some kind of guilt for provoking this Dominick boy into leaving. As far as he could tell, it was just chance that it was Ron and Sissy, instead of Ron and Betsy, or Sissy and Ben Adams, or any other combination, since they were all evidently too drunk to drive. It was kind of a grace of God that the police got to the others before they tried. He had to feel sorry for the Brookes and Stantons and that Captain Dominick and certainly his son, Ron, but he hoped that they wouldn't make matters worse by somehow overreacting to the thing. Just give the reporters the facts, and he was betting they would see it for what it was—another very sad statistic in the fifty thousand deaths by auto every year.

The minute Jim stepped into the study at Brookehaven he knew his fears were well founded. Howard Hilsman wasted no time. Reading from notes he'd made on a long yellow legal pad, he told Jim the official story they had decided to give out. The essence of it was the young people had attended an innocent party with soft drinks and dancing and with their parents present. Since the accident had taken place a couple of hours after the party ended, it was to be presumed that if alcohol was involved, it had been drunk later at the beach and it was improbable that either of them was drunk; the driver, as yet undetermined, must have nodded off or otherwise lost control of the car. An unfortunate tragedy for all concerned. Period.

Through the reading of the hastily drafted statement, Police Chief Santori sat staring fixedly at his shoes. Jim reacted almost automatically. "It won't wash," he said, and the chief looked up with the print of hope on his face.

"Why?" Hilsman asked.

"Well, I'm not a police reporter, but I know that in a case like this the police must have taken blood samples . . ."

Santori just nodded.

Jim went on, "In which case there will probably be shown to be more alcohol than could possibly be absorbed during an hour or so of beer drinking. Is that right, Chief Santori?"

"I'm afraid so."

"Second place, there must have been several hundred people at the party who were aware, as I was, that young people were getting drinks and a dozen or so kids like my daughter Betsy at the beach who knew, as Betsy put it, that Sissy and Ron were 'bombed out of their minds.' "

Judge Brooke took the floor. "I don't believe you understand, Mr. Horner—uh, Jim—that we're dealing with friends here. Isn't that right, Nick?"

When Santori nodded again, the judge continued, "All of the people at that party, including yourself, I trust, were my friends, and all of the young people at the beach, with the exception of the Dominick boy, were their children. Mr. Santori here is one of my oldest associates. So there's really no need for any of the things you mentioned to be discussed with the press."

"But when young Dominick recovers and talks . . . ?"

"I think Mr. Santori and I have reached an understanding about that, and I'm sure Captain Dominick will agree when he learns of it. You see, it's really in the best interests of all of us in this community that there be no scandal of any kind, wouldn't you agree, Jim?"

Jim Horner was fascinated. So this was how they worked, these men of power. "I agree, judge, but unfortunately the thing has happened and—"

"I'm not sure Jim understands the gravity of the situation, judge," Howard Hilsman said. "He hasn't been around here long enough to remember what the press did with that so-called discrimination case. You see, Jim, let a prominent man like the judge here slip a little, and they'll try to make it seem like he fell clear into hell. It is possible, just possible, that the judge could be accused of serving liquor to minors and that all those kids could be charged with illegal possession or some such and that the driver of the car was guilty of manslaughter, at least. Now you wouldn't want your daughter's name mixed up in a mess like that just when *she's* trying to get into college, would you?"

"I wouldn't, but I'm also—"

"You were at the party with all of the rest of us," Hilsman went on. "Andy Wolfe was there. Father Funston. If we did make any mistakes, it seems to us that the least we can do now is to spare the innocent people of Worton the kind of bad publicity that could hurt the whole town. We thought you might be willing to help by handling the press as a kind of spokesman for the families. I'll see to it that nobody else talks out of turn, and the chief here will handle the police, of course. Are you with us?"

It appeared to Jim he was about to become a hero at last—though not quite as his mother had imagined it. Staring into that circle of wary, bloodshot eyes, he couldn't quite bring himself to take a holy stance in defense of truth. Besides, what really was the truth here, anyway? Nobody yet knew for certain. But one thing he was sure of; he was personally involved, as Hilsman said. That remark about Betsy getting into college was on target. With her only average grades it was already a worry. And Susan would be as mortified by bad publicity as anybody in this room. Worse, Jim sensed that if he didn't close ranks with these men now, show his solidarity with them, he would regret it for the rest of his and his family's days in Worton. And Susan would bear the brunt.

"Well, I'm not sure what I can do, but I'll give it a try," Jim said.

The judge got up and took Jim's hand. "Howard said you were a gentleman. Thank you."

It was ridiculous, but Jim could feel himself blushing. It was, for God's sake, as if he had made it through the initiation rites of one of those societies he was never asked to join at Harvard. When he followed Chief Santori over to the police station to confront the salvos from the press, he was set on doing his best, and with apologies to no one, including himself. He didn't know what might happen if he failed, but he had heard enough about Judge Brooke to guess. Except in the case of that strange son-in-law of his, the judge could be ruthless with people who didn't come up to his mark—on the boat, in the office, anywhere. On the other hand there were countless families in Worton who owed everything they had to pleasing the judge. Once, discussing the judge with Jim, Kevin White had paraphrased the Bible, "If Brooke is for you, who can be against you."

54

Evidently the strange power of Judge Brooke was with Jim Horner. He was so groggy by the time he met the press that he couldn't be sure exactly what he said except that, with his crew cut and dark glasses and sharp chin he assuredly came across as sincere; the effect was heightened by the bleary eyes, tired voice and half-day's growth of beard of a weary and worried father. Which, God knew, he was. And although senior editor on *News* wasn't an impressive position in Worton, the reporters respected him. In any event, the first stories on Saturday and on through Sunday were, thankfully, wooden ones—just a few paragraphs reflecting the official story outlined at Brookehaven. By Sunday evening the phone at Bramble Road was ringing with congratulations; Judge Brooke himself was one of the first to call.

Jim Horner should have been happy. He wasn't. At best, the last hours of Sunday are the bleakest in the suburbs; the party is over, and the train pulls out in the morning. For Jim these hours were worse than usual at the end of this emotionally exhausting time. Brooding silently while Ed Sullivan's usual procession of clowns, crooners and comics flickered across the screen in front of him, Jim worried about his denial of his own reporter's instincts; he had, he felt in spite of himself, betrayed his profession.

When Susan suddenly flicked off the tube and suggested going to bed early, Jim gladly agreed. This was usually her signal of willingness, and he craved the blinding relief of orgasm to stop his brain. But instead she wanted to talk. "I'm really proud of you, Jim, the way you helped all our friends this weekend."

"Friends?"

"Yes, friends. Oh, I forgot to tell you. Marguerite Hilsman called and asked us for dinner next Saturday. They thought you might like to meet Fielding Small since you're more or less in the same business . . ."

"Sure. Making fiction . . ."

"Now, Jim . . ."

"I mean it. Playing ball with Judge Brooke meant deny-

55

ing information to my colleagues. What kind of a newsman does that make me? I ought to be out getting this story instead . . ."

"And hurt your own daughter?"

"I've been thinking about that, and I wonder if it would hurt her that much. As the chief told the press, kids will be kids. Betsy ought to learn about consequences. I'm not sure people would hold it against Sissy even if they knew she had been driving. No, the problem is Judge Brooke's sainted reputation—ours, too. The reputations of all of us who stood around watching those kids drink . . ."

"I don't agree at all," Susan said. "Marguerite and I were talking about this on the phone, and she and Howard feel it's better for parents to teach their children to drink than to have them run off down to Port Chester with fake I.D. cards and risk a chance of getting . . ."

"Killed? If Hilsman and the rest feel that way, why lie about what really happened? I'll tell you why—serving drinks to minors is illegal. The man responsible could be fined or sent to jail, or both."

"Could that happen to us?" Susan's voice was now frightened.

"No, it wasn't *our* party. But we stood around and let it go on. And now I've concealed what I knew from the press. There was a story here and I covered it up. I'm thinking of going in tomorrow and resigning."

Susan sat up and turned on a light so she could study her husband's face. "Jim, you aren't serious?"

"I am. Would it surprise you that I actually have some standards, that I even believe a little in my so-called profession, such as it is, and its obligation to tell the truth—or at least try?"

"But you're an editor. It isn't as if you were a reporter or something . . ."

"Susan, I can't believe you . . . you've got to know that it's the editor who decides what should be covered and what should be printed who bears the ultimate responsibility. I just don't know whether I'm fit for that kind of job anymore."

"Give me a cigarette, Jim." Susan hardly ever smoked. Jim sat up, lit a cigarette for her and one for himself. "Jim," she said, "you just did what any decent father would do to protect his child and home. And so did the judge and Howard Hilsman and the rest. I think you ought to be glad to be in such company. I know I am. After all these years, we finally get in with the right, yes, the right people in this town, and . . . and . . . then you want to go and do something foolish that will ruin everything. . . ."

The cigarette didn't work, she was losing control of herself and starting to cry. It had been a long time since Susan threated to come apart like this. Jim was frightened by memories of those bleak months of post partum depression after Julie's birth. He took her in his arms, rocked her and crooned. "Okay, okay, honey . . . I guess we're all upset . . . it'll come out all right . . . don't worry, I won't quit . . ."

"Promise?" she mumbled into his chest.

"Promise."

She turned a wet face up to his, and he kissed her, tasting the salt. He let his free hand wander under the edge of her silk shortie, across a smooth curve of cheek and back and around to cup the warm breasts that had suckled his children. "I love you," he said. She snuggled closer and whispered, "Prove it." He did, and the merciful oblivion he sought came at last.

But walking to the station next morning—Susan was sleeping so peacefully he hadn't wanted to waken her to drive him—Jim felt as queasy of mind as if he had a mental hangover. Like a man who couldn't remember how many drinks he'd had the night before, Jim had a sickening sense of making too many commitments that he might regret. They all seemed right at the time, of course, like that promise to Susan. He just couldn't bear—or risk—making her unhappy, but now he wondered again if he were right. Didn't he at least have a right to ask her to share the burden by trying to see the truth of that ugly nightmare and its possible consequences? Unfortunately, the answer was probably no. Whatever she was now,

Susan was almost as much his creation as her own, and it was too late to change her.

The hell of it was that he wasn't lying when he said he loved her the way she was. He had long ago become aware that Susan was half child, that she thought with her heart instead of her head, that her one real desire in life was to be liked. He appreciated these qualities because normally they manifested themselves in trust, in warmth, in cheerful compliance. If she was sometimes shallow in her judgment of people and events, she was deep in her purity, her almost total innocence of evil. He often thought that putting Susan in Worton, a place designed to protect its citizens from the uglier consequences of human misbehavior, was the smartest thing he'd ever done. So far she seemed truly happy here, and her happiness had been reflected in what he knew from hearing and observing others was an unusually happy home. He couldn't now pretend surprise that Susan, like a child at a horror movie, just wanted to look away from the awful events of the weekend.

Well, maybe she was right. She certainly had lots of company, as she herself pointed out—all the "best" people. The thing that worried Jim was how Susan might react if, in fact, they couldn't shake themselves awake from this nightmare. Because of her innocence and childish desire to be liked, she was far too vulnerable to shame. So this hit her even harder than it did him, because her children were her one creation, her pride. Her concern over them was certainly as logical and justified as his about his work. Loving Susan, Jim had never felt called upon to object to her efforts to keep the girls from harm, even when they took the somewhat superficial form of trying always to put them with the "right" people. Wasn't that what all this was about, his living in Worton? There was no reason to suppose that the girls, following in their mother's footsteps, couldn't also find safety and happiness right here in Worton, or another place just like it. That is, there hadn't been any reason until early Saturday morning. Perhaps Susan, too, had felt the nameless dread that gripped his guts that night. He had found her "settling her stomach" with brandy when he brought Betsy home from the police station, a most unusual thing for Susan to do but understandable then—in fact, he'd joined her.

Yes, it was too late to change Susan, even if he really wanted to change her. He'd have to go on protecting her; it was, after all, her need for his protection almost as much as anything else that had called to the man in him. Maybe this would all just go away like a bad dream, as Susan and the others seemed to feel. His hangover of doubt began to clear, and it vanished almost completely when, on the station platform, George Avery went out of his way to come up and take Jim's hand. "I want to congratulate you, young man, on the way you kept this thing out of the press."

"It's nothing—very—"

"Oh, no. I know what those newspaper fellows can do to you if they get on your back. Listen, I had a son out there on that beach too, you know, and I just want you to know how grateful we all are."

"Well, thanks but—"

"Not at all, Mr. Horner—Jim, isn't it? I think you may be in the wrong end of your profession. If you're ever interested in public relations, give me a call . . ."

All through that party at Brookehaven Betsy Horner could hardly wait for it to end. Ben Adams had passed the word about going to his grandfather's beach, and she knew that something exciting was bound to happen with Ben and Ron getting together. Except for the football season when they lived like monks to stay in training, they weren't like the rest of the dull jocks around school. They made a great pair. Ben, slight and blond, was all cool New England, given to shy understatement. Ron was as Italian as olive oil with his blue-black hair and eyes, muscular body, fast smile and a voice you could hear all over the stadium when he called signals. Despite their differences, they had a lot in common; each in his way was an outsider. Because of his father's drinking, Ben was ruined aristocracy, cut off from the clubby group of preppies who were his natural peers. Ron had a flair for the dramatic that singled him out from the practical peasants among whom his lines had been cast. They were also both poor. In a community where their contemporaries found skis and boats and cars and clothes under every Christmas tree, they had nothing they couldn't earn themselves. As befit a classy quarterback and the end who caught most of his passes, Ron and Ben teamed together off the field to defy the society that threatened to keep them from scoring.

The things Ron and Ben did became underground legend in the halls of Worton High. Stranded one day in New York without funds for the fun they wanted, they lifted a plumed and velvet suit from an outdoor rack in front of a costume shop. Dressed in this finery and wearing dime store dark glasses, Ron stood on street corners belting snatches of Italian opera he remembered from records his grandmother was forever playing while Ben panhandled passing crowds for his friend whose promising career had been cut short by blindness. It was good for about twenty-five dollars before the cops took too much interest. Another time when Ben was invited to a debutante party and in need of tails, Ron insisted that his friend have nothing but the best from Brooks Brothers. While clean-cut Ben kept an exasperated salesman busy trotting out sports coats, cat quick Ron managed to get away with what looked like a suitable dress suit. As it didn't quite fit, Ben simply took the suit to another department which, because of the label, made the needed alterations. Pressed from time to time by the exigencies of romance for a boat in which to take a moonlight sail, Ben, who had learned sailing from his cradle, and Ron, who was fast developing a taste for it, would simply slip the moorings of any convenient yacht whose owner they knew to be safely out of town. By the time they were sixteen, Ben and Ron were doing a lively business in faked I.D. cards which they would rent to classmates in need of a drink down in Port Chester; by the time they were seventeen, they were easing their straitened finances with commissions from friends who were less enterprising in the somewhat delicate operation of obtaining grass. The rather small price they had to pay to remain above the suspicion of family and faculty was to visit the barber with reasonable frequency and make enough touchdowns to send Worton's Crimson Tide surging over the opposition.

Like all the other girls in Worton, Betsy Horner knew that you had to be nervy to get mixed up with Ben Adams or Ron Dominick. It wasn't a matter of sex; they were usually too busy raising hell to get around to the heavy breathing part of a date. But an evening with them was an open flirtation with disaster, embarrassment or arrest. Whenever they took girls to the movies, for example, they never bought more than one ticket for the one who would let the others in through the exit at the first loud part of the show. It wasn't that they were cheap—it was more fun that way. Just having been out with them got to be a status thing among the girls which was, of course, their intention. And until that unforgettable spring night of senior prom it seemed to be the one bit of status that would be denied Betsy Horner.

Like her mother's, Betsy's looks created a clean and wholesome effect. She developed an outgoing personality —it was she who always said "Hi" to everybody in the halls. When they needed a girl to run for class vice-president, Betsy was the natural choice, as she was for head cheerleader. Gregarious by nature, Betsy enjoyed being liked and so went along with whatever was current in speech, music, dress. But underneath the perpetual sunshine of popularity in which she lived, she also yearned for another kind of excitement—she didn't quite know what . . .

She got a feel of it the only time she was ever really out of Worton. When she was about fifteen some rich man at the club lent her father his yacht in the Virgin Islands as a sort of reward for winning the Lightning Championship, and they all went down for a family cruise. At first she didn't want to go and be cooped up for a week in some old sailboat, but, as usual, she wasn't given any choice. "You're going," her father said in that stern way he sometimes had, "because we can't afford to pass up an opportunity like this. I know I never got to any exotic places when I was your age." Well, right away with all those beaches and palm trees she could see it wouldn't be too bad; she'd at least go back with a sun tan that would turn all the other girls in school green with envy.

But that wasn't what made her trip. One night a boy from another boat took her to an authentic native night club on a little island. She got high for the first time, sipping rum and coke out of paper cups, and danced and danced, mostly with the natives because the boy turned out to be clumsy, to the wild calypso of a steel band. The drums got right into her, worked in her pulse, gave her an intimation of a wild, previously unknown passion that might consume her. It was a weird sensation, and ever after that night she had the secret feeling, or hope, that one day she would get hold of whatever it was that lay at the center of her feelings. She couldn't talk about it to anybody. They would think she was crazy, especially her family.

Of course, she couldn't mention she'd been drinking to begin with; her mother would hit the ceiling. Her mother was a "do as I say" instead of "do as I do" person, but then so were most mothers, it seemed. Lately, they could hardly talk about anything without getting around to what was wrong with her—her grades were too low, her friends were too common, the music she liked was junk compared to Beethoven. Her mother was always telling her that she wouldn't talk to her that way except that she *cared,* but Betsy thought she could do with less of that kind of caring. Julie was too young to understand anything except how to bug her by telling on her when she stayed up reading all night or tried to smoke a cigarette. There were times when Betsy thought maybe she could talk to her father. He didn't pick on her as much as her mother—except for her language, but then she guessed he was sensitive about that since language was supposed to be his business—and once in a while even smiled at things that upset her mother, like the time she dropped the collection plate they were passing and said "shit" in church. Maybe it was just that he was a man or maybe her mother was right when she said that her father didn't know much about girls and didn't care the way she did.

Once while they were still on the cruise she almost tried to tell her father about the special, overwhelming feeling she'd had at the dance. They were alone up in the cockpit, the boat sailing easily. Her father was starting again on what a shame it was she hadn't taken advantage of the sailing program at the club . . . and she told him that she thought sailing was a stupid, social thing in Worton and if she heard one more time how he was only trying to give her all the *fun* he'd missed when he was a kid she'd scream. Instead of getting angry, he surprised her by saying quietly, "Well, Betsy, I'm sorry you feel that way. You see I find sailing a special kind of challenge, and I thought you would too. I feel about sailing the way your grandfather felt about fighting for his country and becoming a flyer. . . . maybe I'm like him except I don't have any wars . . ."

It was kind of a strange thing for him to say, and she wasn't at all sure what he meant, except that he too . . . even her father . . . seemed to be looking for something . . . something even he hadn't found . . . and for the moment it made her feel unusually close to him, so that she found herself starting to try to tell him what had happened to her. "You know that dance I went to the other night . . . ?"

"Yes, how was it?"

"Great. You and mother should have come—"

"Betsy, you know your mother and I aren't much for dancing . . . we've told you a hundred times how we met . . ."

And that was the end of that . . . "your mother and I" . . . God! . . . Bringing her mother into it like that, putting them solidly together against her, he'd slammed the door shut again. He was once more a father, half a set of parents. . . .

Betsy assumed she'd forget all about it back in Worton, and she almost did, but once in a while something—a song, a smell, a remembered image—would just drop the bottom out of her stomach and leave her with that voracious hunger again. Nothing, nobody in Worton could appease it. Maybe it had nothing to do with Worton, but there were times when she got to thinking it really did . . . there was this song about "ticky, tacky boxes" that seemed to *fit* Worton, although once when her father heard her playing it he'd said he was damned if he could imagine any ticky, tacky box that cost a hundred thousand dollars. Which was the trouble with Worton, everybody was always measuring things—in grades, points on a scoreboard, dollars, acres, sizes of dresses, years of age. But what she felt, sensed was somewhere out there and couldn't be measured. It was what life was all about, and she had a suspicion that it could only be realized by the ones who threw away the ruler.

Someone in particular, she began to think, like Ron Dominick. And not only because of what she'd heard of him, but by what she closely observed of him, slouching nonchalantly into class, smiling more with the eyes than the mouth, waiting until the very last second to get off a pass. Ben Adams was clear enough; he was, she figured, just plain rebelling against his—as he put it lightly— cruel, cruel fate. But Ron was a mystery . . . never mind that he came from what even in Worton people called the wrong side of the tracks, he had the air and grace of, well, some dark prince not subject to the constraints of the rest of them . . . . As Mike Stark—one of the regular jocks who had invited her to a senior prom even though she was only a junior—put it when they arrived at the dance, "Can you believe it . . . there's Ron Dominick with Sally Holden! I've got to say this for Ron, he just doesn't give a shit . . ."

Inelegant, but apparently true. Most of the kids thought Sally Holden could have stood in for Bugs Bunny. On the other hand, a junior like Ron could only get to the prom as a guest of a senior girl, many of whom considered dipping down below their class instead of up into the pool of boys who had gone on to college a disgrace. Ron, along with Ben who had come with Sally's dumpy friend Terry Black, was therefore one of the few junior boys at the dance. Betsy was just very glad he was there. Lately, she had taken to doing everything short of falling at his feet to get him to notice her beyond a routine response to her universal "Hi!" She'd even bribed a girl going out with him with a promise of a vote for head cheerleader if she'd mention, somehow, her name. The result was a report that was hardly worth the price and delivered, Betsy thought, with an excess of enthusiasm by her informant. "Who—Betsy Horner?" Ron had said. "That little square." Now, though, Ron couldn't help but see her dance, because, dull as he might be off the floor, Mike would show her up well.

Having paid a stiff price for admission by bringing their homely dates, Ron and Ben made the most of the dance by conning teammates like Mike into changing partners. They were particularly interested in junior girls, the courting of whom offered some future. So it happened that Betsy Horner found Ron Dominick holding out his hands to her. "I didn't know you could dance like that, Betsy," he said. "I wonder what other talents you're hiding."

"Well, I guess you'll have to find out." Her heart was, literally, pounding in her ears.

"I'd like to. Listen, Betsy, a few of us are getting together at the mansion after this thing is over. Try to get Mike to come along. . . ."

Betsy wasn't clear what the mansion was, but Mike knew and he was reluctant. "All I have to do is get arrested for breaking into an empty house or being at a pot party or whatever the hell else they have in mind and it'll be the old ball game. I just got into Dartmouth on condition, you know."

Taking a plunge that made her heart jump again, Betsy said, "Okay, if you're scared, just take me home."

Words like that from a girl like Betsy Horner were enough to send the six-foot, four-inch, 250-pound tackle into a concrete wall. "All right, all *right*," he declared (surrendered).

Ben Adams had thrown a kind of road block across the winding road leading out of Worton to the abandoned estate just across the Darien line. To Betsy, it was like a scene out of some movie about Berlin, and it made the adventure all the more exciting. He waved them down and stuck a flashlight in their faces. "Okay," he said. "Lights out and move at idle if you can past the caretaker's house. The old boy's deaf as a post, but we can't take any chances."

After winding through a dozen acres of woods they came out into a clearing where the house stood white and holy as a Greek temple in the moonlight. Ron stepped out of the shadows of the columned porch to greet them. With an elaborate bow, he took Betsy's hand and kissed it. "Welcome to the estate of mind," he said.

"The what?"

"Well, as you'll see, this isn't really real. It's what you make of it in your imagination."

"Geez, you must be already onto the grass, Ron," Mike said.

Ron ignored him, and, taking Betsy's arm, said, "Come into my parlor."

Since there was no furniture, a bunch of them were sitting crosslegged on the floor in front of a little fire that gave out the only light in the cavernous, arched living room. It seemed only to deepen the shadows in the corners and turn the panes of the French windows lining one wall into hundreds of tiny black mirrors. There was, Betsy thought, a strange assortment of kids she'd never expect to find with Ben and Ron . . . like that pimply Avery boy . . . and they were all laughing and passing a joint, all except Sally and Terry who kind of huddled together and looked at the whole thing out of saucer-wide eyes. Mike said right away, "I'm getting out of here. C'mon, Betsy."

"Don't run off. Let me show you around. If you don't like this party, there's always the ballroom," Ron said.

"I'm going," Mike said again.

Ron had rolled a newspaper into a kind of torch, and he was holding out his hand to Betsy. "Coming—or going?" he asked.

Betsy took Ron's hand. She could hear the door bang behind Mike as she followed Ron up the winding marble steps. Shadows dancing in the light of the torch made it seem a romantic passage through a medieval castle. Ron threw open a door and Betsy gasped; she was looking into a ballroom two stories high and half a house long. The tears of crystal chandeliers winked in Ron's light, and one whole wall glowed dully gold from the pipes of an organ.

"People used to know how to live," Ron said. "If I have my way, I'll live this way again. Wouldn't you like to live in a mansion, Betsy—but then you probably do."

"I'm afraid not—just a ranch on Bramble Road, but we like to call it home. Say, does that thing work—that organ?"

"Sure. The old Scotchman who watches this place takes out all the light bulbs, but he has to leave the electricity on for heat. Listen."

Ron gave Betsy the torch to hold, sat down at the keyboard and flipped a switch. After he played a few spooky chords he went into a theme she'd never heard and started to sing something in Italian. The voice Betsy had heard bawling signals on the field was now a tenor so sweet it sent goose pimples running right up from her ankles to her head. His black eyes were looking right into hers as he sang, " 'Mimi, thy little hand is cold . . .' from *La Boheme*," he translated.

When he finished, Betsy half expected him, wanted him, to kiss her. Instead he just grabbed the torch and said, "We'd better get this thing out or we'll burn the place down. Anyway, we're missing the party."

Betsy spent the rest of the night watching his face in the firelight and wondering how it would be if they kissed . . . She wouldn't smoke. She said she was keeping Sally and Terry company, but she was really scared to try. Somebody had brought beer, though, and before long she was lightheaded enough to join in the singing to somebody else's guitar and to laugh at the zingers Ben and Ron kept tossing to each other like a football over everybody else's head. She had, she decided, entered "the estate of mind," and by the time somebody dropped her home, she thought it was the Avery boy, she knew she wanted to go back.

She waited weeks for the phone call. She kept herself together by buying the album of the opera and playing it every night. Finally one day she picked up the receiver to hear a familiar voice. "Hey, you know I showed you some of my talents, but you never showed me yours. That's not a fair deal. What about next Friday night?"

"Sure," she said, trying to sound cool, a hundred degrees cooler than she felt.

Except "next Friday night" turned out to be the night of Brookehaven, and now it seemed very doubtful that Betsy Horner could ever demonstrate her talents for Ron Dominick, who, if she understood it, lay in a coma in the Stamford hospital.

The name of the Hill Club (not to be confused with the Golden Hills Club) undoubtedly came from the fact that the old flour mill in which it was housed sat on a slight rise north of the station. Over the hundred years or so of its existence the building's exterior had been periodically freshened with a coat of barn red paint suspiciously like that on the station and probably out of the same can since the club's founders had all been railroad workers at one time. The old mill's insides had long since been gutted to create a great barnlike hall for dances and large suppers; a kitchen and Ladies and Gents were partitioned off at the rear, and a bar where members normally served themselves occupied one corner. It wasn't exactly homey, but in the days following the accident Captain Lou Dominick spent most of his hours there away from the hospital, staring moodily at the ball game that flickered away on the old black and white screen above the bar while downing an endless succession of boilermakers to ease the pain.

Lou simply couldn't tolerate his home now. Maria who had always seemed a placid, sensible woman was losing her mind over this thing. She was all the time either crying or screaming at him to do something about it. "If you were a man, you'd arrest them, all of them," she'd shout. "They *killed* our boy . . ."

"He isn't dead yet, mother," Lou would try.

"He might as well be. Do you think he'll be any good after this? Do you think he'll play football, go to college?"

"Well, the doctors—"

"The doctors! What do they know? What do they care? They're like all the rest of them. Wasn't Doctor Shepherd at that party himself?"

"Yes, but—"

"There you are. And you listen to him! If you were a man, Lou Dominick, you'd throw them all in jail. Oh, my baby, my baby . . ."

The boys who dropped in and out of the club were more considerate. They might ask, "How's the kid?" to show they cared, but then they would turn the talk to how old Warren Spahn was throwing them or whether the local Little League club had a chance against Milford. Lou had founded the league almost single-handed when Ron had gotten old enough to want to play, and his Joey was warming the bench with the club right now. Though he tried, Joey wasn't any kind of athlete like Ron; he showed alarming signs of taking after Maria's father, who sat all day like a fat Buddha behind the cash register in his liquor store, unwilling to get up even to help a customer find a bottle. The other five were all girls, some of them pretty good lookers, and, although he pretended to be annoyed, Lou was really proud to hear the fellows kid him about his "harem" when they'd see him taking them all to mass.

Maria ought to have been able to understand that this was harder on him than on her. She had all those girls, but he had only the two boys, and Ron was the only one of them who showed real promise. He was going to be the first in the whole Dominick clan ever to go to college; Coach Wilbur Jones at the high school had said even Harvard was interested in him. Now *this*. Nobody was kidding anybody about the fact that it was Ron's touch with a football that would get him ahead, and Dr. Shepherd wasn't holding out much hope that Ron—thank the Lord he'd at least come out of the coma finally—would play again with a fracture in his spine in addition to the concussion. Lou had a lot more faith in Dr. Shepherd than Maria, and for an odd reason—the doctor was a Democrat. Although Lou registered Republican like any sensible man who wanted promotion in the town of Worton, he often pulled the Democratic lever when he got behind that curtain in the booth; the Democrats, he felt, were the party of the people. So even if Dr. Shepherd was at the judge's party, he still wasn't, the way Maria said, "one of them."

Dr. Shepherd's opinion was also one reason Lou had finally been forced to listen to Chief Santori's proposition; the other had to do with his own future, which somehow seemed more important than ever if his oldest child finally proved to be smashed beyond repair. The Sunday after the accident the chief found Lou alone in the club while everybody else was at mass. Lou was already half in the bag, which probably accounted for his first violent reaction. "The fuckers . . . the dirty fuckers," he screamed, and threw his glass at a row of bottles on a shelf behind the bar, resulting in a terrifying crash.

The chief quickly grabbed hold of Lou in a bear hug the way he would a disturbed child. "Calm down, son, calm down. I know how you feel, I really do," he kept saying until Lou broke down and started to cry, sob like a baby. It was what he had wanted to do for days, but in front of anybody else in the world it would have been a shame and a disgrace—a grown man, a tough cop, crying. Nick just hugged him closer and said, "Get it over with, Lou. I'd do the same myself."

Nick Santori was as close to a father as Lou Dominick had ever known; his own had been crushed between two freight cars when he was only six. Santori was young then and still detailed to watching school crossings. He'd gone out of his way to be good to the boy after the tragedy and developed an interest that led him to find a place on the force for Lou and bring him along as his successor. Off duty, Nick stood in for the missing grandfather in Dominick family gatherings, and there was nobody on his feet faster or yelling with greater pride than Nick Santori when Ron Dominick looped a long one into the end zone. So, once he got control of himself, Lou felt obliged to listen to Nick. . . .

"Look, I'm a lot older than you, Lou, and maybe just a little wiser. I guess we could belt those people if we wanted to. Probably Arnold's testimony about where he found the bodies and so on would hold up to prove the girl had been driving. For sure we can prove the kids were getting drinks at the judge's party. You know Stoney was driving the station wagon all night and he told me he saw it himself. So what would that do for us?"

Lou, behind the bar cleaning up the mess he'd made, looked up at the chief's face. Despite his profession, Nick Santori was truly a gentle man. In a small and peaceful town, his chores had been more on the side of helping than restraining people, and he'd developed a live-and-let-live philosophy that glowed through his round features like a candle in a pumpkin. Now, though, the light seemed to have died out. Maybe for once, Lou thought, he could push him in the direction of being tough. . . . "I can see you feel as bad as I do, chief. Well, don't you think we'd be doing this town a service to show these people just because they're almighty rich they can't get away with it?"

"With what?" Nick said. "Ron drank the booze. He didn't have to, you know."

"Chrissake, Nick, he's just a kid. He couldn't get his hands on it if it weren't for—"

"Lou, you should know better than anyone else that any of them can get it anywhere. There isn't a goddamn house in this town that isn't stacked with bottles anybody over the age of three can reach. And, let's face it, Ron's a pretty lively boy, not that I blame him. Hell, you had a beer or two yourself before you were twenty-one—stole some from my refrigerator, in fact, if I remember right. No, this is just a lousy damned piece of rotten bad luck, but the less we make of it the better for everyone, *especially* Ron."

"How do you mean?"

"Well, suppose he doesn't come around and can't play. He's through, and you know it, unless you take Judge Brooke's offer."

"Blood money . . ."

"Don't look at it that way, Lou. They love their kids too, and you can't blame them for trying to protect the girl's reputation . . ."

"At the expense of Ron's . . ."

"Well, people sort of feel differently about a girl being mixed up in something like this. But anyway, I don't think you and Arnold are really even all that sure of who was driving, and, more important, there were no witnesses. If nobody presses charges, there's no reason why we have to make any sure findings. We can just let it drop. Only Ron knows what happened. He could learn to forget for the sake of his own future—and yours too, Lou. Let me give it to you straight—you don't have a Chinaman's chance of being chief if you turn Judge Brooke against you. They also still have time to think up a way of firing me before I qualify for my pension. Think it over— and for Christ's sake, boy, go easy on the sauce."

Lou took the first part of the advice, but not the second. He poured himself another stiff one while he tried to reconcile himself to what he knew as well as Nick was cold reality. The town's governing board of selectmen was split by law into three representatives of the majority Republican Party and two Democrats. Just possibly the Democrats might support an action against Judge Brooke for spite (although Dr. Shepherd was the judge's physician), but there was no counting on the Republicans even though two of them were fellow members of the Hill Club. They owed their positions to Judge Brooke's Republican Town Committee, which over the years had become a hand-picked group of the judge's friends and associates. Yes, Nick was right. But it was a rotten, fucking pill to swallow, even with whiskey.

In contrast to his amiable chief, Lou Dominick was short, dark, quick and hard. A good athlete himself in high school, he was a crack shot in police training, a decorated combat sergeant in Korea. Nick Santori was proud of Lou and admired him and knew just how to use him. Lou was given the job of discipline in the force; at the station the talk was that you could get around the chief, but there was no shitting Captain Lou. When it came to cracking down on some bum or check-kiter or rowdy kid from out of town, Lou usually got the job, but the chief himself tried to handle the occasional unpleasantness involving one of Worton's own. As a result Lou developed into a straight arrow, no-nonsense enforcer of law and order. He had nothing but contempt, hatred, for the people who held themselves above the law because of their position in life (which damn well wasn't God-given), and the one he hated most was William Chesney Stanton, father of the late Sissy Stanton.

Years had done little to ease the hurt from Lou's first encounter with Stanton. He had been on night patrol, following a car that had come out of Golden Hills Country Club when he noticed it weaving all over the road. Honking, sounding his siren, flashing his light didn't slow the other driver. Finally, Lou took a chance and sped around him, forcing him off to the side. Walking back to the other car, a brand new Porsche, Lou was sure it had to be some rich Wortonite; he'd probably just take the fellow home. But whoever it was in the car wouldn't even roll down his window until Lou pounded on it. Infuriated, Lou decided to give him the works, but he began politely, "May I see your driver's license, sir?"

"No need for that," the fellow said. "You must be new on the force. I'm Mr. Stanton."

"Well, I'm officer Dominick, Mr. Stanton, and I want to see your license."

Lou had put his head in the window to have a look at the fellow. "Get your head out of here, Dominick," Stanton said. "I'm going home."

Stanton then engaged the clutch, knocking Lou backward. By the time Lou could catch up again with the Porsche, which was miraculously threading the maze of Worton's narrow roads at sixty or more, he saw it turn into a driveway off Soundview. His instinct was to go in after the fellow but he wasn't sure of his rights. So instead he parked on the road and woke the chief with his car radio-phone. A grumpy Santori made him repeat the story twice and then said, "Let him go, Lou."

"But, chief, it's resisting an officer . . ."

"I know, but he was drunk," Santori said. "Stanton's not a bad fellow sober. In any case, you'd have to go get yourself a warrant to go in there now. Stanton's got a whole law firm behind him, and he's Judge Brooke's son-in-law besides. Forget it, Lou. Oh, and Lou, next time you see something like that, unless the car has a kid in it or an out of state plate, just follow it and see that it gets home."

The worst of it was that when Lou got home, bitching to Maria in expectation of sympathy, all he got was, "I'm glad you didn't do anything to him, Lou. Mr. Stanton's one of dad's best customers."

Now, of course, when Stanton's daughter had hurt her baby, Maria was like a mother tiger; she wanted to claw and bite, to tear them all apart. Somehow Lou had to hold on, hold out against her, be sensible like Nick said. Everything they had been struggling for depended on it. They had never been able to make ends meet, and with seven kids moving into their teens it was worse each year. Only the five thousand or so more he was counting on getting as chief made their debts bearable, and Maria knew that this was the situation as well as he. Maybe she'd come to her senses in time. For the moment, though, booze was Lou Dominick's only solace, and the club his only home.

Chapter IV

Although already in his thirty-eighth year, James Gilbert Horner had never gone through something he was willing to dignify by calling it a moral crisis. Whether it was circumstances of a life that had kept him almost frantically busy or the formidable mental armor with which he had been suited by his mother or just plain luck, he had pretty much been protected from both actual sin and those crippling assaults that come out of the darkness of self-doubt. There were times when he worried about this, feeling somehow deprived of the physical danger and the spiritual agony, and ecstasy, others apparently endured. Still, he couldn't remake his nature, and on the whole he had to be grateful for the fact that it had kept him out of so much trouble—he hadn't, for example, had a fist fight since the age of six, an arrest, a case of clap, a pink slip from the front office, or even a really nasty scene with his wife. Living inside of Jim Horner, it sometimes occurred to him, was not unlike living in Worton, which may have been why escape to that shaded community in many ways felt so comfortable to him.

In not frequent moments of self-examination, Jim acknowledged that a major factor in keeping him out of trouble was the profession he had chosen, or, more properly, fallen into as a logical result of his training. At least up to the level he had so far reached, success in his work depended more on technical competence than the ass-kissing and infighting on which men had to depend in other careers where actual competence was not so easily measured. Jim could ignore the rat race and be as "nice" a guy to his fellows in the office as he was to his family at home; with his serenity, he avoided their malice. While some of his colleagues who regarded themselves as political liberals agonized to the point of drinking themselves to death over conforming to the *News* point of view that a God who looked remarkably like General Eisenhower and Himself Upstairs was in Heaven and all was right with the world, Jim was spared even that. He had personally come so far and so fast from Starkville that he thought, not unreasonably, that it would be churlish of him to complain seriously about the values of a system that made this possible.

Usually Jim avoided those deep discussions with the more bitter of his fellow writers which didn't seem to go anywhere. He was always reminded of a verse out of the *Rubaiyat* his mother had drilled into him: "Myself when young did eagerly frequent/Doctor and Saint, and heard great argument/About it and about: but evermore/Came out by the same door where in I went." Still, one noon, warmed by drinks at Tim Costello's, Jim tried to make a much younger man named Hal Palmer see his light. Palmer, fresh off the police beat of a midwestern paper, was, Jim thought, much too cynical for his age—or his own good. Jim wouldn't have bothered with him except that he admired his work and wanted to see him come along at *News*. So he resorted to his favorite *ad hominem* argument.

"Look at me—or you, for that matter. What's so wrong with a system that lets us get where we are?"

"Get where you are—from where? You try to sound like you're fresh out of a ghetto, but you went to Harvard, for Christ's sake," Palmer said.

"Without a cent . . ."

"Don't give me that poor boy shit, Horner. Your mother was a teacher, wasn't she, and a teacher's never poor in a small town. I know . . . mine was smaller than yours. Your mother never thought she was poor, did she?"

"Well . . ."

"No, of course not. And she raised you to think that you were as good, maybe even better, than anyone else, didn't she? You've never even known anybody who didn't have a chance. I'll bet you don't know one black by name. . . . No, I thought not—or a wop either . . ."

"Worton's full of Italians . . ."

76

"Boy, you sure as hell landed in the right town, Horner. I'll bet even those Italians are Republicans."

Jim understood he was wasting time. "Well listen, Hal, I didn't ask you out to lunch for this. I want to tell you frankly that, regardless of your politics or whatever, you are damn good, and I think you can go places at *News*. But if you'll take it from a young old-timer protective coloration matters around here and you'd fit in better with a bit of a haircut and a different suit. No offense. One of the things I had to learn myself at bad old Harvard that you like to sneer at." He smiled when he said it.

Palmer shook his head as if he had been slapped in the face. He was a big man, big and shaggy and somehow menacing despite the thick glasses he wore. For a minute there Jim thought his long record of avoiding physical violence had come to an end. Instead, Palmer laughed. "I don't believe it, I just don't believe it. If you weren't basically such a nice guy, Horner, I'd either have to cry— or hit you. As it is, I guess I've got to thank you."

A long time later, their conversation came back to haunt Jim some weeks after the tragic accident in Worton. He was summoned to Harry Margolis' office where he found the managing editor surrounded by clippings and in a bad temper, or fine form, take your pick. "Why in the fuck didn't you tell me about that accident up there in your hometown, Horner?"

"Well, Harry, it was just another accident—a couple of kids got boozed up and—"

"I've got news for you. Himself Upstairs doesn't think it was just another accident. He lives up there somewhere, and he's been hearing about it on the train. Seems there's a big coverup going on to save the skin of that old fraud Judge Brooke, and Himself wants it broken. And he wants it done with a story under your byline since you are our house suburbanite . . ."

"Harry, I just don't think—"

Margolis took the ever present cigar out of his mouth, spat so hard he drew a clang from the spittoon he kept at his feet, to the disgust of the young college girl researchers on the staff. "Chrissakes, Horner, you're not paid to think any more than I am. Now get going. You may need somebody to go up and dig for more dirt unless you think it wouldn't be too much trouble to look around your own neighborhood. But let's have something and damn soon."

Jim was so shaken that he could think of nothing to do but take the clippings back to his own office and pretend to get going. When he sat down and tried to light a cigarette, he found that he was literally shaking. This time he was really in a corner; this time, and for the first time, he had to make what, finally, he knew to be a certifiable moral choice. In an unexpected way, it was a chance, at last, to be a hero. He could lead his forces of truth against the powerful of Worton—and probably win. But win what? The kind of story he knew Himself Upstairs wanted would surely bring down on his head the wrath of the very people whom he and—even more—Susan were trying to make their life with. Betsy seemed to be coming out of her shock, and in a few weeks when school opened would be caught up again in all her outgoing activities; Susan was in a cloud of euphoria—the invitation to Hilsmans' had been followed by one to Stantons' and an even rarer one to Whites', and she was making busy plans to repay them. Except for the immediate families of the victims, most people in Worton seemed already to have put the accident behind them. This story would shatter the mirror of their new content like a hard-flung rock.

For a while after he calmed down a bit, Jim thought hopefully that by handling the story himself he could somehow satisfy his boss and still spare his neighbors and family from the prying of a stranger. But even if he could pull it off, nobody, least of all himself, would be happy with the result. Heroism, he reminded himself, also meant sacrifice. The real question was what kind of a hero did he want to be. Perhaps because he had never had to make the choice, Jim had always been scornful of the men he'd heard about who sacrificed their families to their work. Now he was tempted to do the same himself; it would be the smoothest way professionally and personally in terms of seeing himself as a man of principle in his work. Yet wasn't it, in a way, really the coward's way? He would be letting down a lot of people, including those he loved most, who trusted him to try to protect them; moreover, they were people with whom, as Hilsman had put it, he was involved. Could he live with himself if he took a holier-than-thou stance about events in which he had acquiesced and in which his own daughter was involved? He decided that the only right way out for him was "sacrificing" what he had built up for himself at *News*. He would still be, as Palmer had called him, "a nice guy." Jim Horner knew all about the clichéd wisdom that nice guys never win. Well, ironically, in this case that was a comfort. He didn't want to "win." Not this one.

Once his mind was made up, he realized he would have to act fast. Taking the story back to Margolis and refusing to do it would only be half an action, as impossible as being half pregnant. Turning down an assignment was such a cardinal sin at *News* that it would certainly blight his career; in any case, somebody else would do the story, and when it appeared, the angry people of Worton, not understanding Jim's powerlessness despite his title, would also blame him. He would have to get another job and resign—in that order; getting a job was a helluva lot easier when you already had one. If he lost his income too, his sacrifice, to the extent it was one, would turn into a thoroughly hollow thing; having to leave town because they couldn't afford to stay would bring even more hardship and disgrace on his family than being ridden out on a rail—a fate, Jim remembered, that Abraham Lincoln once said he'd rather not endure "except for the honor of the thing." Margolis would only give him a day of grace, or at the most two, before he started bugging him for copy. Jim turned to the only fair bet he had. He dialed the number of Ace Oil Company and asked to speak to Mr. Avery.

Jim didn't feel particularly heroic a day or so later when he walked into Margolis' office, dropped the clippings on his desk, and said in a manner he imagined rather than felt was appropriate for such an occasion, "You'll have to get yourself another boy."

"You mean you won't write this story?"

"Right. In fact, I resign."

"Now, Jim, wait a minute. You're too good. . . ."

It was the first time Margolis, a man sparing of senti-ment, had ever said anything nice to him, and though it didn't dissuade him, it did take him down from his tone.

"I have to. Look, my daughter's mixed up in this, those people are our friends—"

"Even that whited sepulchre Brooke?"

"Well . . . yes . . ."

"God, man, with friends like that who the hell needs enemies? All right, I guess you'd better go. . . . People in our business can't afford to have friends—or families either."

Jim turned and started out, but Margolis called him back. "Jim, I . . . well, I won't say I admire you, but . . . goddamnit . . . good luck . . . Oh, and on your way out, would you give these clippings to Palmer and ask him to come see me?"

Jim Horner's appointment as assistant vice-president in charge of public relations for Ace Oil Company was celebrated in the usual style with a one column head shot and half a column of type on the front page of the Worton *Record*. Everybody in Worton who mattered knew that Jim was no longer working at *News* when its story entitled "A Modern American Tragedy" tore the town apart like an anti-personnel bomb. In a professional way Jim had to admire Hal Palmer's work. His old police reporting instincts had led him to all the right places. Perhaps to cover up the fact that it was no longer news, Hal had written it in a rather florid fictional style, depicting the victims—the Italian boy and the WASP heiress—as a latter day Romeo and Juliet who were forced by the social barriers of Worton society into a tryst in the night. Their love was crossed not by the stars but by the mindless hedonism of adults who encouraged their drink-ing. It was a sin and a shame, and *News* took to task the town's flabby police who were obviously protecting not only one of their own, but, worse, the political and financial powers of the community. Immediate state action was called for to demonstrate to the youth of America that "nobody is above the law. Only if equal justice triumphs can this modern American tragedy be made ultimately meaningful."

At dinner the night the story broke, Jim read it aloud, hoping he would at last get some understanding from his family who had been baffled about his sudden change of jobs. It worked with Susan. "Oh, my God, Jim, it's awful. Thank goodness you're not working there anymore."

"What's the matter with it?" Betsy wanted to know. "Like, it's the truth, isn't it?"

"There are times when the truth hurts too much," Susan said. "You'll realize that when you grow up more."

"I don't get it. You sound as if truth's okay only if it's about somebody you don't know . . ."

"Betsy!" Jim said. "Your mother's only thinking of you, of your reputation. She's worried about college. You're going to have a hard enough time getting in—"

"I don't care about going to college. It seems so unfair, Ron's getting all the blame. He wouldn't even have *been* there if it weren't for me!"

"Now listen," Jim said. "Unless you're holding out on us, you don't know any more than I do, than anybody does, who was driving that car. When you talk about truth, think about that. Nobody wants to hurt Ron, but nobody wants to hurt Sissy either . . ."

"How can you hurt her now? She's dead . . ."

"But her family, Betsy. Don't you see?" Susan said.

Betsy jumped up from the table. "I see all right. We all do. That's what this is all about. You aren't worried about us. You're worried about going to jail for letting some minors have a few drinks . . ."

After Betsy was gone, Jim sighed and said, "Out of the mouths of babes . . ."

"Oh, Jim, she isn't a babe." Susan's face began to crumple and she fought back tears. "She ought to be old enough to understand things better. I always knew that Ron Dominick was trouble—Marguerite Hilsman says he and that Ben Adams are really *wild*. She says Tim says they even steal *boats*. Isn't that right, Julie?"

"Yeah, and they smoke pot too," said Julie, happy to heighten the drama of her older sister's disgrace by showing up Betsy's friends in the worst possible light.

"Well, I hope *you* never get mixed up with people like that," Susan told her younger daughter. "Maybe we'll send you away to school next year where you'll find nicer friends. How would you like that, Julie?"

"Well . . ."

"We'll think about it. . . . You see, Jim, George Avery's generosity is giving us a lot more options, isn't it?"

It was true—thirty thousand was nearly twice seventeen thousand, and Jim had been given to understand it was only the beginning. It did seem a lot of money for writing press releases and drafting an occasioanl speech for Avery, but a few days after the Worton story broke in *News* something happened that made him wonder if any amount of money would ever be enough for the job he was really doing. Summoned again to Brookehaven by a call from Howard Hilsman, he found George Avery sitting in with the group. The judge offered Jim a drink which he refused, thereby earning what he thought was an appreciative glance from Avery, and a leather chair into which he sank up to his spine, giving him a most uncomfortable, and intended, feeling of vulnerability.

"Well, we can see now why you had to resign from that magazine, Jim," Judge Brooke said. "I must say it was the act of a gentleman. I don't suppose there was anything you could have done about that article?"

"A senior editor isn't exactly in what you'd call a policy-making position."

"I see. Well, do you know this fellow Palmer?"

"Yes . . . in a way he was sort of a protégé of mine . . ."

"Good. Excellent," George Avery said, surprising him. "That fits nicely with what I had in mind. I think you could use an assistant in your department, Jim, and maybe you could persuade this enterprising Palmer fellow to join you. Old colleagues . . . it ought to work out fine . . . Would twenty-five thousand be about right?"

My God, these people were not only crude but naïve.

"Well, it's enough money . . . he's only making twelve now. But Hal Palmer is . . . well . . . I'm afraid he'd think this was some kind of bribe . . ."

"That all depends on how you put it to him, Jim," Avery said. "I haven't found the man who isn't interested in money when it's put to him the right way, have you, judge?"

"No. And sometimes you can even put it to them the wrong way." The judge said it with a straight face.

Everybody laughed except Jim. "Well, even if it worked, the magazine would just put somebody else on the story."

"Perhaps, but we have reason to suspect that Palmer's got hold of some inside sources," Hilsman explained. "If you can do your part, we think we can plug any leaks out here."

Jim felt more and more uncomfortable. How could he explain such an offer to Palmer? "I don't see how I can—" he started to say.

Avery interrupted. "Really? We thought you were one of us. I didn't make a mistake in thinking that, did I, Jim?"

"I'm just trying to warn you that it may not work . . ."

"Now we won't know that until we try, will we, Jim?" Avery said. "If we can get this man Palmer off our backs, we can at least buy some time until Dan Parker has a chance to see what he can do on the state level. I'd suggest seeing him as soon as possible."

"I'll . . . try," he said. "But I don't make any promises. Judge, I think I'll have that drink now."

But by the time the lunch date he'd made with Hal Palmer came along, Jim had managed to feel less edgy about the matter. After all, when you looked at it, it *was* natural for him to want his former colleague, whose work he had outspokenly admired, as an assistant. Hal would get a desired opportunity to double his salary in a related field. Jim was just making an offer; Hal could take it, or he could leave it. No sweat . . . right? . . .

No Costello's this time. Have expense account, might as well cut a friend and colleague in on its emoluments. Jim invited Hal to the Skyscraper Club, a place George

Avery used as a tool of his trade. When Jim saw Hal come in, he wondered whether it was in honor of the fancy setting or as a result of the advice he had once tentatively given him that the big man looked somehow less shaggy, almost as conservatively dressed as all the other men around him.

When they were seated by a window overlooking the length of Manhattan, Hal whistled. "Some joint! Hey, isn't that Bobby Kennedy over there?"

"Yes," Jim said, "and don't look around but John Lindsay just came in behind you. They say he's going to run for mayor."

"Well, I guess I can understand a little better why you left *News*—can't afford this kind of thing on peon's pay. Everybody was pretty shook up, you know—we all thought you were a cinch to take over from Margolis."

Jim shrugged, trying not to act—or feel—defensive. "Kids need shoes, as they say, and I've got a daughter about to go to college, and another coming along and—"

"I know. I met your Betsy. Nice kid . . ."

"Oh? Did she talk to you?"

"No, friend, but if that's why you got me here—to try to find my sources—I'm taking off . . ."

"Relax, Hal. Farthest thing from my mind. As a matter of fact, though I can't pretend to like it personally, I thought you did a hell of a job on that story."

"Thanks. Coming from you it means more than the note I got from Himself Upstairs or the grunt from Margolis."

"From the looks of that suit, they must have given you a raise too."

Hal almost blushed. "Jesus, Jim, you know better than that. I doubt if you'd get a raise there for bringing in the first story of the Second Coming. These duds just show I'm not too thickheaded to take advice once in a while."

The talk of money seemed the appropriate opening, especially with the warmth of the second martini. "Hal, I guess we're getting around to the reason for this meeting . . . it would be silly of me to deny that it was the Worton thing that actually shoved me out of *News,* but let me tell you I'm not wringing my hands over it. There *is* the money and, damn it, that's still what we need to raise our kids, our families . . . . anyway, what I'm trying to say is that I've got the T.O., and budget, for a new assistant—"

"Oh, come on, Jim. Me? An old hound dog police reporter like me a flack—"

"Weren't we all flacks, in our fashion? For Himself Upstairs? Anyway, the hell with that, Hal, you've got kids, too. Three, isn't it?"

"They're just babies . . ."

"And they grow up fast, Hal—too fast. I'm talking twenty-five thousand to start, and . . ." He realized he was rushing it ridiculously, and being hopelessly unsubtle, but somehow couldn't stop himself. He wanted to get it the hell over with any way he could. . . .

"Say, Jim boy, you wouldn't be after trying to buy me off that Worton story, would you?"

Jim tried to cover his embarrassment with an anger he felt only against himself. "Christ, Hal, I thought you knew me better than that."

"I thought so too. I happen to know that your boss's son was one of those kids on the beach too. You know, if he had any sense he'd try to bribe me to stay on that story, because I happen to like most of those kids, and, in my way, I've been trying to protect them."

Jim knew he was relieved to realize that his mission was going to fail. No use playing games with Hal any longer. "I was going to thank you for that, Hal—for keeping their names out. Listen, I'm truly embarrassed, but I had to do this. The job offer is on the level, though . . ."

Jim signaled for a third drink. "I'm sure it is. In my book you're still Mister Nice Guy. You may have some peculiar ideas, but you have good instincts. Christ, I know what you're trying to do, and I can't even really blame you. A man will go through a lot to try to protect his family. I suppose I would."

"Thanks, Hal. I used to think I was the all-American exception, but—"

"But now you're joining the rest of the human race. Remember I always used to argue with you that most of the other poor bastards out there on the wrong end of the law couldn't help themselves. Funny you should start learning that in a place like Worton. A pity." Hal held up his glass in a toast, adding, "Here's to Worton. I have a feeling it's going to be the making of us both."

Ever since phlebitis forced him to give up golf, the Reverend Doctor W. Anderson Wolfe had come to look forward to the one sort of outdoor activity he could enjoy, sailing in other people's boats. With Audrey's money pretty much at his disposal, he was in a position to afford one himself, of course, but he reasoned sensibly that this blessing had come along too late in life for him to learn a new sport. So he contented himself with accepting invitations from sailing members of his church. The one he enjoyed most, and the one he could always count on, was the annual Indian summer cruise aboard Judge Brooke's *Helena*. It was just an overnight to one of the ports on Long Island, but the judge was considerate enough to take a few days off in the middle of the week for the occasion since weekends were work days for ministers. Besides, as the judge pointed out, they could anchor in almost any cove without running into the stink pots that were rapidly turning the harbors into seagoing slums on Saturdays and Sundays. The timing of the cruise had evolved naturally enough out of the fact that fall was the beginning of the serious season in church, as in any other Worton organization, and Andy Wolfe found it prudent to discuss plans with his largest contributor privately before getting the rest of the congregation stirred up. Only Bill Stanton or Howard Hilsman or some other younger man who could be relied upon not to count the preacher's drinks went along to help with the crewing on these voyages.

Helena was a schooner, some fifty feet overall, a relic of the past but maintained in such beautiful condition that she was the pride of the port. Judge Brooke, afloat since he started sailing his first dinghy on Brookehaven's tidal pond at the age of four, used his skill to make a grand show of her. Where more timid skippers would bring their yachts in and out of harbor under power, the judge, given any kind of wind, took *Helena* off her mooring with all sail flying, often clearing the club dock by inches and causing ladies on the terrace to choke on their tea.

Andy Wolfe always anticipated an exciting sail with the judge, and this October afternoon was no exception. A brisk northwesterly was keening through the tops of the trees and popping the loose sails that had just been run up when Andy came aboard. Harbingers of clear cold weather, northwesterlies polished the skies above the Sound to a brilliant blue that, by reflection, turned the waters into what Andy imagined he would find in the Aegean or Caribbean, seas he longed to experience if he could ever get Audrey to go anywhere but her island in Maine. Annual isolation on that island, which the Atkins family had bought as a summer place generations ago, was one of the crosses of his marriage that Andy felt obliged to bear. To him it was silly to leave Worton, a summer place itself that time of year, but with five generations in Worton the Atkins had come to look upon the area as a place of toil from which they sought escape after the sale of their old farmland to the likes of G. Hartwell Brooke began to enrich them. Anyway, Audrey's father Bradford, who operated the local oil company, felt obliged to be on deck, as he expressed it in language borrowed from his seagoing forefathers, during heating season. So a lifetime of summers in Maine became an unbreakable habit for Audrey and her sisters even though Bradford Atkins sold the company and put the money in the estate before his death on the theory that none of the girls had a head for business.

"Going to be blowing like stink out there. Are you sure you want all this sail up?" Bill Stanton yelled back from the bow when the judge gave the order to cast off.

"Hell, yes. It'll be a nice reach, and we can keep in

the lee of the Connecticut shore and run over at Port Jeff," the judge said. "Anyway, you know this old girl's steady as a church, if you'll excuse the expression, Andy."

Andy laughed as the *Helena,* her sails filling with a crack, leaped toward open sea. Within minutes, she had such a bone in her teeth that you could hear the hiss under her slicing bow clear back in the cockpit. Judge Brooke, carelessly steering with one hand, waved the other at the weed crop of empty mooring floats through which they were threading their way and said, "Most of these fellows put their boats up too soon. Best sailing in the world this time of year."

Outside the point, the judge turned the helm over to Andy while he went down below to help Bill with lunch. The big schooner settled into a kind of slewing groove in seas that were beginning to roll under the pressure of the wind. Once in a while she would dip her nose and toss a sparkle of jewels into the October sun. With the quiver of her power under his hand on the wheel, Andy Wolfe forgot all about his aching legs. Looking around at sea and sky, he thanked God for leading him out of the grim gothic sanctuaries of his youth into this open world. "This is the life!" he shouted.

The judge's head popped out of the hatch. "What's that, Andy?"

"I said this is the life."

"Sure is, and people wonder why we want to protect it. Now some fool wants to build a bridge across the Sound so that all those cars can crawl back and forth to Long Island. Pretty soon there'll be nothing left in life worth working for."

Andy had to agree. Despite his profession, he wasn't sure about heaven, but he did know that in coming to Worton he had found the next best thing. Sometimes he envied a person like Amos Brooke who had enjoyed it all of his life, but then he was reconciled to the fact that God seemed to grant a special grace to certain people. Perhaps Andy's own reward was a keener appreciation of the good life in comparison with what he had known. Maybe that's what the Lord meant by being born again.

By dusk they were snugged down behind a sand dune at Port Jefferson, and with autumn chill coming up, the judge lit a fire in the cozy, mahogany-faced cabin and decreed it was time to "splice the main brace." Glasses amber with whiskey in hand, they settled back on the cushioned bunks to begin their talk with the judge's ritual question, "Well, what's on your mind, Andy?"

"We've got to fill a spot on the session. Do you have any ideas?"

"I sure do. Horner. Jim Horner."

The minister lifted an inquiring brow. "After what his magazine did to you? I'm surprised."

"That was a shame, but I guess he couldn't help it. He did what he could. Quit his job the day he heard the magazine was going after the story and even tried to get that fellow Palmer off our backs."

"What's he doing now?"

"He's working for George Avery. George says he's a crackerjack at his job, and that's another reason I'm suggesting him. If we decide to go ahead with that new Sunday school wing, we'll need his kind of talent. I'm sure George would lend him to us, he believes in having his people active in community affairs."

"Well, I didn't know all this," Andy said. "Of course, I haven't seen Horner all summer."

"I'm not surprised. He's been sailing Sundays. They tell me he's just about the hottest sailor in the club. Nothing to match Cox and Bavier down at Noroton yet, of course, but they got started in Lightnings too. Kevin White says he regrets the day he taught Horner to tell the bow from the stern," the judge said.

The judge didn't have to explain his allusion to Cox and Bavier. He had taken the minister out several times that summer to witness the trials between *American Eagle* and *Constellation,* trials that had sharpened *Constellation,* with Bavier at the helm, into a runaway winner over Britain's *Sovereign* in the recently concluded America's Cup races. These sailors trailed such glory back to the Worton area that Andy wished he had one of them in his church. So in view of its promise, Horner's preoccupation with sailing could be an advantage provided the man wasn't a skier, too, like so many other sailors. There would be lots of time to get good work out of him in the winter.

"Well, if you think he's the right man . . ."

Bill Stanton added, "I think he's a good choice. George Avery certainly gives him high marks. The only thing I don't like is that I hear his daughter is fooling around with that little wop—"

"Speaking of . . . how's the case coming?" Andy asked.

"Howard Hilsman tells me there won't be any problem on the liquor charges," the judge said. "Sam is going to testify that I gave him orders not to serve any minors. Howard thinks we can get Sam off with a suspended sentence, and as I told Sam, a thing like this will help his trade rather than hurt it. Nobody wants a caterer around who would help put his boss in jail. As to the damage suit, it might be another story if they believe the cops' theory that Sissy was driving," the judge said.

"I hope you're going to contest that."

"Certainly. All the evidence is circumstantial. The boy still can't remember a thing after they left the beach. The whole thing seems such a waste . . . everything seemed settled until that ambulance chaser from Norwalk got hold of Lou Dominick's wife. Three million dollars. Ridiculous. It's a damn shame about the boy, but even if he can't walk he can still earn a living. Look at all those veterans. I was ready to help him, too, as Bill here can testify, if they hadn't turned on us. If only we could have kept the lid on the story. I still don't know who that reporter talked to. The one I really feel sorry for is Nick Santori. Of course, I guess he had to take the blame for negligence when the state moved in with all that hullabaloo, but Nick was just trying to be a decent fellow."

"What's he going to do now?"

"I'm not sure," tht judge said. "George Avery thinks he could find him a good security job at one of their refineries that would bring as much as his pension, except, of course, it would mean moving to Jersey . . .

Well, that's about all we can do . . . the Christian thing, don't you think . . . ?"

Although he nodded assent, Andy Wolfe was thinking wryly that with each passing year he became less and less certain of what "the Christian thing" was in any given situation. Even as his silvering hair and practiced tongue turned him into an ever more authoritative figure in the pulpit, his experience in life upset the sureties his youthful mind had interpreted as a call to preach the Word. With his organizational flair, he could provide his congregation with a handsome temple in which to worship; from the scriptures he could cull the ancient, sonorous phrases of comfort and inspiration with which to marry and bury them; the paraphrases of Biblical stories he learned in seminary served well enough for sermons. In offering people the stuff of faith, Andy Wolfe felt he was doing his duty; let them take away what they would. Of one thing he was certain: he had no right to tell people how to live their lives.

It was this attitude that caused Andy Wolfe to be the one preacher in town who refrained from public comment on the accident and its aftermath. While the news media screamed of sin in the suburbs, the other ministers of Worton, even Father Reardon, felt obliged to join the chorus and remind their congregations that they were witnessing the wages of such sin. Only the Reverend Doctor W. Anderson Wolfe and State Senator Daniel Parker, owner and editor of the Worton *Record,* maintained a dignified silence. Both, of course, were accused of toadying to their benefactor, but Amos Brooke and his whole family were grateful to Andy Wolfe. They felt free to talk in front of him and blessed by his silence. Now, though, Bill Stanton, who had sat glumly consuming two drinks for their one, seemed to want more than silence.

"Christian thing—shit," he said suddenly. "If there's any kind of God, Sissy'd still be alive. C'mon, tell me, Andy, how can your God let a thing like this happen?"

"Now, Bill . . ." the judge began.

"No, judge, it's a good question," Andy interrupted. "But just between us I'm going to have to confess that I don't have an answer. I wish I did, Bill, I really wish I did . . ."

Bill Stanton raised his glass in salute. "In vino veritas," he said. "Now you know why you'll never see me in church again."

There wasn't much Andy could say. One of the few things that really troubled his conscience was the way he had almost dodged the Stantons since the tragedy. Having no consolation beyond ritual to offer, he felt uncomfortable in their presence. Fortunately, Marion Stanton, like her parents, and unlike her husband, bore up with true Brooke grit. Andy saw her around church when she was picking up the younger children from Sunday school and managed to exchange a few pleasantries about the weather with her, and he noticed with relief items in the paper that indicated she had gone back to riding her horses. Bill was the problem. There was much talk, now confirmed in his presence, that Bill Stanton was drinking too much, although Andy wondered how anyone could tell the difference between too much and what Bill Stanton normally drank. The difference was that he was no longer hiding it. A number of parishioners told Andy they had seen Bill Stanton staggering onto the evening train, supported by friends who had found him hunched over the Commodore bar. As his minister Andy was expected to do something about Bill.

What, he couldn't imagine. It did seem presumptuous for Andy Wolfe, son of a New Kensington aluminum worker, graduate of Muskingum and Pittsburgh Xenia Seminary, to give advice to William Chesney Stanton, son of an ambassador, graduate of St. Paul's, Princeton and Harvard Law School. The brightest student in his class, Stanton was plucked out of a Supreme Court clerkship by Judge Brooke's firm for one of the highest starting salaries in the profession. Judge Brooke never regretted the money when he found that young Stanton had been on the sailing team at college. He began bringing the boy home for weekends of crewing on *Helena* and wasn't, of course, surprised when enforced intimacy aboard resulted in what seemed to be a romance between Bill and Marion. Since that time nobody and nothing could touch him, not even his father-in-law who might have been hard pressed to find another mate for his slightly horse-faced daughter. By the pouting, disdainful expression his face grew to wear, Stanton managed to communicate to less gifted people such as Andy Wolfe his sense of immunity from the laws that governed ordinary men. The hard thing Andy Wolfe had to swallow as a Christian was that it not only seemed presumptuous to try to help Bill Stanton but in his heart he didn't really want to. In a way the fellow was getting what he deserved—a terrible thought that could be justified only in Old Testament terms, if at all.

In all of this, the greatest puzzlement to Andy Wolfe was Judge Brooke's attitude. He seemed no more eager than the minister himself to reform his son-in-law, and yet Andy was sure a man of Brooke's power could accomplish the feat. There was plenty of money to ship Stanton off to Silver Hill or any of the other exclusive spots where the rich and famous dried out. And the judge certainly held the whip hand, for it was known that Stanton, despite his background, didn't have a cent of his own. But what Andy Wolfe, in so many ways an innocent, would never understand was that Amos Brooke valued a useful weakness above all other qualities in the people around him. A flawed Bill Stanton was likely to stay meekly in the role the judge wanted him to play—husband to his daughter and father to his grandchildren. It might be hard on Marion at times, but it was better than the alternatives, spinsterhood or divorce.

"Bill," the judge said, "you know the one rule when Andy's aboard the *Helena*. We don't discuss religion. The church, yes, but no theology. It always embarrasses a minister to have to talk about God on his time off. Can you reach the whiskey bottle? At least Andy and I need another round before chow."

When Betsy Horner signed up to be a candy striper at the hospital, her mother was delighted. This was considered the finest form of service for young girls, and they were organized by the Junior League, a group of not-so-junior ladies that Susan Horner wanted to be accepted by. Besides, it showed that Betsy was beginning to think of other people instead of just herself the way she'd seemed to be doing ever since the accident. It did not, of course, occur to Susan that the job might give Betsy a chance to see Ron Dominick, who still lay paralyzed from the waist down, in a room guarded around the clock by an off-duty policeman. The man was instructed to see that only authorized visitors—members of the family and a few trusted friends from the Italian community—got in to see Ron. Marguerite Hilsman said her husband was furious about it; it was obvious that the Dominicks were just trying to make sure that Ron didn't talk to anyone on the other side in case his memory came back before the damage suit was settled, and he failed to listen to the moneyed voice of reason.

At first, Betsy played a very cautious game. She showed no interest at all in the fact that Ron Dominick was in the hospital. Instead, she made it her business to become the most cheerful and conspicuous candy striper of them all. Turning on the tomboyish personality that had made her popular in school, she kidded with patients, doctors, nurses, even the succession of bored cops outside Ron's door. By midfall Betsy's bouncy figure, moving along the halls in a red and white jumper behind a cart of books, was so familiar to everyone that she was part of the scenery. Then, one day, with a familiar "Hi, there!" to the policeman on guard, she rolled right by him and into Ron's room.

"Hi, Ron," she said, loudly enough for anyone in the hall to hear. "I've got a book here I thought maybe you'd like . . ."

Even while she was forcing her brightest tones, Betsy wanted to burst out crying at her first sight of Ron. Nearly six months in bed had bleached his skin and wasted his frame. His dark mischievous eyes were glazed, silent. When he said, "Oh, hi, Bets," his voice was toneless; he didn't seem especially glad, or even surprised, to see her.

Trying to think of what to say next, Betsy noticed a

gallows-like contraption hanging over the bed and asked, "What's that?"

"For exercise," Ron said. "I'm supposed to chin myself."

"Oh, well, let's see!"

"No, I hate it. Anyway, what's the use?"

"Ron, don't talk like that—"

"Would you mind going away, Bets? I'm pretty tired . . ."

". . . Well, all right, sure, Ron . . . here's your book . . ."

Betsy wheeled her cart past the guard, down the hall and into a closet where she could let herself cry. After all these weeks of waiting and planning, Ron's bleak reception was almost more than she could stand. She remembered how awful she thought it was when she heard that Ron's mother was going around town saying he might as well be dead. Now she understood better. But after days more of thinking about it she decided it was up to her to *do* something about Ron; it was the only way she could get over that terrible feeling that if it hadn't been for breaking her date with Ron, and later having a fight with him, he wouldn't have got in this mess. No good that her father kept telling her that Ron drank the liquor, not she, that it was Ron's own choice to go off with Sissy. If she hadn't made him so mad Ron would certainly just have fooled around on the beach like the rest of them and had nothing more than a hangover to show for it . . . Oh, she'd wanted to believe differently, not blame herself, accept her father's reassurance, and then she would remember what Ben Adams had said to her just after they'd left . . . "Well, you've really gone and done it, Betsy, and I hope you're satisfied. First that stuff about his driving—and now this. You know Ron's a funny guy— he doesn't like anybody hassling him, bossing him around, especially a girl that he's trying to impress, for God's sake . . . well, you know . . . you sure blew it, because I can tell you that Ron was really hoping to . . . to get to know you tonight. He had it big for you, *Miss* Betsy Horner . . . damned if I know why. By the way, you loused me up too, and just when Sissy was beginning to give me the time of day . . ." She and Ben had never spoken to each other since. There seemed nothing to say.

Still, with determined cheeriness, Betsy persisted in going into Ron's room every day. He never seemed to want to talk, but he did begin to listen while she chatted about what was going on in the halls of Worton High. At first she would just stand there for a few minutes; then she began sitting on the edge of the bed. Once he asked her to help him readjust his position, and she was startled to feel how frail and bony his arms and shoulders had become. When she came in one day and found Ron trying a few feeble chins on the bar, she impulsively kissed him, and was shocked and hurt in spite of herself at the way he turned his face away.

"Don't do that, don't *ever* do that again, Betsy."

"Why? Am I so repulsive?"

"No," he said to the wall. "And you know it. It's just that I . . . don't you understand, Bets? I'm paralyzed . . . down there."

"That doesn't mean I shouldn't kiss you . . ."

"Yes, it does. I'm no damn good for a girl. I'll never be *any* good for *any* girl."

His voice clotted with something that she recognized as sobbing more by the sight of his shoulders shaking than the actual sound. She had never seen a boy cry, and it made her tremble inside. She reached out and touched the back of his head and neck.

"Don't, Ron," she said. "I mean, how can you be sure?"

"Well, damn it, I can't move . . . I can't move anything, and Dr. Shepherd says I may never . . ."

Betsy's knowledge of male anatomy was considerably more advanced than her mother's had been at seventeen and doubtless light years beyond her grandmother's. Though her experience was limited to trying to ignore the hard and somewhat embarrassing lump the few boys she petted with developed below the belt, she had at least seen enough pictures, read enough in books and maga-

96

zines, heard enough in clinical sex classes to know very well what Ron was talking about. The kids even joked rather openly about "getting it up," and one of her girl friends who had finally agreed to go all the way with a boy later confessed to her with fury and scorn that fear had left him limp as a worm. With Ron still trembling under her touch, she had a sudden inspiration. Burying her face against his neck and ear, she whispered, "Let's find out."

She ran her hand over the shuddering hard cage of his ribs, down the flat of his belly and let it close around the soft, lifeless thing she found. Miraculously, it grew and stiffened under her touch, and she was aware of her own heart pounding. Ron turned the face he had buried in a pillow toward hers. His eyes, still wet, had some of the old life in them. "Bets, oh God, Bets . . ."

Betsy quickly pulled her hand away, as if letting go of a hot wire, took a deep breath, and forced a smile. "There, you see, you're all *right*," she said briskly, in the manner of a nurse having just taken a pulse. Which, of course, in a way she had.

He reached for her, but she drew away. "Oh, God, I am, Bets. Oh, God, oh, God . . . don't leave me like this."

"But I just wanted to see you were all right . . ."

"But I am, I *am*. Don't you understand?"

"Ron, have you ever . . . ?"

"Yeah. Once, just once."

She wanted to ask with whom, surprised at how quickly jealousy could replace pity. Could it have been Sissy before . . . ? She knew she shouldn't, wouldn't, ask . . . she would never want a boy to talk about her . . . "I've got to go," she said quickly. "They'll get suspicious out there."

"Come back, Bets. Promise you'll come back . . ."

"I will," she said, and started for the door.

"Hey, Bets," he called after her in a voice for the first time loud with life. "Ask Ben Adams if he can give you something for me."

"I don't think Ben much likes me. . . ."

"Ah, don't worry about that. You tell him it's for me, and old Ben'll come through . . ."

"Do you think you should?"

"Why not? It looks like I'm going to live, after all, so I might as well get back to enjoying it."

When Judge Amos Hartwell Brooke and the Reverend Doctor W. Anderson Wolfe came calling at the Horners' humble Bramble Road house, Jim was decidedly surprised. He hadn't seen much of the judge since he'd failed, thank God, in his mission to win over Palmer. He might have thought he had been read out of the club except for the fact that Susan was thicker than ever with Marguerite Hilsman and Marion Stanton. The truth was the judge was probably too busy to think about him or much of anybody else, for the Dominick damage suit had been followed by criminal charges brought by the state despite the best efforts of Dan Parker. "Those damn Democrats in Hartford have just been waiting to get something on a good Republican town like Worton," Parker was heard to say, and there was, Jim guessed, a good deal of truth in that. The real reason for the action, though, was Jim's friend Palmer's relentless reporting, and Jim couldn't help secretly admiring, even enjoying, Palmer's stories.

Even though it was the first time the judge had ever entered his house, Jim had a feeling that it would be inappropriate to greet this unannounced call with the usual Worton offer of drinks. He also sensed that the men wanted to see him alone, so he suggested it was time for the girls to do their homework and asked Susan to make more coffee. As soon as she left, the judge said, "No use beating around the bush, Jim. We've come to tell you that we want to put your name up for the church Session at the next congregational meeting."

Jim found it hard to believe his ears. Once their social career had been more or less launched, the Horners had found it easier just to drop the girls off for Sunday school than to get dressed up for church—especially Jim did. For half the year at least he'd had to spend

Sunday mornings tuning up his boat for racing, and Susan had said she was embarrassed to go alone. They did go on Christmas and Easter, of course, and on those Sundays when Jim was asked to usher. They usually found Andy's soothing sermons pleasant but uninspiring. Jim realized that what religion he had, if any, was meaningless to him when, in the midst of his recent moral dilemma, he had never once thought about God.

"How did you happen to pick on me?" Jim asked before they could go on. "I haven't been to church much lately, what with the sailing and—"

"We're aware of that, Jim. Andy and I understand more than a little how sailing can get to you, right, Andy?"

Andy agreed.

"Well, as I say, I'm flattered," Jim repeated, "but I think you've got the wrong man. Don't you have to take some kind of a pledge to be an elder?"

"You have to be ordained," Andy said. "Nothing much to it, though. You just kneel up there in front of the church and confess your faith, and the other elders put their hands on you . . ."

"The thing is I guess I'm not really too sure just what I believe . . ."

The judge enriched the atmosphere with his golden laugh. "That makes two of us, my boy—or maybe three —eh, Andy?"

The minister's responding smile was a bit forced; he hadn't known that his old friend the judge comprehended him quite that clearly. "I wouldn't worry about that, Jim," he said. "I have more trouble with elders who are sure of everything—church lawyers, I call them—than people like yourself. Just think of it as . . . well, joining a board of directors; the Session's job is to make the right kind of decisions to keep the church going."

"That's it—that's what we're getting at," the judge said. "One thing we're thinking about is a new Sunday school wing, and we're going to need your public relations and writing abilities to raise the funds. I was telling George Avery what we had in mind, threatening we might borrow you, and I can tell you he was tickled pink at the idea of one of his people becoming an elder."

The old son of a bitch, Jim thought. No wonder this formidable man had wielded power in Worton so long. Jim had already been given to understand that not the least important part of his new job was to see that George Avery stayed "tickled pink," as Judge Brooke obviously assumed. It was now very clear that the only way he could avoid becoming an elder was to provoke these men into not wanting him, and he wasn't sure how, or whether he ought to do that. But something in him held back. He didn't feel he could stand being another rubber stamp for their plans.

He tried to keep the generally light tone of the talk. "What worries me, gentlemen, is that, if I get into this, I might even get serious about religion."

The judge went right along with him. "Oh, no need for that. That's Andy's job, isn't it, Andy?"

Jim tried again. "Seriously, what I guess I'm trying to say is that I've never considered the church just another organization, or a business. I've always thought an elder should have more conviction. . . ."

" 'More conviction'?" the judge asked. "Andy tells me you were a Sunday school teacher . . ."

"Oh, I was just trying to help out. My own daughters were cluttering up the rolls and I thought it only fair. Anyway, the Bible is at least great literature, and every kid should know some of it."

The judge pounced triumphantly. "Well, of course, there you are. You see you do believe in the institution. You and your family have used it. Don't you think you have an obligation to keep it going and expand it for others?"

Just then Susan came in with the coffee. After a flurry of chatter the judge told her, "We've been trying to argue your husband into becoming an elder . . ."

"Really? Why, that's quite an honor, Jim, isn't it? I hope you said yes."

"There, Jim," the judge said. "With your wife and your boss on our side, I'm sure we can count on you, right?"

Andy Wolfe, who had been virtually silent throughout, suddenly said, "Amos, I think we should give Jim some time to think this over."

"Don't see why, but all right. We'll need a decision in a day or so, though."

"While you're thinking about it, Jim," Andy said, "you might want to consider that the Presbyterian Church is revising its confession to acknowledge that God's word can be reinterpreted in the light of our increasing knowledge. It might make a difference to you."

When the men had gone, Susan said, "What was all that at the end there? You didn't tell them you wouldn't take it, did you?"

"Well, you know I'm not strong on religion . . ."

"What's that got to do with it? It's an honor. Why, Howard Hilsman's on that board, and Kevin White, and . . . Sometimes I just don't understand you, Jim."

"Sometimes I don't understand myself . . ."

Something in Jim's tone or expression evidently moved Susan, because she changed her tactics. She came over and sat on his lap and nuzzled his neck. "Oh, Jim, do say yes. Think what it can mean for the girls . . . all of us . . ."

Jim was sure Susan was speaking for herself, or just possibly Julie. Betsy was another matter. Once she'd gotten through communicants' class and been admitted to church membership, she had pretty much given it up too, except for singing in the high-school-aged choir, which she liked. The one time he'd remonstrated with her, she'd come back with the perfect argument, "Well, you don't go, do you?" Still undecided, Jim didn't feel like discussing the matter with Susan. He did, though, feel like running a tentative hand up under her sweater.

She squirmed a little but didn't get up. "You're not acting much like an elder," she said.

It had been a long time since anything this spontaneous had happened between them, and Jim pressed on, easing his fingers through the mechanism of her bra to the warm flesh of her breast. "You heard Andy say we can reinterpret the Bible," he said. "Well, I think I know now what kind of apples Eve was using to tempt Adam."

When her response was a warm kiss, Jim stood up with Susan still in his arms, but as he carried her toward the bedroom she actually said, "Jim, what about the children?"

"To *hell* with the children," he said, kicking the door shut behind them. . . .

After the storm was over, Susan got up and straightened her clothes. "I've got to finish up the dishes, but you go to sleep," she said. "I'll tell the girls you weren't feeling well, and I had to put you to bed."

"You'd rather they think I was drunk than sexy? Either way, I don't sound much like an elder, do I?"

"Jim, stop being silly," she said, and was gone.

The bland lying Susan could do when she thought it was somehow in her daughters' best interests always amazed him. Susan was not, basically, an untruthful woman. For instance, he was sure that she had never cheated on him in any way, just as he had never cheated on her. This absolute mutual trust was, in fact, the strongest bond in their marriage since in so many other ways they seemed to inhabit different worlds. They often talked past each other and sometimes Jim felt it was as if they were standing in one of those crazy houses each looking into a different distorted mirror.

For instance, nothing in life seemed to matter to Susan as much as the girls. Instinct, perhaps, but in her case no doubt heightened by the fact that she had sacrificed her dreams of a career to their service. They were her achievement, and her acceptance. As they prospered, so did she. And any diminishing of them was an assault on her . . . When he could afford a piano again she had agreed to get one only because it would look so well against the long bare wall of the living room and make it possible for her to give the girls free lessons. "Nobody in this town cares about Bach or Bartók, least of all you," she sighed when Jim suggested mildly that she might want to play herself. Even her concern for what people in the town cared about and the social ambition that went with it seemed rooted in a primitive urge to see her fledglings fly higher and faster. Jim was acutely aware that if he had decided to stay on at *News* Susan would have considered it a fouling of her nest.

It was, in fact, leaving *News* that had really showed Jim the difference in the way he and Susan saw things. Though he tried once, when the girls were out and they were relaxed over perhaps one cocktail too many, to make her see the problem the way he did, as a sort of moral choice, she couldn't understand that at all. When it came to her cubs, at least, she was as amoral as a tigress. White lies such as those she planned to tell tonight, larger lies such as the coverup on the accident or professing a faith one might not have to become an elder, were completely acceptable—not to be questioned— means to the worthiest end of all—family success and security. If Jim questioned them, he was just being plain "silly." If he pressed beyond that point, she would point out that a good many of the best and most respected people evidently saw things the way she did—and so wasn't he, in effect, the one wearing the wrong pair of glasses?

And the worst of it was that he couldn't be sure Susan wasn't, after all, more right than wrong. The Manhattan tower occupied by the *News* was proving to have been an ivory one, and the events since the accident that had taken him away from it were making their own logic of Susan's instincts. The more Jim saw men like Judge Brooke and George Avery in action the more he wondered whether the shining knight vision he had taken away from Starkville wasn't just that—a vision. A jungle world called for jungle reflexes; the toughest animal got to lie on the safest branch of the tree at night. At least there could be no argument that as a result of the decision he had made they were up on a higher limb—more money, more powerful friends, more public respect. Then why didn't he at least feel, as Susan apparently did, that it had been right to do what he'd had to do to get there?

Try as he might to think logically about these things, he was finding it difficult, lying there in the dark unable to sleep, to control that sense of dread he had felt when he'd gone out into the night of Sissy Stanton's death. It was this same gut sensation, he realized now, that had made him indulge himself in that rather tasteless kidding with the judge and Andy about the fact that he might get religion. Except he just might. Perhaps he was just too hopelessly literal minded, the predictable product of a mother who had taught him to believe in the world. Whatever the reason, he felt ill at ease in the presence of men like Judge Brooke, who seemed so sternly unaware of whatever it was that seemed to lurk out there in the dark as long as they could keep the lights of what *they* held to be right and reasonable burning bright. If he kept on trying to be a member of this club of confident men, he was afraid that he would one day commit an indiscretion, knock one of those lights out, and everybody would be embarrassingly aware that he'd never really belonged in the first place.

Despite all his doubts, Jim finally decided that he really hadn't much choice but to go at least a little farther down the Worton road. In view of the other compromises he had made, refusing to be an elder would be a quixotic act that would surely bring him trouble at home and probably in the office too. Maybe, like finally getting into the right clothes at Harvard, this would make him at least superficially more comfortable; nobody would be able to tell by the looks of him that he felt out of step with the others. So when Susan crawled in beside him and, sensing he was awake, asked whether he'd decided to be an elder, he told her, yes, he guessed so.

She took his hand and squeezed it. "I knew you would," she said. "You always do the right thing in the end. You know what—I think they need a sexy elder."

"Could be . . . who knows?"

"*I* know. And I know I love you," Susan said, rolling over with a contented sigh.

He didn't answer.

Chapter V

As the youngest man on the Worton police force, Leo Polchick seemed to get more than his share of the duty of sitting outside Ron Dominick's hospital room. It was supposed to be a volunteer thing, and the older fellows found ways of dumping it on him, once they realized, as fall wore away into hard winter and then dripping spring, that it was a waste of time. Nobody but family and hospital staff ever tried to get in to see the kid; in fact, if the truth were known, most of the people in Worton, let alone Stamford, Norwalk and New York, had forgotten all about him. If Nick Santori hadn't lost his job as a consequence of the state's investigation, he would have put an end to it, of course, but there was no arguing with Captain Lou, now that he was acting chief. Always hard nosed, he had been getting worse every day since the accident. You could tell his nerves were on edge just to watch him chain smoking his way through the day and knocking back boilermakers at the club as soon as he went off duty. He hardly spoke to anyone on the force except to bark orders or deliver a tongue lashing. The smart thing for any of them to do was to keep out of his sight, and the worst part of hospital duty was that the captain showed up there at least once every day and sometimes more.

Captain Lou was always in his blackest mood just after he had been in to see his son. Sometimes he'd study the man on guard looking for dirt on a shoe, a missing button, anything as an excuse to raise hell, even though they were there as a "favor" to him. Leo and the others would have found this intolerable if they hadn't felt sorry for the poor bastard. It wasn't only that the kid in there didn't seem to be getting any better, but the fact that Captain Lou had really put his ass in a sling by bringing suit against the Stantons. The talk around town was that he would be fired the day the case ended, no matter how it came out. Significantly, the board of selectmen had only named him acting chief; the truth was—and everybody knew it, though nobody talked about it—they did this on the advice of the Stantons' attorney, Howard Hilsman, who felt that any reprisals against Captain Dominick at this point might prejudice the case. So Leo put up with the boredom and the captain's bitching as best he could; at least there was always that little candy striper to kid around with on the day shift.

Only twenty-two himself and just back from a year's service in Vietnam, Leo looked on Betsy Horner with a kind of wonder. She was the sort of creature you conjured up in dreams out there in the jungle when you wanted to believe in some kind of future. Clean, friendly, cheerful Betsy seemed everybody's girl next door, the one you wanted to marry after you'd had enough screwing around. If he hadn't known that Ron was paralyzed down there, Leo would have been suspicious of what happened behind the door Betsy so carefully closed every time she went in to see him. As it was, he considered it encouraging that she could be so friendly to an Italian kid like Ron; maybe she'd even give him—a guy from the wrong side of Norwalk's tracks—a tumble.

Day after day while they traded talk about the weather and the latest high school basketball game, Leo tried to work up the nerve to ask her out. One day Betsy herself gave him the chance. He was popping mints into his mouth because he wasn't allowed to smoke in the hospital, and she said, "Hey, can you spare one of those? I'm starved. I didn't have any time for lunch."

"Sure," he said, "take the whole box. I'll be off duty in an hour . . . how about splitting a pizza with me?"

"Gosh, I can't, I've got this dumb play rehearsal right after I leave here and—"

"Another day?"

"Well . . . maybe," she said, and wheeled her cart into Ron's room.

That was also the day Betsy left the door open a crack when she came out, calling over her shoulder, "I'll be

106

back in a minute, Ron." Leo sniffed a familiar smell coming from the room, one he'd recognize anywhere. In Nam they'd called it the evening smell, because it oozed from every hut like the perfume of some strange dusk-blooming flower. No question, it was burning grass.

Leo stuck his head in Ron's door and saw him quickly pinch out a roach. Though it was still almost freezing out, the window was wide open. "Thought I smelled fire or something. You all right?" he asked.

Ron responded with a grin. "Never better," he said.

"Aren't you cold?"

"I've been exercising, I like the air," Ron said. "Betsy's coming back to close it, she just went to get me . . . a record."

Betsy came in then, and Leo thought he detected a little gesture of alarm, although she recovered so quickly he couldn't be sure. She handed Ron the record and said, "Here. Maybe you ought to leave the door open so Leo can hear—it probably gets pretty boring out there, right, Leo?"

"And stir up all the old geezers on the floor? Hunh-uh. Anyway, Leo thinks it smells funny in here. Do you think it smells funny, Bets?"

"Oh, no."

They were kidding no one, of course, and all the way back to the station and all that long night, Leo tried to think what to do about it. Captain Lou was particularly uptight about drugs. Under other circumstances, Leo should have, and could have, busted the kid right there; the evidence was plainly in hand. Leo certainly didn't blame the kid, he'd used the stuff himself, still did when he was damned sure of not getting caught. And you had to figure what it might do to Captain Lou to have his own son busted for doing drugs. If it didn't kill him, he might kill somebody else. Despite the fact that he zonked himself with booze damn near every night, the captain had a horror of marijuana. Every man on the force was in-structed to throw the book at anybody caught with it, and Captain Lou went around boasting to the Women's Club and Chamber of Commerce that, when it came to drugs, Worton was as clean, by God, as a whistle. There was just no way of walking in and arresting Ron . . . he'd have to think of something else. He was surprised even the dumb older cops or somebody on the staff hadn't tumbled to it. The smell was unmistakable. If they ever did, they'd probably panic, and then for sure there would be hell to pay. Because then he, Leo, would be on the spot.

For a while he considered just going in and telling Ron he knew and asking him to cut it out. But the more he thought about it, the more dangerous it seemed. If the kid wanted to be mean, he could tell his old man that Leo was hassling him, had made false accusations against him. No question who Lou would believe and it would be goodbye cops for him. The one sure way of putting an end to it without involving Ron and at the same time maybe earning a bit of glory for himself would be to find out how the kid was getting the stuff. Carefully, Leo examined in his mind everybody he had ever seen going in and out of Ron's room, and his reluctant conclusion was that the supplier had to be none other than that all-American girl next door, Betsy Horner. But arresting Betsy would be as bad as arresting Ron. It wasn't just that he liked her. Her father was evidently some kind of a big shot. He'd seen his name in the papers for being made some kind of vice-president and elected to something in the Presbyterian Church and winning sailing races. Lou taught you to keep an eye out for things like that so you didn't go hassling the wrong people. If he could only figure out a way to warn her—to get her to stop.

Unknowingly, he decided, he'd done the right thing in asking Betsy out for pizza. In the following weeks, she was much friendlier to him. She began kidding around with him the way she would with someone her own age. One day she breezed in and said, "Hey, Leo, ask me what happens when you cross an elephant with a jar of peanut butter."

"Okay, so what happens when you cross an elephant with a jar of peanut butter?"

108

"You get a peanut that never forgets or an elephant that sticks to the roof of your mouth." She even giggled.

"Is that supposed to be funny?"

"Sure . . . don't you think so?"

And suddenly Leo was forced to see Betsy Horner as the kid she was. The couple of years he'd served in the Army had put him forever out of reach of such cute nonsense. And this depressing insight made him realize that there was a gulf of age as well as class between them. He belonged to the adult world—the *other* world. Covering for her and Ron was kid stuff he couldn't afford. For all their sakes, he better stop whatever foolishness these kids were up to before somebody really got hurt.

Leo pretended to laugh and said, "Well, now I think about it, it is kind of funny. Say, how about that pizza?"

"Well . . . okay," Betsy agreed.

When they were settled in a dark booth in the corner of a pizza parlor near the hospital, Leo said, "Say, you must have it in a big way for Ron."

"What makes you say that?"

"Well, I mean smuggling grass in to him. You could get into a lot of trouble."

"How do you . . . I mean, I haven't—"

"Don't try to shit me, Betsy. I was in Nam, and I've got a nose for that stuff like a narc dog. You ought to be glad the other guards are old farts . . ."

Betsy choked so hard on a swallow of pizza he had to jump up and hit her on the back. "You won't tell," she said as soon as she could talk. "I only did it once or twice, it's hard to get—"

"Hard to get? You must be kidding. I know a guy right here in Stamford can get all you want. But you shouldn't . . . it will just get you two in trouble."

"But Ron needs something . . ."

"I feel sorry for Ron. I know what it can do for a guy in the hospital. But he's got to stop. It's too dangerous."

"Oh, please help us," Betsy said, obviously paying no attention to the warning.

Well, he'd tried but she wasn't listening. Better that he

be the one to stop it than some creep out to make a big deal of it. . . . "Okay, I'll put you in touch with this guy if you promise on a stack of Bibles not to tell."

"I do, yes . . ."

But the "guy right here in Stamford" was a plain-clothes policeman, and Betsy Horner was taken into custody immediately after buying marijuana from him on a street corner near the hospital. Leo didn't know exactly when it would happen, didn't want to, and went around for days in dread of it. Although he hadn't felt it wise to explain the whole thing to the boys in Stamford—he didn't mention Ron Dominick at all, for example—he did ask them to go as easy as possible on Betsy. She was really a nice kid, he explained, and he just wanted to see her stopped and scared pretty good before she really got herself all loused up. They said they understood, and he hoped to God they did. When he'd become a cop Leo never expected he'd have to do a thing like this. Lou Dominick was always preaching, "We don't make the laws, we enforce them." Well, yes and no . . . and almost worse than thinking about that kid Betsy was thinking about the fact that he might not really have the stomach for his job after all, and if so, where did that leave him? He finally did manage to talk himself into thinking that, what the hell, nobody would care much about a little pot bust these days, and he really was, in a way, doing the kids a favor, stopping them before they got into something worse. . . .

When it actually happened, Leo Polchick was spending the day off at home, lying on a couch drinking beer and watching the tube. It came over the seven o'clock national news, and it was a real shock. Somehow they'd linked Betsy with Ron Dominick, even though she'd claimed she was buying the stuff for herself, and they made it sound as if every damned kid in Worton was descending to hell in a cloud of smoke. The report of the arrest was followed by a solemn commentary by a fellow Leo happened to know lived up in Weston or Wilton or somewhere and had been arrested a while back for drunken driving. A friend of Leo's on the state police had made the arrest and was still boiling about how it had been hushed up and thrown out of court.

"The arrest of this young lady—Junior League candy striper, daughter of an executive in one of the nation's great oil companies, cheerleader in the high school of perhaps the country's wealthiest and most exclusive suburb is truly alarming," the commentator intoned. "The fact that she was evidently smuggling drugs to the boy involved in last summer's tragic death in a drunken driving accident of another young girl who had everything this world has to offer provides dramatic symbolism none can afford to overlook. If Hamlet smelled something rotten in Denmark, what are we smelling in our own privileged communities? Can we any longer afford the complacent feeling that sin is something that takes place behind walls surrounding our slums and ghettos? While this particular problem may seem to be only the concern of the families involved, or of the town of Worton, where once again police work seems less an enforcement of law than the protection of privilege, is there any one of us who shouldn't be saying to himself tonight, 'There but for the grace of God go I?' "

"Hypocritical pompous son of a bitch!" Leo yelled, and got up to snap the TV off. He felt as sick as he had the time he'd shot what he thought was a Cong coming out of a hut and then found out it was a young girl.

The call from his secretary reached Jim in Houston, where he'd gone on business, fortunately just before he was going to sit down in his hotel room and watch the evening news. He caught the first plane back, and he could only remember the flight as an agonizing, nail-biting suspension in time. He didn't even know enough details to worry intelligently, but the fact that he saw it on the news all the way out in Texas was enough to let him know that it was bad. The commentator had a long reach. The girl behind the airline counter looked at the credit card he handed her and said, "You all from Waahton? That sure must be some sin city."

It was trite to keep thinking as he did that this couldn't

111

have happened at a worse time. When was a good time for bad news? Yet the cliché fit in the sense that this trip had been meant to be a sort of triumph, a first flexing of his power as a full vice-president of Ace Oil. If serving George Avery was less ennobling than serving, as he had once told himself he did at *News,* the great American public, it was certainly more immediately rewarding in the emoluments of money and power. Anonymous though he mostly had to remain, his skillful weaving of the quotations and homilies he'd been brought up on into Avery's speeches was helping turn his employer into a senior statesman of the industry, a man whose name regularly appeared on the front pages of the most prestigious newspapers when he testified before Congress or called at the White House. It was, face it, a heady game Jim found himself playing, and he was, despite his wry awareness, beginning to enjoy it (not to mention justify it); he was even beginning to think about the fact that Avery was aging and that a few members of the company had already suggested that, what with public policy playing such a big part in the energy industry, a new president from the ranks of public relations would be no bad thing.

Timing, time seemed damn near everything. Time had worked its wonders in Worton to the extent that Jim's dark doubts and premonitions and soul searchings were beginning to take on the character of an improbable and dimly recalled nightmare. For one thing, service on the church Session did prove very like sitting in on the board of a small company with matters of faith that might have tested his conscience being left up to either Dr. Wolfe or more likely pronouncements from the National Assembly. The sessions had brought him into such close and evidently impressive contact with Judge Brooke that he had been asked to serve as watch captain on the *Helena* for the long distance racing, which was really getting close to the "going down to the sea in ships" he had fantasized about. And when, in an early warmup race just before he'd left for Houston, he managed to pull off a tactical coup that brought the old schooner her first victory, he apparently gave the judge, in his own words, his "first new lease on life since Sissy's death" and was assured a berth for as long as he might want it.

Further, with more money and new friends, the Horners were finding Bramble Road almost alien territory, and were talking realistically about finding shorefront property where they could build a little house when the girls had gone off to school. Betsy's many activities at Worton High were proving almost as persuasive as good grades, and several of the colleges they had taken her to see expressed real interest. Whether as a result of his example in becoming an elder or simply from peer pressure, Julie was off on what her older sister described scornfully as a "religious kick." In addition to hanging out at the church a lot, she was into a fundamentalist hymn-singing group called "Young Life" that met week nights in various people's homes. Susan was wary of it, there were all sorts of strange people like that Ben Adams at the meetings, but the prospect that it would save Julie from the kind of mess Betsy and poor Sissy had gotten into kept her from arguing about it. Susan herself had joined a couple of tennis groups down at the club and was chairman of the church's white elephant sale and of her music group at the Women's Club, which was threatening to bring culture into the woods of Worton by importing artists from New York for concerts.

Wondering now about what Betsy's new disgrace would do to Susan was almost the worst part of the flight, and Jim got off the plane at Kennedy in a chill of apprehension. Howard Hilsman was waiting for him at the gate. The meaning of his welcome seemed underlined when Howard, shaking hands, said, "Judge Brooke insisted that I come. He's very concerned."

Concerned was an understatement. It was lucky Jim Horner would never know about the conversation in the New York offices of Brooke, Hilsman, Stanton and Seabury when word came through of Betsy Horner's arrest—apparently Betsy or Mrs. Horner or somebody had mentioned Hilsman as their probable attorney, and he had gone straight to the judge. "Oh, my God," was Judge Brooke's reaction. "What have I got myself into with this fellow Horner? You know I sponsored him for the Session, and I've got him on my boat. How in thunder could a thing like this happen? Well, we're stuck with him for the moment, so do what you can. In fact, get out there to the airport and take him in hand so he won't embarrass us any more than he already has."

On the drive up to Connecticut, Hilsman explained that he had got through to Betsy at Stamford police station and instructed her to remain there and say nothing until they arrived; Marguerite was over at the house with Susan who was, understandably, taking it badly. They could get Betsy right out on bail; a reliable bondsman had been instructed to meet them at the station. They'd have to plead her guilty, of course, since the cop who trapped her had posted a witness too, but showing that she was just taking it to the Dominick boy—she claimed it was for herself, but Leo Polchick said otherwise— would probably be held by the judge to be an extenuating circumstance. Hilsman was sure that the worst she'd get would be a suspended sentence and probation. It was fortunate she was picked up in Stamford . . . no telling how Lou Dominick would handle this since any involvement of his son might prejudice the damage suit.

When they reached her, Betsy, sitting on a hard bench and hugging herself as if she had a chill, was white-faced, hollow-eyed, but long past anything like tears. Her only response to their first questions was a motion of her head toward the police. "Ask them. I told them everything."

Jim's first reaction was anger. He frankly wanted to grab the girl and shake her until something came out. Hilsman, sensing this, moved between them and asked kindly, "Now just what did you tell them, Betsy? I thought you promised me you wouldn't talk."

"What's the difference? I was caught . . . I'm a criminal, right?"

"Look, Betsy, we understand that you were just buying this for Ron Dominick—"

114

"No! I wanted it for myself . . ."

"For *yourself*?" Jim said.

"Sure. Why not? Everybody does."

"But—it's dangerous—it's wrong—"

"That's what *you* think . . . I think I just shouldn't have got busted . . ."

Jim felt he was close to violence, or tears, or both in his frustration, and for the moment was saved from them by Howard Hilsman quickly saying, "You two wait here while I take care of the details of getting Betsy out."

Jim sat, sank rather, onto the bench beside his daughter. He was suddenly very, very tired. "What's this going to do to your mother?" he said, as much to himself as to his daughter.

"I knew you'd bring that up . . . do you care what it does to me?"

"Of course I do, that's why I'm here, that's why I wish you would at least try to tell me—"

"Please, daddy, *please*. I just don't want to talk . . ."

So Jim left off, giving her time, hoping her tongue would loosen, but it didn't. The alcoholic tears with which Susan greeted them built into outrage and anger, effectively stifling his efforts to get Betsy to open up. Her peals of "What will people say?" and "How could you do this?" finally drove Betsy to escape to her room . . . and Jim, after consideration, to conclude that his daughter was probably telling them the plain truth. As for the why, he could only guess. Maybe her first encounter with tragedy had gone deeper than any of them knew, and drugs were an unconscious way out. Or maybe it was as simple as her own first explanation that "everybody's doing it," and she was just being a peer among peers. Or one pressure was working on the other? Or . . . ?

Worse in its way than dealing with Betsy was coping with Susan. She couldn't stop talking about it, always somehow ending up with a variation on the unanswerable, "Why us?" To which Jim could offer little more than his own tentative explanation . . . which consoled her not at all.

"I still think," she persisted, "it somehow has to do with that Dominick boy, no matter what she says."

"I'd like to think so too, but one thing Betsy's never been is a liar," Jim said.

"That's true . . . oh, Jim, I *don't* understand, I've tried hard . . . you know I have . . ."

"I know, and you've done a damn fine job, you can't blame yourself for—"

"Then how could this happen?"

"I wish I knew, I don't . . . but, honey, it isn't the end of the world—"

"Maybe not for you, you go off to New York every day . . . *I'm* the one who has to face all the damned gossipy people around here—and I'm the one who has to listen to that awful music all afternoon . . ."

He wanted to be very careful, not accusing but concerned, in the way he said his next words to her. "Do you think drinking is going to make it any better . . . ?"

"Yes—no—I don't know . . . oh God, Jim, what's going to happen to us?"

"Susan, you've just got to pull yourself together. Nobody's blaming you for anything. There are plenty of other parents around here in exactly the same boat. . . ."

"So your *friend* Palmer keeps saying."

She was right. The effusions from Hal Palmer's eloquent typewriter had gone far beyond the early reports and turned Betsy's arrest into a national cause célèbre. He had, of course, resurrected all the gory detail of the night of Sissy's death and then gone on from there. His hound dog nose had ferreted out what he called "the stench" of an almost secret night court session at which Judge Brooke's innocence had been established by the guilty plea of his caterer. Palmer made much of the fact that the man was black and therefore predictably the victim of a system under which justice was "for hire." He had also detected the sweet smell of pot flowing in abundance from Worton High School and sniffed out the fact that at least one Worton youngster, whose arrest had been hushed up to make Captain Dominick's boast of a clean town stick, was doing time in a rehabilitation center for heroin. What made all this news, he had pointed out, was that this wasn't Harlem but the most affluent suburb in the most affluent nation in the world. "If, as they say, our children are our future," he concluded, "we are all in for a very bad time. Bolt the storm doors, batten down the hatches—and, above all, pray."

With Betsy as the centerpiece, Jim Horner no longer took a detached, professional view of Palmer's stories. He was especially upset that Palmer chose to use the fact that Jim was a high executive of an international oil company and an elder of the Presbyterian Church to heighten the drama of his daughter's fall from grace. Palmer was using a standard technique, of course, one Jim probably would have used himself in his *News* days. Nonetheless, he began to have a great deal more understanding of how the judge felt and more sympathy for his almost desperate, even dubious, methods of avoiding such exposure. Instead of arguing as he might once have done, Jim had to give silent assent to a fellow commuter, an account executive, who said to him on the train one day, "Well, Horner, I guess you've got a little different view now of your old business. Those fellows are using all this dirt about your kid and Worton to sell magazines, just the way I use a shot of some girl's bare ass to sell soap."

Regardless of the lack of understanding in the bewildered atmosphere of Bramble Road, there seemed to be a fair amount of it throughout the rest of Worton. Howard Hilsman personally took on Betsy's case for a fraction of his usual fee; Andy Wolfe came calling to assure Jim that he was as welcome as ever on the Session and that this sort of thing "happened in the best of families" (he really said that). And, most surprising of all, Dr. Floyd Shepherd, whom he hardly knew, stopped him one day in the street and said enigmatically, "No matter what anyone says, Mr. Horner, I like that girl of yours. Got to know her when she was a candy striper and . . . well . . . she's a very gallant young lady in my book." You had to fall from grace to make it in the clean precincts of Worton, or so it seemed. Jim had begun by thinking the opposite.

Dr. Floyd Shepherd did not arrive in Worton by accident. During long, wartime years of patching coral cuts and plugging dysentery on a Pacific atoll, he had made up his mind that medicine was medicine wherever you were and that a smart man would practice it in a pleasant as well as predictably profitable place. After a careful study of suburbs in the New York area, he picked Worton because it was the pleasantest of places and because the slow growth there had not yet attracted the doctors who were following the migration of their paying patients elsewhere out of the city. Although some of the big New York men like the famous researcher, Dr. Benjamin Adams, used Worton as a bedroom, the infirmities of the populace were still in the hands of a couple of horse and buggy fellows on the verge of death or retirement. Being young and full of energy, Dr. Shepherd had no trouble establishing himself, although he would shudder at the recollection of those first few years when his practice covered everything—he once delivered a Francetti baby right on the bathroom floor; he sat through night after night helping Bradford Atkins, who refused to go to a hospital, die of cancer; he got to know the Stantons by setting Marion's broken arm on the spot where she fell at the far end of the Hunt Club trail.

As an early bird in the specialty called internist, Dr. Shepherd disliked most of these chores and welcomed the bone men and eye men and baby men and X-ray men and all the rest who followed his footsteps into Worton and surrounding towns. He was, in fact, forever buttonholing young specialists on the loose at alumni gatherings and medical cocktail parties and selling them on the good life in the Worton area. Though before long there were as many doctors' offices as liquor stores and churches in Worton, Dr. Shepherd's year or two of general practice left him with an aura of the kindly family physician in the minds of old Wortonites—an aura he

118

used effectively to light the path to success in his favorite hobby after golf, politics.

Dr. Shepherd's political career began naturally enough with his appointment as town health officer within months of his arrival on the Worton scene. This was not an honor, but a chore the horse and buggy fellows used their own political influence to shove onto his young shoulders. Mostly it involved going about and testing the town beaches for bacteria and trying to get always irate citizens to do something about their overflowing septic tanks. But it also did get Dr. Shepherd's name in the paper, bring him into contact with town officials and awaken a dormant interest in civic affairs. Converted into an ardent New Dealer during the Depression, Dr. Shepherd believed in activist government as the rational man's last refuge against the stupidity and venality of his fellow citizens. In this he was out of step in Worton but delighted to find that his Democratic registration almost guaranteed election to any board of his choice, legal apportionment requiring at least one of his political species. Over the years he had served on the school board, the zoning board, the police commission, the Representative Town Meeting, the board of finance and, finally, the governing board of selectmen. Though always in the minority, Dr. Floyd Shepherd had, as they say, become a force with which to be reckoned, a popular figure whose dissenting opinions, often delivered in the form of wisecracks at open meetings, gave everybody the comforting, even righteous feeling that they were indeed living in a kind of democracy—the right kind, of course.

Whenever an issue polarized the town of Worton, Floyd Shepherd was one of the few people who could carry messages between camps. Liberals like painter Church and novelist Small, who really should have been living in Westport, were more or less stuck with him as the senior Democratic statesman; conservatives like Judge Brooke and Dan Parker had to believe that a man they trusted with the condition of their rich hearts had to be *basically* sound; and enough members of the Italian community had either experienced his kindness in those early days or owed him money for so long that they regarded him as almost one of them. It was natural, then, that, as the malaise induced by Sissy Stanton's death spread slowly through the once spectacularly healthy body politic of Worton, people would begin to look to Dr. Shepherd for some kind of prescription.

At first Floyd Shepherd resented this intrusion on his well-ordered life. He was, in fact, highly annoyed to be awakened that July night by Lou Dominick's call, scheduled as he was to tee off at 8 A.M. in the club's semi-final round and knowing full well he couldn't manage a steady hand on the greens after a sleepless night. From what Lou told him, the smashed body of his son was a matter for surgeons anyway. Still, he knew Lou well enough to tell by the tone of his voice that he would have to go and hold the man's hand no matter who did what with the son. Once it began, it continued. As far as Ron's case was concerned, Dr. Shepherd was rather like a builder, being obliged to orchestrate the plumbers and electricians and carpenters needed on the job but himself having to bring the bad news of rising costs to the family.

Like Ron's mother, Dr. Shepherd soon began to think that Sissy might well have been the lucky one in the accident after all. As an internist who was honest—realistic —enough to admit to himself that he often hadn't much idea of what was wrong with the people who came complaining to him, Dr. Shepherd had early on adopted the philosophy that medicine was more of an art than a science. In the manner of an artist mixing colors, he would try one pill, then another, relying on educated hunch and eternal hope for good results. Since old people who persisted in developing erratic hearts and stubborn cancers couldn't for the most part afford to live in Worton, most of Dr. Shepherd's patients were youngish men and matrons, possessed of the unusual vitality that got them to Worton in the first place. They also had enough money to make him feel at ease about handing them on to a cardiologist, radiologist, gynecologist, dermatologist, psychiatrist (there were more of these per head in Worton than in any town in the country) or even podiatrist if

120

there was any sign of something specific with which the "scientific" part of medicine could come to grips. So Dr. Shepherd was not surprised, nor especially prideful, that his patients usually recovered or at least went on living until they moved away. This record of professional success allowed him to take upwards of $50,000 a year in good conscience, sleep soundly and maintain a reasonably equable disposition. It also accounted for a growing feeling of despair as he watched Ron Dominick's athletic body waste away and with it his fighting spirit die. When the specialists gave up, Dr. Shepherd was the one who had to explain it all to Lou and, undoubtedly, as principal physician in the case, he would be the one that shyster lawyer would put on the stand when, and if, the ugly case the lawyer had persuaded Lou to bring against the Stantons came to trial.

For a while Dr. Shepherd had cherished one small hope. As a man with doubts about science, he had developed a certain respect for medical miracles. He *never* told a patient to give up; he'd seen too many instances when a well-timed divorce or a reversal in fortunes had caused physical problems to vanish. In the case of Ron, a kind of turning point had also seemed possible after that candy striper, Betsy Horner, started visiting him. Dr. Shepherd was glad that the Horners had gone to one of the newer doctors in town, because he knew that Betsy was getting into bed with Ron and wouldn't have liked the problem of what, if anything, to tell her parents. Ron had boasted about it to Dr. Shepherd, thinking the fact that he could get it up might prove to have some medical significance. Perhaps it did, although the specialists didn't agree. Certainly the lift in Ron's spirits and the fact that he went back to chinning and trying to do something for himself were essential preparation for any miracle. So Dr. Shepherd had no intention of telling anybody about the harmless—and perhaps even therapeutic—little affair going on in Room 2103—or the marijuana either, which he had detected even before Leo Polchick. Dr. Shepherd would have prescribed the drug himself if it had been possible, believing that an elevated spirit was far more important than anything regular medicine could do for Ron. He was grateful when Howard Hilsman had managed to get the girl off with a suspended sentence. What irked him, though, was that she was no longer allowed into the hospital, with the result that Ron was slipping back into his former despondency.

Even, maybe especially, that fraud Dan Parker had climbed on the bandwagon this time and was intoning in the *Record* about how the use of drugs showed that the young people of Worton were going to hell. Funny how Dan, a talented man with a bourbon bottle, had kept so quiet when his good friend Amos Brooke was dispensing another kind of drug to the kids. Dr. Shepherd believed that a drug by any other name was still a drug. It wasn't even useful to say so, though, and he was forced to hold his peace. Indeed, he worried that the time might be coming when, as a politician he would have to do more. The aftermath of all the bad national publicity Worton was getting was almost unbelievable. Some families had actually moved out, and according to the people over at Judge Brooke's Sound Realty new sales were off for the first time in the town's history and prices were "on the down side." Worse, during the spring, college admissions directors, who needed only the slimmest excuse to pare the swollen rolls of applicants, had begun shying away from students from the notorious Worton High. They didn't admit it, of course, but everybody knew what was happening.

Dr. Shepherd, therefore, was not particularly surprised when an oddly composed delegation of citizens called upon him in his office just before primary registration time. Spokesman for the group, which included Charles Church, Fielding Small and Judge Brooke, was State Senator Daniel Parker who, though nearing sixty, had such vaulting political ambitions that he didn't even have the grace to laugh when people mentioned the White House. As befit a man who had acquired his money by marrying and burying a series of rich women, Parker was strikingly handsome. Tall, silvered by age but thinned by

122

tennis and swimming (it was said meanly that he threw the power of the *Record* behind the building campaign for a new YMCA in Worton to have a pool where he could swim in winter), Parker had a Roman nose, high cheek bones, riveting blue eyes. Now he had fixed these instruments of persuasion on Dr. Shepherd and was saying, "We're not here to beat around the bush, doc, we want you to run for first selectman as an independent."

"Me? A Democrat? That's pretty funny, coming from you and Mr. Republican over there," the doctor said, nodding in the judge's direction. "Who are you going to let me beat?"

"Francetti."

"Tony Francetti? Dominick's father-in-law?"

"Yes. You know people are blaming Lou for letting all these drugs in and not catching the Horner girl, leaving it to the Stamford police. So we figure Tony'd be tarred by Lou's brush . . ."

"Look," Dr. Shepherd said. "I've had a long day listening to people's stomachs rumble, so maybe I'm not able to hear the message. What are you all up to?"

"Perhaps I should explain," Fielding Small said. "Whether what the papers are saying is true or false, something's gone wrong here, and the place is getting a very bad name. We love this town and I'm sure you do, too. We think the way to reassure not only the people of Worton but all of our critics outside is to have a political sweep. Charlie and I hit on the idea and went to Judge Brooke here and Dan, because we knew it would be impossible in a ninety percent Republican town without some help. They agreed to go along but to be honest, doc, you're the only Democrat they'd buy."

"That's about right," Judge Brooke said. "The way we figure it, if you run as an independent, and the other Democrats get elected as usual, it will . . . well, it will look like a real turnover."

"And Francetti's your sacrificial lamb?"

"Let's say he's not exactly a strong candidate. Too old for one thing," Dan Parker weighed in. "He's been a hard worker over the years and pleading for the chance to run. So now we give it to him. But we'd be irresponsible if we ever let that tub of lard get near the public trough."

"And who's the other Democrat? Who would get my seat? I assume you fellows have the committee sewed up, right, Fielding?"

"We've polled them by phone, and they agree on Professor Loren Johnson. He's a national name with a liberal cast now that he's always going down to Washington to advise LBJ. He's also a sound fellow, and his election would get some *good* national publicity."

Dr. Shepherd rocked back in his chair and laughed. "My God, you're sure of yourselves! And of course you've been counting on my well known vanity . . ."

"I wouldn't put it that way, doc," Dan Parker said. "We honestly think you are the right man at the right time. Everybody knows you've been bitching for years about how this town has been run, so they'll trust you to clean it up."

"Well, I at least might finally manage to get us some sewers, if that's what you mean, but as to legislating against sin . . ."

"Oh, you'll handle it," Parker assured him, "and I can promise you the *Record* will be behind you all the way. The important thing is that we try. There's too much at stake for all of us in our town's reputation. Why, right now I doubt I could even get my state senate seat back, coming from Worton, let alone make a try for Congress as the state committee kindly suggested."

Well, Floyd Shepherd thought, maybe he was getting to the age when you just didn't look a gift horse in the mouth . . . never mind its pedigree or track record. He only hoped this burst of nobility wouldn't louse up his golf time too much, and so with such mixed feelings said, "All right, gentlemen, but don't expect too much," realizing as he said it that he was talking as much to himself as to those assembled, nodding their pleasure at his agreement to serve.

Among the people who were beginning to regret moving

124

to Worton was George Steel Avery, chairman and chief executive officer of Ace Oil Company. True, his wife was comfortable in the brick Georgian house Bradford Atkins had built over the foundations of the old family farm when it burned down because he so admired the one Ben Adams had built down on the point. With true New England reserve, Adams had managed to tuck an astonishing number of rooms behind a compact exterior, but nothing could hide the grandeur of the view out over the Norwalk Islands and the Sound beyond, which was what had sold the Averys. Even a few days of looking out at that water inspired George Avery to acquire himself a big, twin-screwed Matthews cruiser—he was, after all, a man impelled to make use of nature—and he did enjoy plowing up the waters on weekends. He was also gratified that the big men of Worton like Judge Brooke and Howard Hilsman and Dan Parker seemed to recognize him as one of them despite a Texas twang and the fact that he hadn't gone to the right schools. Indeed Worton might well have been the place to be after all if it weren't for his son and only child, a hulking, unattractive—face it—boy of eighteen, George Steel Avery, Jr.

Like many self-made men, George Avery insisted on having somebody more qualified have the making of Steel, as the boy was called. His son was going to have all the mysterious "advantages" he had missed and would, thereby, become the one sort of person he envied, a gentleman. Steel was accordingly sent East to private schools right out of sixth grade, farmed out summers to the fanciest New England camps, given the grand tour of Europe under the guidance of a Harvard senior. Though he would never admit it publicly, George Avery's chief motivation in moving Ace's top command into the New York offices as soon as he had power to do so was to provide his son—hell, not himself—with a more prestigious home address.

Unfortunately, it was at about the time the Averys came to Worton that all the advantages to which he had been subjected rifted on young Steel like an overload of rich food. His body betrayed him by growing pudgy and pimply; his spirit, depressed by seeing himself as a shaggy pony in a corral of sleek young gentlemen in training, rebelled. To gain attention as much as anything else, Steel concocted a scheme whereby all the masters of the small, exclusive school he was attending were locked simultaneously in their rooms or offices and the keys chucked into the nearby lake. During the hour or so of glorious freedom this bought, Steel was actually transported on the shoulders of his fellows like a football hero, but he was forthwith expelled as soon as the local fire department rescued a sufficient number of masters from their cells. For the moment, there was nothing for the Averys to do but insert Steel into the public high school, which was compelled by law to take him.

For Steel this was unmitigated disaster. He knew hardly a soul in a school where tight cliques had been forming since kindergarten. Lacking coordination, as amply demonstrated by the failure over the years of lessons in tennis, golf, swimming, riding he had more sense than to try the one open door to acceptance, athletic achievement. The tempting girls who passed him in the halls without so much as a sidelong glance made matters even worse than they had been in an all male prep school. The only one of them who spoke to him was Betsy Horner, but he suspected darkly that she did it because her father worked for his. Taking an honest look backward over the years, he had to admit that most of his playmates had been children of Ace Oil employees; in fact, when they had been young and mean, a number of them had even told him that their parents made them come to play. And so Steel became a loner, an angry young man who shot the little Kharmann-Ghia his father had given him like a rocket back and forth to school over the curvy roads of Worton and spent an unhealthy amount of time doing God knew what in the room he had selected for himself at the farthest wing of the house from his parents.

With some justification, Steel blamed his parents for the unfairness life had visited upon him. As his father often unkindly said, the boy took after his mother's side of the family physically. Though a yellowing photograph taken about the time George Avery met her in the Texas boarding house her mother ran showed Ethel Sampson Avery as a reasonably attractive girl, she had been a balloon of a woman for as long as her son could remember. Placid and passive, she accepted isolation in whatever huge, empty house George chose for her as the normal lot of a wife, and filled her days with sleeping, eating and viewing TV in near equal proportions. Not surprisingly George Avery spent as little time at home as possible. For what he declared to be business reasons, he maintained an apartment in Manhattan, just as he had in downtown Houston, where he could sleep on nights he worked late during the week. But everybody, including his son Steel, knew that he rarely slept alone: his secretary, Della Sweet, whom he had brought east with him, had been his mistress for a dozen years. In fact the arrangement was so understood that she often came up to Worton for weekends or special days such as Christmas, and Steel was taught to call her "Aunt Della." Steel despised his mother for putting up with this and his father for not being man enough to admit it. Though his parents pretended that they stayed together for his sake, Steel knew it was otherwise: his father had made divorce a cause for firing among the executive ranks of Ace Oil on the theory that the public and customers had more faith in solid family men.

Steel Avery, in fact, had been deceived by very little since the age of six, having at least inherited his father's quick shrewd mind, which enabled him, despite other difficulties, to make excellent grades in every school he'd attended, including Worton High. In his father's eyes, it was Steel's saving grace. The grades would certainly get him into Harvard, where he had been destined to go by parental will from the cradle, and it was likely he would grow out of his pimples during his four years there and another couple of years in Harvard Business School. In view of this hopeful vision of his son's future, George Avery found Betsy Horner's arrest doubly damaging. Not only had it brought Ace Oil the worst publicity in years through the identification of Betsy's father with the company, but the rumors that admissions people in the nation's best colleges were reacting unfavorably to applications from Worton High School jeopardized Steel's chances at a critical time.

Avery's first impulse when he heard the news was to fire Jim Horner; it would serve notice to the rest of the employees and the public just where Ace Oil stood on a thing like drugs. The more he thought about it, however, the more he hesitated. While George Avery wouldn't admit to liking Horner—he didn't believe in "liking" the men who worked for him—he found him useful. Horner knew his business all right; without the image Horner had created for him, George Avery wouldn't be able to walk into the White House and talk to the President, fellow Texan or no. But in a way Horner's position in Worton, up to now at least, had been even more useful to Avery than his work. If it was comforting to see one of his "boys" solemnly passing the communion plate in church, it was even more rewarding to watch him clean up on the Sound. Since he saw to it that everybody in the club knew that Horner got that free time for racing out of Ace Oil's generosity, Avery took the same pride in him another man would in a winning bowling team wearing company T-shirts. Moreover, his open sponsorship of Horner took the curse off the fact that he himself drove a stink pot in a sailing club and had actually, along with the free gas he had arranged for the club's pump, earned his nomination as a director. While Avery knew that his other Worton friends were as upset as he over the bad publicity Horner's kid had brought on the town, he wasn't at all sure how they would react to his firing the man. The thing was that Horner, a Harvard man, seemed one of them; they were all gentlemen, and one reason Avery admired gentlemen was that he never quite understood them.

In the end George Avery decided that he would make use of Horner's embarrassment, as he had in a few other cases where a man's usefulness to him transcended his transgression. In a case like this, you had to do things just right, and Avery began by letting Horner stew for a few weeks. He pointedly ignored him on the train and saw to it that he was more or less divested of work in the office. When he did finally summon Horner into his presence, he made an elaborate show of closing the door, advising his secretary that he was not to be disturbed and otherwise making it clear that grave matters were afoot. Letting Horner remain on his feet, Avery sank into the great leather chair behind his desk and said abruptly, "I'm sure you are aware, Horner, that this unfortunate business with your daughter has brought the worst kind of embarrassing publicity to Ace Oil . . ."

Jim was shaken. Avery had to be sophisticated enough to understand how Palmer and the others were using him in their stories, and how little there was he could do about it. He said so. "I don't see how this really has anything to do with my work."

"You don't? You've been around here long enough to know that Ace Oil prides itself on the clean personal lives of its executives. A man who puts the company's name in a bad light isn't handling his job . . ."

Beneath the flesh of good living Jim could see the square, muscled lines of the oil field fighter Avery once had been. The man had a way of holding his head so that his thick glasses caught the light and became icy mirrors, hiding his eyes. "Well, if you want me to resign . . ."

Avery hitched around slightly so that Jim could look right through the glasses into the magnified blue eyes. "Now, don't be too hasty, fella," he said in a quieter voice . . . "Let's just sit down and talk about this damn thing."

"I don't think there's much to talk about. If you really think I'm hurting the company—"

Avery got up and led Jim over to a corner of the office, where he sat down on a couch, patting the place beside him and talking all the way. "Well, Jim, I think I'm a fair man. Matter of fact, I'm aware you must have some unusual legal expenses—a man like Howard Hilsman doesn't come cheap even at half his fee—I've instructed our treasurer to put through a raise in salary . . ."

Jim sank into the couch. "Thanks—"

"No thanks, Jim," Avery said. "I may be fair, but I'm tough too, and I don't give something for nothing. Worton's in a hell of a mess, as you know, and they're even saying now that the colleges won't take our kids. I've got a son about to graduate from high school there, and I don't like it. You and your kid's future are in this too . . . so I'm sure you'll want to use your talents to help turn this thing around. I understand that Judge Brooke and some of the others are working on the problem, and I think it might be a good idea if you'd put yourself at their disposal. Okay?"

"Yes, I guess so . . ."

"Well, then, go to it."

Jim went back to his office wishing he'd told Avery to shove the job up his ass. And knowing at the same time that no matter how good it might feel at the moment, resigning would just make matters worse. Susan was still so depressed that something as drastic as his being out of work might push her right over the edge. All that money he was supposed to be making just seemed to melt away—higher taxes; inflation; two cars (the wife of a vice-president shouldn't have to get up to drive him to the train); a new boat, to keep up with the Whites. And Susan's old man, obviously growing senile, was so upset by his granddaughter's disgrace that he was threatening to cut them all off without a cent. . . . Jim Horner, face it, needed a job. This job. Okay, climb down off your high horse and get on with it.

Jim had already come to terms with the fact that his daughter Betsy was a very distinct and baffling human being, and one to whom much of what he thought he knew about life made little sense. Oh, when he was her age he'd been guilty of small lapses such as smoking behind the barn and masturbating behind the bathroom door, but he would never—nor, he was certain, would Susan—have thought of doing anything illegal or that might bring public disgrace on his family. Jim had very little to go on to comprehend the difference beyond one small exchange with Betsy. He'd been going on in his most fatherly

130

manner on how kids acted differently in his day when Betsy delivered one of her more portentous curtain lines before exiting to her room. "Except you didn't have the bomb," she said.

At the time Jim thought of it as a meretricious non sequitur, but it kept coming back to nag at him. Betsy had seemed to toss the thing off the top of her head in that irritating way she had, but maybe, even if unconsciously, she had picked a pretty good symbol of the difference between her world and his. The bomb had made a shambles of war. Growing up as he did in a time when everybody was together against the murderous Nazis and the treacherous Japs, war made sense. A gold star in the window was a proud signal—everybody knew that wars were won by the self-sacrifice and courage of individual men like his father; the virtues that produced heroes were daily confirmed. No matter what the agonies of war, most people would live through it—and be better for it. In his day, nobody thought about the world blowing up, just as they didn't think about such things as that blacks might be people, that the world—at least its western half—might run out of gas, that China wasn't Chiang Kai-shek or Charlie Chan, that Buddha perhaps made some sense along with Christ. For Betsy and her friends the difference was no revelation—it was taken for granted.

As he sat there still shaking in the aftermath of his meeting with Avery, Jim began to think he was on his way to answering "Why us?" If he was right about the answer, it could be more frightening than reassuring. Just as he couldn't walk away from his job, he couldn't walk away from what he'd been raised to believe. And it occurred to him that even men of power like Avery and Judge Brooke might be frightened, too. And that frightened men, like frightened animals, usually react by fighting back—and reinforcing their dens. By going up there and doing a job in Worton for Avery, wouldn't he really be helping to fortify *his* den? And wasn't that what he really wanted? Well, wasn't it . . . ?

On the way home that night he wondered whether he

should try to share some of his thinking with Susan, but decided against it. These days he just couldn't seem to get through to her.

Looking around him at the familiar faces, he brought himself back to sanity. Like them, he was a guy with a job to do, a guy with a damn good life. Not perfect—but then, what was perfect except the retreat of the insane or the peace of the dead? So stop scratching for nonexistent answers, he told himself. There was a race coming up next weekend and even though the judge had seemed a little cool to him lately he'd been notified by letter that he was expected to be on deck. Maybe he could bring the *Helena* in first again. Or failing that, maybe he would find, as in the words of one of the few songs Betsy played that he liked, that the answer was, indeed, "blowing in the wind."

Chapter VI

What was left of Bill Stanton's brilliant mind understood that Judge Brooke and his horsey daughter needed him the way he was. They liked to measure their own smug strengths against his weaknesses. He knew they got a kick out of putting their heads together and whispering over the problem of "poor Bill" like a couple of kids discussing the class bad boy. Indeed, in their minds he made the judge's worthless son Hartwell look good by comparison. Hartwell might be pissing his life away running a guest house for fairies on St. Thomas, but at least he didn't drink. Marion and her father thought they had him by the short hairs, whereas it was really the other way around.

Bill's enviable situation was the result of the one legacy he was left by his impoverished diplomat father—a piece of advice. It came from the old man's heart because, despite his exalted title of Ambassador, he had been forced to serve out his life in the swamps of the world where a career man's salary plus expenses would be nearly, but not quite, enough to maintain the office. "Never, for Christ's sake, marry for love," the Ambassador said to his son on one of those interminable nights when they were trying to survive the tropical heat with the aid of cold gin and a feeble fan swinging over their heads, and when a kind of truth oozed like sweat from the pores. "You see what it did to me. Love dies but money grows, my boy. And let me tell you another thing. In any man-woman relationship the whip is in the hand of the one who does not love. So look around until you find a nice homely girl with lots of money and court her like the very devil. If you don't like the thought of this, just keep in mind old Ben Franklin's advice that every cat is gray in the dark."

The first time Bill Stanton stepped off the train in Worton and saw Marion Brooke, who had been dispatched to meet him as the first in a series of clumsy matchmaking ploys by her father, he knew he had laid eyes on his destiny. She was exactly what the Ambassador had ordered. Her dark hair was unattractively cropped—to keep it out of her way while riding and sailing, he later learned—in a way that seemed to emphasize the horsiness of her face with its long nose and lantern jaw. Like many girls who consider themselves too tall, she carried herself with an apologetic slump. Still, dressed in riding clothes and standing beside the old "woodie," she exuded the sweet fragrance of money.

As to his own attraction for Marion, Bill had no doubts. Growing up a "pretty boy" with blond curly hair, dimpled cheeks, full lips and just enough weakness in his receding chin to call for mothering, he had been fondled by women from the cradle. One, the bored wife of the second secretary at his father's last post, had been so hungry for his maleness that she'd nearly injured him for life in an effort to devour it. Bill was intelligent enough to realize early on that such spectacular success came as much from following his father's advice as from his own charms. He had found girls who were shy or less than dazzling far easier to persuade than the popular ones on whom so many of his friends wasted their time. Although such girls had more than satisfied his physical lusts, none so far had been seized of enough possessions to make a permanent commitment palatable. Until he reached Worton. There he wasted no time. Sliding into the car beside Marion Brooke, he said, "Hi, there, I'm Bill Stanton. Your father told me he had a great boat, but he never mentioned a beautiful daughter."

Nothing being perfect, it wasn't long before Bill Stanton detected a flaw in his find. All his life he had struggled with the problem of hiding the fact that he was a physical coward; he simply didn't like to be hurt. During his teenage years at boys schools where contact sports spawned the kind of hero he would have liked to be, he compensated by parading his somewhat astonishing sexual life openly and by seeking out acceptable athletic activity in which brain might beat brawn. Since all the schools he attended were on placid lakes or rivers, sailing turned out to be the sporting answer. There were times when an unsuspected williwaw, threatening to capsize his dinghy, cramped his guts with fear, but it was nothing compared to facing an inevitable clash with 250 pounds of lumbering meat on a football field, and his easy mastery of sailing strategy made him a winner with modest honor among his peers. By the time he reached law school he felt safe in leaving all such nonsense, even sailing, behind, and in fact convinced himself that cowardice itself was nothing but the mark of a superior intelligence that can foresee disaster and subscribe to values in which brute force has no place. So Bill Stanton was more than a little dismayed to discover as early as his first weekend the physical heedlessness of Judge Brooke and his plain daughter. Later he would date the beginning of serious drinking to the need for dulling his superior intelligence during the wild horseback rides and even wilder voyages to which he was subjected. Once, when attempting to get all this across to a psychiatrist, he had said, "Without a couple of drinks, I'd have been scared shitless half the time, do you understand?" And the psychiatrist had nodded sympathetically.

Bill rode his last horse the day before he and Marion were married in the Worton Presbyterian Church. After that, as he liked to put it to himself, he was in a safer saddle and could afford to be blunt the next time Marion asked him to go along. "Listen, honey," he'd said, "I get enough horseshit all day at the office without having to take it on *my* time." The sailing was another matter. Not only did he have a reputation to live up to, but he had to balance the occasional terrors of banging through a squall on the *Helena* against the certain torture he would suffer from the daily drudgery of actually practicing law. Despite, or perhaps because of, his brilliant scholastic record, Bill Stanton found the chores usually assigned to younger men at Brooke and Seabury (Hilsman and Stanton would be added later) tedious beyond endurance. He did, however, enjoy sitting in an office walled with law books and bullshitting about legal theory, taking long lunches at the Princeton Club with old classmates, and wandering Third Avenue and other byways of the city in search of pieces of Oriental porcelain to add to the collection he had started as a child at one of his father's Asian posts. All this could be his, he soon discovered, without really working, as long as he produced grandchildren for the judge and crewed on the *Helena*—an experience he learned to survive by stashing flasks around the hull for use in an emergency.

Bill Stanton detected still another flaw in the smooth texture of his carefully chosen life when his oldest child, named Cecily Helen (for her grandmothers), "Sissy," came into flower. He could only put it down as a miracle that such a child had sprung from such a union, and he was wholly enthralled by her fire and beauty. Here at last in his own home was the enchanting kind of creature from whom he had studiously stayed away to pursue his practical purposes. There being no apparent reason not to worship his own daughter, he did. Still, unaccustomed to love, Bill Stanton found the gnawing pains of concern and jealousy that assailed him when she was out of his protection far more excruciating than another father might. Given his way, he would have kept her up there on a shelf in a glass-fronted case with his fine porcelain. But Sissy, heedless like the rest of the Brookes, tortured him incessantly with the risks she took, not the least of them going out into the night with leering boys who, from the looks of them, could hardly wait to get their hands on her china-smooth flesh. Her father's awkward way of showing love was to rage and fume at his daughter, particularly after a few drinks, until virtually everything she did provoked a contest of wills between them. Actually, the night of her party Sissy had planned to stay home to please her parents and grandparents. When the other young people were pressing her to go, Bill Stanton overheard them and intervened, "You're not going anywhere, Sissy. I forbid it." Tossing her mane of hair like an unbroken pony, Sissy told her father, "I'm taking the Chevy." As she turned to go, Bill reached for her, but Marion nearly pinned him from behind in a kind of bear hug. "Let her go, Bill. Isn't that what this party was for—to introduce her to some young people around here?"

Of course, after her death, everybody said that Bill Stanton ought to pull himself together for the sake of the other children—two little girls and a boy who seemed to have inherited the worst blood of both families and were sent away to private school as much as possible. Bill told them all to go to hell. Instead of pulling himself together, what he really should do was go down and strangle that little wop right in his hospital bed. He was convinced that the story the kid couldn't remember anything was a lot of bull. Otherwise, why did Captain Dominick worry about who Ron might talk to and keep a guard there all the time? Come to that, why did the town tolerate such a misuse of the cops? Hilsman's idea that they should handle Dominick with kid gloves so as not to prejudice the case was infuriating. Wouldn't it be better, he argued, to discredit him? If Dominick were no longer in office, they could probably get that cop who found the bodies to change his testimony—and what jury would be impressed by a police captain who was fired? So he wanted to see the fellow drummed out of town, and when the story of Betsy Horner's arrest broke, he thought he saw his chance.

For weeks, months, Bill Stanton buttonholed everybody he knew or thought he knew, in the club, in stores, on the street, in trains, raising the same questions. Didn't this show that the Dominick boy was just a no-good kid on drugs? Didn't the arrest by outside cops prove Captain Dominick was an incompetent, or worse, covering for his son? What the hell was going on anyway? Shouldn't the town get rid of this Dominick? Stanton soon became a bore to avoid, increasingly drinking in brooding solitude. Sensing that nobody else was interested, he decided that he would have to take care of Dominick himself. His threats didn't particularly worry the people in Stanton's family since they, like him, knew him to be a coward, but they would try to calm him with promises that things would be better when Dr. Shepherd was elected. "What the fuck good will that do? The man's Dominick's doctor," he would reply with some logic.

Bill devoted much of his drinking time to meditating on what was the best thing to do. To find a chink in Lou's armor, he had to know more about his habits. Pretending it had something to do with the case the Dominicks had filed against him, Bill used the firm's private investigating agency to put a tail on Captain Dominick. After studying their daily reports a month or more, he saw an emerging pattern of behavior. Week nights Captain Dominick would go to the Hill Club immediately after coming off duty at five and emerge some two hours later in what the observers thought to be an intoxicated state from the way he walked. He would then drive to the hospital for a short visit with his son before going home. Since he was off duty, the captain was then unarmed and wore civilian clothes. At this point, Bill called off the tail and, driving the old Ford they kept around for the use of their cook so nobody would notice him, spent a couple of evenings himself studying the scene and Captain Dominick's movements from a distance.

One evening he came home to get a little warmth in him before starting his vigil. He'd hoped to avoid his wife, but sure enough, as he was pouring the first drink, Marion came around the corner. "Are you going to pass out before or after dinner—tell me so I can inform the servants."

"Neither. I'm not passing out. I'm going out."

"In your condition? You'll kill yourself. . . . Bill, I wish you'd at least try to get hold of yourself. This has been hard on me too. I'm the one who let her go, remember?"

"And if I hadn't tried to stop her, she wouldn't have gone—"

"Bill, we can't go on blaming ourselves, we have to go on living. I'm at least managing. I just wish you'd show some guts . . ."

"Look," he said, as if not listening to her, "I promised Doc Shepherd I'd help man his campaign headquarters tonight, so I'll just go out and grab a sandwich when I get a chance—"

"I doubt it will do the campaign much good to have the town drunk on exhibition."

"That's enough. One more crack like that and I'm going to walk out of here for good—"

"Not bloody likely . . . where would you get the money to buy your booze . . . ?"

"You're forgetting I'm the best lawyer in the firm . . ."

"And the laziest. Daddy tells me you haven't handled an entire case yourself for years . . ."

"And neither has he . . ." He downed a second drink in a gulp and walked out.

He'd been working at campaign headquarters off and on for a couple of weeks. Around 7:30 he usually went out for a sandwich, often asking the others if he could bring back coffee. He took this opportunity to check up on Dominick as he was leaving his club or the hospital. Tonight Captain Dominick's car was parked in the hospital lot in the lane farthest away from the pale light shed by the hospital windows. Bill sat in his Porsche at the end of the lane the captain would have to cross to get to his car. He felt the familiar rush of rage that always grabbed him when he thought of what the Dominicks had done to Sissy, and what they were trying to do to him.

Within minutes, Bill saw Captain Dominick's familiar figure moving out of the band of light around the hospital and in among the cars. He was alone. Suddenly Bill was gripped by a power that seemed not to be part of himself. Of course, *This* was what he had been waiting for all along. He disengaged the clutch and put the car in gear. When the captain started across the lane, he let the clutch in and tramped on the accelerator. It was a second or so of pure reflex action. All he was aware of was a kind of soft thump on the hood before he was around the bend, lights on and forcing himself to drive normally out of the parking lot. He stifled his panic and continued on to the Worton Diner, where he even made himself take a bite of his sandwich while waiting for his orders of coffee to go.

He was back at Independent Headquarters a little after eight when the call came in to Dr. Shepherd, who kept muttering "Jesus Christ! Jesus Christ!" as he listened.

Hanging up the phone, he said, "That was the hospital. Lou Dominick's been damn near killed . . ."

"What happened?" somebody asked.

"Hit by a car in the parking lot. Both legs broken, concussion, face lacerated. God knows what else."

"Who did it?"

"No one knows. Some hit-and-run, I guess. Lou's been drinking a lot lately . . ."

Fielding Small, his novelist's mind working overtime, said, "There's always the possibility somebody tried to bump him off. Hell, Lou's got enemies, even Bill here—"

"In the name of God, keep those thoughts to yourself," the doctor said quickly. "The publicity on this is going to be bad enough—just another excuse to drag up the whole wretched business again. I tell you our work is really going to be cut out for us if we get elected. But right now I've got to get to the hospital. I'm still Dominick's doctor, you know. I only hope when he comes to he remembers enough so we can get whoever it was. Otherwise too many people are going to get crazy ideas like Fielding here."

Bill Stanton left as soon as he could, afraid that the others would notice his shaken condition. Though it was possible Dominick hadn't recognized his car in the dark, he couldn't chance it. He'd have to get out—of Worton, of Connecticut, of the United States. The way he drove he could reach Canada by dawn, and probably Dominick would be out or under sedation until then. Without being fully conscious of where he was going, Bill found himself on the Thruway heading east and north before he remembered that he didn't have any money or credit cards. He'd realized he must have left his wallet at home when he'd gotten his check at the diner and was barely able to pay it out of the change in his pocket. Well, there was nothing for him to do but to turn around and go home. Now that he thought about it, the reason he'd left his wallet behind was that it was empty too . . . he'd broken the last bill buying a drink on the train. Well, at least it had the cards and maybe he could find some cash in Marion's purse. He wasn't hopeful, though, because she

140

never had any cash—the filthy rich never did. What if Marion was awake? The only good thing about all that horse riding was that she usually went early and soundly to sleep. Of course with his luck this night would be an exception.

The closer he got to his home the surer he became that Marion would be awake and that there would be no way of deceiving her. It was an absolutely eerie sensation. In fact, who could he deceive anyway? His running away would be a confession. Almost completely sober for the first time in years, Bill Stanton saw that he had no choice. Safely encased in steel, his sleek little car responsive to his slightest touch, he was suddenly given the nerve to do what he decided would be the one brave act of his life.

William Stanton's body was found at dawn by the milkman, whose route included Soundview Avenue. It was lying half out of the Porsche, which was wedged between two trees in the Brookehaven woods after evidently vaulting the stone wall on that tricky curve a quarter of a mile from the Stanton place. Everybody was shocked, particularly those at the Independent Headquarters, who agreed that they had never seen Bill Stanton more sober. That was always a dangerous spot on the road, and Dr. Shepherd made it a kind of campaign promise to have it widened in Bill's memory. The thing was, almost everybody in Worton knew that Bill Stanton was one hell of a driver, drunk or sober.

Election nights in the town of Worton were not normally celebrated in hotel ballrooms with balloons and champagne. Most times a few people whose jobs might depend on the outcome would gather in a dank room in the old town hall with the poll watchers and other workers until the count was finished around midnight or a little later. Paper cups and a bottle might be passed around, but that was all. The candidates were almost invariably home in bed since, win or lose, they had to be on the 7:32 in the morning. But Dr. Floyd Shepherd's race with Tony Francetti for first selectman had turned into such a squeaker that quite a few interested people were likely to stay up for it, and recognizing this, Dan Parker sprang for hiring a meeting room in Howard Johnson's, the only place in town that stayed open long enough—to catch the trade off the Thruway. Dr. Shepherd himself offered to pay for the booze. Some twenty people were assembled there, making it the oddest coalition of Republicans and Democrats in the town's history.

The doctor had brought along his wife, who made her opinion of the whole thing clear by sitting off in a corner and issuing loud, shuddering yawns from time to time. Judge Brooke was there alone, of course, since politics was considered men's work in Brookehaven, but Dan Parker's youngish wife was so politically savvy that she stepped into Edna Shepherd's kicked-off shoes as more or less official hostess. Knowing the judge's feelings, Howard Hilsman had left Marguerite at home, but Mr. and Mrs. Loren Johnson and Mr. and Mrs. Fielding Small and Mr. and Mrs. Charles Church were there. Some thought it indelicate of George Avery to bring along his secretary, Della Sweet, instead of his wife, but others felt his doing so in Worton must prove that all those suspicions were unfounded. The way George explained it was that, if Dr. Shepherd won, it would be a kind of triumph for Ace Oil, and he thought that Della should share in that too. And when, toward the witching hour, the figures showed that Dr. Shepherd would win by nearly a thousand votes, the first toasts in the room were indeed offered to George's boy, Jim Horner. He, too, was alone, because Susan was shy of going out with this group ever since Betsy's arrest. Jim, with some pleasure, reflected that the toasts were misdirected—after all, the winning strategy he'd devised was inspired far more by his concern over his older daughter than by any political objective.

In any case, until Lou Dominick's accident Dr. Shepherd had appeared such a sure winner that Jim Horner's contribution to the campaign was pretty much limited to writing press releases. When, as requested by Avery, Jim offered his services to the Brookehaven group they turned him over to Dr. Shepherd, who let him know at once that he had no use for public relations gimmicks. "I don't want to make any promises I can't keep," the doctor had said. "Anyway, there's nothing much wrong with this town that couldn't be cured by a good dose of quiet. My notion is to stay *out* of the papers." Although Jim knew that this wasn't exactly what Judge Brooke and the others had in mind, it gave him considerably more confidence in the good sense of the doctor. His professional instincts led him to hope that just putting the town in the compassionate hands of a folksy physician—a Democrat at that—would in the long run satisfy everybody, and he began quietly feeding Hal Palmer background material for what he hoped would be an election day story.

Jim was encouraged when Hal called one day and asked, "How's the doctor feel about drugs?"

Dr. Shepherd happened to be at headquarters, and Jim said, "I don't know. Hold on and I'll find out."

Without saying who was calling, Jim asked, "Doctor, how do you feel about drugs?"

"Sometimes they're good for what ails you," the doctor said, and quickly added, "but don't quote me on that. If that's somebody from the press tell them that, as a physician, I think all drugs are dangerous but that, as a physician, I also believe they should be handled on a case-by-case basis rather than as a matter of law."

When Jim read that back, Hal said, "Sounds like a good man. Keep me posted."

"I will . . ."

"Oh, and say, Jim, I've meant to tell you how goddamned sorry I am about—"

"Forget it. You were doing your job, now I'm doing mine."

"Well . . . fine . . . and I'm glad you've got somebody decent to work with for a change . . ."

The campaign had been going along so smoothly that Jim began spending most of his time back at Ace Oil until the night Lou Dominick was knocked down in the parking lot. Though Lou couldn't remember what the car looked like, he swore he wasn't drunk, and everybody believed him because he'd been held late on a case that night and hadn't even been to the club. People with less imagination than Fielding Small got his notion that the accident might have been deliberately caused. Men who didn't allow the law to interfere with saving their honor could well understand how the Stantons, say, or the Brookes might feel about a case that not only might cost them a good deal of money but could blacken the name of the beautiful Sissy Stanton. If the injured parent, Bill Stanton himself, had not died tragically that same night, suspicion would have fallen on him, but there were others who had money to hire it done. With such dark suspicions in the air, the election tide changed. Dan Parker's personal polling convinced him that a large sympathy vote for the Dominicks, along with the automatic Republican vote, would put Francetti in office. As if that weren't enough, the media latched onto the Dominick accident for some of the most florid reporting ever—Worton apparently was not only sinful but dangerous.

At a gloomy emergency session in Brookehaven the judge declared, "A general cleanup isn't enough now. What we need is an issue . . ."

"Too late," Dan Parker said. "What we really need is a miracle."

"Isn't that what p.r. men are for?" Fielding Small asked.

Everybody looked to Jim Horner. Jim had known he'd be on the spot, but hadn't been able to think of what to do until a fellow commuter on the Worton-bound train started talking about the trouble he was having with his daughter, who, he said, was forever at the beach or the pizza parlor instead of at home helping her sick mother. It was a situation all too familiar to Jim. There's nothing like having public trouble to attract confidences. Jim was reminded of how it was when Julie as a baby had something called congenital hip dislocation, especially frightening because they'd never heard of it. Within days after mentioning it to a friend, Susan was besieged with calls from a dozen other people whose children had had it or who had had it themselves and who knew all about the best treatment and the best doctors. It was the same way now. More people than he'd ever imagined were upset by the way their kids were behaving, and they seemed to feel safe in sharing their frustrations with Betsy Horner's father, who would, needless to say, have to understand all about it. Of course, few had had anything as bad as a drug bust, but . . . Usually Jim tried to avoid these confidences, but this night the man's story triggered an inspiration. The one subject on nearly every mind in Worton was what Dr. Shepherd called the town's only product—kids. In the end, it was the supposed mishandling of kids that was evoking all the bad publicity. Why not tackle it head-on instead of obliquely as they'd been doing?

Before going to Brookehaven Jim had brought up the subject somewhat hesitantly at the family table. "What could the town really do for young people?" he asked his daughters.

Betsy was bristly as usual. "Well, for one thing, you might stop calling us kids. We're people too, you know . . ."

Julie was eager to get in. "Yeah, we were talking about that at Young Life. God thinks we're as important as anybody . . ."

"Then why don't people listen to us?"

It was Betsy's question and it hung in the air as Jim drove to the meeting. By the time he got there he was ready with his notion, and when they all looked at him he tried it out. "Look, we all know—nobody better than I—that this whole thing's about young people. My idea is that we start building up the doctor as a candidate best able to handle the problems of our kids. Shouldn't be hard because it's true. I know you don't like to make big-deal promises, doctor, but we need some kind of program, say a kind of youth commission that you'd appoint with representation from the young people themselves to advise you. I've got a slogan that's pretty corny, I admit, and that will probably make my older daughter throw up, but . . . well—'Elect Dr. Shepherd and prove that Worton Cares About Kids.' As I said, Betsy may feel it's kind of sappy—at least at first—but we're also interested in convincing people here and out there across the country who are well over twenty-one, actually more like the average age of fifty-odd gathered in this room."

Dan Parker was first to react. "Like you said, Horner, it sounds pretty mushy. This town already supports the best schools in the state, two public beaches, four athletic fields, a YMCA and more clubs than you can shake a stick at. Hell, if that isn't caring about kids, as you put it, I don't know what is. What we really need here is a better police force."

Howard Hilsman nodded vigorous agreement.

The liberal contingent was equally unimpressed. "I always thought Worton was a pretty good place to grow up in," Charles Church said, and Fielding Small only shrugged and muttered, "Well, since I have no children . . ."

Surprisingly—to Jim—it was Judge Brooke who came to his support. "Gentlemen, the hour is late, and since nobody else seems to have a better idea, I see no harm in trying out this one—that is, if Floyd will go along."

"Well, okay, I guess," Dr. Shepherd said. "Of course in my experience town commissions aren't worth much—"

"So much the better," the judge said. "You won't be disappointed if it fails, but meanwhile we've at least got a program. I say let's try it."

And so was born what later came to be called "Jim Horner's Children's Crusade." Though Betsy, predictably, would have nothing whatever to do with anything that had "such an awful slogan," her younger sister Julie and her Young Life friends eagerly rang doorbells and passed out "Shepherd for First Selectman" leaflets. And, to almost everyone's surprise, it worked. Further, the stories Hal Palmer and others wrote about how aroused young people could oust the most entrenched Republican regime in the country suggested that Worton was a portent of things to come in next year's national congressional elections. Hal concluded a front-of-the-magazine interview with, "At last Worton has proved that it really does care about its kids. I'd move there myself if I could afford it."

On election eve, with victory clearly in prospect, men were shaking hands, women kissing. Judge Brooke got to Jim first with a warm clasp. "You keep surprising me, young man. I think maybe you'll make a damn good politician."

The kiss and accompanying direct look bestowed by Charlie Church's ex-model wife set Jim's pulse racing—he was rather glad Susan wasn't there to witness it. "I like smart men," Pauline Church said.

The doctor, standing nearby, interrupted. "I'm going to make Jim pay for this by appointing him chairman of that commission, and it just occurred to me, Pauline, you might want to work with him on it. We're going to need some certified Democrats, and besides you're almost young enough to be part of the problem. . . ."

Pauline Church stuck out her tongue. "I said I liked smart men, doctor, not smart-asses."

All laughed, though some uneasily. "You'll do it?" Dr. Shepherd persisted.

"Sure, why not, might be fun."

When she'd moved away, Dr. Shepherd asked Jim, "And you'll do it, too, of course."

"I just wonder if I'm the right one, I mean considering what's happened to Betsy . . ."

"You're perfect, Jim. If anybody should understand what's going on with these kids, you should . . ."

"Well, I don't."

"Then this will give you a great chance to find out. You pushed me into a campaign promise, now you've got to help me keep it. My first official act will be to announce the appointment in the morning. And you have to admit, at least I've given you the best-looking Democrat in town."

Hartwell Jennings Brooke came home for his brother-in-law's funeral and stayed considerably longer than his father would have liked. Marion's idea had been that she should have a man in the house with her for a while, which Judge Brooke considered almost funny in view of his doubts about whether Hartwell was a man. Still, for reasons the judge could never quite comprehend, Marion was fond of her younger brother. In fact, Judge Brooke blamed the way Hartwell turned out on Marion, who was always protecting him when the boy started going sissy on them. Many was the time Marion had crewed for him because Hartwell was afraid to, or didn't want to, and once she clobbered Benjy Adams so hard for teasing Hartwell that the kid was carted to the hospital. How a girl like Marion could have any use for a brother like Hartwell was an enduring mystery to the one man who should have been able to understand it perfectly.

The trouble was that nothing in Amos Hartwell Brooke's long life had ever made him pause for self-examination. Gifted with boundless energy, more money than he could ever spend and an automatic sense of superiority, he looked out upon life from an unassailable psychological fortress. Whatever enemies he found at the gates were mere problems that always yielded in his mind to rational solutions. If they couldn't be handled physically, a salvo of money usually did the trick. By keeping his fortress in good repair, he was always able, at last resort, to haul in the drawbridge. As a result he had nothing but scorn for the people out there who allowed themselves to be bloodied in senseless combat. He didn't mind manipulating weak people to his ends. He saw it simply as a logical and economical use of his power— and probably a Christian one too, since where would they be without him.

As a rational man, Judge Brooke dealt with his children much as he would with anybody else. Whereas another father might have found Marion's physical deficiencies disappointing, the judge realized that they made it possible for him to control what otherwise might have been a headstrong, rebellious woman. Only within the Brooke fortress could she be a princess, and she was clever enough, consciously or unconsciously, to realize this. It made for a happy relationship, and Marion, sharing his fearlessness, became in a way the son he would never have. That she in turn would find Hartwell's weaknesses useful in securing her position was something too murky for a rational man like the judge to think about.

148

Hartwell, in the judge's view, had simply inherited bad blood from the Jennings side. In marrying Helen, the judge had again acted as rationally as possible. She was delicate and darkly pretty; she came from good New York stock—her father was his father's associate; above all, she was sweetly unaware of possessing any powers within herself, was flutteringly timid and uncertain and in need of a secure man to tell her what she should be. It had made for a most serene marriage, in view of which the judge couldn't, and really didn't, hold it against Helen that some weird strain flowed unbidden through her veins. He could even understand how Helen—dark calling to dark, probably—couldn't help babying her strange son. But as soon as it became evident that Hartwell wasn't like other men, the judge brought rational forces to bear on the problem by supplying enough money to let the boy go anywhere and do anything he desired as long as it was far away from Worton. It was his way of pulling up the drawbridge. People who knew Judge Brooke well never asked him about his son, and there were many who didn't even know he had one. The problem of his son was solved—until son-in-law Bill Stanton's death.

Taking his old spaniel for an airing in the Brookehaven woods one Saturday, the judge was startled to hear shrieks and laughter. At a turn in the path he was nearly knocked down by the hurtling body of Hartwell; behind him was Marion. Both of them were flushed and laughing. "You never would have caught me if it hadn't been for dad," Hartwell spluttered.

"Oh yes I would . . ."

"What the *hell* is going on?" the judge asked.

"Oh, we were just horsing around—like we used to," Marion said. Her father inwardly winced.

"Hartwell and I have a great idea, dad. Tell him about it, Hartie, or do you want me to?"

"I think you'd better . . ."

"Well, with me alone now, we thought it might be nice for Hartwell to come back here to live. . . ."

The judge's silence spoke for itself, and Hartwell, who had no illusions about what his father thought of him, quickly added, "Oh, not in Brookehaven. You know mother wants Marion to move back there since she's feeling so feeble, and it might be a good idea. So I'd buy Marion's place—it's about perfect for me."

"No doubt. . . . That Church fellow must have had you in mind."

The judge, his son noted, was hitting below the belt. Everybody remembered how the judge had argued against hiring Charles Church's brother Hal as architect because he lived over there in Pound Ridge or some such place openly with a decorator fellow. But Marion had insisted. Hal Church was supposed to be the best in the business, certainly the most expensive, which in his field was often considered the same thing.

Marion liked Church's "daring"—his modern designs were always being pictured in magazines like *Life*, and she wanted something like that as a kind of proof that she had outgrown the Victorian pile of her childhood. Hal Church fairly outdid himself. Arguing that the Stanton place would be tucked away from all eyes in a far corner of Brookehaven, he used walls of glass all around to bring in the woods and sea and sky. Building it nearly drove Dan Parker's brother Seth, an old saw-and-hammer man from Worton, crazy. Once he even went to Dr. Shepherd claiming that "that screaming fag" was giving him a heart attack, but it was only gas and Seth was the first one to start bragging when a picture of the house appeared on the cover of an architectural magazine with the legend, "Builder, Seth Parker," in very small type down at the bottom.

Hartwell pretended not to see his father's clear implication. "Yes, I think Hal Church did have me in mind," he said. "You see, I've taken up sculpture—and I can just see my big piece, right in the middle of that glassed living room. . . ." He smiled pleasantly.

"What would you use for money?"

"Oh, I'd sell the island place."

"I can see you don't have any idea of what Marion's place is worth. It's three hundred, possibly four hundred thousand on today's market—and she may need every penny."

This was news to Marion, on whom the judge had settled $100,000 in stocks at the birth of each grandchild. "What do you mean, dad?"

"Well, Howard Hilsman's been talking to me about settling the Dominick suit. He's afraid you wouldn't have a chance with a jury now that Lou Dominick's been badly injured too . . . not to mention the talk about Bill . . . It'll probably take about half a million . . ."

The part about Hilsman was true enough, but until now Judge Brooke had been thinking about putting up the money himself if it came to that. His daughter, flushing darkly with anger, was talking back. "Dad, I thought you promised. I thought you said people like that could never push you around."

"It wouldn't be me; it would be you," the judge said. "Hilsman says that Dominick's attorney is an unprincipled fellow. He'd drag Sissy's name and maybe even Bill's through the mud at a trial—get the town into the papers all over again. I was going to have Howard come over and talk to you, but now that this has come up . . ."

"Well, why sell the house? I've got all that stock."

"Better to hang onto the stock in a market like this, and you won't be needing the house when you move—"

"I thought you said you'd never let a stranger—"

"Oh, we'll find somebody suitable."

Hartwell, whose delicate, handsome features were indeed a reflection of his mother's, was poking the brilliant autumn leaves into patterns with his toe. What his father was saying seemed to make sense; his father always made sense. Although he had spent most of the five hundred thousand settled on him, he could still raise the money—the island place might bring a hundred and fifty by now—but he would be buying back into something he had almost forgotten, a society where appearances meant everything.

"Sis, he's right—what you need is somebody 'suitable' quote unquote. Maybe because I was born here I forgot for a while that I'm not *suitable* for this crummy place. I never was, I never will be. I'm leaving tomorrow, so everybody can fucking well relax. . . ."

When he'd gone the judge sighed deeply. "I'm sorry," he told his daughter, "but I just couldn't stand to have him around. I don't think you should either—he'd be a bad influence on the children. Young Amos is a handful as it is. . . ."

With that, the judge whistled his spaniel to heel and headed back toward his own haven. A good thing too, because he would have been more shocked now to hear his supposedly sturdy daughter crying than he had been when she was whooping with childish laughter. What he most wanted at the moment was something pleasant to occupy his thoughts, and, the afternoon being balmy for November, he knew just what it should be—the *Helena*. She had just been hauled out in a Norwalk yard, and he hadn't yet had time to get his gear off her. Despite his good condition, the judge found climbing up and down ladders a little breathtaking these days, so he usually took one of the younger fellows who crewed with him along to help with this chore. When he got back to the house, he phoned Jim Horner.

If the judge had been one to analyze his own thinking —in which case, of course, he would not have been the judge—he might have spent more time reflecting on his preference for old things. Though there were a half a dozen cars in the Brookehaven garage, he automatically got into the old "woodie" to go down to the yard. The wagon was nearly as old as the *Helena* herself; in fact, he had bought it more than thirty years before for the purpose of lugging sailing gear, and he had used it by preference ever since. To Judge Brooke, the sight and touch of things that had served him well was a continuing comfort, a kind of confirmation of the enduring qualities in a rationally ordered existence. If you chose wisely and spent the money and effort to keep a thing in shape, whether it was a house, a car, a boat, a pipe, a suit of clothes or a body, it was a refutation of your own judgment to get rid of it before all possible usefulness had been exhausted. Judge Brooke knew he probably spent

152

more to keep the *Helena* afloat than it cost these young fellows to run their fiberglass rules-beating racing machines, but it was well worth it, especially when the *Helena* was up there near the front in a race the way she'd been this summer with Horner at the helm.

Judge Brooke was glad he hadn't let that thing about Horner's daughter cause him to do anything hasty. Perhaps having Hartwell around made him feel a little more charitable about another man's problems with his children. From what the judge had heard, Horner's other daughter was a pretty, quiet little thing, and both Helen and Marion liked his wife. What was her name . . . ? He'd had to hand it to Horner, the way he pulled that election out of the hat, and he rather envied George Avery having a man like that in the office. If Horner ran this commission of his as well as he sailed a boat, he'd certainly be a man to watch, or perhaps back, in local politics. With all that said to himself, the judge was still aware of a kind of deep-seated, perhaps unreasonable, uneasiness about Horner. He didn't like to think it was anything so trivial as the fact that the fellow had no background; or that he had put in four years at Cambridge and wasn't on the rolls of a single club. It was something more fundamental, and hard to fault really except out of a vast experience with men and affairs. Horner simply couldn't be relied on to remember whose side he was on—that was closer to it. He wasn't one of them. But Horner was still young, and maybe he would learn in time. . . .

Blocked up in the yard, the *Helena*'s hull with its deep, lead-footed keel was high as a house. Jim Horner, who had never seen her out of the water, whistled when he stood under her. "No wonder she's so steady," he said.

The judge patted the yacht's smooth flank like a lover while Jim fetched the tallest ladder he could find in the rubble of wood blocks, torn bits of canvas and crushed beer cans strewn around in the cavelike gloom created by huge hulls so tightly wedged into the yard that there must have been five million dollars' worth of pleasure craft in that small space. Still struggling to pay off the loan on his own small Lightning on a salary nearing $40,000, Jim wondered for the hundredth time where all the money came from. The answer was probably staring him in the face: across the stern of one large vessel, an honest owner had inscribed the name *Aunt Jane.*

Jim smiled as he set the ladder in place against the *Helena*'s stern.

"What's so amusing?" the judge asked.

"*Aunt Jane.*"

"Oh, yes. Nice little boat. Know the owner well—Harvey Mason."

"Well, he's at least honest. You can't not know where the money came from."

The judge didn't reply. It was the sort of tasteless Horner remark that made him squirm. Gentlemen didn't talk about money that way. Reaching the deck in a pant, he told Jim, "You can see why I need your help."

"My pleasure," Jim said. He meant it. Up there, in the pale orange of an early twilight, he found the *Helena,* stripped of her towering masts and massive rigging, curiously open and vulnerable, like a beautiful woman with her hair down. All around there was a sense of going to ground—the other hulls, some framed but still open to the ravages of weather, some snugged under cocoons of winter canvas; the river flowing by the yard, reduced by tide to a shining ribbon surrounded by flats of black mud on which rusted ground tackle and the hulls of sturdy old lobster and fishing boats that worked through the winter sat like vestiges of a drowned civilization. It was a new impression of the waterfront for Jim, and he liked it. There was a powerful assertion here that, in the end, the sea belonged to itself.

While they sat in the cockpit, resting from the climb and looking about, Jim tried to share some of his feeling with the judge. "You know, judge, I never get down here this time of year. It's so . . . I don't know, magnificently lonely. For me the water's always been a summer thing, full of boats and people like some big amusement park. I envy you seeing it year round."

"Why don't you buy something on the water?" the judge asked.

"We've been looking, but there's just nothing to be had —unless we move out of Worton," Jim said.

From reports the people in his real estate office gave him, the judge knew that Jim was speaking the truth. The wind was a little chillier up here on deck than the judge had anticipated. "Say, Jim," he said, "if you rummage around down below there, you might find a little bottled heat. I could use some, how about you?"

It was while Jim was getting the whiskey that the judge had his bright idea. Why not put Horner in Marion's house? Despite his misgivings about the man, and what he had told Hartwell, he knew that right now, with the market for Worton real estate still suffering from the bad publicity, was not the time to sell. Moreover, these days most of the people with the kind of money he'd want weren't the right kind. The last big sale on the water that Sound Realty had made was to one of the Italian boys from the other side of the tracks who had cleaned up in trucking; the first thing he did was build a swimming pool right on top of his beach, with striped awnings and pavilions like something at Playland.

Lifting the glass Jim handed him in a kind of toast, the judge said, "How would you like to be my neighbor, Jim? Marion's house is for sale, you know . . ."

"My God, judge, we could never afford a place like that."

"Don't be so sure, Jim," the judge said. "Come around and see me Monday—you know I'm up here in the bank Mondays—and we'll have a talk. Well, we'd better get busy unloading before it gets dark."

Yes, the judge decided, Horner might not be quite acceptable, but he was available and right for the job at hand. And thinking of it as a job, the judge thought of the man to fill it as an employee, which was comforting. Employees, after all, could always be fired.

All Floyd Shepherd could think about as he tried to

concentrate on what the girl was saying was, Why in hell did she have to come to me?

Since the election he'd had more than enough damned problems without something like this. Well, the answer here was obvious: she probably thought he knew a lot already from being Ron's doctor and might be sympathetic. The hell of it was that he was. He'd hardly recognized her as the bouncy candy striper he remembered from the hospital. Her hair was stringy, and the skin on her pinched face so pale that the freckles stood out like a case of measles. She wore patched jeans and a man's shirt so oversized that its scalloped tails hung to her knees. He suspected that her costume was more protective than faddish, which led him to wish that, if she had to come at all, she had come to him sooner.

"Betsy, have you told your parents?"

"Oh, no . . . I mean, they wouldn't understand . . ."

"But you think I will?"

"Well, Ron said . . . I mean, you knew all about us and didn't—"

"Didn't tell? That's right. But frankly, Betsy, I thought girls were more informed these days. My OB/GY friends tell me some of you are even coming in with your mothers for fittings."

"My mother isn't like that . . ."

"I dare say not. Or your father, either, from what I've seen of him. But I'm afraid they've got to be told, Betsy. You've waited too long, and there's nothing to do but make arrangements to have this baby. Besides, I couldn't do anything else after what your father's done for me."

Dr. Shepherd, who had been looking away to spare the girl embarrassment, glanced across his desk. All he could see was the wriggly part in Betsy's hair, which had lost all the shine it seemed to have had when he'd seen her going in and out of Ron's room. Of course, that was a long time ago, too long, and far worse than the plight of the girl in front of him was what had happened to Ron since Betsy's arrest, over and above his failure to improve. The boy really wanted to die, and Dr. Shepherd felt that he would soon get his wish. The doctor couldn't tell whether Betsy was crying or not, but he could hardly hear her response. "It'll kill them . . ."

Well, he'd have to turn her over to Bob Stiller, the gentlest of the OBs, but there was one other thing that he could do for her. "Would you like me to tell them, Betsy?"

She now looked up at him, and it seemed she was crying, at least her eyes had a wet, luminous shine. "Would you . . . ?"

If nothing else about the girl was beautiful, those expressive eyes made up for it. Dr. Shepherd looked at his watch to escape them. "What time does your father get home?"

"Usually on the 6:32 . . ."

"All right. We really can't waste any more time, Betsy, so I'll come to your house this evening, and I want you there too. . . . Oh, and one more thing, does Ron know about this?"

"No, and don't tell him. Don't tell him, please. It would really kill him. There's nothing he can do about it . . . and with his father hurt and all . . ."

"Betsy, you're a wise girl, and you're entitled to some honesty from me. It's touch and go with Ron now, you're right, and a problem like this might indeed be too much for him. . . . I'll see you tonight."

Dr. Shepherd was especially apprehensive about his visit to the Horner house. He didn't know Mrs. Horner at all, and what he'd seen of Jim Horner wasn't encouraging when it came to a matter like this. He was certainly a nice enough fellow, but like so many of the young comers around Worton he seemed to take himself—and life—awfully seriously. He even *looked* serious, with those heavy-rimmed glasses and that German haircut. You could see why they had elected him an elder of the church and why George Avery was so high on him. And from what Amos Brooke said, Horner took his sailing as seriously as his work. Dr. Shepherd didn't know much about psychiatry, or for that matter much care, but he guessed that some of Horner's seriousness might come from the insecurity of growing up, as he understood it, without a father—and especially a father who had been some kind of war hero from what Horner had told him one day when he'd made the mistake of kidding about how boring his war service was. Dr. Shepherd also realized, beyond whatever private anguish Betsy's condition might cause, how embarrassing it could be to everybody if Mr. Youth, as Horner was sometimes called these days as a result of being chairman of the Worton Youth Commission, had an eighteen-year-old daughter going around town with her stomach sticking out, and so the doctor regarded a proper handling of the Horner case as much in his line of duty as first selectman as in his professional capacity as Betsy's doctor.

Thinking on all this, Dr. Shepherd found he'd driven to the old Horner home on Bramble Road before remembering that they'd recently moved to the Stanton place on Soundview. In fact, it had happened only about a week ago and so suddenly that everybody was taken by surprise. A lot of people were sore. There was hardly a soul he knew in Worton, including himself, who wouldn't have given all he had to get hold of the Stanton property if they'd known it was on the market. The general assumption was that the judge would buy it back and hold it for Hartwell or one of the grandchildren when Marion and her family moved back into Brookehaven after Bill's death. And how in the world a man like Horner could afford it, nobody knew, although the rumor was that Judge Brooke had made some kind of deal because he liked to have Horner sailing with him. Wouldn't put it past him—Amos Brooke had a way of using his money to get what he wanted, Dr. Shepherd thought as he wound up the long drive to the stone-and-glass house that rode a knoll above the Sound like the bridge of a ship.

Jim Horner opened the door himself. You could tell that he was just back from the city because he was still wearing a business suit and that look of grim determination that carried a man to the end of a trying day. "Well, doc, this is a surprise," he said. "I'm just pouring myself a drink. Come in and join me. What's up?"

Dr. Shepherd followed Horner into the glassed living

room that would have seemed cold this fall night except for the fire hissing and crackling in an opening in the one wall of solid stone. Nobody else was evident, but he could tell from the smells and sounds that Mrs. Horner was busy in the kitchen. The room still had an empty look—the Horners might be living there but they hadn't had time to do much settling in. It was that in-gathering, feeding hour when even the most sorely tried of families seem to come together, and Dr. Shepherd wished mightily he did not have this mission to perform.

"Jim, I will have that drink—Scotch, light on the water—but then I think it would be best to have Mrs. Horner and Betsy in to hear what I have to say."

"Oh, I thought it was town business . . ."

When Jim came back with his wife and daughter, Dr. Shepherd, still standing with his back to the fire, took a quick sip and a firm grip on his glass, and began. "Betsy came to see me professionally today . . ."

Betsy had slumped onto a couch and was examining a crack in the stone floor as if she expected it to move. Her mother—in Dr. Shepherd's eye exactly the kind of a wife a fellow like Horner ought to have: not striking but pleasant and round and rosy, with a bright eye and perhaps under other circumstances a bright laugh—jumped in right away. "Betsy, are you sick? Why didn't you tell me? I'd have taken you to Dr. Hammond—"

"Mrs. Horner, she's not sick . . . She's pregnant." He said it flat out, what other way?

Jim dropped the glass he was filling; it shattered against the slate floor like an exclamation point. Susan's hands flew up as if to keep her eyes from seeing. "Oh, my God, oh, my *God* . . ."

Betsy lifted her head just enough to give the doctor a didn't-I-tell-you look as he quickly went on. "The reason she came to me, Mrs. Horner, instead of Dr. Hammond, is that with all the identification of my campaign with youth, she probably thought I would be more, well, understanding. Is that about right, Betsy? And then, of course, she knows that you and I are working together, Jim . . ."

But Jim wasn't listening. His eyes, large behind the glasses, were fixed on the crumpled, inelegant form of his daughter. He couldn't help himself—he felt the same stab of anger he'd felt when he'd seen her down there in the Stamford police station. "Who is it?" was what he let out.

"Oh, my God," said Susan, starting to cry. "What will people think *now*?"

"Who is it? Tell me who it is," Jim shouted and started moving toward his daughter.

Dr. Shepherd slipped between them. He put a hand on Horner's arm and could feel the tension. "Calm down, Jim," he said. "Betsy told me she doesn't want to give the father's name. She doesn't love him and doesn't want to have anything to do with him, and I agree with her. Getting some other kid mixed up in this would only make matters worse."

Susan's mind moved to the practical faster than her husband's. "What can we do? Is there . . . can you arrange an operation, doctor?"

"I'm afraid not, she's too far along, but we can find a place where she can go . . ."

Suddenly, Jim went back to the little bar he had set up in the corner. "I'm going to have another drink. You, too, Susan?"

"Oh, yes . . . please." And saying it, sank into a chair near the fire, tears running down her cheeks.

Having no children of his own, Dr. Shepherd hadn't quite known what to expect of this scene, but he did note that neither parent went to comfort their daughter. But then it was quite probable that he knew more about what was inside this girl than they did, a situation too common in his practice. One thing he liked about Betsy was the way she kept her mouth shut to spare Ron. He sat down on the couch beside her and took her hand. She gave him a glance he couldn't interpret.

"As far as I can tell, Betsy's perfectly healthy and shouldn't have any trouble," he said.

And then Susan Horner completely broke down, burying her face in her hands. "I can't bear it . . . I just can't . . ."

160

Jim went over and put an arm around her. "Here, drink this. Can you make the arrangements, doctor?"

"Well, yes, I guess so . . ."

"If you want, you can have my resignation from the commission. I don't see how I can be much use to you there, after this . . ."

"I wouldn't dream of accepting it," Dr. Shepherd said. "That's one of the reasons I wanted to be here when you got the news—so you wouldn't get any foolish ideas like that. This happens, like they say, in the best of families . . ."

Jim's smile was a crack. "That's a hot one, doctor. That's just what our good pastor Andy Wolfe said about the drug thing. Apparently my family's getting better and better all the time . . ."

"Now, Jim, listen. What I'm telling you is the truth. You ought to talk to my OB friends, they get a couple of kids a month in the same fix right here in Worton. But there's something else you ought to know about Betsy that I'm guessing she's never told you. I'm betraying a confidence here, but under the circumstances . . ." Betsy's nails were suddenly digging into the flesh of his hand, but he went on. ". . . I feel I must. Whatever she told the press or the police or you, Betsy was not using marijuana. She was taking it to Ron. I personally give her credit for keeping him alive. . . ."

Susan looked almost indignant. "But *why*, Betsy, why didn't—"

"That's it!" Jim interrupted. "That Dominick kid. That's who it is—right?"

Now the digging nails were really causing pain.

"A paralyzed kid?" Dr. Shepherd just let the question hang there in the air. The digging stopped.

"I just don't understand . . . I just don't . . . why us? . . . why . . ." Susan Horner kept saying, over and over.

Dr. Shepherd risked a glance at Betsy, and she responded with the faintest suggestion of a smile. See? it said.

He saw. The Horners were obviously decent people,

161

people who believed in the right things and had come very far from where they'd been—as far as this house they were sitting in—during their comparatively short time in Worton. Like himself, they'd probably come here to live the good life in a pleasant place. Unlike himself, part of that life, as promised in the ads, was to be the production of pleasant children. Given the right environment and isolated from the weeds of life, children ought to bloom at the right time and in the right way, just like plants. When one of them was twisted out of shape by the heat of some passion or another, it was a reflection on the gardener, an aberration that destroyed the whole effect and made you wonder whether even nature, or God, or whatever you chose to call the force that shaped life, was reliable. Dr. Shepherd had seen this happen so often that he no longer regretted at all the early hysterectomy that had left Edna sterile.

Dr. Shepherd got up. "I have to leave you now," he said, "but remember, Jim, I'm still counting on you. Nobody needs to know a thing about this. I'll call Stiller and get Betsy an appointment as soon as possible—he's reliable and can arrange for a place where she'll be comfortable. . . ."

Silence was what Dr. Shepherd heard as he let himself out of the Horners' glass house.

162

Chapter VII

If there was one thing that the Reverend Doctor W. Anderson Wolfe had never wanted, it was an assistant minister. He was happy to have a choir director since he couldn't carry a tune himself, a janitor and a couple of good secretaries. But the idea of having someone else messing around in the murky area of the faith he was dispensing was unsettling. Over the years, he had managed to fight off a number of efforts by the session to provide him with an assistant, but the phlebitis was his undoing. While it didn't keep him from performing his duties, it was an intimation of mortality that caused even his good friend Amos Brooke to turn against his position. One night at a secret meeting at Brookehaven to which Andy Wolfe was not invited, the session voted unanimously that for the good of the church an assistant was needed to take over in case Andy should be incapacitated or—God forbid—die.

A pulpit committee, including Jim Horner, was appointed to scour the seminaries for a likely candidate. Andy Wolfe fought a delaying action by finding some fault in each young man who was brought up for his inspection—one had been clubbed in one of those freedom marches in the South, and "you wouldn't want that kind of radical around here, would you"—another was suspiciously without a wife or fiancée though he was all of twenty-seven—still another came right out and admitted that he didn't believe in the Virgin Birth and thought Bishop Pike was "the greatest theologian of our times." It was Jim Horner who finally found a man Andy Wolfe could hardly turn down. Jim was attending one of those businessmen's prayer breakfasts in New York to which he was assigned by George Avery as what one of his fellow executives called the "house Christian" on the theory that it was good business for an Ace Oil Company executive to be rubbing shoulders with the likes of attorney Richard

Nixon, preacher Norman Vincent Peale and banker George Champion. One morning the speaker turned out to be a somewhat overaged graduate of thirty-five from Princeton Theological School by the name of John Peters—and Jim knew that he had found his man.

When John Peters rose to speak it would have been hard to distinguish him from any of the audience. He looked like an IBM salesman—vigorous smile, neat hair, white shirt, dark tie and suit—and talked like one too, which made sense in view of the fact that he had indeed been a member of that company's Hundred Percent Club until he found Jesus, or vice versa. He was a little emotional—but then good salesmen usually are emotional—as he told how it had happened at a Billy Graham rally. Jim Horner had watched some of those curious events on TV and had often wondered what kind of people they were who streamed down the aisles of great stadia toward the altar while the choir sang, "Just as I am without one plea . . ." He had never imagined that among them there would be a man like this John Peters. Once he got over that business about giving his life to Jesus, Peters actually made a good deal of sense, telling his audience that he could see now the need for closer bonds between religion and business. This, he said, would be his ministry; because of his special background, he hoped to serve in a big suburban church where he would be working closely with "fellows like you out there." Toward the end, just to show he was still a good fellow despite his conversion, he tried a little humility and humor. "I don't know yet whether I've got what it takes," he said. "I know the Lord didn't give me Billy Graham's golden tongue, but He did give me a lower handicap on the golf course."

Golf had been Andy Wolfe's game before his legs went bad, and, like any good executive, he had used the game to cement relationships with a number of the better-paying members of his congregation. Now that he couldn't play, he had noticed a few of them falling away. So when John Peters spent most of his first interview talking about golf instead of religion, as Jim Horner had suggested he do, Andy saw immediate possibilities in this particular assistant and finally approved of hiring him. It cost the church a little more than they had anticipated, since Peters had five children, but for a while it surely seemed worth it. He was runner-up in the Golden Hills (ministers received complimentary memberships) championship his first season and thereby convinced a number of people that it didn't necessarily hurt your game to spend Sunday mornings in church.

The few times that Andy Wolfe allowed Peters to take over the pulpit, his sermons were a bit simple and disconcerting to a congregation accustomed to Andy's gentle and scholarly Biblical paraphrases. Peters tended to run a service like a sales manager warming up the staff. Preaching on worry, for example, he said: "Are any of you worried out there? Of course you are. I can see it in your faces. You, there, you're worried about your sales conference tomorrow. You back there, madam, you're worried about whether your son will pass the college boards. You up there in the balcony, you're worried whether that special boy is going to ask you out. Well, friends, if you're worried, you don't have Jesus in your hearts. Jesus told us not to worry, to be like the lilies of the field. A few minutes ago we all sang, 'What a friend we have in Jesus, all our sins and griefs to bear . . .' We sang it with our lips, but did we sing it with our hearts? I tell you, my friends, to be a Christian you have to learn to let go and let God. Did you get that? Let go and let God. Now say it after me—let go and let God . . ." You could see people squirming, looking archly at each other all over the church, though a few did murmur the words. "Come on, you can do better than that! You can sing louder than that! Let's make this our slogan for the week—let go and let God . . . Once more, let go and let God . . . Again, and louder this time, let go and let God!" By now he was getting a chorus of sound from red-faced people who realized that they were not likely to get out of there unless they responded.

Later, a number of people in the congregation were heard to say that they thought Peters' performance was "cute," but a larger number, including such influential elders as Judge Brooke, thought he was making fools of them. The judge, remembering that Horner had found the fellow, wondered whether it wasn't another sign that Horner suffered from some baffling lack of judgment. But when Andy Wolfe, who had been away for the weekend, heard about it, he tried to calm the waters by pointing out that anyone with a handicap of six had to be pretty steady at the core and that Peters would settle down in time.

Privately, though, Andy was beginning to have some doubts, since in too many ways Peters was exhibiting the fanaticism of the newly converted. There was that thing about the car, for instance. For a number of years now, the church had been providing Andy on an annual basis with the smallest, most conservative Cadillac to bear him on his missions of mercy. It was felt that it would be appropriate to arrange for an Oldsmobile for Peters since Al Cranshaw, the Cadillac-Oldsmobile dealer and a trustee of the church, could provide that at cost too. Al was the first to admit that it was no sacrifice on his part; people were waiting in line each year to pay the highest prices for the preacher's "cream puff" when it came back in on trade. So the trustees voted the money, and Peters was informed at a session meeting that the car would be available as soon as Al got hold of the right model.

Everybody was a little shocked when Peters said, "I can't accept that, gentlemen. I've got my little Volkswagen that runs perfectly well. A little expense money for gas is all I need."

"I think you'd find the Oldsmobile far more comfortable," one man said.

"Too comfortable," Peters said, and, forgetting about Andy's Cadillac, went on, "Jesus told us to sell everything and give it to the poor, and I just don't think it looks right for a minister to be going around in a big car . . ."

"Well, as far as I'm concerned," said another elder, "I don't think it would look right for a minister of this church to be going around in a beat-up Volkswagen. I know I wouldn't want you coming up to my house in that thing. The neighbors would all think we can't afford to keep our preachers in proper style. Don't you agree, Andy?"

This was exactly what Andy Wolfe had feared about bringing another minister aboard. Any answer to that question could make him look bad. Wondering how Solomon might handle it, Andy had a sudden inspiration. "I think Mr. Peters has a good point," he said, "but he's going to be working a lot with our young people and what he really needs is a large station wagon if Al can find one for him. We could stencil the church's name on the side like some businesses do, so it would be perfectly clear that it was a piece of equipment Mr. Peters was using in the Lord's work. How does that strike you, John?"

"Well, on that basis . . ."

"Good, that's settled," said one of the elders, who added with a wink at Peters, "but just don't let us see that thing parked up there in the lot at Golden Hills."

Though that meeting broke up in general laughter, Andy Wolfe had the uncomfortable feeling that more problems would follow. And so he wasn't surprised about the sermons. He found that he could handle that one easily by keeping Peters busy with the Sunday school and getting guest preachers when he had to be away, except during summer vacation when there weren't enough people in the pews to make much difference. The real crisis, though, came when Peters discovered Young Life. A national evangelical group working outside the church, even though it had been founded by a too earnest Presbyterian minister, Young Life was recruiting kids from all over town and filling them full of God knows what kind of stuff at meetings in people's homes. For a number of people, having their kids turned on to Jesus was almost as frightening as having them turned on to drugs; some even feared there might be drugs involved too, since the group improbably included characters like that wild Ben Adams. Because *some* kind of religion seemed to be going on, disturbed parents naturally went to their pastors for advice, with the result that a good part of every regular monthly meeting of the Worton Ministerial Association was devoted to a frustrating discussion of what to do about Young Life. These good men were loath to denounce publicly a group of young people for enthusiastically professing the religion they preached, and therefore fell back on exchanging ideas for beefing up the youth programs in their various churches. New to all this, John Peters listened patiently for a few meetings. Then one day when the Congregational minister was enumerating the perils of a proposal to organize an ecumenical ski weekend to compete with one scheduled by Young Life —broken limbs, consummated sex and, God forbid, smuggled booze or drugs—Peters exploded.

"You don't have to worry about things like that when you have young people who have really taken Christ into their hearts," he said. "The trouble with us is that we are jealous. We're just like my competitors used to be when I was with IBM. I'd say Young Life is selling the goods better than we are, and I say more power to them! In fact, I'm telling my own young people to get into Young Life."

There was a shocked silence, during which the other ministers stole curious looks at Andy Wolfe, who was most stunned of all. He hadn't known Peters was up to this, and now he wondered who of the young people whose parents had complained to him might have been influenced by his own assistant. He hoped mightily that one of them wasn't Felicia Marden, Dan Parker's stepdaughter by the most recent of his felicitous marriages. The last time Dan spoke about it he warned Andy that, if the ministers didn't do something about it soon, he would turn the *Record* loose on this suspicious youth group and lay the blame right on the town's pulpits. Not wishing to reveal before his colleagues his ignorance of his own assistant's activities, Andy held his peace and was most grateful when the Episcopalian rector, Father Archibald Funston, was moved to speak. While his pillowed figure and veined nose and lively brood of four daughters bespoke a less than ascetic journey through life, Arch Funston liked to be called "father" to emphasize the height of the rites pursued by his particular congregation. A Rhodes scholar and author of essays, one of which had appeared a dozen years ago in *Atlantic Monthly,* Father

Funston was a leader of what intellectual life Worton could boast. People listened when he spoke.

"My dear young man," Father Funston said, "I was not aware that we are engaged in some sort of sales contest. I think I may be speaking for most of us here when I say that our principal purpose is to preserve the church, without which all the fruits of Christendom will one day surely rot. While an emotional conversion such as, I gather, you yourself experienced and to which these young people are being subjected can sometimes benefit an individual, only the church with its enduring rites and sacraments can save a civilization. The greatest enemy of the church is heresy, and our objection to this group is not that it is necessarily harmful to the young individuals involved but that it may, in standing outside the established churches, constitute a heresy."

"But Father Funston, they urge their young people to go to church, just like Billy Graham does," Peters argued. "From what I understand, half their kids weren't going to any church at all, and some of them were Catholic. I talked to their leader and he'd like nothing better than to be invited to use our churches for meetings. Wouldn't that solve your problem?"

"Not mine, certainly," Father Funston replied, "and perhaps not the others'. While we believe in ecumenical action on secular matters—otherwise we wouldn't be meeting here today—we are, as priests, dedicated to upholding the peculiar rites of our several traditions and to passing them on to young people reared within the faith."

"I thought our job was to bring souls to Jesus," Peters said.

Father Funston sighed, shrugged, rolled his eyes toward heaven. "Well, gentlemen, I propose we table the ski trip until next season while we have a committee study the very real problems Mr. Harding has raised. Any more business?"

Andy Wolfe had just about decided that the Young Life thing was cause enough to ask the session to remove his increasingly embarrassing assistant when Jim Horner came up with his idea for a "children's crusade,"

169

using the group as a nucleus. Felicia Marden won a prize for passing out more "Worton Cares About Kids" leaflets than anyone else, and Dan Parker did a complete turnaround, praising Young Life to the skies in a *Record* editorial. Then Peters' Democratic registration (it was only when Andy Wolfe learned that IBM's founder Thomas J. Watson was, incredibly, a Democrat that he understood this anomaly) earned him a seat on the new Youth Commission, which made him sort of a civic asset to the church. A move to get rid of him at that point would have been viewed as fear, or jealousy or just plain bad taste on Andy Wolfe's part.

His dilemma did not go unnoted. One afternoon over sherry in the privacy of the rector's lead-paned study, Arch Funston said to his old friend Andy Wolfe, "You know, I don't envy you that Peters fellow. These Johnny-come-latelies never do under Christianity."

Betsy hadn't liked the move to Soundview. Among other things, it made getting to school a real hassle. Back on Bramble Road, she'd had lots of friends with cars. Now she had to wait out in the woods, often in predawn darkness, for the bus. It was not only chilly, it was humiliating. You'd think if daddy could afford to live in a place like this he could afford to provide his daughter with a car, but he was worse than ever about money now. He kept telling them that buying the Stanton place was an opportunity of a lifetime, and they'd all have to tighten their belts. She thought it was peculiar, showing off in a glass house like that when it was so obvious they couldn't afford it. People in glass houses . . .

Under the circumstances, it was natural that Betsy should stick out her thumb when she saw Steel Avery come tooling along in his little Karmann Ghia. She thought him an awful lump, but she also felt kind of sorry for him and always tried to say "Hi!" to him in the halls. He had, after all, been at the mansion with Ron that magical night, so he must have something there that boys at least could see. One good thing she did know about him was that he was smart, and she figured that, if he would start giving her rides, maybe he would help on her homework. The car stopped with a smoking screech that must have cost him an eighth of an inch of rubber. Betsy started to run, and Julie, who was standing with her, started to run too. Betsy waved her back. "Get your own ride, Goody."

Betsy wasn't about to have Julie tagging along and crowding into that tiny car with them. It was bad enough living in the same house with her these days, and the best thing about the new house was that their bedrooms were farther apart. Ever since Betsy had been busted, Julie had been playing up to their parents in a way that turned Betsy's stomach. Julie had even started taking sailing lessons and crewing with dad, though she hated every minute of it, and now she was into this Young Life trip through that weird new assistant minister that dad had brought to the church. They had tried to get Betsy to join too, but she wouldn't join anything Ben Adams was part of. If getting religion meant ratting on your friends the way Ben did when he testified against her, she didn't want anything to do with it. Ben would probably have told on Ron too if he hadn't known that some of Ron's Italian friends would beat him up.

That first ride worked out just the way Betsy had hoped. Steel offered to take her home too, and from then on it became a regular routine. He was a funny kid, sort of silent and sad. She was glad she had thought about the homework because it gave them something to talk about—they didn't know the same kids or go to the same places or anything. He didn't even like her kind of music, and would have something by Bach or someone like that running on the tape deck all the time. Though Steel's pimples and flab put her off, she was surprised to find that he had nice, kind gray eyes and a soothing voice. When she didn't have to look right at him, she could imagine that she was with somebody she could really like. And when she was alone in her own room listening to Simon and Garfunkel singing about how hard it was to relate to anyone, she often found herself thinking more about Steel than anyone else—except Ron.

When she skipped her second period Betsy knew for

sure that she was pregnant, and the worst part was that she didn't feel safe about talking to anybody, not even one of the other girls in school who, everybody said, had gone off somewhere to have an abortion. For a while she thought about trying to sneak in and talk to Ron, since she knew the hospital so well, but the stories she'd heard about how sick he was made her wonder whether he would really care, or maybe care too much and get worse. And then when his father was injured, she *knew* she couldn't let Ron know. So she got to thinking about Dr. Shepherd, since Ron had told her that he was a good guy. He also didn't look like all the other doctors she knew, grave and grumpy and tired around the eyes; he was always smiling and shaking hands and making corny cracks. She remembered seeing him stand up there in front of senior assembly after her father got him going on that dumb children's crusade and saying, "There's a comedian you young people wouldn't know about named W. C. Fields (that showed how far out of it he was, not knowing about the old movies on TV) who used to say something like, 'People who hate dogs and children can't be all bad.' Well, I'm afraid that's the way people out there think about all of us in Worton, but we're going to show them they're wrong. We're going to show them that Worton Cares About Kids, and you're going to help me." Stuff like that. Made you wonder whether he really would understand, but Betsy tried to make herself go to him. Sometimes she'd walk back and forth in front of his office on the Post Road four or five times before she would chicken out.

Maybe it was all the throwing up in the morning— thank God she had her own bathroom in the new house so there wasn't much chance of Julie or her mother catching her—that gradually gave Betsy the feeling that, no matter what happened, she was ruined. She couldn't imagine letting someone cut or scrape down there, or whatever they had to do, and even less going around for months, sticking out and finally having a baby. Feeling as she did, she stopped putting her hair up at night or wearing makeup or even washing very carefully. At the same time she started wearing jeans and outsized shirts or baggy sweaters to school, which Steel Avery was one of the first to notice, or at least to mention.

"You trying to start a new style or something, Betsy?"

She had rehearsed for that and answered with unconscious humor, "Oh, no, it's just that I don't think it really matters what a person looks like, do you? It's what's inside that counts."

"You really think that? So do I, but nobody else seems to . . ."

"Well, now you know I do."

"Then you don't care so much the way I look?"

"I wouldn't be riding with you all the time if I did, would I?"

After that, Steel was considerably warmer and started telling her more about the life he had led in all those schools and camps and now in his wing of the Georgian house on Soundview. He didn't hide much of anything from her, and one morning she got into the car and smelled the smell. Steel was dragging on a homemade cigarette. "Hey, I didn't know you were on grass," she said.

"Sure," he said. "I don't usually turn on in the morning but I've got an interview with this Harvard guy coming up and I'm nervous . . ."

"You—nervous? Why? You've got the highest grades in the class."

"I know, but I'm no jock or anything, and they want everything these days. The thing is, I don't give a damn whether I go to Harvard or not, but the old man has his heart set on it."

"Hey, I thought you didn't care what your father wants."

"I don't. I probably wouldn't go even if they let me in. It's just that I don't want to give him the satisfaction of saying they turned me down because of what I am. He already goes around saying I take after my mother, and this would clinch it. . . . Here, have a drag."

"No, thanks. I don't . . . I mean I never have."

"Ah, c'mon, Betsy, you don't have to be that way with me. I'm your buddy."

"No, really . . ."

"Then all that stuff about you taking it in to Ron Dominick was true?"

Betsy was trapped, but she didn't much care—she was tired of lying. When she didn't say anything, Steel went on, "Hey, you really must have had it bad for him—to take all the blame like that."

"I did . . . I do," Betsy said, and her hands, lying on her lap, moved up to try to ease the waist of her jeans, against which her stiffening belly was pushing more persistently with each passing day. She'd have to do something about letting them out, but then maybe it wouldn't matter since now she'd seen Dr. Stiller, he had fixed it up for her to go away to some place down south very soon now. She didn't want to go away, and she didn't want to stay. The idea of killing herself had also occurred to her. . . . "Here, let me try it," she said. "I might as well . . ."

Betsy gagged and choked on the smoke. "No, you take a deep drag like this," Steel said, demonstrating. "Like with a regular cigarette."

"Oh, I don't even know how to smoke," Betsy said, and began to cry.

Steel pulled the car over to the side of the road and put a tentative arm around her shoulders. "Betsy, what's the matter? Are you sick?"

"Oh God, I just want to die—"

"Don't talk like that." He smiled at her. "I do too sometimes . . . it's nothing—"

"Except you don't happen to be *pregnant*. . . ."

That shut him up, but Betsy realized what she really wanted was to talk, to spill it all out to someone who just might understand. It was godawful around the house . . . Sometimes she wished the doctor had never told her parents the reassuring truth about the drugs—all it did was confuse them. If they thought she was smoking, they could have blamed her pregnancy on that and just figured she had *really* gone to pot. The un-

174

expected pun made her smile in spite of herself. At least that way they could have stayed furious with her, instead of acting hurt and wondering how in the world she could ever have let some boy do that to her. . . . Actually her father didn't *say* anything . . . it was her mother . . . My God, you'd have thought sex was the crime of the *ages*. . . . Sometimes she nearly did blurt out how it really was, how it felt to have Ron be alive for a little in her arms, saying, "Oh, my princess, my angel, my Bets . . ." and know she could help him like that even if he was so badly hurt. But because protecting Ron was the last small thing she could do for him now, she kept silent. Anyway, how could her parents understand her feelings? They'd told her a thousand times how they'd waited two years before they could get their parents to let them marry, and they were just as young and full of beans as any kid nowadays. She wondered. Her mother still seemed so ashamed of going to bed with her father that she'd lie to them about what was happening as if they were too dumb to know. No . . . it was easier just not to talk, though it put a terrible strain on everybody. . . . She didn't know whether Steel would understand her either, but at least he'd understand why she was going away. She figured she sort of owed it to him. She knew she was letting him get a lot of wrong ideas about her out of wanting not to hurt her feelings. She spared him the intimate parts, just saying that she was in love with Ron, and when she'd finished Steel just sat there a while and then asked, "Do you really want to go wherever it is they're sending you?"

"No."

"All right then, why don't you go away with me? I'll take you somewhere and you can have the baby and we'll tell people it's mine . . ."

"Steel, what a crazy idea! I mean, it's wonderful of you, but you know I don't love you and—"

"So what? Lots of couples are living together, some are even rooming together in college, and they aren't getting married and maybe they're not even in love, whatever *that* is."

"But they're not having babies—"

"We could manage. It would be a lot better than going off somewhere where you don't know anybody and . . ."

Her tears began again, in spite of herself, and Steel rolled another cigarette and lit it and handed it to her. "Here, you'd better learn how to smoke, you need it."

"We're going to be late for school, you'll miss your appointment—"

"Who gives a shit? Listen, Betsy, like the song says, I know I'm not much to look at and all that, but . . ."

She managed to get down a drag, which burned and made her a little light-headed. She looked at Steel. "Stop talking about yourself like that," she said. "I'm not much to look at myself." And again she was able to manage a smile. "Maybe if you grew a beard—"

"Hey, that's it— Seriously, Betsy, you're the only person who's been really decent to me in my whole life, and if you'll just let me, I'll—"

"Where would we get the money?" In some ways she was more her parents' daughter than she knew.

"I'll get it, don't worry. How long do we have?"

"A week, maybe two, I'm not sure—"

Suddenly Steel put his little car in gear. "If I step on it we can still make it," he said. "The big thing now is to stay strictly out of trouble, until . . ."

Jim Horner had never been much on politics. As a magazine writer he took the position that it was his professional duty to be more or less neutral, but in all honesty he had to admit that it was his personal preference too. He always liked to think that he was for the best man, not the party. Actually, he and Susan hadn't bothered to register when they were in New York but decided they had to when they moved to Worton because they were taxpayers. Jim argued that they should sign up as Republicans; if you registered Democrat or Independent all you did was disenfranchise yourself in a town where the only possible contest was in the Republican primaries.

Of course, for a long time they really didn't know the

names of anybody running in Worton, so they often just skipped the local elections. It was a struggle then for Jim to get to the polls either before or after train time, and Susan always had to figure out something to do with the kids. In national elections they voted a straight Republican ticket. As their parents, and their parents before them, had. In this, the Horners seemed comfortingly like the people around them; politics like religion and what you did for a living figured very little in the dialogue of Worton during those early years. The first time Jim began to hear any serious political argument in town was after Goldwater got the Republican nomination. Even people like Howard Hilsman were talking openly about voting Democratic, and Jim joined them. Ballots were split like cordwood in Worton that year, but locally every single Republican won. Now that Johnson was escalating the Vietnam war faster than Goldwater had dared propose in his campaign, Jim wondered if it wouldn't have made more sense to go on pulling the same old lever.

If Jim found broken promises, compromises, cynicism and outright thievery disillusioning on the national political scene, he found it worse on the local level after circumstances had involved him. Dr. Floyd Shepherd, the white knight of reform in Worton, seemed to be turning out to be not so different from the rest. Jim had allowed himself to hope for a commission of people who would at least try to discover what was going wrong with the care and feeding of young people in Worton and take some swift actions to change the situation. Instead, Dr. Shepherd's main concern in selecting members was what he called "political balance." By law, as the doctor explained to Jim, any town commission had to include a certain representation from the minority party, their parents' registration being used to label the young people. But the doctor went further than that in asking the Democrat and Republican town committees to vet the names —"just to stay plugged into the power." Because of her husband, Pauline Church passed with flying colors. It was thought expedient to have a representative of the cloth on anything having to do with the nurture of the young, and, the Republican posts having already been filled, the doctor had to pick John Peters as the only member of the clergy on the Democrats' roll, Father Funston having registered Independent on the grounds that a representative of the everlasting church should not take sides in matters as transient as politics. The biggest disappointment was Dr. Shepherd's naming of his defeated opponent, Tony Francetti, to the last vacant spot.

"Judge Brooke and Dan Parker thought Tony should be given a consolation prize, and I owed them something," the doctor said when Jim protested. "Besides, I figure he'll keep your commission sort of tied into the police through his son-in-law and take the heat off any suspicions that we're somehow messing around with their kids."

Now, half a year later, as he sat behind a cigarette-scarred table in a steamy little room in Town Hall, Jim felt that his worst doubts about the group being workable were coming true. It was not easy to concentrate. Betsy's precipitous flight with Steel Avery somehow made a mockery out of the commission. . . . "The thing is, we gotta do something about these fucking cops," said a boy whose long, tangled hair made Jim yearn to pour a bucket of disinfectant on him. Jim was startled—he wasn't used to hearing such adjectives in a meeting of people of both sexes ranging from sixteen to sixty-eight. The other young people didn't so much as snigger, but Tony Francetti, the oldest in the room, said, "Watch your language, young fella—"

"Well, what I mean is," the boy went on, "if you have long hair or something, they just pull you over whether you're doing anything wrong or not and search your car—"

"My mother'd a washed my mouth out with soap if I'd talked like that," Francetti said. "I'll bet that young fellow over there don't . . ."

Francetti was nodding in the direction of one of the youngest boys, a sophomore with a crew cut, round, peach-fuzzed cheeks and glasses that made him look like an adolescent owl. The boy was polite but firm. "That's not the *point,* Mr. Francetti. Jeff is trying to tell you, nobody cares about our rights—"

"Rights? Rights? Nobody ever talked about rights when I was a kid, and nobody had no cars either. Why, I used to walk all the way from my house over there by the Hill Club down to the old Beach School."

Jim rapped his pencil on the table. "Excuse me, Mr. Francetti, I'm afraid this isn't getting us anywhere—and that goes for your point too, Jeff. We've been asked to come up with a program. Let's stop wrangling and get to it."

"I couldn't agree more, Mr. Chairman," said John Peters. "Now, the way I look at it is that we already have a nucleus of committed Christian youth here in Young Life. Since they are outside any one church, they have shown us the way by themselves, and I think this commission ought to work with the churches to put together an ecumenical young people's movement with the help of Young Life. If we could achieve all that, all the problems we're talking about would disappear."

"What about us Jews?" Jeff asked.

Everybody laughed since Jeff was obviously not Jewish, nor were any but a handful of the town's young people. Only one girl didn't join in—a girl who never seemed to laugh. She was a senior who always looked immaculate in her matched skirts and sweaters and seamless silk stockings and whose brow was forever furrowed with intense concern. Jim had heard that she made all A's and had been admitted in her *junior* year to Smith. She was just Betsy's age, the daughter Susan would have liked. . . .

"Jeff's made a point," the girl was saying. "He wasn't being funny. We don't have enough Jews or blacks or chicanos or anything in this town. We don't even have a clue about what their life is about."

This girl even sounded like Betsy, Jim thought, at least in the days when she would deign to talk to them. A chorus of "Right ons" from the young members of the commission greeted her little speech. Francetti decided to try to beat them at their own game. "We've got plenty of wops like me. Ain't that enough?" he asked, and let his Buddha belly shake with laughter.

There was a kind of embarrassed silence before a woman's voice said, "We're not helping Mr. Horner at all. He's trying to get a job done and I think if we really put our minds to it we just *might* come up with something practical."

It was Pauline Church, and Jim gave her a smile of gratitude. He realized that he had been doing that more and more at these meetings, and was becoming acutely aware that her presence was about the only thing that made them tolerable. Only the lank length of her and the perfect features of her high-cheekboned face would suggest that Pauline Church had ever been anything as glamorous as a model. She wore no makeup, pulled her long hair severely back into a bun or a kind of pony tail, dressed in slacks and sweaters. Like an eager student, she sat alert on the edge of her chair, notebook on knee and pencil in hand; Jim had made her secretary to provide a Democratic balance to the student vice-president, whose parents were Republican, and himself. He was learning, or trying to . . . Still somewhere in her late twenties, Pauline seemed poised between the two worlds swirling around each other in that little room. She could catch the allusions of the brighter kids because she had read Ferlinghetti and Ginsberg and *Ramparts,* listened to Bob Dylan and Joan Baez, seen every James Dean movie, but she could appreciate too the bewildered rage these complaining kids evoked in Tony Francetti, since Charlie had told her all about how Tony really did walk two miles to school, lugged papers in the early dark, carried other people's golf clubs, mixed mortar, drove spikes along the tracks, all the while saving up the pennies that enabled him to buy the liquor store where he today sat grandly immobile listening to the cash register ring; even though he had to find the bottles himself and hated the man's politics, Charlie still wouldn't buy his booze anywhere else. So it was usually Pauline who, uncommitted to either side of the generational wrangle, at least tried to help Jim

180

keep the meetings targeted on finding some practical notions to make Worton a decent town for kids.

Despite her efforts, this meeting began to break up as inconclusively as usual when one kid after another shrugged into his jacket and, mumbling about homework, lunged out into the hall, and right after one of them left she made a face and said, "There goes my ride . . . he must have forgotten."

"Don't worry, I'll take you home. We ought to talk anyway," Jim said.

In the car he told her, "Thanks for trying. Sometimes I don't think we're ever going to get anywhere. If Francetti would just shut up—"

"He's no worse in his way than Jeff . . ."

"Well, you're right. God, without you there I think I'd go out of my mind."

"That's the nicest thing anybody's said to me all day. Got a lighter in here?"

Jim pointed to the button on the dial, and, when she leaned close to use it, was aware of a subtle fragrance, a kind of milky perfume that had to belong to a very feminine body. Those eyes of hers that he had noticed so long ago when he first saw her at Brookehaven seemed to give off a kind of teasing mischief in the lights from the dash. Though he was only driving a married female friend home from a boring, frustrating meeting, he seemed to be breaking out with the same prickly sensation he used to get taking a strange girl home from the first date and wondering whether he should try anything or not. It was pretty silly. He put it down to the fact that this was the first attractive woman he had really been alone with since his marriage. Which, he supposed, made him not only square but some kind of artifact. He was disappointed when from the proper distance of her own side of the car and through a cloud of smoke Pauline said matter-of-factly, "Better slow down. Our drive's next on the right."

The Church house was a pre-Revolutionary Colonial, expanded through several generations of Churches from a salt-box core into a romantic rambling jumble of clapboarded, shuttered wings. It sat in a copse of white birch and pine trees along the eighth fairway of the Golden Hills Country Club, most of which had been laid out on the rocky farmland that Charles Church's grandfather was only too happy to unload. After the sale, the old man put the proceeds into five percent gold bonds, got rid of his cows and chickens, deeded the house and a few remaining acres to his son and took a train to Florida, from where he never returned. The son, Charles' father, conveniently drank himself to death about the time Charles came back from his art studies in Paris with the first of his many brides, leaving Charles not only with the house but what remained of the gold bonds. The fact that Charles Church could now command $2500 to $3000 for one of his slick portraits or seascapes was taken as proof that he had the soul of a true artist, and the fact that he continued to paint when he obviously didn't have to work for a living was considered a sign that he had inherited some of the good blood of his Puritan ancestors. In view of this, people were puzzled at how Charles Church could have turned so queer politically as to take a job in the Roosevelt administration helping with the WPA art program and act as county chairman for *Henry Wallace.* When Church would stomp out of Ye Olde Liquor Shoppe after a hot political argument over the cash register, Tony Francetti, who had known three generations of Churches, would jerk a thumb in the direction of the artist's receding figure and explain it all to whomever was still around: "He's all right, Charlie. The thing is he never had to work for a living."

As they pulled up in front of the house Pauline said, "I hate to ask this, Jim, but do you mind going in with me? I don't like to go into the house alone at night, which is why I always ask Colin to drive me when Charlie's away."

"Not at all," Jim said, hoping his tone sounded more casual than he felt.

"I'm a city girl, used to apartments. This old place creaks at night like a ship in a gale. It's damned spooky."

While she fumbled through her purse for a key, Jim

read a plaque beside the door, put up by the local historical society, that informed anyone who might venture this far from the main road that the original house had been erected circa 1773 by one Ebenezer Church. The lintel was so low that Jim banged his head going in. It made him feel awkward and outsized as he stood in the little entrance hall with its sloping, wide-boarded, foot-polished floor and wondered exactly what he should do next. Pauline solved the problem gracefully. "Come on back and have a nightcap," she said. "You said you wanted to talk to me, and we haven't had much of a chance."

"Well, that's right—okay, just one."

"Just drop your coat on that old cobbler's bench there, if you don't mind," she said. "Charlie keeps all the booze back in his studio, so follow me. I hope you won't be shocked by what you see."

Jim trailed her along a low-ceilinged rippling hall to the one room that Charles Church had added to the expanding house. It was clear at the back where the property opened onto the treeless, light-drenched expanse of the golf course, and the whole north wall, including the sloping ceiling, was glass. Except for a couple of chairs and a sofa, aged to comfort and grouped around a free-standing fireplace, the room was a working studio, cluttered with easels, canvases, brushes, paint jars. A bar of adjustable spot lights, like something backstage in a theater, hung overhead, and, coming into the room, Pauline switched this on. The lights played on a dozen or more pencil studies of a long-legged nude figure that clearly was Pauline's. In his realistic style, Charles Church had left little to the imagination.

Waving at the pictures, Pauline said, "Charlie's latest studies. Much too realistic, but he's probably too old to change his style, poor man."

More to cover his embarrassment than anything else, Jim said, "I hear he sells very well."

"Fantastically. Isn't it an irony? Charlie's one artist who could have afforded to do his own thing all his life. I think it's the Yankee peasant in him—nothing's good if it doesn't bring in a buck. But here, let me get these lights off so you don't have to stare at my navel, or whatever."

The whatever was what he was looking at, and he was grateful for the comparative obscurity when she switched on a small lamp by the fireplace and turned off the overhead spots. The sketches, receding fuzzily into the background, were, if anything, even more alluring for the accent of mystery they now took on. Watching Pauline move to the little bar set into the wall behind the fireplace, Jim had to admit that old Charlie had at least caught some of his wife's grace. Charlie's interest in Pauline was clear enough, but like his wife and others in Worton, Jim now wondered what the hell a girl so young and beautiful and bright saw in that old lecher.

When she handed him a drink Jim sat down in one of the chairs and Pauline perched lightly on the edge of the couch nearest him. "All right, so talk," she said.

"Well, I was wondering whether you think there might be something in John Peters' idea of getting the churches together—not the religious thing, but . . ."

Pauline laughed. "God, you really are as serious as you look, aren't you?"

His reaction was more instinctive than comprehending. "Well, I don't see—"

"I'm sorry for teasing," she said, reaching out and putting a hand on top of his. The touch started a not unpleasant tingling along the length of his arm. "The fact is I like your sincerity, Jim. It's the only reason I keep going to these stupid meetings. You don't really think they're going to do any good, do you?"

"I'll admit I'm beginning to wonder . . ."

"The beginning of wisdom. The problem is that nobody's listening to anybody else. The kids pop off and shock Francetti and that dear Mrs. Lamb and even you— don't deny it, I could see it in your face. Francetti lectures them, and they get mad. Peters wants to turn them into little Christians. They don't even know what they want, but it isn't more basketball courts or revival meetings. You know, what the older people in this town don't, or

184

won't, understand is that they aren't dealing with specific acts but a whole change in attitude."

"Funny. I was thinking something like that myself not long ago . . ."

"Well, there's hope for you yet . . ."

"But not much for the town? I had the idea you felt we could really come up with something."

"Well, we're supposed to be listening to each other. There ought to be a way to make that a reality . . ."

"That's kind of vague, Pauline."

"I know it, but I've got an idea cooking. Let me think about it. Maybe by the next meeting . . ."

Jim had finished his drink. Now he looked at his watch. "Say, I ought to be going. Susan will be—"

"Do you have one of those wives who waits up to hear how you wowed them at the meeting?"

"Oh, no, I've been going to so many of these damned things that Susan usually goes to sleep unless there's something good on the late show. . . . She trusts me, I guess."

"I can see why. So come on, have one more for the road. Please. You know, you're about the only person I've talked to in this town besides the butcher. I don't know why, but they don't much like me. . . ."

"Jealousy. You're too young and pretty."

She got up to make another drink. "It's funny," she said, "I thought being the wife of *the* Charles Church . . ."

"No offense," Jim said, "but Charlie's somewhat of a character around here, people have stopped counting his wives."

And suddenly, she was angry. Jim liked the effect, which brought instant color to her rather pale cheeks. "That's the trouble with this goddamned town," she said. "Nobody can be different, not even the kids. Charlie tried to warn me but I wouldn't believe that a whole town—"

"Well, I think you're being a little harsh—"

"You do, do you? Then tell me—why did your own daughter feel she had to run away?"

"That's hitting pretty low . . ."

She touched him again. "You're right, Jim, and I'm truly sorry. It just shows you how upset I get when I think about all these stuffy people. I know how it must hurt. But seriously, what's wrong with a *girl* having a *baby*?"

"At eighteen? Unmarried?"

"But she went off with him, didn't she?"

"If it's him . . . I'd hoped Betsy had better taste—"

"Oh, Jesus! You sound just like my parents. When they found out about Charlie they made such a scene, calling him a dirty old man and other charming things to his face, that they've been embarrassed even to come to see us, which is just as well as far as I'm concerned . . ."

"If we're going to be so frank, Pauline, I've got to say I think they do have a point. An old man like Charlie—"

"My God, my dad could have said that. Hell, he did. Want to know something funny? Dad's in public relations too—for General Motors. It was their idea to send me east to this fancy school where they manufacture ladies. I think they thought there was a Ford in my future. Well, if you want the story, Dr. Freud, Charlie was my art teacher. He saw I couldn't draw worth a damn so he turned me into a model. All of a sudden there was a hundred dollars an hour, my own apartment, thousand-dollar dresses—and then he offered me all this. Pretty heady stuff for a little girl from Detroit. He called me his Galatea. You know, Charlie can really be charming, and he thinks young . . ."

She started to laugh. "Hey, you know that's really good —thinks young. Do you know where Charlie is now? He's in his New York apartment—shacked up with a *younger* girl . . ."

"And that doesn't bother you?"

"Sure, but I'm a modern girl and I try to believe in everybody, as they say, doing his own thing. That's Charlie's thing."

"And what's yours?"

"Being me."

"And who are you?"

186

"I don't know, I'm still trying to find out. Charlie's great about that. He's got me back in college again—a real college, Barnard—and he talks to me, about everything. Funny thing is that he really isn't jealous, not even when I had something going there for a while with a Columbia professor, so I guess that's why *I* can't be. Maybe what Charlie and I have isn't love the way you and my parents look at it, but *maybe* it's something better . . . we don't own each other."

"I've really got to go, Pauline . . ."

"All right, sure. I wouldn't want to get you in trouble." She smiled. "Thanks for listening, anyway."

"Thank you, and . . . any time."

"If you mean that, you know where to find me. I'm alone a lot . . ."

Jim was standing, and she got to her feet too. Tall enough to look him in the eye, she took both his hands in hers and kissed him gently on the mouth. He flushed, and she laughed. "Just a way of saying thanks. I don't want to scare you, but something about you makes me want to shake you up."

Jim left the house in a state of emotional confusion he'd not experienced since, for God's sake, high school. The smell of Pauline was still in the car, and he thought several times of turning back. She had, after all, told him in every possible way that she was available. Exactly why, he didn't know. Maybe she was one of those women who just had a thing about father figures, which wasn't particularly flattering. Still, the chance to possess the lithe young body so fully revealed in Charlie Church's sketches was damned compelling. Jim had deliberately avoided all the usual traps—the convention call girls, the late nights on business trips that ended in some whorehouse, the willing secretary. Now to run into this thing right in the middle of Worton, in the oldest house in town, just by taking a woman home from a weeknight meeting, was incredible. All those clucking matrons must be right about her—or were they? Was she that kind of woman, or was there maybe something between her and Jim, some mysterious chemistry that made her open up to him? He liked to think it was the latter, and he knew it was the most dangerous thought of all.

Unfortunately, Susan was not asleep when he crawled into bed. "Where have you been?" she asked. "You smell like a saloon. Some way for Mr. Youth, the big elder, to be coming home."

"I just had a drink with one of the commission members. We had some things to talk over—"

"Who was it?"

"Pauline Church, matter of fact."

"Really? Worton's shining example to youth!"

"She's not so bad, Susan, when you get to know her—"

"Well, don't you go getting to know her too well. All we need in this family is another scandal . . ."

"Susan, that's really not like you. Try to understand—"

"I *don't* understand. It seems to me that's all everybody's been saying to me ever since Betsy got into trouble. Well, I don't understand where we went wrong, and I certainly don't understand how you and a woman like Pauline Church can sit around drinking to all hours and pretending you're helping the kids . . ."

"Because she's the only one I can get to even *think* seriously about what the commission is supposed to do. Come on, Susan, we're not children. It's my job to take help where and from whom I can get it—"

Susan rolled over and flung her body on top of his. She buried her tear-wet face against his and said, "Oh, I know, Jim. I'm just . . . just kind of scared . . . Nothing's turning out right, is it? . . . And if you . . ."

He didn't say anything. There seemed nothing to say. Nothing to do except hold her close and rock her until they fell asleep.

Chapter VIII

The funeral mass for Ronald Dominick was far and away the biggest thing that had ever happened in Worton's Roman Catholic church. Nearly the whole high school turned out. If the day hadn't been bright and warm for early spring, it would have been a disaster; they had to string loudspeakers out to the steps so that the overflow crowd could hear. All ten of Ron's teammates on the offensive lineup managed to get back from the colleges they were attending to carry the casket, and Coach Wilbur Jones delivered a eulogy in which he pointed out that Ron had been more of a star in the game of life than on the gridiron. People in the crowd that gave way to let the family pass after services commented on the fact that Lou Dominick, who had recovered and recently been appointed chief of police, hardly limped at all and that from what you could see through those dark veils all those girls were turning into real beauties. It wasn't really a sad occasion since everybody agreed it was a blessing the boy had passed away even though it was generally understood that the settlement in the Stanton case would have kept him for life. Now the Dominicks could use the money to send the other kids to college, and it couldn't have happened to a more deserving family.

Mingling with the mourners and studying the whole scene with a keener eye than anybody else was a shaggy-headed, bearded young man in jeans and leather jacket who even on his home turf went unsuspected in his true identity. He was Leo Polchick, Worton's newest police sergeant, and he was very much on duty. News of Ron Dominick's death had naturally been carried, though in only half a column or so, widely in the press as a sort of mournful coda to the opening movement of what was becoming a symphony of sinful youth. The story about Ron didn't get much play since worse seemed to be hap-

189

pening every day on campuses, at concerts, wherever youth gathered. They were forming marches, burning draft cards, dropping out, turning themselves into "acid heads" with LSD. Their activities were so startling that *Time* departed from tradition and named the whole generation of twenty-five and under as its "Man of the Year." Still the old echo of Sissy's and Ron's rendezvous with death stirred enough notice that Leo felt sure an interested eye—such as Betsy Horner's—might fall on it and that Betsy might well be moved to come back for the funeral. So Leo studied every youthful female face, almost to the point of embarrassment, in hopes of recognizing the outlines of Betsy he remembered beneath whatever mask a hard two years of life might have given her.

No luck—or rather, maybe good luck. Leo wasn't at all happy with his assignment, although it was regarded as a windfall by the rest of the men on the force. He had no set hours, wore his hippy disguise continually and was encouraged to indulge in his favorite smoke and some not unpleasant liaisons with girls on the loose as part of his pursuit of leads. He could travel almost at whim to such haunts of the young as Boston's Cambridge area, New York's Greenwich Village, San Francisco's Haight-Ashbury—the notorious "Psychedelphia." Whenever he came in with another negative report, as he would have to do after the funeral, Lou Dominick would just say, "Keep at it, Leo, you'll find them." The point was that he didn't *want* to find them, never had. He was haunted not only by the dream of the Betsy Horner with whom he'd fallen half in love but the shame of the rotten deal he'd laid on her. Moreover, like a sports writer assigned to cover a particular team, he had grown more loyal to the people he was meant to watch than to his employer. He really liked a lot of these kids, and he hoped that Betsy and that Avery kid were making out okay. . . . God knew what they'd face when . . . if . . . he brought them back, but the grim determination he'd seen in Lou and that Mr. Avery, the one time he met him, was damned scary. They weren't people to horse with.

190

When First Selectman Dr. Floyd Shepherd questioned the expense of assigning an officer for so long just to look for two young people, Chief Dominick defended it on grounds that the crime young Avery had committed was a large one in terms of money, Betsy's was a serious one in terms of her probationary status, and bringing them back would serve both as a lesson to other Worton young people and as a way of restoring confidence in the local police. It was a line of argument with which Dr. Shepherd could not, publicly, disagree. Just before the young couple disappeared, Steel Avery had forged something like $5000 worth of checks in his parents' names and passed them off on nearly every merchant in Worton. Despite his obvious ability to do so, George Avery had refused to make good the money, arguing that his son was a criminal who should be brought to book and knowing, of course, that the angry merchants would support the police effort. This sort of crime, along with breaking into private homes to lift TV sets and other valuables, seemed to be growing in Worton and was attributed by Lou Dominick to youngsters needing money for drugs and other expensive bad habits. As the town's leading public official, Dr. Shepherd was obliged to deplore this trend despite the fact that, in this particular case, he hoped with all his heart that the kids would get away.

More than once Dr. Shepherd wished he hadn't felt ethically bound to hold in confidence what he knew of Ron's relationship with Betsy. He could tell that Lou had it all screwed up. Somehow Lou had wormed an admission out of his son that Betsy had been bringing him marijuana, and so he attributed Ron's decline and death to some kind of effect from the drug. None of Dr. Shepherd's efforts to convince him that this was medically unsound did any good, and so he suspected that Lou's real reason for keeping Polchick on the job was a kind of personal vendetta against Betsy Horner, a wish to bring her to more disgrace. Once he thought of telling Lou that the child Betsy had carried was his grandchild, but he realized that with a man like Lou such news could make matters worse. With all those daughters to protect, Lou

Dominick took an even dimmer view of sexual license than he did of drugs. None of that "kids will be kids" philosophy of his old boss Santori for Lou, but then, as Lou always pointed out, "Nick don't know a damn thing about kids, he never had any himself."

On an official level Dr. Shepherd was finding his new chief a difficult man to keep in line. Lou Dominick didn't seem to realize how lucky he was to have a job at all. There had been quite a movement on foot to get the new administration to fire Dominick as well as a few other top officers in retribution for the department's failure to act in both the Sissy Stanton and Betsy Horner cases. But whoever had run Lou down and thereby turned him into a victim of misfortune or attempted murder also had put an end to such a possibility, despite the outcome of the election. About half the town still thought that somebody was "out to get" Lou Dominick, and so under the circumstances firing him, or even failing to promote him, would have been an extremely unpopular act. Dr. Shepherd often thought what a blessing it was for the peace of the town that Bill Stanton's whereabouts were well accounted for that night and what an irony it would be if Stanton had anything at all to do with the accident that made Lou Dominick's position so secure.

In any event, Lou did not feel at all obliged to cooperate with Dr. Shepherd's effort to show that "Worton Cares About Kids." Lou wasn't going to have any truck with any commission that included that fellow Horner, who couldn't control his own brat, and that whore that Charlie Church had married. "These kids around here are bad enough without having people like that messing around with them," Lou told Dr. Shepherd. "You know what my father-in-law told me? He told me one kid sat there and talked about the 'fucking cops'—how do you like that?—and that Horner and the rest didn't do anything about it. I tell you, if there's a criminal element in this town it's those kids. You want to do something for this town, doc? Just get all those damned women away from their cocktails and bridge tables and tennis courts and back home where they belong, taking care of the kids.

Meantime, I'm going to bust every damn one of their brats I can catch."

It did make Lou Dominick actually grind his teeth to drive by the Golden Hills Country Club of a nice afternoon and see the courts so aflutter with women you'd think a flock of white birds had descended on them, or to go to the beach and find the place littered with baking female flesh. They should be home like his Maria sweating over the ironing board or stove so the kids would at least know where to find them. When they did pick up a kid, they usually had to hold him in the station house half a day before they could reach the mother at home or locate the father in New York. Then, chances were, if it was afternoon, either or both of the parents would be half in the bag and come charging into the station with a lawyer and screaming, "How can you do this to my son?" before they'd even found out what had happened. Half the time the kid was more embarrassed by the way his parents carried on than by what he had done. One actually begged Lou just to lock him up without bothering to call home.

The way the Horners and Averys acted when their kids ran off was typical. Think they'd call the cops for help? Oh, no. It was three days before Lou knew about it, and the word came to him through one of the merchants when Avery stopped payment on a forged check. By then the trail was already cold. Lou put out a nationwide alert, but those kids were smart enough to have ditched the Karmann Ghia and changed their looks and clothes and names. Of course, the parents were full of excuses. The Horners said their daughter told them she was going to visit a girl friend in college up in New London, and they didn't suspect otherwise until they found the Avery kid was gone too. Avery said he was away in Houston on a business trip and that big fat wife of his was so upset that she just collapsed in a heap. Lou could tell that Avery was furious with her. If it hadn't been for his bank calling his secretary in New York who called him in Houston about a suspicious check, he might still be down there. One thing Lou would say for Avery—once he did get onto it, he wasn't one of those parents who tried to protect his kid. He was tough. The eyes behind those big glasses of his were cold when he told Lou, "That boy of mine's nothing but a common criminal, and I want you to find him and throw the book at him."

The Horners, on the other hand, just seemed upset and confused. They agreed that they would like to know where their daughter was; they were worried about her because she had some kind of a health problem. So they cooperated as much as they could by giving him pictures of her, taking him into her bedroom where the other daughter, Julie, went through everything and figured out what clothes she had taken, listing names and addresses of friends and relatives she might be in touch with. They didn't seem to think that she had committed any crime until Lou reminded them that she was still on probation for her drug bust. It was then that Mrs. Horner broke down and started crying a flood, but Lou couldn't feel sorry for her. Anybody who could afford to live in a house like that Stanton place and let a daughter get away from them had to have something wrong with them.

Whatever the parents thought about it, Lou had his own reasons for wanting to get his hands on that Horner kid. He was sure that she was somehow responsible for Ron's death, and this time he wanted to see her in the jug. When it came to assigning the job, Leo Polchick was a natural choice. A lot of fellows on the force blamed Leo for giving the Worton police a bad name by letting Stamford arrest that Horner kid, but Lou appreciated Polchick's motives—and his method. He had, after all, in a way managed to save Ron's neck, whatever the nasty rumors, and had also spared Lou the embarrassment of moving in on one of that Brookehaven group at a time when his own position was more than a little shaky. Besides, Polchick was the only man on the force young enough and savvy enough to go underground, as he might have to do to find the kids. What surprised Lou, though, was Leo's first reaction to the assignment.

"Jeez, I don't think that's for me, chief," he said.

"Why? You're the only one who really knows that kid well enough to spot her."

"That's just the thing. She knows me too. She'd see me coming a mile off."

"Not if you disguise yourself enough. I'd think you'd jump at a job like this, Leo. Just think—no more traffic patrol, no more school guard duty, no more—"

"Yeah, and no more moonlighting either. Nobody's going to hire a hippy to drive them to the airport. What the hell am I going to live on?"

"A sergeant's salary. You're promoted as of now. Unless you refuse, in which case you're fired for insubordination."

"Well, in that case, I guess I don't have much choice . . ."

"I thought you'd see it my way, Leo. Now get going."

The chief would be disappointed about the funeral, and Leo wondered just how many such negative reports he could absorb before he finally gave up. Knowing he'd probably find the chief having his own private wake at the Hill Club, Leo went up there and got himself a boilermaker and watched the game while he was waiting. Old Whitey Ford was on the mound for the Yanks, looking pretty good despite all that trouble he'd had with his circulation. When you were as young as Leo, it made you feel good about the future to see how a guy could hang in there as old as thirty-eight. The drink and the game almost made him forget why he was there, until he felt a hand on his shoulder and turned around to see Lou's face. The chief had an eyebrow raised in silent query, and Leo said, "Nope. No sign of her."

"I never thought there would be," the chief said. "The little twat's too smart for that. You know, I'm beginning to think they've skipped the country."

"How, for Christ's sake? They'd have to get passports and all that . . ."

"There must be some place they could have gone—slipped into Canada maybe and joined all those deserters. They did have five thousand dollars, you know. I think you'd better get onto that."

195

"Listen, chief, why don't you drop it? We're never going to find them now—talk about needles in haystacks . . ."

Lou Dominick looked queer. All the muscles seemed to be twitching around his mouth and up through his cheeks. His voice was queer too, like he was talking with a mouth full of water. "You don't seem to understand, Leo—*that kid killed my son.*"

"I thought it was Sissy Stanton. . . . Anyway, I don't think you realize, Lou—Betsy was in love with Ron. That's how I trapped her, and if you want to know the truth, I don't feel so hot about it."

"Love? Some kind of love, getting him on drugs . . ."

"Lou, whatever the law says, grass isn't as bad for you as this stuff." He lifted his glass.

"You sound like Doc Shepherd, but I don't believe you—either of you. You didn't see him, watch him like I did, day after day, slipping away . . ."

"I think he died of something else."

"What?"

"How about not wanting to live?"

"Why, you—"

"Easy, chief . . . please . . . I'm just trying—"

"Easy? How would you feel burying a son? Huh? How would you *feel* . . . ?"

Lou wasn't going to hit him, as Leo had feared. Worse, he was going to cry. It was terrible to watch a tough guy cry—the last time had been out in Nam. Leo knew it was time to get the hell out. "Okay, chief, okay, I'm on my way. I'll let you know what I find out. . . ."

Susan Horner could remember exactly the day, the hour, the place she had felt herself coming apart. But every time Dr. Bruno asked her to tell him about it she couldn't bring herself to speak the truth—it seemed too trivial. God knows, she'd had enough shocks—the time the police called to say that Betsy was in custody for buying drugs, the night Dr. Shepherd told them Betsy was pregnant, the day George Avery steamed in and accused Betsy of seducing his son. But when she recounted one of these experiences, Dr. Bruno would say in that irritating purr of his, "Yes, yes, of course, of course, but that can't be it, can it? Please, Mrs. Horner, just let your thoughts drift, don't try to control them. Now . . ."

"What difference does it make?"

"Well, Mrs. Horner, we might know better what's really troubling you. Other people manage to go through things like this without such distressing symptoms. You say your husband seems to be carrying on as usual. Would you object to my seeing him?"

"Oh, don't. I don't want him to know . . ."

"Well, he must know how you feel if you are crying the way you say you are and avoiding sexual relations . . ."

"He knows I'm not feeling well, but he doesn't know I'm seeing you. He doesn't believe in psychiatrists."

"I see. Well, Mrs. Horner, I must tell you that you are wasting your time and money if you refuse—"

"Oh, all right, all right. But it just seems so silly . . ."

She couldn't start right at the time it had happened and have it make any sense at all. She had to begin back somewhere to set the scene. He'd have to understand a little about the club and sailing and all—he was a tennis player—for it to make any sense to him. She began by trying to get across what seemed to her Jim's sort of small-boy enthusiasm for messing around with boats. In all their married life she'd never seen anything get to him quite like that. After Kevin White started asking him to go crewing he could hardly wait for weekends to roll around. Weeknights he kept his nose buried in *Yachting*, and in the fall he enrolled in Power Squadron classes at the high school. At parties he'd get in a corner with anybody who owned so much as a canoe and be lost for the rest of the evening. It was kind of an obsession, but she could understand it . . . Jim had really had a very strict childhood, he'd always worked and studied and never had time for enjoying himself. Before they joined the yacht club and had a boat of their own, it seemed a harmless enough thing and, of course, right for Worton.

To be frank, she had to admit she was more interested in getting into the club than into a boat—Worton Yacht

Club was the hardest club in town to join. The roster of its membership—Brooke, Stanton, Hilsman, Atkins, Adams, White—was a kind of unofficial Worton blue book; there were none of the executive drifters, the expense account members that kept Golden Hills going. Jim thought that the limited membership was just a practical way of avoiding strain on the limited mooring and dock facilities, but she suspected he was wrong. She was sure of it when they met the membership committee. Trying to drink tea, with cup nearly rattling against saucer, she had to cope with women whose glib speech was laced with words like spinnaker and genoa and reef and galley, while their wise, x-ray eyes seemed to take in everything she wore right down to the garter belt. Still, it all seemed worth it when, the second time around, they were finally admitted to that privileged knot of people who gathered on the club's windy terrace for opening day ceremonies. While the flag officers, handsomely erect in their blue blazers, white pants and white hats, stood at attention, the flags were raised to the sound of cannon and Andy Wolfe recited the words of the Navy hymn for "those in peril on the sea." Right after the ceremony Marguerite Hilsman, who was standing beside her and who had ignored her a hundred times at church or Women's Club or wherever, turned and said, "Well, Susan Horner! Welcome aboard! Is that your husband Jim over there? Kevin White says he's turning into one of the best sailors around." Susan had to confess that she had the same kind of triumphant good feeling of acceptance she'd had way back when she first learned she had been admitted to Wellesley.

She really didn't want to bore Dr. Bruno with too much detail of the next years. The strain had set in when Jim borrowed money they couldn't afford to buy a brand new Lightning and then insisted they spend every waking weekend moment in it to make it worthwhile. Worse, Jim, who was pretty easy to get along with around the house except for his passion for neatness and punctuality, had turned into a sort of tyrant at the helm, ordering everybody to jump here or there, grab this or that. He some-

198

times frightened the girls and often infuriated her, and more than once after these "pleasure" cruises they hardly spoke to each other until the middle of the next week. Well, eventually it seemed better for Jim to find his own crew and for her to be a sailing widow. There were compensations, though. She found a few women to play tennis with during the week and, when Jim began winning races, they started to invite her down Sundays to sit at the end of the table and pour tea. Even the oldest members felt obliged to be nice to the champion's wife, and she began to enjoy a pleasant sense of importance—even if vicarious—whenever she was around the club.

Thinking about the club, she wondered now if that wasn't where their troubles with Betsy began. When the girls got a little older Jim wanted them to enroll in the sailing program and, frankly, so did she—although for different reasons. Jim was determined that his daughters should have the things in life that he'd missed; she thought it would be a way for them to get to know the . . . well . . . better sort of young people, the ones who went away to school. Betsy didn't want to go—none of her school friends were there; the sailing kids her age already knew everything and were stuck-up about it. Jim signed her up anyway, and every day Susan would have to endure Betsy's tears and stomach aches as she drove her down for lessons.

One day Susan arrived early, while all the kids were still out in boats, and found Betsy, sitting alone and sniffling, in the girls' locker room. "What are you doing here?" she wanted to know.

"I . . . I didn't have any lunch."

"Why not? I gave you five dollars this morning. Remember, I didn't have any change?"

"It was stolen . . . out of my locker while I was out sailing this morning."

"Who would do a thing like that?"

"Lib White. I know; she was the only one who wasn't sailing—"

"I can't believe it. She must have her own money. Her parents . . ."

"Oh, she does it for fun."

"Didn't you ask her to give it back?"

"Sure, and she just laughed at me. So did the other girls. They told me not to be a baby."

"Why didn't you tell the mother of the day?"

"You wouldn't want me to do that, would you? Anyway, the mother of the day is Mrs. White. Oh, mother, I just *hate* them, all of them . . ."

So, maybe because it was easier on her, Susan started allowing Betsy to stay home. When Jim found out about it he was furious. "The trouble with all of you is you're too sheltered. You just don't understand that's the way life is—in school, in business, everywhere," he said. "Hell, you wouldn't believe it if I told you his name, but I saw one of our most respected club members clip the buoy last Sunday and go right on racing. He beat the hell out of me, and I could have lodged a protest with the committee. What I did instead was force him over the line on the next start so he ended up last and ruined his average, and I'm sure he knows why. That's what you have to do. Betsy's got to learn to fight back . . ."

She didn't know what Dr. Bruno thought about all that, but she was beginning to think Jim had been right. If they'd made Betsy go back and fight maybe she wouldn't have slipped into that other high school crowd; maybe she would have got interested in some nice boy like Tim Hilsman instead of Ron Dominick. If they'd been stricter with her she might have learned to obey them, might have become interested in . . . well, healthy things instead of all that awful loud music. But Betsy wasn't easy, she just stood right up to her father and said, "Daddy, I can't believe you. I thought we were supposed to do unto others what we wanted them to do unto us."

"In an ideal world you might be right, Betsy, but I'm just trying to tell you how the world really is."

"Well, how can it be better if people just go on doing things like that?"

That's when Jim gave up, because, after all, what could he say? . . . What Susan couldn't understand now

200

was how a girl who could talk like that could do the things Betsy did. She only wished Dr. Bruno could be seeing Betsy too. Maybe he could explain it all. . . .

Anyway, after Betsy got into that trouble with the drugs, Susan stopped going to the club, stopped going much of anywhere. She was never sure of people, particularly the women. There was the time that neighbor on Bramble Road, frankly a rather common woman, called when her daughter was over at their house. After asking Susan to send the girl home, she said, "I hope you won't take this wrong, Mrs. Horner, but we don't think Dorothy should be seeing so much of Betsy after . . . well, you know what I mean, and I do hope you understand . . . I mean, we all know Betsy's a sweet girl—" Susan had hung up, but she couldn't hang up on people she saw, and she was happy to escape into the beautiful seclusion of the place on Soundview, where about the only people she met were Marion Stanton and her nice little mother who would drop in for tea and chat about flowers and horses and food like the real ladies they were.

What the doctor had to understand now was that their Julie was very different from Betsy. Dark and shy and silent like her father, she had been afraid of that club crowd too. Because of what had happened with Betsy, they couldn't very well force Julie to go, but when Betsy dropped out and Julie could see how estranged she was getting from them Julie made up her own mind to go into sailing just to make her father and mother happy. This was important to the story, because it got Susan into going down to the club again. She must say she was surprised at how warmly the women greeted her. They were impressed with her new address on Soundview, openly admiring about what a beautiful girl Julie was turning out to be, congratulatory about Jim's new prominence as "Mr. Youth" . . . Whenever Susan would come down on a nice afternoon and bring her knitting to wait for Julie to come in from sailing, the terrace-sitting mother—Jim and some of the other men called them the "sea gulls"—would make room for her and include her in the lazy gossipy talk. It was like old times, like the beginning, and she began to enjoy the almost animal sense of security in being in her own place, among her own kind. . . .

Then came all that business about Betsy's pregnancy and running away with the Avery boy. Who would ever have thought—an unattractive boy like that when she was so popular? Anyway, thank God it happened in winter when she didn't see much of anybody anyway. By the time she started taking Julie down to the club again she had forgotten about it—well, not forgotten, because you never forget a thing like that, but stopped thinking about it every minute. She was sorry to bother the doctor with all this background, but she was getting to it now—to the thing that happened that was so silly.

It was on an afternoon when she'd come down to the club and begun to go over to the regulars clustered in the sunny corner of the terrace. Come to think of it, they did look a lot like seagulls, perched around a small table with their heads together as if they were all picking from the same cracked clam. When they saw her coming toward them, they fluttered apart and stopped talking, and she knew at once that they had been talking about her, and her and Betsy. And that's when it happened. She came all over queer, felt like her body was turning into jelly or liquid, felt as if her heart would rattle right out of her chest, felt like she would cry or faint or throw up, or all three, right there in front of them. She could close her eyes now and see every detail of their faces, with their caught-in-the-act expressions, and start feeling queer all over again. She didn't know how long she just stood there while they looked at each other, but she did know that she turned and ran, actually ran, back to her car in the parking lot. She didn't even have the strength to drive away. She just sat there and cried, cried like she had never cried before, cried uncontrollably. It was like having hiccups you couldn't stop. Afraid somebody would see her, she stretched out on the front seat and went on crying until she kind of passed out. Julie found her there.

Scared to death, she kept shaking her and saying, "Mom, are you sick? Mom, what's the matter?"

Well, she was sick all right but not the way Julie thought or, later, Jim thought. "Is there such a thing as being sick at heart, Dr. Bruno?"

"It's an old-fashioned way of putting it. I'd prefer mind . . ."

"But isn't that silly? You see why I didn't bother telling you about a thing like that."

"Not silly at all. Now I think I know how we can get started. Time's up now, I'm afraid. Next week I hope you'll agree to use the couch."

"Oh, I wouldn't feel right about that. I don't have any hidden sex things or anything like that. You can see I'm really a very normal ordinary person . . ."

"None of us is what you call normal, Mrs. Horner, and the sooner we learn to accept that, the better off we are. As for ordinary—that's in the eye of the beholder. See you next week."

Every weekday morning there took place on the Worton station platform a curious ballet in three acts. The curtain raiser was low-keyed and mysterious. Out of the pre-dawn darkness most months of the year would slink the shadows of lean, hurried men, the kind of men who, driven by insomnia or insecurity, felt compelled to reach their places of work before anybody else. They would slink, silent and sullen, into the dusty seats of the 6:30 and wait for the day to arrive. In the next, and main, act, hundreds of young and vigorous warriors would descend from chariots driven by females in helmets of curlers and advance on the waiting 7:30 train. Their voices were hearty in greeting as they moved with precision through the steps that would bring them to the same seat in the same car every morning; stagehands or spectators who got in their way would be ruthlessly shoved aside by briefcases wielded like shields. The third act an hour later brought a more varied cast in view—men of splendid costume and kingly gait, women wobbling uncertainly atop unaccustomed heels, aging citizens shuffling through their last routine.

It was in this last act that George Steel Avery always played a part on the infrequent mornings when he had spent the night in Worton. Unlike regular commuters who moved blindly through their appointed roles, George Avery always looked brightly around for an opportunity to insert himself into the drama. What he hoped to spot was a man from Ace Oil Company. It was mean of him, he knew, but he always enjoyed the man's embarrassment at being discovered taking a train that would inevitably get him late to the office; some of the excuses they produced were highly inventive. Besides, George Avery often found an hour's conversation with a sweating, overeager junior executive very useful in finding out things about his corporation that he would never have known otherwise.

On a morning when the other actor in this little skit turned out to be Jim Horner, George Avery was not amused. In fact, he was upset. He had hardly exchanged a word with the man since that awful shouting match in the Horners' house when they'd argued over whose kid had done what to whom, and he wasn't enthralled at the sight of him now. He had got him out of his sight in the office by transferring him to the international division, which was ten floors below, and seldom ran into him in Worton now that he had tired of driving around the Sound in his cruiser and gone back to golf. He would have fired Horner outright if it hadn't been for Della's cool head. Funny, people probably thought that he and Della were having some kind of hot affair when their relationship was as old shoe as any marriage. He couldn't even remember the last time they'd slept together; most evenings they just sat with their feet on the coffee table watching TV and talking business, something Ethel never could do. Della's reasoning about Horner was hard to argue with. Like Dr. Frankenstein, he'd created a sort of monster in reverse by pushing Horner into civic affairs up in Worton—a Mr. Good Guy whose removal for such

204

evident personal reasons would look bad for both the company and Avery himself. All that national publicity Horner's children's crusade got was exactly what Avery had wanted—it really wasn't Horner's fault that it had come too late for them both.

Well, Horner still worked for him and, from the looks of that Stanton place he'd bought, needed every cent he was getting—and more. "Good morning, Horner," George Avery said, tugging up his coat sleeve to look at his watch.

"Morning, Mr. Avery. I don't usually see you here. Susan was sick this morning and . . ."

Jim hated himself for even half-apologizing to the man, but he was less than ever before in any position to be out of a job . . . And although the move to international had been a step down, or at least sideways, he'd been happy that at least he no longer had to see Avery. The man had proved out to be unbelievably vicious. When he'd been arguing with him that it must have been Betsy who'd gotten Steel into trouble, Avery had said right there in front of Susan, "That fat slob son of mine couldn't screw a knothole in a fence without its coming after him."

Jim had come close to hitting him, to throwing him out of the house, but then the man had suddenly humbled himself in front of them and pulled the vibrato stop on his emotional organ. "Don't you see—everything I've ever worked for gone, shot to hell. Look at this, look what I found . . ." He shoved a letter at them. It was from Harvard, informing Steel that the admissions scout to Worton had been very impressed and asking him to come up for more interviews. "He'll never make it now—a damned criminal. . . ."

Perhaps because he'd experienced it, Harvard didn't seem all that important to Jim, at least not at that moment. "We've got more immediate problems, Mr. Avery. Betsy is pregnant—"

Avery hardened up again. "So you're going to try to stick my boy with the kid?"

"I'm not trying to *stick* anybody with anything, Mr.

Avery. That seems to have been taken care of already—"

"Very funny, Horner . . . well, we'll let the police sort it out when they catch up with them . . ."

That had been Jim's last real conversation with Avery, but he didn't see how he could avoid having another one now. When they were seated together on the train Avery said, "About that youth commission, Horner. I think you're wasting your time anyway, but when it comes to wasting company time—"

"I believe you asked me to do all I could."

"That was before . . . Besides, I gather from Dan Parker that you might be getting yourself into a peck of trouble—"

"What kind of trouble?"

"Something about bringing some psychologist in here to run a hot line for kids on dope . . . Parker says the whole thing would have fallen through if you hadn't voted with the Democrats. . . ."

"I don't think of the people on that commission as belonging to any party. The young people wanted it and—"

"My God, Horner! 'The young people wanted it.' You of all people ought to know now that what young people want sure as hell isn't what's good for them. It's time we stopped indulging these little brats. Look at the way they're cluttering up the streets and wrecking universities. I'm not a Harvard man like you, Horner; I didn't get a chance to go to any college, but if I had I damn well would have treated it with some respect. This town doesn't need a long-haired shrink. It needs more cops . . . and what's this about bringing a lot of niggers to Worton?"

Jim winced. "So far it hasn't gone beyond the talking stage . . ."

Actually Jim was pretty sure it would prove to be more than talk, but there was no use trying to explain it to Avery. The notion to invite a Harlem high school class up for an exchange week in Worton came from the serious, silk-stockinged girl, and Jim would probably have to vote for it just as he had for Pauline Church's idea to establish a "listening post" with a hot line. The young people on the commission had voted at once and unanimously for Pauline's proposal; by law no motion could carry without a majority of the adult members also approving. Tony Francetti, of course, didn't want any "psychowhatchamacallit messing around with our kids," and little Mrs. Lamb still thought there ought to be "tea dances at the high school—that's the way *we* used to stay out of trouble." John Peters thought there ought to be a man of the cloth on the receiving end of confidences, if it came to that. The young people said that if their vote for Mrs. Church's plan didn't carry they'd take a walk and expose the whole bullshit "Worton Cares About Kids" for the phony it seemed to be. That decided Jim and even persuaded Peters, who felt he'd lose face with the young people at the church if he didn't go along. When Dr. Shepherd heard about it, he sighed and said, "Democracy's so damn difficult . . . there are times when I wish I didn't believe in it."

George Avery didn't, of course. "Well, talk or not," he said. "I don't want any representative of Ace Oil Company mixed up in a thing like that. I suggest you resign from that commission, Horner . . ."

"Maybe I should resign from Ace Oil instead . . ." He hoped Avery couldn't see how shocked he was by his own words.

Avery was pleased . . . his calculated provocation had brought even swifter results than he'd expected. "Maybe you should," he agreed.

He enjoyed the surprised look on Horner's face—surprise tinged, as he saw it, with dismay around the eyes. In his long executive life he'd cut the ground from under hundreds of young fellows like Horner who thought they could bully him with a threat to resign. If they left, good riddance; if they crawled back with an apology, their chastened attitude about who was boss made them more valuable. Right now he was enjoying watching smart-ass Horner struggling for the right words.

"I'd like a month or so to look around," Jim finally said, fighting to sound calm.

"Why not? It's your idea to resign. I've no fault to find with your work."

Avery's enjoyment with the cat-and-mouse game was disrupted when Horner got up abruptly from his seat, took his briefcase off the rack and said, "You'll have my letter today, Mr. Avery."

Watching Horner sway his way down the car, Avery took out his second cigar of the day and lit it with a feeling of satisfaction. It had turned out to be a fruitful meeting after all; hell, even Della couldn't blame him for accepting a freely offered resignation. He really didn't want to have anything more to do with Horner. Since Steel had messed up his life, Avery had no further need of Horner's image-building or the prestige of living in Worton either, for that matter. He would already have sold out and moved back to Texas if it weren't for that stupid wife of his. Ethel had some crazy notion that she had to stay right there in that house so that Steel could find them, as if the kid couldn't find his way to the Ace Oil Company's offices. Under the circumstances, though, staying in Worton was a small price to pay for keeping Ethel quiet. Once they got the matter of the boy settled they could move the whole works back to Houston, where there weren't so many soft-headed Harvard gentlemen like Horner and their rotten kids to deal with. Watching the crumbling warrens of Harlem slip by, George Avery smiled to himself. When he'd first moved to Worton, everybody warned him that commuting was a waste of time. Nothing ever happened on trains, they'd said. . . .

Jim Horner could have told him differently, even then. He'd met Kevin White on a train, for instance, written many of those essays that had made George Avery famous, thought up the notion for a so-called children's crusade—and now had resigned. Jim didn't try to find another seat, preferring to stand in a vestibule between cars where the clatter of the rocketing train insulated him against everything but his own thoughts. Soon he was also insulated by the darkness in the tunnel under Manhattan. It seemed eerily symbolic of what he had just done to himself. The exhilaration he'd felt momentarily had given way to the plain old sweats.

Why in hell *had* he let Avery goad him into such a rash act? He'd long ago thought he'd come to terms with the fact that you don't have to like a man to work for him. Any other point of view would be hopelessly immature —a naive expectation that you could somehow escape the fate of at least half of mankind. He would like to have believed otherwise, but in these first moments of self-confrontation he felt anything but heroic—gripped as he was by fear that he had done something damn foolish and imperiled his whole family in the consequence.

The train was still moving, though so slowly now that you could see the shapes of the individual little light bulbs that struggled against the dank dark. Still time to go back and apologize. He actually put his hand on the door, then faced another piece of reality—there was no way he could make himself do it. Call it pride, or stupidity, Jim Horner would never again kiss George Avery's ass. By the time the train stopped, Jim had got himself reasonably together, and plunged through the crowds like a fullback, more eager to get to the office than he had been since his first day at *News*. Writing that letter of resignation would be a goddamn *pleasure.*

In the end, though, it wasn't. He went through draft after high-sounding draft. He informed George Avery that, working with young people, he had discovered that there was a lot more to life than preserving order to sell more oil, that there were such things as compassion, integrity, honesty—or, as Jeff put it in meetings, "no bullshit." But reading over each new effort caused him to think that he was as guilty of bullshit as anybody. He'd initially taken the job there on the suggestion of Avery himself; expediency had often dictated the votes he'd cast in commission; only the bad luck of getting the wrong train and bumping into Avery had provoked this resignation. He wasn't really such a crusader for truth and virtue. What he definitely was was a guy in a hell of a hole. He had exactly $372 in the bank until his next pay check; the interest on Judge Brooke's loan to him was so high that he hadn't been able to pay a cent of principal—now there, spelling aside, was a real principle to worry about—knowledge that he was out of a job would probably push Susan, who was steadily drinking more, right over the edge. What's more, Avery surely knew, or suspected, all this. Finally Jim wrote: "Owing to personal reasons as discussed, I hereby resign as Vice President of Public Relations International of Ace Oil Company. James G. Horner."

He put the letter in an envelope and asked his secretary to hand deliver it to Avery's office. Then he went out to lunch in a bar where nobody would know him. For the first time in years, Jim Horner got so drunk that he played the last, most revealing act in the commuting ballet: on the way home he slept through Worton and woke up with a hangover in New Haven at 7:32 p.m.

Chapter IX

When people asked Judge Amos Hartwell Brooke how he felt these days, he would always grin and boom, "Pretty well for an old man."

Actually, he didn't feel much different physically at going on seventy-three than he had at seventy, or sixty-five, for that matter. He was still able to take long walks, swim, handle the *Helena*'s helm in a fair breeze of wind. He could eat almost anything except baked beans and onions, which tended to turn him literally into an old fart, and he could still down a couple of bourbons although a third one before dinner usually put him to sleep in front of the TV. At his last examination, Dr. Shepherd assured him he was in remarkable shape for a man his age except for a touch of emphysema. One thing he liked about Shepherd was that the man didn't take medicine so all-fired seriously. When he asked whether he should give up smoking his pipe, Dr. Shepherd said, "Well, you're going to die some day, judge. The question you've got to answer for yourself is whether you want to die happy or miserable." So he compromised by smoking one or two less pipes a day.

The thing that was turning Judge Brooke into a self-confessed old man was a kind of feeling he found hard to describe. In the last few years—ever since Sissy's death, in fact—he had begun to experience a sensation that the very ground of his being was giving way. The nearest he could get to it was a memory from very early childhood. Back then, they had one of those iron-hard winters—the kind of winter that seems to come along only in everybody's youngest years—when the tidal pond at Brookehaven froze over. Already physically fearless, he'd ventured clear out to the middle before he was aware of ominous cracking sounds. As he turned to run back, heart pounding, each footfall created a small spider web of hairline cracks until the whole surface shattered and dropped him, screaming, into the icy water. Fortunately a servant heard him and managed to fish him out with a long extension ladder, but ice remained the one fear that Amos Brooke could never quite handle. And it was like that now, like being trapped on cracking ice where the very weight of his wealth and power worked against him.

The trouble was that nobody seemed to respect tradition and position, nobody acted the way you expected them to anymore. Especially the young people. That thing at Harvard where the Secretary of Defense was mobbed and chased around like a character in an Our Gang comedy was just typical. He wished he had accepted that invitation to serve on the Board of Overseers up there; he'd show those unwashed students and their weak-kneed professors what for. Matter of fact, what Harvard and this whole country needed was some men of strength and dignity in leadership. You could hardly blame people for losing their bearings when you had an oaf in the White House—imagine, a President of the United States pulling up his shirt to show his scars to photographers, and picking dogs up by the ears. The fellow had no background or education or even guts. Judge Brooke agreed with him that we ought to win this war—in fact, he'd drop some bombs on Hanoi they wouldn't forget if he were in there —but any man who had ever owned a dollar—and those Johnsons had skimmed off quite a few of them from the looks of that ranch down there—ought to know the nation couldn't afford a war on poverty too. Even the Bible said that the poor would always be with you, so all you did by giving people something they hadn't earned was create false expectations. No wonder those blacks on relief out there in Detroit tore the town apart—wasn't the President himself going around saying the country *owed* them? Unless they got a good tough Republican in the White House next time and a Congress to back him up, Judge Brooke could see everything he owned melting away in the heat of rising taxes or inflation, or both. Worst of all . . . nobody seemed to care a damn.

Even at that, Judge Brooke thought it might be possible

to weather the economic storm, the way they had back in the thirties when Roosevelt damn near wrecked the country, if they could keep Worton on an even keel. But they'd had a different crew aboard then—the kind of fellows you could count on to stick to their homes and jobs and pleasures through thick and thin. Look at the way this fellow Avery and Horner were reacting to their runaway kids. Just because his son had gone off, Avery was actually talking of selling and moving out. It had never occurred to the judge to abandon Brookehaven on Hartwell's account. And Horner. The damned fool had let it all affect his business judgment, and nobody knew better than the judge how thinly stretched the young man was. Unfortunately, this wasn't the only sign of that fault in Horner that had kept Judge Brooke so uneasy and puzzled. From the rumors he heard, Horner was letting that youth commission of his get out of hand. It was a clever idea to get Floyd elected, but the judge had thought that Horner—and Floyd too, for that matter—were smart enough to understand that you don't actually allow a commission of that sort to *do* anything. Sensible executives—especially presidents—always understood this. Whenever they saw the spread of an ugly stain that only time or God could wipe away, they just papered it over with a commission.

Well, if Horner was fool enough to get himself into trouble, the judge would just have to deal with it as it came along. Now that the judge was beginning to think that he ought not to commit the *Helena*—or was it himself?—to the strain of racing much longer, once they got through this season, he probably wouldn't have much more need of Horner. As for Marion's house, if Horner couldn't keep up the payments—an eventuality he'd always anticipated—it would come back into Brookehaven under the agreement and could be turned over at a good profit or held against this infernal inflation. All this Judge Brooke had in mind the day he and Floyd Shepherd and Dan Parker met in the editor's little office at the *Record.* "He don't look old to me, does he to you, Floyd?" Dan said. "You know, I tell everybody there's one thing as changeless as the tides around here—Amos Brooke."

"Right you are, Dan. He's got the spirit at least of a thirty-year-old, so no more of this talk of being old, judge. Horner tells me you've entered the Vineyard race, and old men don't enter races."

"Well, we'll see for sure," Dan said. Getting up to close the door against possible intruders, he took a bottle of Jack Daniel's from a file cabinet drawer and set it on his desk with a stack of paper cups.

The judge, helping himself, said, "All right, you win— I can still splice the main brace. Must be serious business, Dan, if you think we need fortification."

"It is," Dan admitted. "Remember, doc, I promised your administration the *Record*'s support? Well, I'm going to have to go back on that."

"Why?"

"This Horner fellow you were just talking about. Tony Francetti's been to see me, and you wouldn't believe what goes on in those meetings. Kids, including girls, using words like fuck and shit right out loud. And I tell you I just can't go along with what they've planned this fall."

So the rumors the judge had heard were true. "What's going on?" he asked.

"Some kind of busing, for one thing—bringing nigger kids in here so our kids can find out what they're like. Can you imagine?"

"What do you know about this, Floyd?" the judge asked.

"From what Horner tells me, I'd say Tony is going a bit overboard. All they're going to do is bring some kids from Harlem as guests for a week—"

"What about that hot line with that kooky psychologist Pauline Church found down there at Columbia?" Dan Parker asked.

"He's well qualified, I've checked him out," Dr. Shepherd said. "I also happen to think it's a pretty good idea. There are a lot of young people in this town who don't know where to go for some help—"

214

"Why not?" Dan Parker asked. "They've got parents, haven't they?"

"Unfortunately. The parents are usually the problem."

"You wouldn't talk like that if you had children of your own, Floyd. Anyway, I agree with Tony that we don't want any long-haired psychologist messing around with our kids. I'm just telling you, doc, if you don't keep Horner in line I'm going to have to blast him—and you too. As Amos well knows, I've finally got the inside track for Congress in '68 and I'm not going to lose it over this kind of thing."

"It might turn out to be a plus, Dan," Dr. Shepherd argued. "The way I see things going, people are getting some different attitudes. Including me . . ."

"Well, not the people who vote for me," Dan shot back. "There's a big backlash going on out there. Talk to Francetti and his people. They're tired of these niggers and draft dodgers and hippies."

"I'm afraid I basically agree with Dan," Judge Brooke said. "What this country needs is some strong leadership, and we need it right here in town, Floyd."

"Which is another way of saying that you want to dump me?"

"Unless you dump Horner," Dan Parker said.

"That's real fine of you fellows. If I recall correctly, *you* came to *me* with your hats in hand. I didn't want this job—hell, I haven't been out on the course a dozen times this summer—but I've done what you all wanted, and needed, thanks largely to Horner, and now you want me to turn on him and call off the game."

"Now, Floyd, be reasonable," the judge said. "We all agreed that setting up a commission like this would possibly turn the publicity around on this town, and it did. So that job is done, and it's time to put the lid back on. If you keep things quiet the way they used to be, you could be first selectman forever—and play golf too."

"Mighty appealing, judge . . . except something's happening here . . . I don't say I really know what it is, but—I hate to remind you of it, judge—it all seemed to start with Sissy's death, which all of us tried to shrug off as an accident. Looking at it now, though, I think it was more like the top of a pressure cooker blowing and giving us notice that we had to do something to turn down the heat. I'd say that's what Horner's group is at least trying to do—"

"But that's just the point, Floyd. You're not turning the heat down, you're turning it up," the judge said. "When the taxpayers of this town find out you're spending money for things like this, they'll revolt. You'd do much better to stick to those sewers you always wanted —at least it would be something they could see."

"Well, judge, you don't get a very good picture of what's going on in the world or even in Worton out of the *Wall Street Journal, Yachting* and the bar at the Harvard Club. Try being a doctor *and* first selectman sometime. I hear more confessionals than Father Reardon. You'd be surprised at what goes on in some of our families around here . . ."

"I don't think families are any business of the people in government," the judge said, clearly speaking a speech rather than reacting to what Floyd had just said. "It isn't the job of government to peek through windows . . ."

"But it is the job of government to protect people's rights," Dr. Shepherd said, warming to his own speech, "and I'm beginning to be of the opinion that even young people have some rights—"

"Nonsense, Floyd!" the judge said. "You're going soft . . . worse, you're sounding like a *real* Democrat." Parker joined him in an appreciative laugh.

"Well, have a talk with your friend Horner, then. As far as I know, he's as Republican as Herbert Hoover. But let me warn you, gentlemen, if you want to be practical and even cynical, attacking Horner right now might be like going up against mother, or God. Worse, it would be going against kids. However much trouble they're having with them, most of the people in this town think kids are damned important, sort of their nugget for the future. In fact, that's why they moved here—to protect the investment. Unfortunately, it may be the source of the problem too . . ."

216

"Well, if Horner's got everybody buffaloed, there may be another solution. What if he left town?"

"He'd never do that," Dan Parker said. "You saw to that yourself when you let him have the Stanton place. I never did understand—"

"He seemed a sound enough fellow then," the judge quickly explained. "But now I hear he's lost his job with Avery, and if I were to start pressing him on his note . . ."

"You wouldn't do that, judge," Dr. Shepherd said.

"Not before the Vineyard race," the judge admitted, "and maybe by then you can do something about him. I can't afford to have a couple of hundred thousand idle, especially after that Dominick settlement. And don't forget, Floyd, I did *that* mostly for you, for the town, because you'd have had another ugly mess on your hands if that had gone to trial. So maybe getting rid of Horner would be the best thing all around for all of us. Think it over . . ."

"I don't like the sound of this, judge . . ."

"Floyd, I don't know whether you're in a position to like it or not. The way this country is going it's a lot more important to get a man like Dan here into Congress than to worry about the delicate feelings of a fellow like Horner, who came from nowhere and could as easily go back there. I'm willing, and I think Dan is too, to keep you in office because you've been one of us for a long time, but there is a limit, Floyd . . ."

"Judge . . . Dan . . . I've got some awful news for you. I *am* a Democrat. I don't want to see Dan elected to *anything*." Dr. Shepherd got up without finishing his drink. "And as for being one of you, as you put it, I think you might find yourselves more comfortable consulting Dr. Hammond in the future. He's perfectly competent, I can assure you . . ."

When Dr. Shepherd had slammed the door behind him, Dan Parker poured another drink. "What's got into him?"

Judge Brooke sighed. "You see why I say I'm feeling

old? You can't rely on anybody anymore. Do you suppose this Hammond is any good? At my age . . ."

"I'm sure he is. My wife goes to him . . . Tell you the truth, I never did think much of Floyd as a doctor. Know what he said to me last time? He said my trouble was I couldn't keep up with screwing a younger woman. Of course, he was always kidding . . ."

"I don't think he was kidding today."

"Neither do I."

"There's one thing the doc may have been right about, though," the judge said. "You might hurt yourself by attacking Horner until he actually pulls one of those stupid stunts. Hold off a little while until we see what can be done about him."

"All right—and thanks, Amos."

Thinking later of Dan Parker and what he was willing to do for him, Judge Brooke was reminded of the truth of that old adage about politics making strange bedfellows. There was a time when he wouldn't have spoken to Dan Parker in the street, and he could remember his mother, like some character out of Dickens, packing a Christmas basket of food in Brookehaven every year to senl over to the "poor Parkers." Dan's marriage to old Mrs. Bradbury was the scandal of the time—a grocery boy of twenty and a widow of sixty. Lawyers for her children went to court to try to get her declared incompetent and failed. In revenge she used all her money to buy the *Record* for Dan and left him the house besides when she conveniently died of a heart attack brought on by all the bitterness. Dan found out quickly that the *Record* didn't make any money—it still didn't—but he had fortunately developed a taste, or at least a tolerance, for older women; so he sold the Bradbury place and moved in with Mrs. Cadmon, a richer and older friend of his former wife. This being more or less what people had come to expect of Dan, the marriage to Mrs. Cadmon caused far less of a sensation. More than one person even exhibited grudging admiration: "You've got to hand it to Dan Parker; he knows which side the bread is buttered on."

If Mrs. Bradbury's gift to Dan was a profession, Mrs.

Cadmon's present was a style. She personally picked out his clothes from the best New York stores, saw to it that the professionals from Golden Hills (where her late husband had been a charter member) schooled him in the fine points of swimming and tennis, sports more likely in her opinion to maintain his slim, youthful body than golf. She took him to plays and operas in the city and at least once a year, usually in spring, on a voyage to Europe. On these occasions Dan would use his ownership of the *Record* to arrange interviews with high European officials, and it was apparent from his "letters" back to the paper that the two who especially impressed him were Adolf Hitler, who kept young hoodlums busy marching, and Benito Mussolini, who made the trains run on time. By the time Dan Parker presented himself before the Republican Town Committee as a possible candidate for the legislature, most members saw only a cultured, well-dressed squire who owned the only public voice in town. They'd either forgotten, or didn't know, how he'd achieved that image. Though Amos Brooke considered Parker little more than a gigolo, he went along with the others in endorsing the candidacy for a very practical reason: they needed the *Record*'s strong support for local Republicans ever since the town had missed by a hair going Democratic in Roosevelt's '32 sweep.

Judge Brooke never regretted the decision. Using the same personal charm with which he won the hearts of old ladies, Parker turned into a vote getter; as a respecter, even worshiper, of wealth, he was suitably conservative on every issue. And he exhibited the kind of loyalty to persons and institutions Judge Brooke most admired. Instead of turning his back on his own family, he brought them along with him: he found good jobs in Hartford for his sisters' shiftless husbands and took his brother Seth down off the scaffolding and set him up as president of Parker Brothers Construction. With admirable patience he nursed the ex-Mrs. Cadmon through her final illness (there were pictures of him taking her off the *Queen Mary* in a wheelchair) and elected to stay on in the old Cadmon place, a Victorian horror on the Post Road, "just to keep it out of the hands of developers." He spent the Cadmon estate selflessly, being one of the largest contributors to the YMCA (where he could swim in winter), the new Presbyterian church (whose pastor, the Rev. Dr. W. Anderson Wolfe, was the only minister who would consent to marry him to the present Mrs. Parker) and the Republican Party. Amos Brooke was among those who felt that Dan Parker had earned a change by the time he induced a matron twenty years younger than he to leave her husband and move into the Cadmon house with her three children. She had been an assiduous campaign worker who understood politics, and a handsome ready-made family would be an asset when they finally got Parker onto the national stage. The husband was one of those faceless commuting executives from somewhere else, a heating engineer or something like that, who disappeared from Worton without a trace, even taking the memory of scandal with him. Whether Parker's marriage was causing him the troubles Dr. Shepherd so crudely alluded to, nobody could know, but it was a socially accepted fact in Worton. There was little choice: it was said that Lilly Atkin's obituary was omitted from the *Record* because she had snubbed the new Mrs. Parker coming out of church one Sunday.

Altogether, Dan Parker seemed to be an exception to Judge Brooke's usual rule that gentlemen are born, not made. Perhaps the thing that separated him from other opportunists like George Avery was a pride of place, a sense of belonging somewhere and an instinct for protecting that somewhere. At any rate, the thought of being able to help put Parker into Congress lifted Judge Brooke's sagging spirits. Maybe he wasn't so old after all. Maybe there was a way off the ice.

A man in Worton might not mind that people knew, or suspected, that he kept a mistress in New York, or stayed overlong at the Commodore bar, or cheated on his income tax, but the one unforgivable sin that he tried mightily to conceal from everybody, including his own family, was being out of work. When, as it not infrequently happened,

220

a Worton man was "between jobs" he did not take advantage of the situation to sit around the house in a comfortable sweater and read the want ads. What he did was carry out a more than usually elaborate charade of doing business in town, rising and catching his regular train and setting up a cover in the city worthy of a CIA agent. The reason he did this was his well-founded fear that the tolerance for his lapses and oversights thus far exhibited by bankers and tradesmen and even his wife was based on their certainty of getting eventual reward from some part of his presumably large and steady paycheck. Moreover, when it came to getting a new position, a man known to be without a job was in the same sorry situation as a girl leaning against the gymnasium wall at a high school dance. So, like others he had heard about, Jim Horner pretended, even after his time or grace ran out, that he was still in business.

In his case, the charade was not too difficult to arrange. Because he had dealt directly with the chairman of the company on largely personal grounds, his resignation wasn't widely known. The understanding girls back at Ace agreed to field his calls and transfer messages to the Harvard Club, where he had fortunately paid his dues in advance and could hole up between job-hunting forays. With this setup even Susan didn't have to know for the few weeks or months it would take him to get something else, unless, of course, Judge Brooke spilled the beans to Helen or Marion who then spilled them to Susan. Obviously, that bastard Avery must have leaked the news to the judge in some kind of clumsy effort to get the judge upset about him and the Youth Commission, too. Otherwise there was no accounting for the brief flurry of conversation they'd had in the church parking lot after a session meeting one night.

"Jim," the judge said, "if you want a word of advice from an old man, I think you are carrying this youth thing much too far."

"There isn't much else I can do."

"Oh, come now, Jim. From what I heard you could have voted with Tony Francetti and Mrs. Lamb and—"

"Judge, we've just about convinced these young people that we're making an honest effort. They'd be dangerously disappointed if we sat on every idea they're for. Besides, I don't see any harm in it—"

"You don't? All else aside, I see a lot of harm in something that causes you to lose your position. I have an investment to protect, you know."

"I'm very aware of that, *sir*."

"Well, fine. Just take a tip from me, Jim. Life is long and youth is short. You put those youngsters in their place and they'll forget all about it in a month or so. You're too good a helmsman to get yourself off on the wrong course like this. Well . . . like they say, a word to the wise . . . Goodnight, Jim."

Jim wasn't too surprised at what the Judge had said. He was, after all, an old man, set in his ways. He couldn't be expected to understand, or care, that there was something new in the way young people were acting and looking at things these days—even though they could sometimes get pretty tiresome in their flights of self-righteousness. What really bothered Jim was the judge's bringing Jim's personal obligations into the picture, as if he were making some veiled threat. As Jim understood the agreement about the house, his main obligation was to keep up his interest payments. How else could he have afforded such a place? Furthermore, Jim was only doing the job the judge himself had seconded at that long ago meeting at Brookehaven. Well, still bearing in mind that he was no hero, he somehow didn't find the judge's backside—for all its long acquaintance with fine old money—any more prepossessing than George Avery's. He guessed he'd go along with what he was doing . . . Meanwhile, though, he had even more pressing things to worry about.

Finding work at close to forty, he soon learned, was harder than working. He sent his first hopeful feelers out through the oil business, where he'd gained considerable reputation as the author of the essays that had made an energy statesman out of such uncharismatic material as George S. Avery. It was a delicate business—trying to let people know he was available without revealing that he was also at liberty and, therefore, of doubtful value. For a while he thought his hints weren't getting through until one night a fellow Wortonite who worked for another oil company opened up to him in the bar car.

"Jim, I don't know what the hell's gone wrong for you over there at Ace, but I can tell you right now, if you're out at Ace, you're out of gas, so to speak. There's a gentlemen's agreement that one oil company doesn't raid another for people, and then of course nobody wants a fellow who's fucked it up somehow. See that guy sitting over there—the one with the half glasses. A few years back you'd have known him, because he was a hell of a sailor. He was also one of the best goddamned engineers in the oil business. Well, his boss ordered him out to some Christforsaken place on the Persian gulf, and he said, no thanks, he liked living and sailing in Worton, and he'd get himself another job. The poor bastard was on the street for more than two years, had to sell his boat and damned near lost his house. Know what he's doing now? He's secretary or something like that for the rubber *heel* industry at about half the dough he was making. But he's lucky at that. He got it through his wife's cousin who's a big shoe manufacturer up Boston way, I gather. Take my advice, Jim—stay where you are. Avery's a son of a bitch, I know, but like Roosevelt said about some dictator down there in Latin America, he's *your* son of a bitch."

The only comfort Jim got out of that speech was that other people thought Avery was a son of a bitch too, and that it evidently wasn't generally known that he was already at liberty. But he was obviously wasting his time on oil, and so he turned to the only other profession he knew. Remembering Harry Margolis' rather clumsy attempt at understanding when he left, Jim called his old boss who, as he'd noted on the masthead, was now executive editor of *News*. He probably should have called Hal Palmer, who had been promoted to Margolis' former job, but somehow he couldn't face Palmer under these circumstances. Harry sounded grumpily friendly on the phone and, fortunately, asked him to lunch. "Never let a flack buy me a hot dog," Harry said. Same old Harry, but not quite. When Jim arrived at *News,* he found Harry in a corner office on a floor above the editorial department. His gates were guarded by a toothpaste ad secretary, and his floor was softened by high-pile carpet. Although he was chewing a cigar, no cuspidor was in sight. The material of Harry's dark striped jacket actually matched that of his pants, and the tufts of gray hair that used to look as if he were trying to yank them from his scalp were trimmed and smoothed. Jim was a little depressed by the "hot dog" line since Harry used to lunch standing up at Nedick's, but Harry's eating style had changed too. He led Jim to the Waldorf where they were met at the door of the Bull and Bear by an obsequious head waiter who showed them to what was obviously Mr. Margolis' regular table. The head waiter even lingered to take their drink order, and Jim was moved to say, "Some class, Harry."

"Goes with the job," Harry said. "I'm nothing but a fucking figurehead. So how's the black gold flowing?"

"Stuck in the pipes as far as I'm concerned," Jim said. "I'm fed up."

"Oh?"

Obviously Harry wasn't going to help much. "Yeah. Remember you used to tell me the news business was better than working for a living? Well, I've found out you were right, and I'd like to get back into it."

Their drinks had come, and Harry took a meditative sip while he studied Jim with shrewd eyes. "Fired, eh?"

"No . . . I resigned . . ."

"You must be getting pretty good at resigning by now. It wouldn't have anything to do with your daughter running off with that Avery kid, would it?"

Jim flushed. "How do you know about that?"

"Oh, Hal Palmer's a kind of professional Worton watcher. You know it was that story got him started on his way to pushing me upstairs. By the way, he says you're doing a hell of a job with the kids up there."

"Well, thanks. Actually, it's my work with the kids that got me into trouble with Avery. He thinks they all ought to be thrown in jail."

"If the man thinks that way, he can't be all bad," Harry said. "If I believed in God, I'd thank Him that Betty and I never could have kids. All they do is break your heart. But this isn't solving your problem. I think you ought to go around to *Time* or better yet, *Fortune.* Here's a couple of people you ought to see, I'll give them a call."

Harry took a card out of his wallet and started scratching down the names. "Thanks, Harry," Jim said, "but I really had something at *News* in mind."

"Sorry, Jim, but no chance. You've got to know you can't go back again. Anyway, Hal's got his ass glued to that old chair of mine, and he's brought a lot of even younger guys along into the other slots. Besides, and I think you know this, I'd as soon marry a whore as hire an ex-flack. . . . Well, see anything you like on this menu? The filet mignon is good if you get it rare enough . . ."

Thank you, Harry. Old Buddy . . . it's always good to get it straight from the shoulder.

Jim did go to *Time*. The young man from personnel who prevented Jim from getting to see Harry's friend looked about the age of Betsy. He was very polite but he "would be less than honest with you, Mr. Horner, if I didn't point out that with our pension plan a man of your age . . ." His reception was better at *Fortune,* where anybody remotely connected with the heavy Ace Oil account had to be handled carefully. Harry's friend there spent more than an hour with him and agreed that energy was going to be a big story in the next few years and that Jim's background in the field was impressive. "But you of all people have to be aware, Mr. Horner, that our man has done some of the best reporting on the subject, and we might not be able to handle another expert." He was shown to the door with a don't-call-me-I'll-call-you handshake. Even the head hunters were discouraging. "If you'd come to me before you—uh, resigned—it would have been a leadpipe cinch," one of them told him. "Our clients like to think they're getting a live one, you know."

Jim now took to playing a new game he'd invented to take his mind off his troubles as he rode the trains and walked the streets. By studying other men carefully he tried to spot those who might be in the same fix as himself. One clue for a commuter was casual, near-conspiratorial attention to the want ads instead of the crossword puzzle in the morning paper. Jim followed a couple of men he'd caught at this activity when they left the train but was disappointed to see them disappear behind the revolving doors of a normal office building instead of into a phone booth at the station or into a nearby restaurant or bar. His mind was still on the game one midmorning when, waiting in boredom at the Harvard Club for the call that never came, he gave in and went to the bar. A lone man was sitting there nursing a bloody Mary, and Jim was sure he'd caught his prey.

After a little careful probing had confirmed his suspicions, Jim and his new friend, who had been a couple of classes ahead of him at college, opened up with each other. They had a lot in common, including the fact that the man had been a magazine space salesman whose job had gone down under the weight of competition from TV and that he lived up near Jim, in Darien, and was acting out the same charade. As they traded first jokes and then not so jokey confidences about the problems of job hunting, Jim began to get the nudge of an idea. There must be a lot more of them out there . . . if they could get together and pool contacts and other resources they could help each other. By the end of the third drink, Jim and his new friend Paul Richards had turned alcohol-supported euphoria into a whole plan of action for a new organization. They even had a name for it—Job Hunters Anonymous—and they'd start recruiting by small ads in the *Times*. Going home that night, Jim felt some real hope for the first time in months. He needed it.

If the days of deception in New York were wearing, the nights of deception in Worton were worse. The whole thing would have been considerably easier if he could have shared it with Susan—the old long-ago cheerful Susan, that is, the one who always was sure everything would turn out all right. . . . While he'd tried not to think too much about it, Jim had been aware that these last couple of years had turned Susan into a person he hardly knew. Not that he blamed her. Not a bit. The whole thing with Betsy had been, to her, a proof of failure that had left her bitter and bewildered. Still, she had seemed to be riding it out pretty well, and he was hopeful when she started going down to the club again with Julie. But after that night when a frightened Julie came running to him with the story of whatever it was that had happened in the parking lot there, Susan had gone steadily downhill. The crying jags nearly drove him out of his mind, and almost every evening now Susan insisted on having one, maybe two more cocktails than he. The only good thing about it was that the drinks put her to sleep, and he didn't have to struggle not to talk about what was on his mind, or try to make love to her. He felt guilty about not wanting her, although he told himself he really shouldn't . . . She had always been a little "casual," as she called it about her appearance but she was now simply letting herself go, not washing her hair, her face increasingly puffy from drink and crying, broadening in the rear. But he could hardly blame her either, considering everything that had happened. All he could really do was try to keep hoping that it was something that time, or medicine, could eventually cure.

Since Susan was also one of those people who had never so much as had a hangnail in her life, he had a terrible time getting her to a doctor. He didn't dare suggest Dr. Shepherd, whom Susan was now blaming for somehow turning Betsy's head. She didn't want to go to Dr. Stiller either, because he knew all about Betsy and would start blabbing it around town that the whole family was strange. Finally Jim got from Floyd Shepherd the name of a New York gynecologist she could go to more or less anonymously and took her in with him on the train and sat there in the waiting room to make certain she saw him. When she came out she said, "He says it's probably just menopause. But how could it be at my age when I'm still flowing like a river? I told you it was a waste of time, Jim. I think something's wrong with my head. Maybe I ought to go to a psychiatrist." Jim exploded at that. From stories he'd done about psychiatry, he considered the whole thing a form of expensive quackery. . . .

The night Jim came home filled with hopeful excitement about Job Hunters Anonymous, Julie met him at the door. He knew immediately something had to be wrong because Julie had been making herself scarce all summer the way Betsy used to do. If she wasn't mooning in her room, she was out until all hours with that Ben Adams, about whom Susan was forever complaining even though he had become a leader of Young Life and the Youth Commission. "Mother's really sick," Julie said. "In the bedroom . . ."

When Jim rushed in, heart pounding, Susan looked up at him with such a goofy smile that he knew immediately she wasn't sick—she was drunk. Stretched out beside her on the bed was Rusty, the setter who had long since replaced Noel. Evidently, the dog had been roaming the marshes on the edge of the property because her coat was matted and reeking and the sheets were streaked with tidal mud. "Get that goddamned dog off there," Jim said. "Come on, Rusty, get down!"

Susan put her arms around the dog and nestled her face into the fur. "You leave her alone, Jim. She loves me . . . don't you, darling! . . . of course you do . . ."

Sweet Jesus. He didn't know whether to weep or curse. Now that he'd hit on a way to maybe at least start to improve his professional life, the personal was hitting bottom. It was like being on some dizzying seesaw.

He looked for silent minutes at the pair on the bed. "Oh, shit," he finally said, and walked out.

That night Jim Horner moved onto the Castro convertible in his study.

Ben Adams was back to doing drugs. Everybody knew it except his parents, his grandparents, his teachers, the leader of Young Life, the Rev. John Peters, Police Chief Lou Dominick, Youth Commissioner James Horner, the paid captain of the Worton Yacht Club, First Selectman Dr. Floyd Shepherd and *Record* editor Senator Dan Parker. If any one of these people found out, it would go hard on him, and so he was considerably more careful as to sources and where and when to turn on than he was in the good old days when he and Ron lived it up without giving a damn about anything or anybody. One reason he stuck to grass instead of trying LSD like some of the other guys was that he knew he could control it the same way so many of the old farts around town could control their drinking. It was a dirty shame that his father couldn't be like them—or that his father hadn't grown up at a time when he could have got started on grass, which, from everything Ben read, was a lot less damaging than alcohol. At least it made you feel kind of peaceful inside. Anyway, aside from staying out of trouble, he especially didn't want adults to know about the grass because he was ashamed of wanting it, needing it. It wasn't the same feeling he used to have, when getting away with smoking a joint had been a kind of status thing, like catching a touchdown pass. For him, at least, he was into the habit because he needed it, and needing it was letting down the people who were trying to help him, people like Hal Evans at Young Life and John Peters. Worse, it could put Julie in trouble, even though she knew about it and said she understood.

There was a time when Ben really had stopped smoking and was convinced down deep that he had been saved by Jesus. Looking back now, he guessed that it was more fear and shame than anything religious that drove him into Young Life. When the cops got hold of him and threatened to bust him too if he didn't testify against Betsy Horner, he felt he had little choice—his grandfather was dying and Ben couldn't stand adding another disgrace to the old man's sorrow over his drunken son. Still, even though he felt he had good reason not to give a damn about Miss Betsy Horner, he didn't feel too good about ratting on her. . . . Anyway, he finally decided he had to talk to someone about himself, and went to that new young minister, John Peters, who introduced him to Hal Evans of Young Life. For a while Young Life was terrific, like standing under a shower after you'd been playing on a muddy field. Evans had been a better football player than Ben had ever thought of being and was a hell of a skier and mountain climber too. In summer Evans took them all out to a camp in Colorado, and one of the things he made them do was go mountain climbing. Ben, who thought he wasn't afraid of anything, was about half way up a steep rock face when he made the mistake of looking down, and he was so scared he just froze. Evans came back to him, put out a hand and led him to the top. That night Ben tried to hide in his bunk, but Evans found him and said, "Everybody's scared sometimes, Ben. That's why we need Jesus. If you had faith enough to take my hand out there, don't you have faith enough to take the hand Jesus is holding out to you now?" That did it—he went out with Evans to where all the kids were gathered around a bonfire and stood up and confessed how scared he'd been and how he knew now that what he needed was Jesus' help. He proved to himself that it worked next morning by helping another kid stuck on the same mountain. Her name was Julie Horner.

Julie fascinated him. Totally different from her sister, Julie had a dark, delicate beauty that reminded him of Sissy Stanton, a girl he had carried the torch for almost all his life. He'd only just gotten to know Sissy and found out how much fun she could be the night she died. He still couldn't really believe it, kept thinking he'd wake up some day the way he did from a terrible dream and find out it was all in his head. . . . It was supposed to have been such a super night. The moon was out and everybody was feeling just high enough. He and Ron had planned to get everybody going on their favorite game of "pirate." You began by sitting around a beach fire drinking beer and yo-ho-hoing and telling pirate stories, and then you got one of the girls to walk the "plank," right off the little dock there at the beach and into the water with all her clothes on. You could almost always count on one being in the mood—they'd sort of figured Betsy Horner for that night because of the way she was dancing—to go first and shame the others into following. After that it was usually easy to get them to go skinny dipping while their clothes dried by the fire so that they wouldn't have to go home

wet. But the game never got going that night, because of
that thing between Ron and Betsy. Ben was sore as hell
because he'd been counting on seeing a lot more of Sissy,
in more ways than one, and by the time the cops came
down to the beach that night he was drinking himself
blind.

For a while, Ben blamed Betsy—if she hadn't had that
silly fight, Sissy and Ron would still be alive—and feeling
that made it easier to tell the cops about her getting grass
to Ron. It was only after Betsy's arrest and when he
finally got in, disguised as a hospital orderly, to see Ron,
and realized how much Ron and Betsy were in love that
he began feeling badly—but by then it was too late. Betsy
would have nothing to do with him, and he could hardly
blame her. When he started seeing Julie at Young Life
and got that eerie feeling that Sissy had somehow risen
from the grave, Ben was understandably shy of her. He
was certain she must hate him too for what he'd done to
her sister. Still, he tried to stick near her unobtrusively—
at meetings, on the bus, on the mountain—hoping for a
chance . . . and when it came, it did indeed seem a
godsend . . . a gift of God.

Whether it was just the closeness of touch or something
in the thin Colorado air or the atmosphere of spiritual
confession around the bonfire, Ben and Julie rather as-
tonishingly found themselves telling, confessing to, each
other everything. He told her of his shame over Betsy, his
upset and real sense of depression over Sissy and Ron, his
misery about his drunken father—but then set her to
laughing with reminiscences about the crazy things he and
Ron had done in the golden days when they'd seemed to
have life by the old tail. On her part she revealed what a
miserable brat she'd been to her sister and wondered out
loud whether Betsy, let alone Jesus, could ever forgive
her. But she'd also been trying, in her own way, to ease
the pain Betsy had caused her parents, even if she hadn't
meant to. They agreed then that by being real Christians
they could both help the reputations of their families,
which made them feel good about themselves. And close,
very close. They were in love, they decided, by the time

they got back to Worton, and for a while Ben was almost glad he wasn't going off to college with all of his classmates. After all, Julie still had two more years to go in high school. Her mother had wanted to send her away, but Young Life had kept her from that. Another reason to praise Jesus.

In the end, though, it was missing college as much as anything else that made Ben begin feeling so sorry for himself that he slipped back onto grass. There was just no way for him to go as all the rest of his graduating class did except for a few Italian kids and a couple of morons like Buddy Phelps. One big problem was money. His grandfather Adams' estate, what there was of it, was tied up in a legal hassle between his father and aunts, and his father spent so much time in the saloon next to his real estate office that he hardly earned enough to keep them in food, let alone pay college tuition. Although he'd earned his letter at Worton High, Ben was too slight to be of any interest to football scholarship scouts from college, and his grades were too low for scholastic aid. All the guidance people warned him not to try to work his way through, considering the competition these days; he'd surely flunk out carrying such a heavy outside load. Money, though, was only one problem. His father was another, and worse. Several times now he'd had to manhandle the old man into bed or out of the house to keep him from slapping his mother and sisters around when he was in his cups. Sometimes he couldn't blame his father; the girls were forever shrilling at him that he wouldn't have to be fighting for his inheritance and they'd all be on easy street if the old doctor hadn't been so disgusted by his drinking. Still, Ben was actually afraid of what might happen to the women if he left home, and so he stayed close. Being prime draft bait, he wasn't even a good candidate for a permanent job. He pumped gas in the winter months and fixed old power mowers in his grandfathers Atkins' (the poor branch of the family, naturally) service station, and summers he ran the launch down at the yacht club where his father, who had once been more of a championship sailor than any of them, including

Mr. White or Mr. Horner, was no longer welcome—not only for being irregular in his dues but also because he and Mrs. Johnson had gone skinny dipping one night right off the end of the dock in the middle of the commodore's dance. Ben's very presence in the streets of Worton when nearly everybody else his age had gone off made him feel like a walking advertisement of his family's shame.

Peters and Evans were the only ones who had any faith in him, and now he'd let *them* down. All right, part of their interest in him was that as a jock with a wild reputation they considered him a useful catch for the Christian forces, an example to the younger kids, but at least they cared—if they were using him it was for a good cause. They got him into everything—the church young people's group, Young Life, Mr. Horner's Youth Commission. And, admit it, it did make him feel a bit of a big shot when he got his picture in the paper, which wasn't difficult since Dan Parker's stepdaughter was his co-leader in Young Life, but he also knew the publicity helped his mother and sisters. Once when he was down patching up the seawall below the terrace at the club he overheard one of the "sea gulls" saying, "I think it's marvelous the way Benjy Adams' son is turning out with all he's had to put up with. His mother must be an angel. I think he's cute, too. I just wish Marcia could get to know him." Not if they knew him, they wouldn't. . . .

Aware that he was splitting himself in half, feeling a hypocrite but feeling equally helpless to do anything about it, Ben went along with the Christian bit by day and escaped into drugs at night. Somehow when he was alone and staring at a wall solider than the plasterboard siding of his room the vision of a Jesus with outstretched hand just wasn't there. He found considerably more comfort in listening to the Beatles sing about, "It's getting hard to be someone . . . It doesn't matter much to me. Let me take you down, 'cause I'm going to strawberry fields . . ." They really knew what it was like when your chances of being someone seemed shot to hell, and they knew how you got to those strawberry fields. So did he.

Maybe there was a Jesus who knew too, but he wasn't the kind of Jesus that Evans and Peters seemed to be talking about. Theirs was the kind who was all for getting into the game and charging down the field, never mind those fellows left on the bench. Now Ben knew how some of his friends must have felt when the coach would pace up and down looking for a substitute but never glance at them. If it weren't for Julie . . .

Julie wouldn't smoke with him, or even drink. She'd only let him get away with a few damp kisses and a caress or two through her clothes. Sometimes it was awfully hard for him to stop, but he felt better about it when she told him it was hard for her too. "Oh, Ben, sometimes I'd like to . . . well, you know . . . but when I remember what happened to Betsy and how it hurt my parents, I just can't .. . ." He understood. Funny how they always seemed to get around to talking about their parents almost the way the "sea gulls" were always talking about their kids. Julie admired him for staying around Worton to protect his mother and sisters, but she told him he ought to feel sorry, not scared or mad, about his father—"alcoholism is a disease like cancer or anything." Her situation was harder to understand. Ben often thought she must be making it up . . . her family had to have plenty of money to live in a big glass house like that, and her father was a pretty good guy from what he saw of him at meetings. But Julie said her mother was drinking too much too, and crying a lot, and the worst thing was that her mother and father weren't sleeping together anymore. He said that it was just while her mother was "sick," but she was afraid it was something more. They'd always been so much together on everything that it used to drive Betsy and her wild, but now she'd rather see them that way than this. . . . About money, well, she just didn't know; her father just didn't talk about things like that. Losing his job was hard on him but then he had this new business, this Job Hunters Anonymous thing, going, and they seemed to go on living pretty much the way they always had except that he was always at her to turn out the lights and told her she ought to carry her lunch the way he used to do when she wanted more money after the school cafeteria raised its rates.

"It's really sad," Julie said. "My parents don't seem to be happy and yet they think I ought to be just naturally happy because they've given me so much. Would you believe it, Ben—I think they actually think Betsy would have stayed out of trouble if she'd only gotten into the *sailing* program? I guess that's why I joined, to make them feel better. . . . It didn't hurt me and it seemed to please them. Sometimes, though, I wonder if they understand *anything*. . . ."

Well, never mind the reasons, Ben was grateful Julie was there. He'd spend some time with her every day he was working at the club and when he had an afternoon off she'd play hookey from the program and they'd go out in the Horners' Lightning. Usually they'd sail down to a cove in a little island off the coast, which was especially private in the middle of the week. They'd swim and then bake on the beach and talk and talk and talk. Now that she knew about it, he'd sometimes have a joint. "I don't know why you need it," she would say. "It isn't much of a compliment to me, Ben. I can be turned on by a Coke when I'm with you."

"I don't know why either," he told her on one of those afternoons when he was lying flat out and gratefully inhaling whatever it was that seemed to make the blue infinity above him even more so. There was no blemish within the sky's perfect bowl except for a tiny black anvil of a thunderhead rising slowly out of the north. They would have to go back, but not for an hour or so, and meanwhile maybe she could help, or understand at least. "It's like my mother's always yelling at my father that he's been babied all his life and is still trying to suck on the teat. Maybe this is my teat. I don't know . . . I wish I knew something about psychology. Do you?"

"No," Julie said, "but my mother is going to a psychiatrist. She thinks nobody knows, but I saw his card one day when she emptied her purse—Dr. August Bruno. You know, the one on Dean Street."

"My mother thinks Dad should go to a psychiatrist too. He says my grandfather—you know, Dr. Adams—used to tell him shrinks were phonies. But I think he's afraid to find out he's really sick. I'd be, too . . ."

Julie, who had been lying flat beside him, rolled over and brought a pretty, worried face between him and the sky. Her long dark hair, straight and still slightly damp from swimming, hung in silken curtains, making a delicious mystery of her eyes. "You are *not* sick, Ben Adams," she said. "Like Mr. Evans says, everything is going to be all right. You'll be going to college and—"

"Going to college? No way, Julie, and you know it. It's almost two years now. And Dad's worse, if anything, and the case about my grandfather's estate hasn't even come to court. What's going to happen is that my number is going to come up, and I'm going to be sent off to Vietnam and—"

"Ben, hush. Don't be so bitter. . . ."

"Why not? I'm perfect fodder for that stupid shooting match out there. You'll never see somebody like Tim Hilsman, who'll get his master's and doctor's and God knows what until it's all over, going to war. No, it's guys like me and dumb little Buddy Phelps—they called him the other day, you know. Some terrific future."

"I think you've got a beautiful future. You've got me."

"No, Julie. You'll be going to college, and I want you to. I don't want to be a drag on you—"

"You a drag? Ben Adams, I *love* you. I really do," she said, and the curtains came down, whispering across his cheeks, as she kissed him softly on the mouth.

It was like the approaching storm. The sea in which their island simmered lay still and shining, the grasses and scrub growth beyond the beach curled and shrank in the breezeless heat, a lone gull screamed in nervous apprehension. Ben reached up and pulled Julie's light, moist body full length onto his own. He kissed her hungrily on her eyes, ears, neck, everywhere his lips could reach while his fingers fumbled loose the ties of her bikini. "Ben, no . . . we shouldn't . . ." but she didn't really struggle when he rolled her over and stretched her out on

236

her towel, his eyes devouring those milky banded parts of her he'd never seen. He could hear the first low mutterings from the ugly black wall rising at his back, as, kissing her quiet, he let his own private storm break over her.

If it was sandy and sticky and awkward, they would never know; they had no way of comparing it with anything else. The enormity of what had happened overwhelmed all other sense. Ben whispered, "Oh, God, Julie . . . how I love you . . ." and then the sky cracked, like the voice of God. . . . Julie was the first to come back to reality. "Ben, we've got to get back . . ."

They swam, reaching their anchored boat which had been lifted beyond wading depth by the rising tide. While Ben hauled in the anchor, Julie raised the main and jib. Only the lightest of whispers caught the sails; the wind was still lurking behind the clouds which were now filtering the sun into light as eerie as that in an eclipse. Taking the tiller, Ben worried that unless they got more breeze before the storm hit, they might well not make it. He looked at Julie, silent, huddled into herself, staring down at the floor boards. "Julie . . . I'm sorry, I couldn't help it, I . . ."

Julie was shivering, though it wasn't yet cold. "Oh, God, Ben, I'm so frightened . . . what if I get . . . you know, like Betsy . . . it will kill my parents—"

"You won't. I mean, you don't have to . . . Isn't there some kind of pill?"

"Not afterwards."

Silence. Ben prayed for wind, not so much to get them home as to break the awful tension. His prayer was abruptly answered in full measure. It was a "door slammer" when it came, a giant hand of wind. Before he could get the main sheet off the jam cleat, the wind's heavy hand flipped the boat over like a toy. Ben, sitting on the deck, rolled backward onto the hull without so much as wetting his feet, but Julie, sitting down in the cockpit, disappeared below a tangle of rigging and sail. Ben dove and struggled frantically against the bursting of his lungs to help free her, which he somehow did, and

237

when they were clinging to the hull and gasping for air he noticed his hands were torn, bloody, salt stung.

"Julie, you all right?"

Still breathless, she nodded, then managed to get out, "Your hands . . . look at your *hands* . . ."

"They're okay, keep kicking, try to stay warm . . ."

The Sound warmed slowly in early summer, and the chill of the water was already getting to them. Even if they could have balanced on the upturned hull, it would have been worse, since the storm had now broken in sheets of rain colder than the sea. Fingers of lightning reached into the trees and buildings huddled along the dark line of shore, and thunder muttered angrily through the sky. In their preoccupation with themselves, neither had noticed any other boats around them before the storm, but even if some other imprudent sailors were still afloat they couldn't be seen through the curtain of rain. Though the island was less than a mile behind them, both had been schooled that swimming was never to be considered as long as there was something to cling to. In any case, the wind had already whipped the water into a frothy, choking chop. Ben dove and damaged his hands even more wrenching life jackets from their storage under the seats. As he helped Julie struggle into hers, he could feel the shivers running the length of her thin body.

"Swim. Kick. Keep *moving*," he said again. "Somebody'll find us as soon as this lets up."

"I'm scared, Ben. Oh, God, hold me, I don't know how much longer . . ."

Ben pinned her between him and the hull, got her tight within the circle of his arms and wrapped his legs around her in an effort to share heat he no longer possessed. He was shaking himself. Isolated in their small gray circle of storm, they might as well have been in mid-Atlantic.

"I'll hold you, Julie," Ben said, not believing he could last much longer either.

The club launch was almost on top of them before they heard or saw her. The captain, standing at the controls, his yellow slicker and sou'wester streaming with rain, maneuvered carefully into position to pick them up.

"Thought I'd find you somewheres along this course," he said as he helped Julie aboard.

Ben took off his life jacket, tossed it over into the launch. "I'll get the sails off this boat, Captain Boynes, and then we can tow her up."

"Not with hands like that, y'won't. We'll anchor her and pick her up later. Anyway, Mrs. Horner's havin' a regular fit back there at the club. Hadn't been for her I'd a let you cool off out here till this blows over," the captain said.

When Ben had gotten aboard, the captain made them huddle under a blanket he'd brought that, soaking as it was, still let their young bodies recover some heat. "Don't know what gets into you goddamned kids," the captain said. "You've been around water long enough, Ben, and your father before you, to see a storm like this comin'. Can't imagine what the hell you were thinkin' of; don't make sense."

Ben looked at Julie during this tirade, and detected a smile, which he returned. And then they quickly reverted to straight faces, afraid the captain would pitch them back into the sea, where he obviously thought they belonged.

But they had made love and survived death. Born, and born again . . .

Clearly nothing could touch them.

Chapter X

As time went by, the Rev. John Peters discovered that bringing the Word to Worton was a far more frustrating exercise than he could have imagined. Like a fencer up against a superior opponent, he found every thrust and lunge delicately parried, usually by the very people who should have been most open to him. He hardly even exchanged words, for example, with his own superior, the Rev. Dr. W. Anderson Wolfe, who, maintaining a kind of distant dignity, communicated even such matters as church schedules through notes or his long-time secretary Mrs. Lydia Dolcetti, a converted Catholic in need of the job to maintain her fatherless brood. Coming in one Tuesday morning, John Peters stopped by Mrs. Dolcetti's desk on the way to his own office. "What's he got lined up for this week?" he asked.

"Well, let's see. Tomorrow he'd like you to take the hospital rounds because he has to go to the Chamber of Commerce lunch," Mrs. Dolcetti said, shuffling through her notes. "Then Thursday there's the Hanson funeral. It's going to be a big one, and he thinks it would look better if both ministers were there, and . . . oh, yes . . . he'd like you to talk to Mrs. Hilsman. She's complaining again about those Negro children, and he thought because you were on the commission . . ."

John Peters groaned. "He would . . ."

Looking over her glasses, Mrs. Dolcetti said, "If you don't mind my saying so, Mr. Peters, I wonder sometimes why you stay on here."

"So do I. You've been here a long time, Mrs. Dolcetti —what am I doing wrong?"

"Well, it's not my business . . ."

"No, tell me. I mean it."

"People here just aren't used to your kind of preaching, Mr. Peters. They don't think they need it."

"They do, though. I'm only preaching the gospel of Jesus. You believe in Jesus, don't you, Mrs. Dolcetti?"

"I was raised a Catholic . . ."

"I don't mean it that way. Don't you think Jesus can change lives?"

"I don't know, Mr. Peters. I'm having a hard enough time living my life the way it is, without changing it."

"Well, why are you working here—in the church?"

"I need the money. I'm sorry, Mr. Peters. You won't forget about Mrs. Hilsman? She's been calling Dr. Wolfe every day . . ."

In the quiet of his own office John Peters tried to figure out for the thousandth time why he couldn't seem to make anybody else hear that clear call that had caused him to overturn his own life. The only people he could reach were the young ones like Julie Horner and perhaps Ben Adams. If it weren't for them he long ago would have gone to greener fields. It was fear of losing even the young people's allegiance that caused Peters finally to go along with the plan to import the black children. When he had argued that the town wasn't ready for it, that the first priority was getting people to accept Jesus in their hearts, the kids turned on him. That foul-mouthed Jeff Jones, who certainly wasn't any kind of a Christian, thank God, shouted, "What's the use of preaching all that shit about brotherly love if you don't practice it?" The other young people, including Ben Adams, agreed, and in the end Peters and Horner, who had been trying to stay neutral as he apparently believed a good chairman should, felt obliged to join Pauline Church and vote with the kids. He doubted that trying to explain all this to Mrs. Hilsman would do much good.

An aggressively sweet woman, Mrs. Hilsman was descended from a long line of ministers and, therefore, had her religion more in her blood than in her mind. The church was something you were born into, like the right class in society, and the object was to keep it untainted by those "lesser breeds without the law," as Kipling so well described everybody else out there in the "Recessional," which she used to sing in the Sweet Briar chorus. It was all right to send missionaries out to the heathen as long as they were as far away as China—an aunt of hers had romantically drowned in the Yangtse—but she saw no need for bringing fallen people in off the streets. She was even upset when young Ben Adams, as head of the youth group, was asked to read scripture at a service. "His father's never been inside the church—not that we'd want a man of that type—and his mother's people are . . . well, you know. . . . I just think there might be more suitable representation of our own fine young people. Now if Tim were home . . ." But Tim was seldom home and, as a result, could be held in her mind as the perfect son, the yardstick against which she measured and found wanting the unruly and messy young people she saw around her.

None of this would have mattered much except that Mrs. Hilsman through long and devoted service at baking cakes, selling antiques and mending choir robes had managed to get herself elected as the first woman elder in the church's history. Sitting in session, she annoyed them by directing their attention to the deplorable state of the communion silver, the ragged edges around the tulip beds and the need for new wallpaper in the downstairs ladies powder room. But they couldn't ignore her, since her constituency was their wives, the women who kept the church humming with sewing circles during the week and who, of course, provided the seemingly endless march of young people that filled the Sunday school rooms and ultimately swelled the church rolls as they passed through membership rites. Peters knew that Mrs. Hilsman had opposed the idea of his serving on the Youth Commission. "I think there is enough for him to do right here with our own young people," she was supposed to have told the rest of the session. Now she would be quite capable of causing him real trouble, and he wondered in his present mood whether it wouldn't be better just to resign in a righteous huff rather than risk being kicked out and carrying the damaging record through his whole ministerial career like a dishonorable discharge from the army.

John Peters paced his study and prayed. If God answered him, he did so in the curious form of old Thomas J. Watson, whose act Peters had been lucky enough to catch before the great salesman went to his reward. Good salesmen never quit; when the going gets tough, the tough get going. Working himself gradually into a fighting mood with a mantra of slogans, Peters sat down and dialed the Hilsman number. The voice that answered was soft as the fall of magnolia blossoms. "Why, John Peters, I'd just love to talk with you. You come right on over here and I'll have coffee waiting."

The Hilsman home was located, suitably for that of a junior partner, across Soundview from Brookehaven. It was a rambling ranch house the Hilsmans had built on a level stretch of filled-in marsh land that Judge Brooke sold them for a knockdown price shortly after Howard joined the firm. They had no access to the water, not even a view of it, but it made little difference now since Hilsman had poured his expanding income into turning the place into virtually a private club with swimming pool and pool house, tennis court and paddle tennis court. Over the years they had added so many boxcar like wings to the house that Peters would not have known which door to approach if he hadn't seen Mrs. Hilsman waving to him from the entry to a glassed-over greenhouse on the southeast corner. "I thought we'd have our coffee in here among the plants," she explained. "You don't mind if I do a little working while we talk? You know, with serving on the session and all, I'm just so busy these days . . ."

Inside the greenhouse, the air was warm and moist and so clotted with the mingled exhalation of plants and flowers that it reminded Peters of all those funerals where he would have to stand and pray over caskets banked with dying blossoms. "Isn't this divine?" Mrs. Hilsman bubbled while she poured the coffee at a little wrought iron table. "I do so like to be among living things. You know, when nobody's around, I talk to them. There was a man on television who said there's scientific proof that plants understand you. I think they're God's creatures just as much as people, don't you, Mr. Peters?"

"I suppose you could say so . . ." He felt that he was beginning to sweat with the first sip of coffee and wished they could move outdoors, anywhere.

"I do say so. I declare the world would be an ugly place without flowers. You know Jesus talked about the lilies of the fields and said we should all be like them . . . I do hope you'll forgive me for fussing while we talk," she said, putting a white smock appliqued with tiny water can, trowels, forks, clippers and other garden implements over her go-to-luncheon silk dress. She picked up a shears and began snipping at the nearest plants while she went on: "I suppose Andy sent you over to talk to me about those nigras you all are planning to bring up here to Worton?"

"As a matter of fact, yes, Mrs. Hilsman . . ."

"Well, I told Andy, and I want to tell you that Mr. Hilsman and I think it is a very serious error. We can't understand how a sensible man like Mr. Horner and a man with your business background would let a thing like this go on."

"I was doubtful about it myself, Mrs. Hilsman . . ."

"Then why didn't you stop it? Do you have any idea what this is going to do? I don't see how you and Mr. Horner can call yourselves Christians and let those young people of yours use those poor nigras that way . . ."

"But I thought . . ."

"I know just what you thought, Mr. Peters. You thought because of my accent that I just don't like nigras. Well, you're wrong. I was practically raised by the blackest woman you ever saw, and I still send her a little card and present every Christmas after thirty years. It's because I do know them so well that I know they like to be among their own people just as much as we do. Why my Tim—he's at Yale now, you know—tells me that the nigras there have formed their own Black Student *Alliance*. Now, don't you see? All you're going to do with these children is make them unhappy by showing them things they can never have."

"I confess I never thought of it precisely that way . . ."

"I didn't imagine you had, Mr. Peters. That's why

245

Andy Wolfe sent you over here to talk to me. He agrees with me, and so does Judge Brooke. We're going to ask the session to take action so that our church won't be part of such an un-Christian thing even if we can't stop it in the town."

"Have you talked to Jim Horner?"

"Judge Brooke said he's already spoken a word to Mr. Horner."

By now, sweating profusely and a little nauseated by the heavy aroma, Peters had lost all desire to pursue the selling mission that had brought him to the Hilsman home. He only wanted to get out of there. It would be no use talking Jesus to a woman who already based her reasoning—however falsely—on her special understanding of the faith. It was obvious, too, that she had powerful support. So he was now in the position of standing up against the powers of his own church or letting down the young people he had brought to Christ. He was back to quitting as the only way out.

He stood up. "What would you expect me to do, Mrs. Hilsman?"

"Why, I just think you should go back to those young people and tell them how foolish and unfair they're being."

"I'm afraid you don't know those young people, Mrs. Hilsman."

"They can't be so much different from my Tim. Children want you to tell them how to behave. When Tim was smaller, Mr. Hilsman used to tell him, 'This is our house, and we're bigger than you, so you do what we say.' Well, Mr. Peters, this is our community, and I hope we're, so to speak, bigger than they are."

"I really should be getting back now, Mrs. Hilsman."

Mrs. Hilsman, who had been clipping away at a stand of chrysanthemums brought early to bloom in the controlled environment of her greenhouse, bunched the flowers and handed them to Peters. "Here," she said, "take these back to Mrs. Dolcetti and tell her to put them in a vase on Andy's desk. He so loves flowers."

The letter arrived at the office. It was addressed in a hand that Jim Horner didn't recognize, marked "personal" and scotchtaped so securely that he could hardly open it. Until he started reading, Jim hadn't the slightest suspicion as to the contents—it was not at all unusual for one of their furtive executives just turned loose to approach them in a secretive way. But the first sentence started Jim's heart pounding.

"Dear Mr. Horner," the letter said. "Like I promised, you are now the first person to know that I have found her. Maybe after you read this letter, you will be the only person. It's up to you . . ."

Jim knew at once that he was reading the words of Leo Polchick. In recent months he'd come to know Sergeant Polchick very well. The town's Board of Finance had put a lot of pressure through the Police Commission on Chief Dominick to stop wasting the salary of a sergeant exclusively on the pursuit of a couple of juvenile fugitives; as a result Lou assigned Polchick to a new post as head of the department's youth division with the particular task of acting as liaison with Horner's Youth Commission. "Keep those goddamned do-gooders off my back," was the way he put it to Leo. So Leo had started coming to many of their meetings, and he and Jim would often exchange a few informal words about the search for Betsy and Steel. Jim could tell that the sergeant had little heart for the mission, but his instructions from Dominick were still to follow up every lead, and, as he confessed to Jim, "better me finding them than some out of town cop who doesn't give a damn." One night Leo produced a picture of Betsy from the police files—his favorite; standing on a beach lined with palm trees in a bikini, she had that special glow he remembered so well—and asked Jim where it had been taken. "In the Virgin Islands," Jim said, and then the meeting started and he forgot all about it until now. Before reading on, he looked at the smudged postmark on the envelope again. It was St. Thomas.

"I came down here," Leo wrote, "because I had a hunch she just might go somewhere she knew. Well, I was wandering around down here when I bumped into this fellow from Worton, Judge Brooke's son, you know.

As soon as he found out who I was he just laughed and took me right up to this little hotel he runs and there was Betsy big as life. I know people back in Worton say Brooke is a queer, and maybe he is, but they really like him down here. This hotel of his is like a refuge for every kind of stray cat—you know, hippies, draft dodgers, fairies, girls in trouble. So there was Betsy, happy as a clam helping him run the place. Hart thinks it's a big joke to have this girl with the worst reputation in Worton, and who was living in the house he says his father wouldn't let him buy, working for him, and I guess it is. The reason he wasn't worried about showing her to me is that all these black cops down here like him for keeping the oddballs out of their hair and they're not about to cooperate in arresting some little girl who didn't do anything to them.

"Well, after I got to talking to Betsy, I didn't want to arrest her either. I don't know how you are going to feel about this part, Mr. Horner, but she has been through a lot. She and the boy were holed up somewhere in Greenwich Village when the baby came, and the only doctor they could trust was some guy into drugs. He sort of botched things and the baby died. She damned near died too, and I guess the whole thing got to the Avery kid so much he went over the deep end—into LSD and then heroin. Buying his drugs was eating up their money and watching him go was more than she could stand, so one night Betsy took what she could of the money that was left and got on a plane for here. She didn't know why exactly except that she'd once had some kind of good feeling down here and hoped it would come back. At least that's what she said . . . I really shouldn't be writing you this at all because I promised Betsy I wouldn't tell anybody where she is. But from what I've seen, I think you're a pretty straight guy, and I know that if I was anybody's father I would want to know. Maybe I can get her to write to you herself later on, and I'm really trusting you not to do anything until she does. You see, Betsy and I are—well, living together and maybe we might get married sometime and I think some day she might want to get back with her family because she doesn't hold anything against you, she really doesn't. She just isn't ready for it yet.

"What I did about Dominick was write him and tell him I didn't find the kids but that I liked it so much down here I was resigning. I told him I'd run into Hart Brooke and he'd found me a job as security officer at one of the big hotels, which is true. You can check all this with Dominick if you want to, but I have to warn you he's pretty damn sore. He got me on the phone after he read my letter and called me a liar and a traitor and a pansy who'd fallen in love with Brooke. I told him to blow it out his ass and hung up. So that's the way things are, Mr. Horner. I'll try to get Betsy to write to you, I really will. Sincerely, Leo Polchick."

When he had read the letter over three times, Jim Horner put it in a plain envelope, wrote his name on it, sealed it elaborately and hid it in the office safe. He would have to think a long time about whether he could share the news with Susan in her present state. Having Betsy just vaguely out there somewhere had become almost tolerable; the way you handled it was just to stop mentioning her name. Lately they'd been avoiding Susan's parents because the old people wouldn't even try to get over it. Though he'd stopped talking about cutting them all out of his will, Susan's father would sigh heavily, shake his head and forever be asking, "How could she ever do such things? What's the world ever coming to?" Before she died, his own mother was worse. She'd already found it hard to explain to her neighbors the disappearance of Jim's name from the *News*. Then at the time of Betsy's arrest, she'd written, "I can't imagine what your father would say. I'm so ashamed . . . That girl is no granddaughter of mine. . . ." It became suddenly inconvenient to make the long trip between Worton and Starkville, and Jim didn't force it. The thing to do was to forget and go on living, and now that his new business was finally getting off the ground, he had real hopes he could eventually get Susan back to normal (except precisely what was that?). In any case sharing the news in Leo's letter would certainly not help.

He didn't have much more time to brood about it because Angie, the secretary and all-around girl Friday and only employee of Job Hunters Anonymous, had buzzed him several times to tell him that there was a client waiting in the outer room of the little suite they rented above a Chinese restaurant in Stamford. As soon as they began getting replies to their ads Jim and Paul had decided to set up in Stamford not only because the rent was cheaper and it was near their homes but because they found that most of their clients were from the suburbs too. Though it was slow business placing people and they were still just scraping along, they did have one early break that got them off the ground.

Just about the time they were signing all the papers and incorporating, Jim got an unexpected call from Hal Palmer. "Say," he said, "that old fox Margolis just told me about seeing you a while back. He said you wanted to get back into the news business. No matter what he told you, I could use a man with good instincts—particularly the man who taught me how to write. Of course I couldn't offer you what you've been getting . . ."

For a minute Jim was tempted. He could still tell Paul to go it alone on their still uncertain venture and hedge back to safety and considerably more respectability. He also knew that it wasn't possible, that Margolis had been right in saying that a man should never turn back, couldn't. He'd be an embarrassment around the office that Palmer would come to regret—and hate. So he countered the offer by playing it big about his new business.

"Sounds great. You know, that would make a nice feature for the business section. Mind if I send a fellow up there to talk to you?"

"Thanks, Hal. That would put us on the map."

"No thanks needed, Jim—for a lot of reasons. Still wearing Brooks Brothers suits?"

"No, as a matter of fact I—"

Hal laughed. "I told you Worton would be the making of you . . ."

250

Partly because of economy, Jim had taken to wearing old jackets, elbows patched with leather, or sweaters to the office. He had let his hair grow some and even started a beard. Since his business was to operate a sort of clearing house, by phone and file, he no longer had to pass personal muster in front of vested personnel men. It was the client who had to go forth properly suited for the fray, and Jim often felt sorry for these men who, long out of work, had to beg or borrow from their families to go on looking prosperous. The *News* piece flushed more wounded corporate birds out of cover than Jim would have imagined existed. A number of them came from right around the Worton area—some he'd briefly envied when he saw them descending from the train into the arms of some cheeky girl in a tennis dress standing by the family station wagon. To hear what had really happened to them was to become freshly aware of the way people actually lived behind the facade they offered the world. It was, in fact, the same other side of the story he was gradually getting from the young people, as they came to have some confidence in him.

The man Angie brought in this morning was, fortunately for Jim's mood, a stranger. Fortyish, vigorous, gray-templed, handsome in full executive uniform, he came on strong. "Name's Black," he said, and named a little Pennsylvania town as home. "Read about your thing in *News* and was just driving by, left the family up on the Cape for a few weeks. Thought you might have some interesting openings."

"You're out of work, Mr. Black?"

"Well . . . let's just say looking around. Fellow wants to improve himself, you know. Got a couple of kids coming on to college, and—"

"Mr. Black, we've got one rule here: tell the truth. It's a little like Alcoholics Anonymous. We've found we can't do anything unless we know exactly where a man is and why. Sometimes it helps to talk anyway. Mr. Richards and I have been through this ourselves, and we like to think we understand. Let's begin with your real name."

"Schweitzer. George Schweitzer. Pennsylvania Dutch, you know."

"Yes" (but we have Jewish clients, too, he'd like to have said). "Now what's the situation?"

"Well, I was telling the truth—about the family up on the Cape and coming through. They don't know, you see, and I wanted them out of the way until I can find something . . ."

Jim nodded.

"I was purchasing agent for this little machine tool company—Danver. You probably never heard of it, but it's a goddamned gold mine. Wholly owned by Danver, who gets a pile out of it for himself and his worthless family. But I'll say he was pretty good about sharing with a few of us he considered top men. I got twenty thousand dollars and of course something on the side . . ."

"What do you mean by that? We've got to have the picture of your total income to know where you might be placed."

"Well, you know, Mr. Horner—kickbacks. It's the way the business is done. I must have got twenty thousand more out of that, not to mention the Cadillac parked outside here and that place on the Cape some fellow who doesn't know I've lost my job is lending me. I hope I'm not shocking you . . ."

"Nothing much shocks me anymore, Mr. Schweitzer. What happened?"

"You'll hardly believe this. I still can't. This Danver fellow liked to think of us all as his family. I remember he had to see my wife before he'd hire me. Well, he was always throwing parties for us. A while back he got a case of hot pants and he shucked his old wife for a goofy blonde and built her a new house way out of town. Well, he had a big wingding to introduce the new wife and show off the house, and of course we went. This girl decorated that house worse than her face. I mean, it was full of leopard skins and white couches and all that stuff, and when my wife went up to the bedroom to powder her nose she got talking to the wife of another old friend who didn't work for the company and they started to talk

252

about what bad taste this woman had. Just then they heard the john flushing and out comes the new Mrs. Danver, who sails past them with her nose in the air and they know she's heard everything. Well, when my wife was telling me about this on the way home, half laughing and half crying, I didn't feel too good but tried not to think too much about it. The next day Danver calls me in and says, 'Schweitzer, I think you'd better find yourself a job in a company where your wife can enjoy better taste.' And that was that. Do you believe it?"

"I do," Jim said.

"The thing is I just can't tell my wife. I mean, we've been married twenty years, and I . . ." Schweitzer started to choke up, but he managed to get it out. ". . . I love her and I know what it would do to her to think that she . . . well, you see . . ."

Jim stood up and took Schweitzer's hand and led him toward the door. "I see, Mr. Schweitzer. Keep in touch. We'll do what we can do."

The poor bastard, Jim thought—obviously a get-along type when it came to thievery but a guy who would do anything for the wife and kids and keep it all to himself. How well he knew about that; oh, how well! If anybody thought Abe Lincoln had abolished slavery, they ought to get to know the American executive life as Jim was getting to know it. Oh, it could look good in terms of owning houses and cars and backyard barbecue pits and boats and college degrees, but in terms of owning anything like a soul, it was worse than life on any plantation. The only men who could call themselves men from what Jim was seeing were the people in business for themselves, running the store or the garage or the laundry, or the so often despised blue-collar workers who had a skill and belonged to a union and got as much as they could for a day's wages never mind who kissed whose ass. And once more Jim realized his thoughts were drifting in the same current with those of the young people he knew. Once he remembered Jeff Jones, whose father was vice-president to a large advertising agency, breaking up a meeting with: "Be like my old man? Not on your life. He takes a screwing all day and gets no screwing at night, which if you ask me is the wrong way around."

The remark naturally upset Mrs. Lamb and Tony Francetti, but Jim, thinking of it now, and of all the Schweitzers of the world, appreciated it and allowed himself the luxury of a laugh. It made him feel better about the letter locked up in his safe. At least Betsy seemed to be alive and well and maybe happy, which was more than could be said for most people. He felt bad about young Avery, but at least he was out of reach of his vengeful parents. Leo Polchick had been right in his trust. Jim would keep the news to himself. In his new business, he was getting good at that.

One reason Fielding Small went on living in Worton was that he enjoyed the look on the faces of his acquaintances in the literary circles of New York when he pronounced the name. "You can't mean it!" a girl in harlequin glasses toying with a cigarette in a long holder would say. "Up with those Philistines? I mean, who do you *talk* to?"

Of course, since they seldom saw her, his city friends tended to forget about his wife Anna, who pulled her hair into a bun, wore rubber-soled shoes, counted her day made when she spotted a red-winged blackbird on her morning walk, typed his manuscripts, cooked gourmet food, warmed his bed and listened and listened. And they had no way at all of knowing about the Tuesday Club, which was by far the most exclusive club in Worton, so exclusive, in fact, that people like First Selectman Dr. Floyd Shepherd and Judge Amos Hartwell Brooke were not aware of its existence. Now that Dr. Benjamin Adams had died, its permanent membership was down to four—Fielding Small, Charles Church, Loren Johnson (adviser to L.B.J.) and Father Archibald Funston. Their gathering place was a back-corner booth in a bar on the Post Road called Tony's, a saloon so grubby and evil-smelling that mothers took their children across the street to avoid the aroma oozing from its doors. The club had discovered this refuge by trial and error. Meetings at homes were imperiled by the interruption of wives or the noisy distraction of children; in the better clubs and restaurants, friends were wont to drop by their table uninvited. The beauty of Tony's was that the honest working men who crowded the bar three deep at six p.m. were all gone to make amends to the missus by seven or eight at the latest, leaving the Tuesday Club in splendid isolation. They all humored Father Funston by referring to Tony's as "the pub," since the ring of English tradition made it seem more respectable, and Tony always left the back door unlatched Tuesday nights so that the good father could slip in from the parking lot unmarked by any parishioner who might be abroad at that hour.

The function of the Tuesday Club was talk—endless talk lubricated from the pitcher of beer Tony kept filled in the center of the table. Occasionally they would pass resolutions for the sake of the minutes that Fielding Small insisted on writing up when he wasn't in the middle of a novel. One night, along about midnight and half way through the fourth pitcher of beer, they voted three to zero, Father Funston abstaining, to declare that God was, in fact, dead; more recently, they voted three to one, Loren Johnson opposing on account of his close association with the President—"a much misunderstood man, I can assure you"—that the United States should pull out of Vietnam. The Tuesday Club had to be the only place in Worton where current books, plays, art exhibits and even musical compositions were discussed; where names like Warhol, Rothko, Bergman, Fellini, Martin Luther King, Jr., Harvey Cox, James Baldwin, Mailer, Robert Lowell, Kennedy, Bernstein, Friedan were uttered without derision; where names like Joe Namath, Bus Mosbacher, Jack Nicklaus, Richard Nixon, Hubert Humphrey, John Wayne, Nelson Rockefeller, William Westmoreland, Norman Vincent Peale were uttered not at all. Of late, though, possibly influenced by Pauline Church's pillow talk, the Tuesday Club discussions seemed to be more and more concerned with local affairs, particularly the controversial activities of the Youth Commission.

"I get a laugh out of this, I really do," Fielding Small said. "From the buzzing I hear about, they've busted open a real hornets' nest. I'm only afraid that Floyd will be stung at the polls this fall."

"Not only him," Loren Johnson said. "The whole board of selectmen is shook up. We had a knockdown that lasted till two o'clock the other night about whether to put this commission out of business—ended up in a three-two vote, of course, to keep it going. Floyd told us bluntly that he'd been warned that Dan Parker is going to start blasting the commission—and us—in the *Record*."

"That horse's ass . . ."

"Now wait a minute, Charlie, I've learned a lot about politics around here since you fellows got me into this," Johnson went on. "Parker's heading for Congress in '68, and I'm not sure he hasn't sniffed the right wind shift. Besides, he's got Judge Brooke with him. So you can't exactly blame him. What's the Christian line on all this, Arch?"

"Troubled," Father Funston admitted. "They tell me there's a movement on over in the Presbyterian church to repudiate this invitation to the black kids. Of course, they've got a problem since that young Peters got so many of his own flock mixed up with Young Life, and they've got more hosts in their congregation than the rest of us. Their sanctuary is going to look like a checker board for a couple of Sundays—so there goes what used to be called the 'most segregated hour of the week.'"

"But isn't that good, Arch?" Fielding Small asked. "We've all agreed here there isn't much future for this country unless we all develop a good case of color blindness. Isn't this a perfect place to begin?"

"I don't know, I just don't know," Father Funston said. "Of course, it isn't Christian to exclude a person for the color of his skin, but I just hope the Presbyterians—or my vestry too, for that matter—don't do anything rash that would make us all look bad. Still, I wonder whether we're doing our black friends a favor by forcing a thing like this, by bringing them into an unnatural situation . . ."

"You know what Chief Dominick told the selectmen the other night?" Loren Johnson said. "That all those nigger kids, as he called them, would case the house they were living in and come back and rip it off. 'If I catch one smoke in this town after that bus pulls out for Harlem, I'll jug him,' he said."

"Well, you can't blame somebody like Dominick—or Tony over there—for his prejudices," Small said. "It's people like Marguerite Hilsman, who I understand is back of the thing at the Presbyterian church, who really get to me."

"The one I feel sorry for is that Jim Horner," Charlie Church said. "Pauline tells me he's a regular square—certainly looked it, until recently at least—yet here he is the lightning rod for this whole storm . . ."

"You're right," Johnson agreed. "He's damned if he does and damned if he doesn't. If he tried to put those kids down now, they'd howl so loud it could be heard all the way to CBS or *News*. If he doesn't, he'll have trouble with every one of his neighbors down there on Soundview."

"I don't know—I'm kind of enjoying watching him squirm," Small said. "Horner's one of those smart-ass p.r. guys. Maybe I'm just jealous because they make a thousand bucks a word, but it's fun seeing one of them have to live with his own bright idea."

"Don't you have any sympathy, Fielding? I've heard Horner isn't a p.r. man anymore, lost his job over this. I thought great writers were supposed to be men of compassion," Father Funston said.

"Well, I do feel sorry about what happened to Horner's kid. The way Floyd talks, there's a lot of mystery around that whole thing. It might even give me a novel one of these days. The interesting thing is that the Horners are such *totally ordinary* decent people, such "squares," as you call them, Charlie. You can understand how young Ben Adams, or the Dominick kid, or even Sissy Stanton might get all mixed up, with families like they have, but why a kid like Betsy Horner would suddenly go off the rails—"

"What makes you think she did go 'off the rails,' as you put it?" Church asked.

"Getting busted for drugs and running off with the kid next door isn't exactly standard behavior for a Worton teenager even now," Small said. "I suppose you'd say this is some kind of judgment of God on the poor Horners, Arch? Or are you ready to agree with the rest of us that God is dead?"

"I'll take the fifth on that," Funston said. "Whatever I say would be bad for my business."

They all laughed, and Loren Johnson stood up. "Hate to break this up," he said, "but I've got to catch the early shuttle to Washington. L.B.J.'s still under the gun on inflation and needs some moral support from us Keynesians."

Driving home, Fielding Small felt that wonderful sense of excitement that came for him with the birth of an *idea*. He'd just tossed off the thing about doing a novel on Betsy Horner to make conversation, but now it began to take hold in his mind. It was the paradigm of the American Dream turned nightmare. The characters were perfect: Jim Horner, clean-cut young executive; his wife Susan, sweet matron; Betsy, cheer-leader; Ron Dominick, football star; Steel Avery, poor little rich boy; Julie, Young Life sister; and Fielding Small understood, even a dog named *Rusty*. What really happened—and why? If he could answer these questions even in fictional form he would have something. His answers might speak to millions of middle-class Americans asking: "Where have we gone wrong?" And these days they were really asking—on the couch, in the office, over a million martinis and in loveless marriage beds.

At least it was worth a try, Fielding decided, and the obvious first step was to get to know the Horners better. The opportunity was at hand. Judge Brooke had called him just the other day and asked him to go along on the Vineyard race. Until now Fielding had been trying to think of an excuse to get out of it because he didn't fancy being cooped up for days within range of the judge's booming voice or being subjected to what he heard was iron discipline under way. Sailing in his mind was a memory of delight, a savoring of one youthful escapade when, just after World War II, he and a couple of fellow air force officers ran a rum-soaked old schooner through the Caribbean's blue seas. Fielding had avoided involvement with the sailing crowd in Worton, as well as the Golden Hills and Hunt Club sets, because he couldn't afford his own boat and didn't like racing, though he and Anna had gone for an occasional Sunday sail with the Brookes on the *Helena*. As for sail racing, he considered it absurd, agreeing with a fellow writer whom he hated for saying it first that it was "like watching the grass grow." But now the chance for close observation of Jim Horner in action outweighed all this. It should be especially interesting this time out, since the judge and Horner were known to be locking horns over this youth business. Maybe one would throw the other overboard, though Fielding doubted he'd have the luck to witness such a drama among gentlemen.

Anna was waiting up for him—not in front of the flickering tube but in quiet perusal of a novel. She waved it at him. "You really ought to read this, Fielding. If this can make a best seller, you ought to be able to do it too."

"Well, at least I think I maybe got me a story. Remind me tomorrow to call Judge Brooke and tell him I'll go along on the Vineyard race."

"I thought you didn't like racing."

"I don't—but anything for my art."

Chapter XI

Charlie Church was up against something new in the way of women, and there were times when he wasn't at all sure he would survive it. His Galatea had come to life in the most amazing ways, not all of them pleasing. As a nineteenth-century gentleman born a dozen years too late, and a New Englander at that, Charlie Church was an instinctive believer in the double standard. While his artistic eye and temperament might demand refreshment from time to time, any woman bearing his name was expected to stay home and darn his socks and tend his fires against the time of his coming. All his other wives had done that until, out of sheer boredom, he sent them packing with the smallest possible reward that the prestigious firm of Brooke, Hilsman, Stanton and Seabury could browbeat their usually second-rate lawyers into accepting.

If Pauline was turning into somebody else, it was his own damned fault. What he had taken for innocence in the shy skeleton of a girl who caught his eye in art class turned out to be a cunning sense of self-protection. He could see now that while he thought he was busy fashioning her into a new object of pleasure, she was teasing and tricking him into playing the role he was now finding more than a little wearing.

Pauline had jumped at the chance to start modeling not because, as so many he had known before her, she was vain about her body but because she saw in it the quickest way to establish her independence from her family. Actually, she made most of her money working for other people as a sort of animated clothes rack, but she undressed for him with such humorous detachment that it unmanned him. "I can't imagine what you see in a skinny thing like me, but go ahead and look," she said the first time. What he saw in her was the long cool look of an Egyptian princess who had just stepped down from a thousand-year-old temple frieze. This coolness, remoteness seemed emphasized by the smooth, marbled texture of her bare skin. He wanted badly to touch her, to animate her, to possess her, but something always held him back. He could see now that it was her clever flattery in treating him casually as a contemporary, a professional, a friend. From the very first she had looked right into his eyes and called him "Charlie," leveling their ages with a name. She wasn't anything like the giggly, girlish ones who would call him "Dr. Church" or "Professor" even in bed, and carry on about just *loving* "older men."

"If there's anything I hate worse than a dirty young man, it's a dirty old one—you know, the kind who pinch you in the elevator while they're pretending to read the *Wall Street Journal*," Pauline would tell him. "What I like about you, Charlie, is that you can work with a girl without making her feel like a sex object."

He'd nod, pretending to paint, and she'd go on. "You're a real friend, Charlie, you are—the only one I have. The thing I like is that I can talk about everything to you, but I guess there isn't much a girl sitting around in her birthday suit can hide, is there? What I want to know is what I ought to do about Bob . . ."

"That photographer fellow?"

"No, the one from Grosse Pointe, the one my parents sent around to see me. He's in some big Wall Street law firm or something. He's always trying to sleep with me—"

"I don't blame him."

"Why, Charlie Church, now don't go ruining everything."

"Do you think I'm over the hill, Pauline, just because—?"

"Never. You're the youngest man I know, Charlie. Why you ought to hear Bob talk. He thinks they ought to take these draft card burners out and shoot them—of course he got himself out by staying in school until he was too old. And the other day he referred to Dr. King as an uppity nigger . . ."

"He'll go far."

"But not with me. The thing is that I don't quite know

262

how to get rid of him—he's so persistent and he's always calling his mother and passing on things about me that I'm sure she passes on to my mother. If he knew, if they ever found out I was sitting here in the altogether in front of you, they'd be on the first plane."

"Well, you are twenty-one . . ."

"Once a child, always a child. Maybe the thing that keeps you young, Charlie, is that you don't have to be stuffy for the benefit of your children. You don't have any, do you?"

"Not for want of trying."

"Careful, Charlie! I think you really are trying to convince me that you're a dirty old man after all."

"Never with you, Pauline. I'm the last of the Edwardian gentlemen."

And so it would go. Once she said, "You know, if I ever sleep with you, Charlie, it would have to be right out in the open. I wouldn't like this business of sneaking behind your wife's back. There's no double standard for me, Charlie, and I'm never going to be anyone's back street girl like in that movie I saw on TV the other night."

When his then current wife finally got tired of darning socks for a man she hardly saw and moved out of the old house in Worton, Charlie invited Pauline up for a working weekend. "I need my studio there to do the job right," he argued persuasively. He was surprised at her reaction to the place. She fell in love with the old house, with the woods, with the Sound. But most of all she was entranced by the huge fraying Church family Bible in which the names of Churches had been inscribed for three centuries. She would sit with it in her lap while she was posing and read aloud the Abigails, Contents, Sarahs, Marthas, and pump him for details about these long-vanished women. "How come none of your wives are here, Charlie?"

"You have to bring a new Church into the world to become *the* Mrs. Church of any generation," he said.

She snapped the book shut and gave him an unfathomable look from those teasing eyes of hers. "So somebody could still become *the* Mrs. Church?"

"Not without trying . . ."

"Then why don't we try, Charlie?"

And that's the way it happened—in the middle of a dull afternoon, in the creaking, canopied four-poster in which Charles Church himself had been conceived. She gave herself with such maddening reserve that he felt he had to have her again and again and perhaps forever. "I really do want to make you *the* Mrs. Church," he said.

"On one condition . . ."

"What?"

"That I can go on being Pauline Thompson too, the way you've always gone on being Charlie Church . . ."

"What's that all supposed to mean?"

"I'm not sure. I don't know, but we can find out. Want to try?"

"Yes," he said, and, amazingly, he was able to, and she said, "Didn't I tell you that you are as young as you think?"

But something about her eluded him then and still eluded him. He never did feel she was really his, and they had not been able to write her name in the Bible. For years he had suspected that the problem was his but he would never go to a doctor to find out—there were some things in life better left unknown. When, after a fruitless season with Pauline he began drifting back to his old ways, he was somewhat surprised, despite all the brave talk, at her attitude. Always before, his conduct had produced a kind of satisfying jealousy at home that ultimately led to a parting of the ways—and new opportunity. Pauline was just amused.

"They say you can't teach old dogs new tricks, Charlie, and I always knew it applied to you," she said. "I never expected you to change. I don't think people should. I think they should be themselves. One reason I married you was that I didn't think you were in any position to act like some jealous young prig of a husband and because I already knew there was no way I could think of owning you."

It was certainly a new thing, all right, and sometimes he thought the timbers of the old Church house actually trembled at the talk that went on in the four-poster bed.

Instead of letting him hide his tracks like any civilized man, she'd coax him into confessing his conquests. She could never seem to understand that a pinch of dishonesty was the salt of what he had been brought up to think of as good taste. It was also, unhappily, a good part of the sweetness of forbidden fruit. Somehow his misadventures lost their savor in the telling, particularly when she'd counter with, "Thank heavens it wasn't a meaningful relationship. It hardly ever is when they're as dumb as all that. Sometimes it doesn't even work when they're smart. Paul—that professor, you know—wanted me to . . . well, you know what . . . and I had to tell him where he could put it. But I'm afraid there is this man here in Worton . . ."

"You don't mean Jim Horner?"

"The very same."

"Nothing's happened between you, has it?"

"I wish I could lie and say yes, but like I told you he's a perfect square, the most married man in town, if you ask me."

"Thank God. You know, Pauline, people are already getting ideas. The other day I met Mrs. Andrews out at the mailbox, and she said—you know, real sweet the way she can—'Mr. Church, would you mind asking your wife to have her friend drive out more quietly so *late* at night? You know, it starts our dog to barking, and Mr. Andrews needs his sleep.' Well, you know damned well what she was saying."

"I don't see that it's anybody's business but mine—and maybe yours."

"Worton isn't New York, Pauline, whether you like it or not. People believe in the old-fashioned virtues up here—"

"Including Charlie Church, the big bad bohemian?"

"It's the way it looks . . ."

"That's the trouble with this whole damned town. It's built on appearances. The kids can see right through them . . ."

"That's another thing. Whatever you and Horner are getting into with each other, you're going to tear this town apart with that commission of yours. The other night at Tuesday Club we were talking about bringing these black kids up here—"

"So the big liberals are scared their talk might turn into action? Is that it, Charlie? You men give me a laugh. You're like those high-talking chiefs they have out there in Polynesia who sit around and settle the affairs of the world while the tribe stays stuck in the stone age. None of you really want to see Worton change, do you?"

"Hey, Pauline . . ."

"All I can say is that if you don't want this place shaken up, you brought the wrong girl up here . . ."

"I'm beginning to agree with you."

"Oh, no you don't, Charlie Church. You don't get rid of me that easily. You know, despite everything, I'm beginning to like it here, and I still want to be *the* Mrs. Church—unless you're tired of trying."

The damnable thing was that he wasn't. And maybe, just maybe, it would work this time. Then lying awake, once more unsated, once more feeling he had somehow failed, Charlie began to laugh at the thought of this strange woman's name going down at the bottom of that long list of sharp-faced Puritan women, some of whose portraits still chilled the walls of the old house. What would they ever think of her? Hell, he didn't even know if she believed in God.

Sleepily, Pauline asked, "What's so funny, Charlie?"

"I was just wondering if you believe in God. I never asked . . ."

"I'm damned if I know, Charlie. Why . . .?"

"Well, you want your name to go down in the Bible along with old Martha and her prayer book . . ."

"Listen, Charlie, there are lots of hot names in the Bible—Jezebel, Salome, Mary Magdalene . . ."

"Pauline, you're goddamn impossible."

"Goddamn right."

Marion Brooke Stanton had been able to take everything. Armed with no particular feminine graces, she had made a fine art of fortitude when she discovered it would earn almost as much admiration as beauty. She was "good old Marion," and hers was the shoulder people cried on. Since she knew that Dr. Floyd Shepherd had counted on this attribute when he chose to break the news to her, she struggled to live up to her reputation. But for some reason she was finding this more difficult to take than all the other hurts, disillusionments and shocks in the night that had made her life much like riding the jumps at the club.

"You know, I'm glad you brought her to me after all, Marion," Dr. Shepherd was saying. "I think I lost my head back there when I was talking to your father and let politics interfere with my profession. Hammond's one of those modern young fellows, and he'd have her in the hospital right away. While I hate to say this to you, I see no use in it. I honestly think she'd be happier at home for whatever time she has . . ."

"How long . . .?"

"If I were a religious man, I'd say it's up to God. I just don't know. Six months perhaps. The radiologist says there's evidence of it all through her—lungs, liver . . ."

"Oh, God . . ."

Marion had buried her face in her hands, and Dr. Shepherd was uncomfortably afraid she was going to cry. It had never occurred to him that this big, solid woman he'd seen cope with so many crises would be so affected by the not surprising news that her aging mother had cancer. He had counted on Marion to tell the judge, with whom he hadn't spoken since that morning in Dan Parker's office, and of course Helen Brooke, herself. Bad enough to give this news to strangers, let alone old friends, and he'd felt lucky to have an ally in good, old Marion.

"Now, Marion, she is seventy-two," he said. "I can give her something to keep her comfortable; she shouldn't have much pain. Pull yourself together; she's really going to need you."

Marion managed not to cry after all. "You're right, Dr. Shepherd. Will we need a nurse or anything?"

"Not for a while. I think with the help you've got there you can handle it until she has to stay in bed."

"Do I have to tell them right now?"

"Use your judgment, Marion. I think she knows already—people usually do."

Dr. Shepherd was right again. Marion got home just in time for the Brookehaven nightly ritual of cocktails in the den. Her mother didn't want one, and her father fussed, "What's the matter, Helen? Turning down a drink's a sure sign of age, you know."

"I'm just not myself tonight, Amos," Helen said.

"Huh, seems to me you're never yourself lately. Ought to see that Dr. Hammond. Floyd was right—the fellow's good. 'Course he couldn't find anything wrong with me."

"Maybe I will. If you don't mind, dear, I just don't feel like dinner," Helen said. "Would you see me up to my room, Marion?"

In her bedroom, Helen made it easy for her daughter. "He told you, didn't he?"

Marion started to deny it, but her mother waved her off and went on, "Well, *don't* tell your father—at least not until after the race. It may be his last, you know, and I don't want to spoil it . . . Now run along, or he'll suspect something."

It was a trying, silent meal, ending with the judge's order: "See that your mother goes to the doctor. Probably that gall bladder kicking up. She should have had it out years ago."

Marion, glad her children were away at camp until after Labor Day, went alone to her room. The impulse to come apart and weep had gone, but she wanted to think about why she was so unstrung by this news. She'd survived what should have been more damaging deaths before. But she'd had to handle them after the fact the way you had to keep a boat steady when you were hit by an unexpected squall. This was different, this knowing it was coming, this having to watch its certain ravages. But it was more than that, she knew, and it had to do with the strange feelings she had been experiencing ever since she'd moved back to Brookehaven.

At first she thought it was nothing but a normal and comforting reaction to all she'd been through. Without any thought or discussion she'd moved into the bedroom she had occupied all her youth, just on the other side of the tower from her parents' rooms. The very first night, lying in her old bed and aware of the familiar shapes looming around her, watching a flicker of moonlight reflected off the pond pick out the old crack in the corner of the ceiling, she felt safe and sure again of the future. When she'd heard her father harrumphing past her door on the way to bed, she'd rolled over and slept like a baby.

Instead of resenting it as she once had, she found the orderliness of life in the old house—sitdown breakfast at nine, cocktails in the den at six, dinner promptly at seven, dog out at eleven, lights out at twelve—a soothing change from the shambles of coping with a moody, drunken husband and four unscheduled children. And there was something else. Doors closed in Brookehaven. Unlike the sliding windows of her glass house, they made private lives possible. Except at the cocktail hour, the den was her father's; nobody invaded the tower sewing room where her mother played solitaire or watched TV. A large dressing room separated the high-ceilinged bedrooms to which her mother and father—he with his spaniel on the floor—had retired separately for as long as she could remember.

There was a time when she—and Hart, especially—considered themselves children of a loveless marriage. Old photographs of their mother—in long-waisted middy blouse and sailor hat in the cockpit of the first *Helena,* in cloche and tight skirt awkwardly swinging a golf club—were proof that she had tried the judge's way of life. But she literally had no stomach for the sea and no skill at sports; besides, she tired easily. So except for church and parties and the formal ritual of the house, the judge and his lady went their own ways. Marion's fierce reaction was to join what she considered her lonely father; Hart's was to comfort his gentle mother. But nobody spoke a word about it. You did the things you did because they seemed right at the time—and not unlike everything you learned about life in the English novels they made you read in school. Love was something for a season; marriage was for life.

Only when she returned, running unconsciously for shelter from the storms of her own life, did Marion begin to appreciate her parents' relationship. The distance and doors between them lent a dignity to their feelings. They had never been awash in that murky sea of magazine togetherness that lured so many people of Marion's generation; they accepted as given the separateness of individuals, the difference of male and female. Each never expected more from the other than he or she had to give. Looking back, she couldn't recall her father's ever uttering a word of reproach when her mother declined to join this or that expedition, though disappointment may have shown in his eyes; nor did their mother nag him to stay at home, though sometimes she wept, according to Hart, when he had gone. Once when she was young and impressionable the judge had broken down and taken the whole family over to experience spring in Paris. While mother and Hart dawdled in galleries, she and her father walked and walked. Going through the Tuileries one day, they surprised a couple aggressively caressing each other, and the judge said, "See that, Marion?—they're trying to get more out of life than there is in it." She'd thought then it was a simply awful thing to say, proof of the lovelessness from which she'd sprung.

She thought differently now, because, whatever you called the thing her parents shared, it endured unchanged and unchanging. In another family, the way Hart turned out might have torn them apart. You could laugh about the judge's old-fashioned and unscientific opinion that there was just some bad Jennings blood in Hart's veins, but it was part of the judge's ability to accept things and people as they were and go on from there. "I don't hold with so-called liberals—they think everything and everybody can be changed and made better," she could remember her father's saying. "Call me conservative, if you like, but I prefer being called a realist." Marion thanked God that she had absorbed enough of the judge's temperament to look at her own life, for the most part, with a cool eye. Otherwise, she might be all terribly mixed up by some psychiatrist, like poor Susan Horner.

Marion had no respect for people like Susan. She'd had some troubles, but her daughter was at least alive, as far as anybody knew, not dead like Sissy, and she still had that pretty little Julie around the house and a regular rock of a husband. Marion and her mother had stopped dropping in on Susan for tea after the time they could smell the gin clear across the table and Susan rattled the cups and saucers like castanets. Old Mrs. Brooke didn't need that kind of grief. Marion wouldn't have known about the psychiatrist at all if Susan hadn't come running all the way over to Brookehaven one day. She was out of breath and thrown together like a rag doll and told Marion she was just too shaky to drive herself to the doctor's. Marion took her, of course—it was the only decent thing to do—but felt it was a waste of time when she found out it was Dr. Bruno. Although Susan wouldn't tell her what went on in there, she seemed even worse when she came out. She didn't talk all the way home except to beg Marion not to tell a soul. "Everybody'd think I was crazy if they knew I was going to Dr. Bruno," was the way she put it, and she was probably right.

Marion had no doubt that somebody like Dr. Bruno would make a lot of the way she felt about her mother's dying. There had been a time—years, in fact—when she and her mother could hardly talk to each other without a fight. They disagreed on everything, beginning with what kind of clothes she should take to school ("They'd never let me wear a blouse like that—it's positively indecent"), running through the raising of children ("I don't see how you can let them cry like that; I always had nurse take you away") and care of husband ("How can you let Bill make a fool of himself the way he did at the club last night?"), to the feeding of plants ("If you don't give those poinsettias more water, they'll die"). Maybe she felt guilty about the time when, seized by inner rage, she wished her mother, if not dead, at least as conveniently far away as China.

But those times were long past. After Sissy's death—so

many things seemed to come after Sissy's death—her mother changed, or maybe she changed. They began talking to each other like friends, even exchanging shy confidences about things as intimate as sexual relations. Marion was, for example, pleased and surprised to learn that the judge, though somewhat ceremonial in his approach, could still be ardent on occasion, making even more mysterious and inviting the relationship from which she'd sprung. It was her mother who, apparently sensing what was going on inside her, suggested, even pleaded, for the move back to Brookehaven. Marion could see now that they needed each other—her mother needed her strength, and she her mother's comfort. But the terrible thing was that she no longer felt that she had the strength to give. Sinking back into Brookehaven, surrounded by ceremony, servants and certainty, she had allowed herself the luxury of becoming something like a child again. She had come to live for the small delights of the day—the morning ride at the Hunt Club, lunch with a friend at Golden Hills or on a nice day on the Yacht Club terrace, dinner with her parents and any children who might be home under the steady gaze from the family portraits. Behind Brookehaven's solid brick walls everything seemed as safe and sure as it had been when she was a little girl—until Dr. Shepherd broke the news. She hated to admit it to herself, but she knew the real blow was having to grow up all over again.

After the first shock wore off, Marion began to find her mother's resigned acceptance of her condition infuriating. People with money didn't have to die of something like cancer these days. She argued that Dr. Shepherd was a quack, more interested in golf and politics than in medicine. Maybe they should go to Dr. Hammond. When her mother refused, she went herself to the specialists upon whose tests Dr. Shepherd had based his opinion. They agreed with Floyd Shepherd's evaluation of their results, but then people, particularly down in Memorial in New York, were doing miraculous things these days. Armed with the reports, Marion went herself to see a leading surgeon at Memorial. "From the looks of these and without seeing your mother, I'd have to say it wouldn't do much good to operate," he said. "We could try radiation. It might give her more time, and you never know . . ."

"How much time?"

"A year, perhaps two. Of course, it can be painful and produce nausea . . ."

"And it can cure?"

"Cure isn't a word we like to use, particularly in a case as advanced as your mother's."

"But there is hope?"

"Mrs. Stanton, if I didn't believe in hope, I wouldn't be in this business."

Helen Brooke made a great show of breakfast, of every meal, in fact. She would munch her way through enough toast and take enough sips of tea to keep the judge happy until he got up and left her with an affectionate peck on the cheek. Then she'd go upstairs and lose most of it in the basin before crawling back into bed again. Marion knew what was happening and always followed her mother up after the judge left the house. It was then that they had most of their talks. The day after she'd been to New York, Marion sat on the bed and said, "We're going to get you into Memorial, and you are going to beat this thing."

An odd look, like that of a fearful child, came into her mother's eyes. "Oh, no . . ."

"Why *not*, mother? You want to go on living—"

"Marion, you might not understand this, but I think I've lived as much as I can."

"Nonsense. If it weren't for Floyd Shepherd you wouldn't feel that way. I don't know what he's giving you, but it's taking the fight out of you. Oh, I agreed with him at first until I talked with these other doctors."

"I never did have much fight, not like you and your father . . ."

"That's what I'm talking about—father and me. Brookehaven wouldn't be the same without you. Aren't you being . . . well, selfish? Daddy would be furious if he knew—"

"I don't think so, Marion. Your father and I have

273

always understood that a person has a right to be selfish at times . . ."

No matter what her mother said, Marion was sure that the judge would want to take action if action offered any hope. Often she yearned to tell him, to get him involved, but she knew it would destroy her relationship with her mother and take away the one drive that seemed to keep her mother going at all, the desire that the judge go on his race with peace of mind. Until that was over, she'd have to get some other help . . . maybe from Andy Wolfe.

Religion, like sex, was something that was practiced, not preached, in the Brooke household. For as long as Marion could remember, her parents had gone to church together, unless the judge was off cruising somewhere. The fate of the Worton Presbyterian Church had often been decided in the Brookehaven den or over the dining table where the Wolfes were the most frequent guests. Marion herself had gone to church until she could get away to school and seen to it that the children got most of the way through Sunday school. Sometimes she thought that her father just looked upon the church as a useful organization, like the bank or the town government, but she had a feeling that her mother had a more simple faith. It was worth a try.

"Mother, do you think it's Christian? I mean it's almost like commiting suicide not to try something when the doctors say—"

Weary of arguing what her body told her was un-arguable, Helen interrupted impatiently, "I don't know. I just don't know. Now please leave me alone, Marion. I'm tired . . ."

"Would you . . . would you just talk to Andy Wolfe, mother?"

"Oh; all right, all right. But I'm sure he'll agree with Floyd and me . . ."

It wasn't until she actually got to the church that Marion remembered that Andy Wolfe was up at that place in Maine and wouldn't be back until after Labor Day, after the race. Mrs. Dolcetti told her that John Peters was in—wouldn't she like to see him? She wasn't sure. She didn't know Peters herself, but she was aware that her father didn't think much of him. She'd overheard the judge grump that "the fellow takes his religion too seriously"—an odd comment about a preacher but the kind of thing she loved about her father. Still, Marion remembered her mother's defending the young minister. "'I think you're just being cynical, Amos,' she'd said. "I think he's a nice looking young man, and I do like the way we sing all the old hymns when he preaches."

Waiting for Andy Wolfe to come back seemed too long, so Marion found herself seated across the spare steel desk they had moved into an old Sunday school room to make an office for John Peters. It was as far removed as possible in both space and atmosphere from the book-lined, carpeted study where she had often gone to consult with Dr. Wolfe, but it seemed to suit the no-nonsense personality of the young man in front of her. He had the handshake, the smile, the voice of a salesman. "Well, Mrs. Stanton, what a wonderful surprise! What can I do for you?"

While she unfolded details of her mother's illness, he seemed to go through a kind of change. Impatient of hearing her out, he asked almost before she'd finished: "Ah, so you've heard of my healing?"

"Healing? Well, no, I . . ."

"I've been practicing the laying on of hands. Some people in the church don't like it—your father's one, I'm afraid—but it's very respectable," he said, and picked a magazine off his desk and waved it at her. "Right here in *News,* it tells about an Episcopal bishop doing it. I've had some astonishing results—you know old Mr. Kruger, the one with the arthritis? Well, he can walk right into church now with the aid of canes, and Miss Atkins says she can hear again though the doctors told her there wasn't anything they could do for her . . ."

"That's interesting, Mr. Peters, but I didn't have anything like that in mind. I just thought maybe you could persuade Mother it was her Christian duty to go to the doctors in New York."

"Perhaps that, too, Mrs. Stanton. But don't you think we should try God's own power first? Think of the suffering we could spare her. I've never had a terminal case, but . . ."

"Oh, I don't think so, Mr. Peters. Talk like this would scare her to death."

"Maybe you, Mrs. Stanton. Oh, I can see from your face how skeptical you are. But I can see, too, that you are a strong woman—I know you are from what you've gone through. Perhaps you don't need God now. But the sick are different. I visit them every day, and I know. They know they can't do anything for themselves . . . they're willing to let go and let God. I'm sure you know how it is with alcoholics; you can't help them until they admit they're helpless. Well, it's like that in my healing too, and I'm willing to bet your mother would have a very different reaction to it than you. I don't see how you can lose by letting me try. I ought to visit her anyway . . . I would have been there already if I had known she was ill."

The thing about alcoholics reached her. She remembered her fruitless efforts with Bill. Maybe he did know what he was talking about, and he was certainly right about there being nothing to lose. She shrugged. "All right, if you promise to try to get her to go to the doctors too . . ."

"That may turn out to be God's way of doing the job, Mrs. Stanton. I'll look in tomorrow."

"No, wait till I call. It would be better some day when Daddy's in New York. You see, she doesn't want him to know until after the race. You've got to promise me you won't tell him."

Having won his point, John Peters seemed suddenly relaxed again, almost wistful. "No fear, Mrs. Stanton. The judge and I seldom speak these days."

"Far out!" the young man whistled, and you could tell by watching his bright eyes soak up the scenery around him that he really meant it. For just a second there, Jim Horner was transported inside the stranger's mind, seeing the view through fresh eyes—the sinister stand of wind-sculpted pines, the rocky point jutting out like the bow of some clumsy ship into a froth of sea, the wide expanse of blue water beyond with its summer infestation of sailing ships hovering like butterflies on spinnaker wings. It was sad to realize that though his own windows held a view very much like this he had become almost oblivious to it . . . too often now it seemed only a mocking backdrop to the ugliness within those glass walls.

"Thought you'd like it," Benjy Adams said. "Best damned place in this town, with the possible exception of Brookehaven."

"Oh, I like it even better—it's more rugged somehow," Pauline Church said. "Listen—you can really hear the sea here."

"Yeah, some nights when there's a good northeaster blowing, it can keep you awake," Benjy said.

"You're talking to a guy who's been sleeping above Third Avenue. If anything, it'll be the quiet that gets me . . ."

Jim Horner and Pauline exchanged looks of satisfaction. It had been a trying morning, and there was a real question of what they could do if Arnold Schine hadn't liked the place. It appeared to be the only one available to him in all of Worton. Now that Schine seemed satisfied, Jim could relax and appreciate the irony of the fact that the quarters for the young man brought in to help cope with the town's troubled youth were not only in the first, or second, loveliest spot in the community but directly above the little Adams Point beach where the whole story had begun.

When Pauline Church had called to tell him that Schine planned to arrive in town, Jim took time away from the office to help with the official greeting, another advantage of not being in the city. And it turned out to be fortunate, because it was Jim who finally thought of Adams Point. At first they innocently marched Schine right into Judge Brooke's Sound Realty Company, which was known to have the largest number of listings in town. The judge wasn't there, of course, and all of his good lady salespeople fluttered up at the sight of Schine like a flock of disturbed chickens. The beard and the long black hair pulled back into a pony tail tied with a ribbon would have been enough in themselves without the fact that the fellow was so obviously Jewish. When they came back to roost, the ladies made a great show of going through their books, but "there isn't a thing. You know, with no multiple housing, we have so few apartments. Well, you understand, Mr. Horner . . . Mrs. Church. Even most of our teachers live in Norwalk or Stamford or somewhere . . ."

After much the same treatment in other offices, they were about to give up when Jim remembered that Julie had told him that just before Ben Adams was drafted into the Army he'd been living in the apartment above the garage at Adams Point to keep an eye on the place while it was still in litigation. Maybe they'd need somebody to take his place, and it could be a good deal for Schine for whom they'd been able to scrounge only $7000 in salary out of the Board of Finance. He'd never met Ben's father, Benjy; these days Benjy Adams wasn't the sort of man you went out of your way to meet. Though Jim had been intrigued by some of the legends of the days when Benjy Adams was the golden boy of the Sound, perhaps the best Star sailor in the world, he wasn't anxious to see what he had become. Only the kind of ghouls who used to divert shipping onto the rocks along the Carolina coast enjoyed examining wrecks . . .

Although it was still midmorning, a scribbled note scotchtaped to the window of Benjamin Adams, Jr., Real Estate, read: "Next door." Through light as stale as the smell of last night's beer, Jim saw a graying man running to flab toying with a glass on Tony's bar. He approached and said rather tentatively, "Mr. Adams?" He was sure when the man turned watery eyes, still webbed with sailor's crinkles, toward him. He got off his stool and held out a shaky hand. "That's right, Benjy Adams."

"I'm Jim Horner."

"Good to meet you. Have a drink."

"No thanks, I've got a problem . . ."

"Well, shoot. Anything I can do for you. You know, my kid thinks the world of that girl of yours, she's done him a lot of good. And I don't mind telling you, Jim, I've been impressed with what you've done with the old *Helena*. You know, I tried her once, came in dead last. But I never was any good, 'cept round the buoys. Well, what can I do for you?"

Benjy Adams was delighted with the prospect of installing Arnold Schine at the Point—for all the wrong reasons. "I sure need somebody," he said, "and just wait till they hear there's a Jew boy living at the Point. My sister Betty'll flip."

"Now wait a minute, Mr. Adams, we don't need that, he'll have enough trouble doing his job here as it is . . ."

"Oh, I won't say anything," Benjy Adams assured Jim. "I'll just let it surface, like an old body, and wait for the stink. The board'll probably go after my license again, but this time the law's on my side and I'll make the bastards squirm. I could take you into my office right now and show you three vacant apartments on the multiple listing, including my own at the Point. But don't worry, nobody'll bother him down there."

When they got Arnold settled and were about to leave, Pauline asked Jim, "Do you have any plans for lunch?"

"Well, I thought I ought to get back to the office . . ."

"On a day like this? C'mon, I'll build you a drink and make a sandwich and we can sit in the sun a while. Charlie's in New York."

It was an invitation hard to resist, and Jim thought he really ought to talk to Pauline about something all of them, even Floyd Shepherd, had overlooked when they hired Arnold Schine. He was certain the news would be around town in hours, and for once he was almost grateful for the blackout Dan Parker had ordered the *Record* to put on Youth Commission news in lieu of an outright attack. When he mentioned it in the car Pauline said, "So what? My God, Jim, this is the twentieth century, isn't it? I just can't believe these people. I'm for ignoring it because I know it won't make any difference to the kids. They'll be more interested in his beads and guitar—and the fact that he talks their language."

Pauline settled him in a comfortable old Adirondack

chair on the little terrace outside Charlie's studio and went off to make drinks. Watching a foursome of women work their way down the fairway in front of him, Jim got a delicious feeling of playing hookey, of being in a day world of women few Worton men ever invaded. He had a sense that anything could happen. . . . Pauline came back not only with drinks but with a good deal more of herself on view, having changed into a bikini. "Can't afford to miss this sun," she said. "Why don't you take off your shirt—or anything else you like, for that matter?"

Jim was clearly unsettled. Stretching her long body out on a lounge, Pauline said, "Don't tell me I've embarrassed you again, Jim Horner. You've got to be the squarest man I know—in the good sense of it too. So you'd better get some of that drink down because I'm really going to shock you. The other night I confessed to Charlie that I have a thing about you . . ."

"You what?"

"Well, I think I explained about Charlie and me. I just don't believe in being sneaky, so if I'm going to seduce you—"

"Pauline—"

"Oh, come off it, Jim. I know you want me, and now I think you may need me. You've been having a pretty terrible time of it, haven't you? I can see it in your eyes. Do you want to talk about it?"

"No."

"Good. But let me guess one thing—you haven't been sleeping with your wife, have you?"

"Well . . . she's been sick . . ."

"Then you do indeed need me?"

"Pauline, I can't . . . I'm a . . ."

"I know—an elder in the church, a husband, a father. But you're a man, too—and I'm a woman, in case you haven't noticed."

"My God, Pauline . . ."

She got up and took his hand. "C'mon, let's go inside the studio. It's air-conditioned. Besides, we need another drink."

He wondered if she could feel his hand trembling as he

followed her. He had no idea of what would happen or how, but no will to turn back. Inside, he was aware of the nude sketches of Pauline still friezing the walls. Pauline acknowledged the pictures with a nod while, deftly and simply, she undid the patches of cloth that had been barely covering her and tossed them aside. "With all those things around, these don't make much sense, do they?"

The sudden cool of the air-conditioning was more than his nerves could take. He was shaking, almost out of control. She came to him, tall enough to look into his eyes. "You're cold, poor man," she said, and, putting her arms around him, pulled him close and kissed him. He could feel her lips parting, inviting; his hands, with a life of their own, roamed the silk of her skin. She led him over to the couch, helping him tear and struggle at his clothes.

It was over soon, too soon, and he nearly wept. "God, I'm sorry, Pauline, it's been so long . . ."

"Hush. You're like a boy. I love it. . . . The important thing is that we can be friends now, really friends."

"I'm afraid I want to be more than that, Pauline. I think I've been . . . falling in love with you—"

"Don't spoil it with talk, Jim. Love can ruin a beautiful friendship . . . Do you know what, Jim Horner? You have the most beautiful eyes without those awful glasses."

"And," he said, surprising himself, "do *you* know what —you have the most beautiful hair—everywhere," and he buried his face in it.

And luckily he was like a boy another time . . . When finally they were lying together quietly, he asked, "Can I come again, Pauline?"

She laughed delightedly. "That's a pretty good pun, Jim Horner. I didn't know you were a funny man. Seriously, if you don't, I guarantee I'll kill you."

Chapter XII

First Selectman Dr. Floyd Shepherd was almost ashamed of himself for thinking that it was about the best news he had heard since Harry Truman beat Dewey. Summer sessions of the board were always trying, sweaty affairs in the stuffy meeting room of the Old Town Hall, and he usually kept to the shortest possible agenda. Without too much difficulty he managed to get the chairmen of what Dan Parker always sneeringly called the "do-good committees"—conservation, youth, recreation, arts and the like—to hold their fire until after October. So when Youth Commissioner Jim Horner sent word that he wanted to report an important matter to the selectmen, Dr. Shepherd anticipated the worst, a long session with tempers rising like the heat. He was already getting flack about Arnold Schine. None of the complainers had the guts to tell him what was really on their minds, of course, talking about the fellow's beard and clothes, as if he didn't look like their own sons. Now Horner was no doubt going to give them the gruesome details and date of the Harlem visitation. It didn't help that Dan Parker had heard of Horner's appearance and was sitting there to cover personally the meeting for the *Record*. Except for one stout and perspiring woman, Parker was the lone onlooker; the sensible citizens of Worton were down at the beach or enjoying a tall, cool one on the terrace at home.

Dr. Shepherd decided to get the lady out of the way first. She rose ominously, as if to address a public gathering, put glasses on her nose and repeatedly glanced at notes in her shaking hand. "I am Mrs. John F. Bridges of Hawks Hill Road, Worton, Connecticut, and I have come to register a formal protest against the dogs roaming at will through my neighborhood. I should like to suggest to the Board of Selectmen that an ordinance be passed—"

"Just a minute, Mrs. Bridges," Dr. Shepherd interrupted. "Where did you say you live?"

"Hawks Hill Road . . ."

"Ah, yes. And do you have a dog?"

"No sir, I don't need a dog. My yard is full of other people's dogs, tearing up the rose bushes, trampling the petunias and—"

"I can imagine, Mrs. Bridges," the doctor said. "Well, Mrs. Bridges, we do have a dog warden in town and—"

"Oh, I call him all the time. Most of the time he isn't home, or by the time he comes the dogs are gone. Once he caught a dog depositing its matter right on my white gravel driveway, and he said, 'Oh, that's just Gyp, madam, he don't harm nobody,' and went away. I think dogs should be kept on a leash the way they are in other civilized communities."

Loren Johnson, fresh from large affairs in Washington, stepped in. "Mrs. Bridges, I'm afraid this board cannot take action on a single complaint. If you feel so strongly on the subject, perhaps you should circulate a petition to determine whether a significant number of citizens agree with you. I think I should warn you, however, that in my observation freedom for dogs is one of the aspects of this community in which most of us take pride."

"Well, I think it's a disgrace."

"Yes, thank you, Mrs. Bridges," Dr. Shepherd said. "I think you should take Mr. Johnson's advice, or perhaps you could interest Mr. Parker over there in making it a campaign for the *Record*."

"Not me," Dan Parker protested. "I'm running for Congress, you know, and a man who's against dogs around here couldn't get elected dog catcher, to coin a phrase." He even smiled.

Mrs. Bridges departed in a fury at the laughter that followed her out of the room. Dr. Shepherd sighed; he'd surely hear from her again. Meanwhile he decided to face the worst. "All right, Jim," he said. "What's on your mind?"

"Gentlemen," Jim Horner said, "I regret to inform you that the Youth Commission's plans for bringing a number of guests to town from Harlem have been indefinitely postponed."

With a quick glance around the table Dr. Shepherd could tell that his colleagues, even the liberal Loren Johnson, had reacted with as much relief as he to the news. In fact, he had a feeling they were having difficulty restraining themselves from clapping. "Best bad news I've heard in months," Dan Parker said from the sidelines.

"Mr. Parker, may I remind you that this is an official meeting of this board," Dr. Shepherd said. "Do you mind telling us what happpened, Jim?"

"Well, we made up a subcommittee consisting of a couple of young people and John Peters to go down to Harlem to issue the invitation to this high school principal there. I get conflicting reports of what actually happened, but in the end he turned us down."

"Conflicting reports?"

"Yes. The kids seem to think John Peters put this idea into the principal's head that he would be subjecting his young people to embarrassment if he sent them up here. Peters denies it. He says the fellow was hemming and hawing around, and he just figured he was trying to say no without hurting the kids' feelings," Jim said.

"Nobody at the end of the pipeline," Loren Johnson observed. "It's the way it always happens. I remember a while back a group over there in Darien got together and told some Negro organizations they'd help their people find homes. Nobody even came to look."

"It isn't quite that bad," Horner said. "The principal was intrigued enough with the idea to play turnabout and invite us to send some of our young people down there. We'll be discussing it at the next meeting . . ."

"You're not serious?" Dan Parker exploded.

"Please, Mr. Parker, the press is not a participant in these proceedings," Dr. Shepherd said. "But I have to agree with Mr. Parker for once, Jim. Maybe some private group like a church could get involved in a thing like that, but not a town agency. If anything happened to one of those kids, it would not only mean political suicide for all of us here but perhaps invite some kind of suit against the town. I think you're going to have to be firm on this, explain to your young people that any activity beyond the borders of Worton is beyond the jurisdiction of the commission. Do you agree?"

"I'll tell them—"

"Well, then, let's get on to other business. The public works department has put in a request—"

"Just a minute, Floyd," said one of the minority selectmen, Rocco Finch. "Before Horner gets out of here, I'd like to know what this Schine—excuse the expression—is up to."

Dr. Shepherd wasn't surprised at the interruption. Out of the corner of his eye he'd seen Dan Parker whisper to Finch and pass him a slip of paper.

"He's got a telephone line—perhaps you've seen the number advertised, Mr. Finch—so young people in trouble can call."

"Where's he working?"

"Well, temporarily out of his apartment at Adams Point until we can find a place to rent . . ."

"That's what I've heard. That's a good neighborhood, and it don't seem right to have a bunch of kids going in and out all hours with the mufflers off their cars and all. Don't we have some empty office here in the hall?"

"I don't know, but the idea, Mr. Finch, is not to have this hot line identified with authority. Otherwise the young people would be afraid—"

"You talked to Lou Dominick about this, Horner? He says this Schine has a whole lot of hippies and drug addicts down there answering phones."

Jim reddened. "One of them is my daughter, Mr. Finch, another is one of Father Funston's daughters . . ."

"Yeah, well what about that Jimmy Wilson? Lou busted him for drugs, and he's been in some kind of institution. And that Harold Chase . . ."

"The theory, Mr. Finch, is that kids in trouble would rather talk to other kids who have been through trouble and understand. It's sort of like Alcoholics Anonymous."

"This Schine been in trouble?"

"Not that I know of, specifically. Oh, I suppose he's

tried a few of the drugs like most young people today— otherwise he wouldn't know what he's talking about. But Dr. Shepherd can verify that he's got the best credentials —a master's degree in psychology and—"

"How come he ain't in the army?"

"He's still enrolled in Columbia, working toward his doctorate."

"Well, I don't mind telling you, Horner, I wouldn't want a kid of mine calling them."

"Mr. Finch, I profoundly hope none of your children, none of any of our children, will have occasion to use the service. From what Julie tells me, the calls already coming in are pitiful—a terrified _kid_ going through an OD alone . . ."

"A what?"

"An overdose of drugs. They've already saved one life that they know of."

"Are you sure you know where those calls are coming from? This here's _Worton,_ not Stamford or New York—"

"I'm afraid it's Worton . . ."

"If you ask me, those are matters for the police . . ."

". . . or a father with a good old-fashioned razor strap," Dan Parker put in.

This time Dr. Shepherd just looked at him. "We're not getting anywhere with this talk," he said. "We agreed to start this hot line program . . ."

"I didn't," Finch said.

". . . by a majority vote, and Mr. Horner has promised to give us a full report once it's fully under way in the fall."

"After elections?"

"This is one thing I'd hoped to keep out of politics, Rocco," Dr. Shepherd said.

"Wishful thinking, Floyd," Loren Johnson said. "There's nothing that's ever out of politics. I think we should let Horner go now and get on with that request from public works . . ."

After the meeting, Dr. Shepherd found himself alone with Dan Parker, whom he'd not spoken with since the meeting in the editor's office. "Well, I guess Horner's news will spike your guns, Dan," he said.

"Not all of them. I agree with Finch about that Schine fellow."

"You ought to. You fed him the ammunition."

"My duty, Floyd. I don't think the people of this town know what's going on, and I intend to tell them."

"Whose fault is that? You're the one who put a black-out on Youth Commission news. But go ahead. I'm getting damn tired of all this. The best present I could get election day would be to find myself out of this job."

Dr. Shepherd kept a yawning wife awake another hour while he tried to share his problems with her. "One thing this does for me, though, Edna, is make me glad that we never had any children." Suddenly Edna started to cry, and, turning over to go to sleep, Dr. Shepherd decided that it definitely wasn't his day. He forced his mind into an exercise he had found far more valuable than counting sheep. Visualizing the Golden Hills course, he began to play a perfect round of golf—a 225-yard drive off the first tee, a nicely lofted five iron to the lip of the green, two putts, on to the second hole . . . On bad nights he sometimes had to get as far as the par three on fifteen before the sedation of perfection put him to sleep.

Andy Wolfe paced the porch of the little store on the mainland, waiting for his calls to Worton to come back. The fog was so thick he couldn't make out the end of the dock where he'd tied the skiff he'd brought over from the island. Somewhere out there the engines of the early-morning lobster boats returning with their haul gurgled as if running under water, horns squawking like lost birds calling to their mates. A Maine morning . . .

Until he talked to a few more people he couldn't be absolutely sure about what Mrs. Dolcetti had hinted at in her confusing card, but it certainly sounded as if that fool Peters had finally gone and torn it. It was one thing to play around with old Kruger's arthritis but quite another to get involved in some healing nonsense with Helen Brooke, the wife of Andy's best friend and the church's staunchest supporter. When he'd left for Maine Andy hadn't even known Helen was sick; now it seemed she was dying. Why? Of what? Andy had got to the point where he liked to think that seventy-two wasn't really so old, and there was no doubt that the Brookes could afford the best medical service in the world. Why, then, get John Peters mixed up in this? When would that fool phone ring? If there was anything more isolating than the fog here, it was the service on the community's lone pay telephone; even when you got through, words were garbled by static the way they used to be on those old crystal sets.

Andy's impulse when he got the card was to jump on the first train to Worton. Audrey, of course, argued against it. She had never left the island until after Labor Day in all her years, and she certainly didn't want to be left alone up here to do all the packing. Besides, Marion Stanton was just about the most sensible woman she knew, and she certainly wouldn't let anything harm Helen. The least Andy could do was find out more about the situation before he lost his head. So Andy found himself persuaded to make the call, not so much by Audrey's logic as his own basic reluctance to get involved down in Worton.

Dying was always an awkward matter for Andy Wolfe, and he was glad to be in a ministry of relatively young and vigorous people who for the most part were forced by economics or a hankering for sun to move on before their times had come. He had to endure only three or four funerals a year. Fortunately men more sanguine about the process than he had provided a beautiful liturgy which he could intone for the comfort of the bereaved on these occasions. His hardest season of preaching every year was Easter when he was expected to summon up a resurrectional joy in mortality—"O death, where is thy sting? O grave, where is thy victory?" He saw the victory and sting right there in the coffin or the urn, and while he could quote the words of other men like Paul, he could not bring himself personally to promise the dying *anything*. If he was uncertain about resurrection—though there was always that element of mystery that could not be denied— he was sure that God should not lightly be summoned to intervene in the processes of nature. The religion Andy preached was not designed to change men or work miracles but to make tolerable the enduring human condition so ably illustrated in that compendium of saints and sinners known as the Bible. If he was, as he knew John Peters thought of him, nothing but a comforter, so be it.

The first call was from Floyd Shepherd. Through the static he managed to catch the vital words "terminal cancer" and "nothing to be done." Hard to imagine in this day and age, but Floyd had always seemed as skeptical about medicine as he, Andy, was about religion when it came to the working of miracles. Marion Stanton was easier to hear. Yes, Peters had been over. He did seem a comfort to her mother, so she didn't see much harm in it except that he wasn't persuading her to go to Memorial. Should Andy come down? Only if he could do it without making the judge suspicious—"It would really kill mother if he finds out before the race . . ." The race? As soon as he hung up, Andy Wolfe knew he had the key to opening the right door. For years, incarcerated here in Maine, he had reluctantly passed up Amos Brooke's invitations to go along on a race. This time the judge had been especially insistent because he thought it might be the *Helena*'s last. No use trying the phone again, especially since he had enough time. He bought a card from the rack in the old store, which was also the post office— he noticed wryly its depiction of a sparkling sea and sun-drenched coast and figured the photographer must have camped a month in Maine to catch that hour—and scribbled, "Dear Amos: Joining you for Vineyard race after all. Save a berth. Andy." Then he chugged home in the skiff to fight it out with Audrey.

Andy's intention was to surprise John Peters, and he succeeded. In addition to arriving unannounced, by appearing in Peters' makeshift office in the bowels of the church, a thing he'd never done before, he shocked the young man so much that he almost forgot to get up. "Sit down, John," Andy said, still standing himself to keep a literal upper hand. "I've come all the way down from

290

Maine to tell you something and I want it to sink in—stay away from Helen Brooke, I'll take over now—"

"But Dr. Wolfe, Mrs. Brooke wants me—"

"I don't know what kind of mumbo jumbo you're doing, but from what I hear that woman belongs in the hospital and I'm going to see that she gets there. Not only that, but I'm going to the session's next meeting and ask them to relieve you of your duties. Can you imagine what would happen in this church if Helen Brooke dies because of your—"

"But what if she lives, Dr. Wolfe, as she's showing every sign of doing? I don't think you'd find the session going with you then."

"Oh, so that's it . . . well, you've brought us enough other problems, what with those black kids and—"

"They're not coming, *thanks* to me."

"Thanks to you?"

"Yes, I followed Mrs. Hilsman's advice and talked them out of it . . . for their own good."

"I'm relieved to hear it. But I'm instructing you as minister of this church and pastor to the Brooke family to leave them *alone*."

Peters rose. He was flushed and obviously struggling for control. "Dr. Wolfe, you've made it clear in every possible way, including sticking me down here in this hole, that you don't approve of my ministry. Well, I don't think you even have a ministry, and if this were a matter of any less importance than the life of that good woman, I would resign right now. But God is calling me to her. I know it, and I'm going. As a matter of fact, I'm going right now since I've heard the judge is away in New York. I challenge you to come with me—and see the Lord work."

"I'll be no part of this—"

"You don't have to be. I'll make a deal with you. Come with me and we'll put it up to Mrs. Brooke. If she no longer needs me, I guess the church doesn't need me either."

Andy resented Peters' dictating terms but he felt obliged to accept. He couldn't, even if he wanted to, physically prevent this young fellow from going, and he felt that the more chances Peters had to weave his spell or whatever it was, the harder it would be to do anything about it. Andy knew enough about the peculiarities of cancer to be aware that the disease itself might play into Peters' hands. Floyd Shepherd used to call it the "optimist's disease" since patients in remission would sometimes feel so well that they were sure they were cured; this was, in fact, the basis of cancer quackery in medicine and the same phenomenon could apply as well to faith healing. Andy's hope was that Helen, who had always seemed a most sensible woman, would listen to him as her long-time spiritual guide.

Andy could tell from her expression that Helen was genuinely glad to see him, but her words weren't reassuring. "This dear boy has been so good to me, Andy. I don't know what I would have done without him. Why, you know I'm feeling so well I was able to have a cocktail with the judge last night and even eat most of my dinner. . . ."

Looking at her, Andy couldn't bear to come right out with what he thought. She had visibly wasted since the beginning of summer, but the thing that disturbed him most was her eyes. Almost too bright inside the deepening sockets surrounding them, they held that shine of desperation he'd tried not to notice before in the eyes of the dying.

"That's good news, Helen," he said. "Marion tells me the doctors at Memorial think they can do something for you, and I hope you'll go down there as soon as you can. I understand about the race, but I'm sure when Amos hears—"

"Oh, I don't need those doctors. Ever since Mr. Peters has been coming I've been feeling better and better. By the time you all get back from the race I'll be down on the dock to meet you with a bottle of champagne."

"But Helen . . ."

"I know how I feel, Andy. Now Mr. Peters is here to pray. Let's get about it before I get too tired."

Peters invited them all to kneel, and Andy, feeling most uncomfortable, felt that he had no choice but to go along.

He and Marion exchanged looks as Peters, the only one still standing, put a hand on Helen's head. "Dear Lord Jesus Christ, send thy healing balm through this, my palm, that your servant Helen Brooke may be restored whole to her loving husband and family. We ask this in thy name and in the name of the Father and of the Holy Ghost. Amen."

That was all. Nothing sinister beyond the slight vibrato in Peters' voice. Andy must have been so busy silently communicating with Marion that he missed the passage of God. As soon as they were off their knees, Peters said, "Now that he's here, Mrs. Brooke, Dr. Wolfe feels he should take over visiting you. I've told him that I'm willing to go on, but . . ."

Helen Brooke recoiled in that old instinctive gesture of fear. "Oh, please do, Mr. Peters. Andy's a dear friend, but I'm sure he doesn't feel as you do . . ."

"That's right, Helen, I don't," Andy said. "In fact, as your pastor as well as your friend, I feel obliged to point out that not taking advantage of what medicine may have to offer you could be considered self-destruction, which, as you know, is also considered a sin in our faith . . . and most all others as well. It's no accident that it is. Life and death are matters for God to decide, not people. It's a good arrangement, Helen . . ."

"You see, Mother?" Marion said, relieved at Andy's, for him, long speech.

"But I am seeing Dr. Shepherd, and he's keeping me from pain," Helen argued. "If he felt I should be doing more, wouldn't he say so?"

"Floyd is not exactly the last word," Andy said.

Helen sank back in her chair and closed her eyes. "I wish you'd all leave me. I'm so tired . . . please . . . and do come back, Mr. Peters . . . I'm sure Andy can spare you."

Andy would have to credit Peters with not betraying any sign of the triumph he must have felt even after they got outside. At the door Marion said to Andy, "You see what we're up against? You can't even argue with her; she always gets tired."

"But she *is* feeling better, isn't she, Mrs. Stanton?" Peters asked.

"Yes, I've got to admit it. I don't know why . . . will you come back?"

"It's up to Dr. Wolfe."

Andy knew when he was beaten. "Well, I guess until we can get Amos involved—that's only a week now . . ."

As he left Brookehaven that day with Helen's haunted eyes imprinted in his brain, Andy Wolfe's strongest wish was that the damn race were already over.

Although she was eager to pick it up, Julie Horner always let the phone ring at least two or three times. It was her own variation on the technique, feeling as she did that it gave whoever was calling a chance to chicken out without being embarrassed if they wanted to. It was hard to resist the ring—the thing about the hot line was that you never knew what might come over it but you could be pretty sure in its way it was important. Once she felt she'd managed to keep a kid on the phone for two whole hours until she could be reasonably sure from the way he was talking that he wasn't going to carry out his threat to commit suicide. Now after the third long ring, she took the receiver off the hook. "Hello. Hot line."

"Hey, uh . . . uh . . ." It was a boy's voice, cracking from excitement.

"Would you like to talk? What would you like to talk about?"

"Aah . . . I like your voice, baby . . . aaah, just talk . . ."

She listened a minute to the sighs, the heavy breathing. "I can't talk if I don't know what you want to talk about."

"Just talk, baby . . . aaaaah . . ."

She hung up the phone so gently he probably couldn't hear it. For her this was the saddest kind of call. In the log she wrote "getting his rocks off," which was the way Arnold talked about masturbation. When she got calls like this, Julie was always glad she'd gotten to know Ben well enough that he'd talked to her about how it felt for a boy to be always wanting a girl. Otherwise she'd probably have been disgusted the way Ruth Funston was, even though the minister's daughter pretended not to be. Julie just felt sorry for whoever it was . . . Sometimes, admit it, it was a little creepy going around school and wondering if one of them had recognized her voice and was watching her and then thinking about her when he did it. But from what the other girls on the phone reported it didn't seem to matter whose voice it was, and maybe that was the saddest thing of all . . .

Julie didn't know what she would have done if Arnold Schine hadn't come along with this hot line thing soon after Ben was drafted. She hadn't wanted Ben to go, and even had gone so far as to try to argue him into telling them he was on pot or paying some shrink to say he was a fairy the way some of the guys did to get out of it. In the end, though, she had to agree with him that he just couldn't do that to his family—it would be too much. If they'd only stayed in Young Life, he might have tried to get out as a conscientious objector, but neither of them had felt like going back there after their sexual experience on the island. Hal Evans of Young Life was always talking about the temple of the body and how you had to keep it pure. They felt so good with each other that they knew it couldn't be all wrong, and they laughed at Ben's stories of how Hal Evans would call the boys aside and say, "I know how it is, we're all human. The thing is that you can't stop a bird from flying over your head, but you can keep it from getting in your hair. When you really feel that way, just go and do a dozen push-ups. It works every time."

Dear Ben . . . he tried to look on the bright side of things. He argued that he could save money in the service and get educational benefits so that when he got out they could get married and go to school together. He could be somebody even if he never got a cent of his grandfather's money. So he went off, and they wrote to each other almost every day, and he kept telling her how his bank account was slowly building and how the blank spaces on a calendar he'd made up of every day until his discharge were slowly disappearing. When they told him he was

headed for Vietnam, he wrote, "Just think of it this way—
there won't be any chicks out there in the jungle to give
you any competition." She knew that there was no competition—there had never been, there never would be.
She knew it as she knew the yearning of her body. She
and Ben were an article of true faith.

She doubted there'd ever been another love like theirs,
except for Betsy's . . . Betsy—she often wished she
knew where Betsy was now so that she could at least
talk to her, tell her that now, thanks to Ben, she could
understand how it was for her with Ron . . . why she
did what she did, felt what she felt. Betsy was an early
casualty . . . two people in one body . . . and with
nobody around to help. Now it was easy to get the pill
from that Planned Parenthood doctor, but when Betsy was
growing up it was a long time ago, almost the dark ages.
Say this for her father's Youth Commission, they'd brought
Arnold Schine to town, which made all the difference for
her.

Before he'd allow them on the phone, Arnold held
sessions in which he told them, "You can't help other
people if you can't be honest about yourself. What we
want to do is to keep people from getting themselves really
messed up—going onto hard stuff, getting busted, killing
themselves or bugging out the way your sister did, Julie."

Although the other kids were always talking about
their hassles with their parents, Julie never did. Arnold
didn't press her, and she knew why when he told her,
"You know, you're pretty lucky, Julie. I haven't met your
mother, but your father seems like a guy who's got it
pretty well together."

It was the highest kind of compliment, but she wondered whether her father would appreciate it. The fact
was, she really couldn't talk with her father. Even though
he looked more relaxed with his longer hair and clothes
to shock the man in the gray flannel suit, she could feel
that he was as tense as she around the house. If either of
them said the wrong thing, it could send her mother off on
a crying or drinking jag, or both. So they never mentioned Betsy anymore. Sometimes Julie had the feeling

that her father wanted to talk to her even more than she wanted to talk to him, but that he didn't know how—maybe *they* needed a hot line. He and her mother had always seemed to think that being "good" parents meant shielding Betsy and her from what they already knew; she could remember hearing them talk in their bedroom for hours into the night when anything important happened like changing jobs or buying a house or Betsy's bust. That didn't happen anymore, of course, now that they were in separate rooms, which maybe was one reason why her father was so tense. She could tell his business wasn't going well because he'd sold one car and then the Lightning, but when she tried to ask him about it he'd just said, "Oh, that's not your worry, we'll get by . . ." He'd always been like that about his work, and in fact she'd never really understood what he did. All she'd known when she was little was that he was gone, often before she got up, and she could still remember being packed into a snowsuit in the dark when all she'd wanted to do was go to bed and carted to the station where they'd sit in all the steam and glaring lights waiting for his train to come in. When he'd get into the car and give her mother a peck, she'd always ask, "Have a good day, darling?" and he'd nod and say he hoped she had the gin out . . .

The night Arnold told her that he liked her work enough to hire her if they could get money for an assistant she had a terrific idea on the way home of how she could help her father and maybe get him to open up and talk a little. She was glad to find that her mother had already gone to bed. Her father was sitting watching an old movie on TV, but she could tell that his mind wasn't really on it. She sat down beside him on the couch. "Guess what, Daddy? Arnold wants to hire me next year as an assistant. That means you won't have to spend all that money to send me to college."

Her father jumped up and snapped off the set; at least he was going to take her seriously. "Julie, you get that idea out of your head, and for God's sake don't let your mother hear you talk that way—"

"Why? I know you're not making all that much money and—"

"I've got enough to send you to school, and we'd sell this house if it came to that. You know your mother and I always wanted you girls to go to college."

"I don't think she cares so much now, as long as there's booze—"

"Julie!"

"I'm sorry, but it's true, isn't it? All right, Daddy, what *is* wrong with Mother? Do you know?"

He seemed to slump back into the couch, rubbed his eyes as if they were misting. "The doctor says it's menopause, maybe it is. A lot of women have a rough time with it, and if that's it she'll get over it in time. Meanwhile . . ."

"Dad, I'm trying not to rock the boat, but—"

"I know, but please no more of this talk about not going to college. Aside from the fact that it just might kill your mother, you've got to know from the way your friend Ben Adams feels about the importance of college. You can't get anywhere these days without it."

She wanted to ask him where *anywhere* was, but she was afraid that she knew the answer. For him, anywhere was here in Worton in a glass house by the sea. Though she didn't hear them talking about it much anymore, Julie could remember when she and Betsy were little how her parents would congratulate themselves on being in Worton. Her mother was forever saying, "You girls just don't know how lucky you are to grow up in a place like this." Maybe so, they *didn't* know. What her parents didn't understand was that for her and Betsy and almost all the kids she knew, anywhere was somewhere else, *not* Worton.

"But, Dad, what if I don't really want to?"

"Isn't that being selfish, Julie? You know . . . well, your mother's counting on you. You can't let *her* down. Now, it's late . . ." He got up to switch the movie back on.

She couldn't talk over that, in more ways than one. And in a way he looked so beat—but she felt even sorrier for herself. Their problem, though, seemed to be the same—whatever it was that ailed her mother. She didn't think that was fair. . . .

Neither did her father. He disliked himself for dumping a load of potential guilt on his daughter instead of talking more honestly with her, particularly when she had offered to help. He seemed not to be able to stop spouting the lines of the father role that had become nearly rote over the years—hide your own terrors (there probably won't be enough money for college), protect your wife (it just about would kill Susan if Julie dropped out too), stand by the accepted values (anybody who's anybody has to go to college) and so on.

While the movie flickered before his eyes, unseen and unheard, Jim smoked cigarette after cigarette and thought, really, who the hell was he to lecture anybody . . . especially his daughter . . . on her obligations to her mother . . . ? In the past he'd made compromises he wasn't proud of—though he'd been able to rationalize them—had told white lies, had drunk too much at parties, but he'd never knowingly sinned until he started sleeping with Pauline. Talk about Julie letting her mother down, what would it do to Susan if she knew about him? Yes, it was a sin. It was an old-fashioned word, he knew, but it was the only one that seemed to fit, even if Pauline did laugh at him whenever he used it.

"Oh, come off it, Jim," she'd say, "that's just an ownership thing. People are always trying to find ways to own something, to hold onto it. So some old boy made adultery a sin as a form of protection back in the days when women were valuable property like cattle."

"That's clever, but you don't really think that's all it is—"

"What else? I'm not leaving Charlie, you're not leaving Susan. In fact, I'll bet you're a lot better around the old homestead than you've been for a long time. I know I am."

"It doesn't work that way with me. Born twenty years

299

too soon, I guess. People believed in being faithful, for good or bad, and I'm afraid I caught it."

"*Some* people, sure, some people always have—but it was for the poor peasants, who were fed a lot of crap by their priests and rulers. But it wasn't for the kings, oh no! Take a look at David in your Bible, or Henry the Eighth, or Jack Kennedy for that matter. Are you a peasant or a king, Jim Horner?"

He had to laugh . . . he always did with her, and that was one of the most wonderful gifts of this strange and special girl. She was impossibly immoral by any standards —face it, *his* standards—other than her own, yet oddly this seemed to give her a purity as evident as the milky whiteness of her skin. She gave of her body and took of his so completely without shame that the idea of sin did indeed seem silly when he was with her. It was only when he slipped back into the realities of his own life that it confronted and upset him.

One thing he was certain of—he'd have to do something about it before Susan found out, before it became a public scandal . . . like daughter, like father, he thought wryly . . . At the same time he knew that breaking off their affair would be terribly painful. Whether his love for Pauline was true or not, his craving for her was as strong as for a drug. Their meetings were what gave his days meaning. He had never felt so physically alive as in their uninhibited lovemaking. Still . . . he'd have to give it up, but not now . . . maybe after the Vineyard race, after Labor Day, when it could come to a bittersweet end like the old summer romances of youth or something . . . Or something, indeed. He'd never known something to compare to it. . . .

He decided that he would look in on Julie and if she were awake apologize and suggest more of a talk tomorrow. When he opened her door the shaft of light from the hall fell across her face. She was asleep and so sweet and childishly innocent-looking that he couldn't bear to disturb her. As he closed the door and went on to his own bed he thought about Julie so suddenly having to absorb the knowledge of misery over the hot line phones and in her own home, and he wished that he could bring back those days of serenity that stayed in memory like one long summer Sunday when they'd be off to church, the girls starched bright in their Sunday school dresses, with no more pressing issue before them than whether to have their picnic in the backyard or at the beach. Before he went to sleep Jim Horner prayed, not as a proper elder but as a man in anguish with nowhere else to turn. It did not occur to him that he might have done better to have awakened his daughter and told her how he felt.

Still feeling trapped the next morning, Julie did something she suspected she shouldn't: she went to see Dr. Bruno. Maybe, she thought, if she could find out what was really wrong with her mother she could help both her father and herself. She was surprised somehow that, except for a leather couch along one wall, Dr. Bruno's office looked pretty much like any other doctor's, and so did he—a balding man with glasses and a soft voice. "What you're asking, Miss Horner, is rather difficult for me as your mother's doctor. I'd rather your father came to see me—"

"Oh, he doesn't know she's seeing you. It would make things worse to tell him."

He nodded, and reminded himself that the treatment, not orthodox doctrine, was the issue. It was a fact that Julie Horner, young as she was, was the only "family" to help him in the treatment of her very sick mother. "Well, perhaps I should try to give you some explanation, Julie. Your mother is in a state of depression. Part of it is normal considering her time of life . . . and what has happened in her life. It *feels* worse to her, though, because of a deep fear of rejection that she has. Some such fear, of course, is normal too—most of us have it. Hers seems to come from her parents, especially her father, making her feel they wouldn't love her if she was bad in any way. She can even remember as a baby being picked up and carried away somewhere in the night when she cried, so her father wouldn't be disturbed. She learned to feel it was easier to be *good* and cheerful and do things that made them proud. . . . Even her music came from that —pleasing them by practicing and being in recitals when she thought she had failed them by not being pretty. That's why it wasn't hard to give the music up when she had daughters and found that being a mother and giving her parents grandchildren was something they and most of her friends thought was the very best thing a good girl could do. You know, that was back in the days when we didn't worry about overpopulation and being a mother was just about every young woman's ambition. Well, and then she brought you here to this fine community, and she was getting along well and everything was turning out like a dream come true . . . until your sister got into some difficulty. She tried to carry her head high for a while, but her spirit was too fragile. It broke, Julie, like a piece of delicate china, when she realized that people were whispering about her, disapproving of her, rejecting her. . . . Maybe in her depression she doesn't *seem* to care about you right now, but I know from what she tells me how very much she does care (cares too damn much, he thought to himself). She's really proud of you. I know it will seem unfair to you, but if you can just help to keep her that way—well, it will help buy some time for her to work things out."

"Well, I'll try, Dr. Bruno, but I have my own life and—"

"I know, young lady, I know. We all do . . . but none of us is ever free from our responsibilities to other people, particularly parents. You know what they say, none of us has to have children, but all of us have to have parents— they're here when we arrive. All we can do is make the best of them. . . . Now, I'm afraid you'll have to excuse me, I have a patient waiting. By the way, he's a man who's coming to me because he felt he didn't have any parents, at least none that he knew of . . ."

It was heavy, heavier than what her father had put on her. And she began to think it would be better to have a mother at least strong enough to hassle her like some

302

of the other kids did, one you could really hate and not feel guilty about it. For now, there seemed no good way out of her bind. No good answer for her. She needed Ben for that. She too made a calendar and began checking off the days.

Chapter XIII

Standing on the after deck of the *Helena* as she maneuvered through a fleet of more than a hundred yachts assembling off the Cows at Stamford, Fielding Small was glad he had decided to come. It was a golden late afternoon in early September with a brisk northeasterly flinging diamonds across the water and stretching the canvas aloft until the rigging sang. From the stable teak platform of the aging *Helena,* most of the boats, ranging down to thirty feet or so, all fiberglass and aluminum, looked like the expensive toys they were. The excited boys from the club, whom Judge Brooke had recruited to do the heavy work of handling sails, kept pointing out the famous ones: "There's *Thunderbird!*" "Hey, there's *Nyala*—over there!" "Look—*Bacarrat!*" But the biggest cheer went up aboard the *Helena* when they spotted another grand old lady of a schooner, DeCoursey Fales' *Nina.* She would be their real rival, and as the two boats crossed tacks they saluted each other with a dip of the ensign and a doff of the skippers' caps. "Watch our wake!" Judge Brooke boomed across the water in friendly challenge.

Here in the melee of jockeying boats, the image of grass growing faded from Fielding's mind. Six or seven knots seemed speed enough for these awkward sea birds as they winged down on each other, their helmsmen yelling "Starboard!" for right of way, their winches screaming and sails crackling as they came about through the wind. Actually Fielding's mouth was already dry with excitement, and he marveled at the way Jim Horner, who seemed a slight and vulnerable figure under the towering rigging, steered calmly through the confusion. Listening to one man call the time, watching the boy on the bowsprit for signals of danger ahead, keeping an eye on the rest of the fleet, calling orders for sail trim, Jim kept working the *Helena* into position for the start. When the time was being shouted in heart-stopping seconds, Jim had the *Helena* tearing down on the line—no way now of stopping her if he had miscalculated. Gun! They were off, to windward and ahead of all the yachts in their division.

Old Judge Brooke was literally jumping up and down, pounding Horner on the back. "Best damned start ever, Jim! We'll bury them all."

Jim ignored the compliment. He was busy telling the boys to haul in on a sail here, let out on a sail there until he was satisfied that the *Helena* was making maximum speed. Then he called to one of them. "You want to take her for a minute, Tommy? Try to hold on 100 to 110. I think I could use a beer. Anyone else?"

When Fielding Small followed Jim down below, he decided that, like his own, all the other throats had grown cotton in the excitement of the start. There they all were—the afterguard, as Judge Brooke called them, because age and presumably wisdom allowed them to stay comfortably back in the cockpit and steer the boat while the youngsters worked the deck. The judge had a better idea than beer. He was holding a whiskey bottle and pouring into plastic cups.

"Don't usually do this on a race," he said. "But that was such a grand start it deserves one splice of the main brace—just one, mind you." The drinks poured, the judge raised his to Jim. "Here's to Watch Captain Horner. Good going, Jim. And while I'm at it, let me congratulate you on handling that business with the black kids . . ."

Jim should have let it go, accepted the praise gracefully. But something, perhaps a feistiness born of the good start, made him want to smash the judge's bland assumption that he'd followed his "word to the wise" like some craven underling. "It wasn't my doing, judge," he said. "I wanted to see those kids come up here, do the town some good . . ."

The judge choked on his drink, had to wipe his chin with his sleeve. "Do the town some good? Why it would have torn the place apart. I'm surprised at you, Jim. I thought you understood . . ."

"I guess I don't understand, as you put it, judge. What

I've been learning the hard way is that we're living in a world with values different from Worton's, and we might as well get used to it. One reason it would be good to see some blacks in Worton is that they're going to be living here soon anyway."

"Not while I'm alive," the judge said.

"Then you might need an act of God to stop it, like the one that stopped this. Or is that putting it too strong, Andy? At least it was God's newest agent around here—John Peters."

"Well, I'll be damned," the judge said. "You know I always thought there was something odd about you, Horner . . ."

This was getting to be more drama than Fielding Small had bargained for. He could see Horner getting red in the face.

"If you feel that way, judge, I suggest you sail your own damned boat," Horner said. "If we weren't so far out, I'd swim ashore."

"Why, I'd think a nigger-loving saint like you could walk on the water."

Truly alarmed, Andy Wolfe stepped between them. "Please, both of you," he said, "if you want to discuss these mattters when the race is over, that's your business, but you both owe it to the rest of us to make peace now."

"I don't owe anything to anybody," the judge said. "I'm captain of this ship, I own it, and I'll do as I damned please. If Horner wants to take that attitude, he can spend the rest of the race in his bunk."

"Now, wait a minute, Amos," Andy said, taking a deep breath. "If you don't owe anything to us, you owe something to Helen . . ."

"What's she got to do with this?"

Andy felt that he couldn't let the judge drop Horner when so much depended on his help. "Everything, Amos. No way to keep it from you now . . . your chance of doing well in this race is all that's been keeping her alive . . ."

"What the hell do you mean by *that?* There's nothing wrong with Helen."

"There is something very wrong with Helen, Amos. She has cancer and—"

"Cancer! You've known this and you didn't tell me?"

"Yes, Helen made all of us—Marion too—promise not to say a word until after the race. She didn't want to spoil it for *you*. That's why—"

"But, my God, man, why isn't she in the hospital?"

"Well, Floyd says—"

"Floyd? I thought she was going to Dr. Hammond. Why didn't you—"

"Well, I was away, and Peters—"

"She hasn't been seeing *him,* has she? He hasn't been fooling around with that mumbo jumbo of his . . ."

"Well, he's been praying . . ."

"Oh, my God, I'm going back right now!"

"Amos, if you do that I think you'll really kill her."

Suddenly the fight seemed to drain out of the judge. He looked around at all of them as if he'd never seen them before, poured himself another drink and downed it like medicine. "Look, fellows, I don't feel so well . . . you'll have to excuse me . . ." And like a wounded animal he sank into his quarter berth aft of the chart table.

Understandably—if uncharacteristically—the judge seemed to have forgotten that he hadn't posted watches or charted a course. But navigation was the judge's traditional task and expertise—in all the times Jim had been aboard the *Helena*, nobody else had ever attended the charts, least of all himself. Now, though, somebody had to take over. His anger at the judge was completely washed away by the news of Helen's illness.

"I don't know how the others feel, Jim, but I wish you'd take command for a while," Andy Wolfe said.

"Don't you think we ought to turn around?" Jim asked.

"Not yet," Andy said. "I meant it when I said how important it is to Helen that the judge have this race—and probably to him too in the long run, since it might well be his last on the *Helena*. I think he'll be all right in a while. Floyd Shepherd said the judge is sound as a dollar. I think there was too much excitement there at the start and then the shock—maybe I shouldn't have told him about Helen but under the circumstances I felt I had to—and then that second drink didn't help. But a little sleep ought to fix him up. You can hear he's snoring now."

"Well, under the circumstances maybe Kevin should take it," Jim suggested.

"Oh, no, not me," White said. "I can hardly find the weather mark a mile away in a fog, and you damn well know it."

"Well, I've never done much myself," Jim said.

"But you took all those Power Squadron courses, didn't you?" White said.

Jim looked at them. The consensus was clear enough. "All right, I'll do my best but—"

"Thanks, Jim, and when he hears of it I'm sure the judge will be grateful to you," Andy Wolfe said. "I wouldn't worry about that other thing. You know, he is an old man and set in his views, but most of all he loves this town, and, well, he just lost his head a little . . . I'm sure he didn't mean it—"

"Oh, he meant it all right," Jim said. "He tried to warn me a while back, and I ignored him, which I gather is something you just don't do to Judge Brooke. But don't worry, first things first . . . I won't let it interfere with my sailing, if that's what's bothering you. All right, let's set watches. How about you going on Kevin's, Andy, and I'll take Fielding here on mine. Divide the boys any way you want."

Because of the slant of the wind, Jim figured a course to bring them to Plum Gut, one of the narrow bottlenecks through which the Atlantic tides boiled in and out of the Sound, would give them the best speed. It would be a reach, with the wind coming well aft of the bow, so sheets could be eased allowing the big schooner's great clouds of canvas to make the most of the wind. It was just right for the *Helena*; the wheel hardly needed a touch to keep the big hull on course as it frothed onward into the darkening east. Fielding and Jim Horner traded tricks at the helm every half hour, mostly keeping a silence inspired by awe at the sheer beauty around them. Reflecting the sunset at their backs, the sails of the early-starting smaller boats they were overtaking burned like small bobbing fires on the slate blue field of water. The stars began to bloom in the slowly rising night ahead. On either hand the silent shores shrank into dusk, isolating the men aboard the *Helena* from all the normal uses of their lives.

Fielding began to understand how sailing could get to a man. There in the cockpit that dwindled in size by the minute as stars deepened the heavens, he was caught up in all the remembered romance of youthful voyages toward delights the world didn't hold. The past was slipped with the moorings, and all that mattered now was what lay ahead. A voyage was like war, like love, probably like crime—a measured time out of time when to live was simply to do.

Whether Jim Horner, beside him, shared such feelings was hard to tell. In the round eye of the binnacle, its light ever sharpened by the dark, Fielding could see the keenness of Horner's sharp features, the flash of eyes always moving from sail to sail and out across the water where the fleet, sunset fires banked, had turned into a field of fireflies with their winking masthead lights. "Better let off that staysail a hair, Tommy." "Try falling off a little, Fielding—that's it, hold her." "I think we're picking up on *Nina* but *Nyala*'s way out there."

It didn't seem the proper time or place to bother Horner with the probing questions the novelist had hoped to ask. Already, though, Fielding felt he'd learned a good deal. He had been impressed with the way Horner stood up to the judge about those black kids and even more impressed with the way he handled the boat and quietly accepted and then assumed responsibility. If this was what people meant by Horner's being square, then the world could use a lot more four corners. One thing sure—Horner's troubles evidently didn't stem from being ineffectual. Fielding began to worry that there was no novel in Horner. The kind of tragedy he'd had in mind demanded a motivating flaw in character—greed, ambition, dishonesty, intemperance, cowardice, something. A thing like

310

plain rotten luck wouldn't do. Well, maybe if he waited, the flaw would show.

"Looks like Orient Point Light off the starboard bow. Next watch'll take us through the gut. Don't envy them," Horner said.

"Why?"

"Pretty narrow in there and tricky if you don't know it. Well, time to sack out."

"Shouldn't you take her through?"

"No. Kevin White's the best helmsman in the business, and I've given him a course. Besides, on a long race like this, you simply have to stick to your watches and grab some rest or you'll get foggy in the head and that can be really dangerous."

Tired as he was when they went off watch, Fielding Small, so long a fastidious loner, could not sleep in a bunk still warm and redolent of another man's body. He lay rigidly still, aware of every sound—the rush of water against the hull, tense voices on deck discussing sightings and headings, the pound of feet as the boys went forward for sail changes on a changing course, the screech of blocks, the catching snores from a bunk across the cabin where Jim Horner lay, disciplined to sleep when sleep was in order. The voices on deck tightened to the unmistakable pitch of anxiety. "That's got to be the light, Andy? Isn't that the light? . . . Ever been through here at night, Andy? . . . No . . . any of you boys been through here at night? . . . Take her, Andy, while I have another look . . ." Down the hatch, flashlight sweeping a white band across Fielding's closed eyes, then probing the chart. Back on deck. "God, I'm not sure, Andy. Let me take her. Get Jim up here—or better, the skipper." Andy Wolfe's mellifluous preaching voice. "Amos! Amos! We need you on deck." The judge's grumble. "Let me be . . . let me be . . . I feel awful . . . my chest . . ." The preacher entreating now. "Amos, please. We're heading for the gut, and we're not sure . . ."

The smell of disaster was sharp as smoke in the air, and Fielding was half out of his bunk when the *Helena* struck. She rose straight in the air and came down with a splintering crash that sent him sprawling on the cabin sole. Jim Horner's body landed on his. The old hull was writhing and groaning in the teeth of the rocks like a dying animal. Yells, curses. "All hands on deck!" The boys of their watch leapt over their sprawled bodies and popped out of the hatch. "Get the goddamned sails off!" Above a stricken body, the schooner's great wings flogged in mindless menace. Coming apart like the boat, White clutched the useless helm and cursed into the night.

Scrambling up, Horner handed Fielding a flashlight. "Search the bilges for holes, I'll get the radio." While he frantically pulled up hatches to look into the rusty bowels of the boat, Fielding could hear Horner calling out methodically, "Mayday! Mayday! Schooner *Helena* aground off Plum Gut. Mayday! Mayday!" Up forward, the feeble beam of Fielding's light revealed a steady rise of water. "We're leaking, must be a hole somewhere," he called back, and heard Horner's instantly amended message. "Mayday! Mayday! Schooner *Helena* aground and taking water fast . . ." Fielding got back to the cabin just in time to see the judge trying to struggle out of his bunk. In the glow from the chart table light, his eyes looked popped, wild. "What the hell have you done to my *Helena?* You've killed her, Horner. You've killed her . . ."

The judge fell back, and Horner went right in on top of him. My God, the man's lost his mind, Fielding thought . . . he's going to strangle him. He could see only twitching legs as if a struggle were going on. Fielding stooped and shot the beam of his flashlight into the narrow cave of the berth. Horner had the judge in a grotesque embrace, jaw in hand, mouth over mouth. It took less than a second for Fielding to feel as foolish as he'd felt frightened and then frightened again as he realized what Horner was up to. Before he had got control of himself, Horner had crawled out again and called the Coast Guard. "Mayday! Mayday! Schooner *Helena* aground and taking water . . . dead man aboard repeat dead man aboard . . ."

Seeing Fielding's eyes on him, Horner turned away from the radio and motioned toward the bunk. "It's no use, he just went out . . . so fast . . . get the boys to start manning the hand pump on deck when they have the canvas off, and bring the others down here."

By the judge's preference the *Helena*'s cabin was lit with kerosene lamps, one of which Jim had going by the time the afterguard assembled below. The light flickered, flared and fluttered as the big hull lifted and dropped with teeth-shattering thuds against the unyielding rocks. It was worse than no light at all . . . the rich dull gleam of mahogany and brass it evoked from the fittings of the snug cabin made the fact of their disaster and the judge's death even more incredible. Kevin White was in shock, and Jim wrapped him in a blanket and handed him a cup of whiskey. Andy Wolfe, looking for the first time merely old instead of old and distinguished, kept intoning, "Amos . . . Amos . . ."

"As far as I can tell it was a massive heart attack, and he just went right away with no pain," Jim said. "I don't know whether you feel you should say anything, Andy . . ."

"I can't . . . He was my friend . . . it was my fault for not letting him turn back. . . ."

At this White seemed to come alive again. "No . . . my fault . . . whole damned thing . . ."

"Look," Jim said, "if there's any fault around here it's mine. I was supposed to be in command of this boat, and it was my course . . . As for the judge, well, I guess he was beyond his Biblical allotment, wasn't he, Andy, and so I suppose it shouldn't be any surprise that the excitement was too much for him. Now I'm going on deck to see how bad a fix we're really in."

Within minutes Horner was back with a report. "We're holed badly up forward. One of the boys went over the side and said he could practically stick his fist in it. That means we can't be towed off, we'd go down like a rock—I'm afraid the *Helena*'s a goner. If we have to we can get ashore, water's only about waist deep at the bow. But it's cold and rough and the tide's rising, and I don't think we should risk it with Andy's legs and Kevin's chills and the problem of getting the judge over. I suggest we try to keep her afloat with the pump—thank God for those kids with muscles—until the Coast Guard gets here. They ought to be able to pick us right off the stern with the tide coming up. Keep yourselves warm, I'm going on deck with flares to signal when I see them."

Fielding followed Horner up into the night. Out there in the dark, with the beam of Plum Island light sweeping the rigging that shuddered every time the sea dropped the *Helena*, the mood was more appropriate to the event than down in the still cozy cabin. Here the ship that had seemed such a magnificently powerful thing an hour ago was puny in the vise of nature. Fielding thought of the men who had regularly perished on coasts like this in the centuries before engines and lights and radios. Jim Horner shattered Fielding's thoughts with a flare that burst aloft and for minutes lighted the scene of the *Helena*'s death like some movie set. Below the radio crackled with the impersonal Coast Guard voice . . . "Thank you, *Helena*. We see you . . ."

"Well, I guess that's it," Jim said. "They'll be here in about fifteen minutes. Forget the pumps. Go below and get yourselves something to eat or drink."

When he and Horner were left alone on deck, Fielding said, "At the risk of insubordination, I'd like to protest your proposal to take all the blame. How do you know White was steering the right course? He was having lots of trouble seeing lights and things, I could hear him . . ."

"White's a fine sailor, he taught me all I know."

"Well, what about Andy? He probably couldn't even see the compass through those trifocals of his."

"No, I know what went wrong. I didn't figure the tide right. It was lower and coming in stronger than I thought, and it just set us against the shore. That's what's supposed to be so damn intriguing about sailing—there's always some force you can't predict. Except this time it killed us."

Fielding had a sense that the moment he'd been waiting for had arrived. "A little like life?" he said.

"A lot," Jim agreed.

"A lot like your life?"

"Maybe . . . how come you know enough to ask?"

"I don't, I'm just guessing. A novelist's business, you know. Would you think it strange if I told you that I had an idea of doing a novel on . . . well, you and Worton? I don't think I can now . . ."

"Why not?"

"Well, for one thing, nice guys don't make heroes unless they win through in the end, and frankly I doubt you're going to. . . . The way I look at it, you've managed to rig all the power in town against you—Lou Dominick, Tony Francetti, Rocco Finch, Dan Parker, Judge Brooke. . . . I know you don't think this way, but the judge's death might seem a break, almost as if God were on your side the way it happened, except I doubt it. The power from men like the judge hangs around. I've lived a long time in this town, Jim, and that different world out there you were telling the judge about is exactly what they want to keep out—at all costs."

" 'They'? How about you?"

"All right, maybe me too. But the thing I really can't understand, Jim, is how you got into all this. You're such a damn straight arrow—ex-writer for a conservative magazine, oil company flack, corporation head hunter, elder in the church. It doesn't fit."

"I thought I had a job to do—some people needed help . . ." He was talking as much to himself as to Small, whom he suddenly disliked intensely.

"Well, that fits, but a lot of people thought you'd done enough when you got Floyd elected. There was no reason for you to go along with Charlie Church's crazy wife and a bunch of kids too—"

"I lost a daughter—*remember?*"

"Yes, and that's the most intriguing part of it all. But I don't suppose you want to talk about it?"

"No. Listen, you go ahead and write your novel, Fielding, and I'll read it and maybe it'll be so fucking brilliant that even I'll understand why I fuck up, the way I did this race—" A huge spotlight interrupted, and Jim now ordered Small to get the others on deck. "And we'd better put the judge's body into something. That sail bag will do."

Chapter XIV

The funeral for Benjamin Adams III was by all odds the largest in the history of Worton, surpassing even those of Ronald Dominick and Judge Amos Hartwell Brooke. For convenience, it was held on an October Saturday and people were sitting on the balcony steps, standing along the walls and jammed into the narthex of the Worton Presbyterian Church. Every minister in town, including Father Reardon, graced the pulpit, and a color guard of veterans in uniform, one an echo from the First World War, held themselves as rigidly at attention as age would allow behind the altar in honor of Worton's first Vietnam war hero. Ben Adams had not only managed to get himself killed in a fire fight, but he had done it so spectacularly that he was recommended for the posthumous award of the Silver Star. First Selectman Dr. Floyd Shepherd voiced the town's pride in her native son, and G. Carswell Putnam, Brig. Gen., USA (Ret.), commander of the local VFW post, gave a military eulogy. Sitting in the front row were the father, Benjamin Adams, Jr., sober since the telegram arrived, and his family, their good name redeemed in blood.

Despite the numbers, veteran crowd watchers took more note as always of those who were not there. Sitting together, two of the club's "sea gulls" who had watched the romance between Julie Horner and Ben Adams with consuming interest exchanged lifted brows and whispered words over the absence of Julie and, in fact, all the Horner family. "Wouldn't you think . . . ?" It was almost as bad as Hartwell Brooke's not turning up for his father's funeral. But the ladies would have been even more shocked if they had known where Julie Horner was on that bright morning. . . . Arms linked with Arnold Schine, she was strolling beside the reflecting pool between the Washington Monument and Lincoln Memorial in the nation's capital. Julie and Arnold were clinging together so as not to be separated in a crowd of more than 50,000 people. Speakers on the steps of the Lincoln Memorial were reminding them that they were all troops in a march on the Pentagon, an assault against the symbol of America's misspent might. Julie couldn't really hear the speeches because she was too keyed up, too nervous to concentrate. But when one of the speakers got the crowd going on a chant "Hell no—we won't go!" she and Arnold joined in . . . were taken over. Up there on the steps were Dr. Benjamin Spock and his wife, and for Julie it was like seeing her mother's God come to life, and there was Chaplain William Sloane Coffin, Jr., from Yale, who had brought Mrs. Hilsman's son Tim down with him. Julie knew Tim a little from the yacht club and, when she ran into him in the crowd, he'd said, "For God's sake, kid, don't tell anybody back home you saw me, Dad would have a stroke." . . . And there was somebody Arnold said was a poet named Robert Lowell, and Norman Mailer the writer . . . Nobody knew exactly what would happen when they all got across the river and over to the Pentagon, but with so many of them and such famous people . . .

Coming down here had been Arnold's idea. Certainly not Julie's. She had wanted to kill herself when Mr. Adams had called and told her about Ben. Arnold was the only person she could talk to, the only person who knew what had been happening between her and Ben. Making it even worse, she'd gotten a letter from Ben a few days *after* she'd heard the news of his death. She could not open it at first, and when she did she wished she hadn't. As usual he was trying to make *her* feel good . . . saying how big his bank account was getting to be and how short the time was growing . . . and then, "Hey, guess what, I've stopped smoking. It isn't easy, because sometimes it's just like one big pot party around here, but I think I've decided what I want to do and turning on all the time could ruin it. I want to be a doctor like my grandfather and maybe come back over here when this is all over and do something with these people.

There's this young medical officer here in camp who spends his time off duty going around to the villages, and I've started helping him, and I sort of like the way it feels . . . hey, how'd you like to be Mrs. Doctor Adams? Or a nurse or a doctor too. If you like working with kids on the hot line the way you say you do it might be your thing. Wouldn't it be great to go to med school together? Don't worry about me, Julie. I go out on patrols every so often but I'm a born coward and hide behind every tree. You won't catch Ben Adams making a hero of himself for a war like this one, and most of the guys feel the same way . . . which is why it's such a temptation to get stoned all the time. I just wish people back there would wake up and get us out of here."

When Julie read this last part of Ben's letter to Arnold he told her about the people planning to go to Washington and suggested that they go along, it might be something she could do in Ben's memory that would mean something—to Ben. Up till then she hadn't thought much about the war except that it was keeping Ben away from her. Hardly anybody else she knew in Worton had been drafted . . . they were all in college or graduate school. The history teacher at high school was all worked up about it and kept talking about "America's moral dilemma" but she didn't listen to him all that much . . . it was the last period in the day and she was usually writing the letter she would mail to Ben on the way home. After she got Ben's letter, though, she started watching the war news on TV and talking to the teacher and decided that going to Washington for the peace march was the only thing to do for Ben, even if it meant missing his funeral.

She was uneasy about sneaking out on her mother, but her mother would have put up a terrible fuss, not so much about protesting the war but leaving her alone and "going off down there with that . . . that . . . Ben Adams was bad enough but at least he came from a good old Worton family . . ." So she'd gotten up very early Saturday and left a note for her mother where she would be sure to find it, under the whiskey bottles in the bar.

She said she was going with "a bunch of people" and would be back Sunday. It might have been easier if her father hadn't had to go to that meeting down in Miami because, although she'd never really talked to him about the war, she did know that he was friendly with Mrs. Church, who had become so against it that she wore a "Get Out of Vietnam" button and once when they were watching the news he'd shaken his head and said, "I wonder what makes us think we can run the whole world." . . . But with all her father had on his mind she guessed he couldn't worry about something like the war, which was too big to do anything about. . . .

Being in Washington with all these people gave you a different feeling . . . They hadn't had anything to eat except a doughnut and a cup of coffee at the airport in New York, and Julie began to think she was going to faint from hunger or die of thirst. When they got to a big parking lot across the highway from the Pentagon there was so much going on Julie forgot about herself. They were carried along like chips in a stream over to the Mall in front of the Pentagon, and suddenly they were right there in the front line looking into the faces of the soldiers. Julie suddenly thought they looked the way Ben must have looked and began to wonder how they really felt inside those uniforms. When she said something about it to Arnold and Alice, a girl Arnold knew from Columbia, Alice said, "Okay, let's see," and danced over right in front of one of them and said, "C'mon, join us. Don't just stand there——" and she put her fingers to her lips and threw the soldier a kiss, and then some other soldiers grabbed her and dragged her off. Julie was horrified. It had never occurred to her that they could actually be arrested. Now, though, she could see that it was happening all down the line. "I can't get arrested," she told Arnold, "it would really kill Mother," and he understood and pulled her back into the crowd, where it seemed safer.

It was beginning to get dark now, and chilly, and somebody had built a fire, so they went over and sat near it with a lot of other people. One of them was a teacher named Mac. "Here's some real fire," he said, and took out his draft card and stuck it in the bonfire. Finally Arnold got his out and lit it too and said, "This one's for Ben."

Julie cried then and Arnold put his arms around her and she let him because something had made her feel more alone than she had ever felt in her life, and right there in the midst of all those people. When Mac saw them and said, "Atta boy, Arnie, make love, not war!" Arnold let go of her and jumped up and pulled her up by the hand. "Let's get out of here," he said.

Away from the crowd, moving back toward the bridge, Arnold apologized. "I really didn't mean that, Julie, I'm sorry, I was just carried away—"

"Don't," Julie said. "I'm not a child. Besides, I was feeling so . . . so terribly alone . . . when you burned your card, I finally knew that Ben is never coming back. . . ."

Arnold took her hand and Julie squeezed his in response. They stopped momentarily and she kissed him and said, "Arnold, I'm so damned afraid . . . you're going to be in trouble—for burning your card—"

"I don't know, I don't care. For sure, I'd rather go to jail than fight this war."

"I'm glad, Arnold. I only wish—"

"I know—that Ben had had the chance to say it."

It was Pauline's idea. When Jim had told her he was going to Miami for a meeting of management personnel consultants, she'd said, "Let me meet you there. Do you realize that we've never spent the night together?" It was true, and Jim decided that it might be a good way to end the affair that he didn't want to end. It didn't work that way. It was like honeymoons would be if they weren't so often wasted on the wrong people. . . . Jim didn't go to many of the meetings, and when the Assistant Secretary of Defense canceled out as speaker on the final Saturday session because of that Washington peace march they just stayed in their room all day, and Jim felt that it was getting to be more like a beginning than an end to whatever it was they had between them. . . .

There was something just right about the impersonality of this room, which was just one of a thousand similar cells in a high rise looking out on an empty sea. They were as cut off from any relation to their past and separate lives as they would have been in a space capsule. It was so hot—they opened the windows to the sea and turned off the air-conditioning—that they didn't bother putting on clothes the whole day, except when the bus boy came with drinks or meals. "When we're like this we can't hide anything from each other," Pauline said when they awoke from a soft after-lunch after-lovemaking nap and she found Jim's eyes delighting in the sight of her.

"You're right," he said, feeling uneasy in spite of his pleasure with her.

"But you're trying, aren't you? You've been wanting to give me that crap about, 'Darling, we can't go on like this,' haven't you?"

Not now, not now . . . he thought, but when she persisted he told her some of it, about what Fielding Smith had said about him having the whole town against him—and her too—for bringing up things they'd rather not think about . . . "It seems we're a threat to their world . . ."

"I'm afraid he may have a point, Jim. You know Fielding is in with Charlie in that Tuesday Club—and they call themselves the town liberals. Well, I know from the way Charlie talks that even those big-deal so-called liberals are upset with what we're doing. I can get away with it because I'm just another one of Charlie Church's crazy mistakes, but I don't know about you . . . in fact, I often wonder why you're being such a hero about it."

"A hero? Funny you should use that word. My mother wanted me to be a hero, except I think she had something more like General MacArthur in mind. Well, I'm no hero. You know I got into this business in the first place mostly because George Avery told me to, or else—and at least at first I probably stayed in because I didn't want to give him the satisfaction of telling me to get out, or else."

Pauline reached over and traced the outline of his sharp

322

chin with her delicate fingers. "Come on, Jim, there's more to it than that, more to you than that."

"Well, maybe so. I guess when I began to get a clue about how miserable so many young people were feeling, I realized that I wouldn't have had to lose Betsy if I'd understood a little more a little better. You know, I ache when I think of what that girl went through because she didn't think there was anyone around she could really talk to. . . ."

"Jim, do you have any idea at all where she is?"

Lying naked in a naked room where it did seem foolish to hide anything, Jim broke his vow of silence and told Pauline about the letter from Leo Polchick. No word had come from Betsy, and he was beginning to doubt that it ever would.

"Jim," Pauline said, "call her, call her right now—from here. It's better than Worton—at least there's no chance of anybody but me ever knowing . . ."

"Do you think she'd be willing to talk?"

"I don't know. Neither do you. But I do know that you're a different man from the one she ran away from, and maybe she'd sense it. Here . . ."

Pauline was handing him the phone. The operator had no trouble getting through to Hartwell Brooke's hotel . . . and Betsy herself answered the phone. "Carib Coast."

"Betsy, this is—"

"Daddy! My God . . . how did you know I was here?"

"Never mind, I'm down in Miami at a meeting and thought I'd call . . . I could just come down there and—"

"*Don't* Daddy, please *don't*. I . . . well, does Mother know?"

"Not yet. She's in pretty bad shape, Betsy, and—"

"I'm sorry, Daddy, but don't tell her, it would only make things worse . . ."

"I just thought if she could know you're all right . . . you are, aren't you?"

"Yes, oh yes, but mother wouldn't think so. I'm not living her kind of life. She's got Julie—"

"Julie's changed too, Betsy . . . I think we all have . . ."

"Daddy, it wouldn't work. I can never go back, and if you come here, I'll have to run again. I swear I will . . . Daddy, I've got to hang up—" and the phone was dead.

Jim handed the dead phone back to Pauline and began swallowing hard against the tightness in his throat. Pauline put her fingers against his lips. "Don't try to say anything. I don't need to hear, I know . . ."

Jim rolled over, wrapped arms and legs around her body still moist and ripe with the smell of love, and buried his face in her long hair. "Pauline, if I didn't have you . . ."

Responding to his embrace, she said, "Maybe I shouldn't argue with a professional word merchant, but you're using the wrong one here. I don't like that word 'have.' People ought to stop trying to *have* people."

"Now *you're* trying to tell *me* it's over . . ."

Pauline turned, pressed his face and lips against her small, stiffening breasts. "Oh, no, I'd just like another word, Jim. What about *enjoy*? You can *enjoy* me—"

The phone's ring interrupted, and she quickly reached out and knocked it off the hook. Jim reached over her to grab the dangling instrument. "We can't," he said. "Nobody knows we're here, it might be Betsy . . ."

But there was only a buzz, so he dialed the operator. "My phone just rang, I knocked it off the hook . . ."

"Long distance from Worton, Connecticut. Dr. Floyd Shepherd calling . . . he said he'd call back in an hour."

Pauline pulled him down against her and held him with a sudden strength that nearly took his breath away. "One hour . . . then we'd better make sure it's one to remember."

On that Saturday afternoon, after helping to conduct the body of Benjamin Adams III to its hero's grave, Police Chief Lou Dominick was having a beer in the Hill Club and trying to argue Rocco Finch out of his crazy idea.

"I know you're not on the ballot, Lou, but this town's small enough so we could put you over with a write-in,"

Rocco was saying. "Hell, with that Stanton settlement you don't need your crummy job, and you're the only one who could possibly beat the doc, with all due respect for your father-in-law."

"That's just it—Tony would never forgive me, or Maria either. Anyway, I'm no politician. I'm a cop."

"All the better. That's what people around here want—a good shot of law and order. Dan Parker told me he'd go all out for you in the *Record* if you just say the word. You and me and Harold Hastings, voting together, could get rid of that Horner and run that Arnold Schine right out of town. You'd like that, wouldn't you, Lou?"

"Damned right."

"Okay, then . . ."

They stopped talking at the sight of Sergeant Grimes, on duty and in uniform, coming over to the bar. Lou knew right away that it had to be something pretty important . . . they'd have phoned him on a routine matter. Grimes half saluted. "Sorry to bother you, chief, but I just got this weird phone call from Mrs. Horner down on Soundview . . ."

Though his style was different, Lou had copied one rule of procedure from his old mentor Nick Santori. The whole force was instructed to bring any matter that had anything to do with the rich and powerful of Worton to Lou personally. You never knew, as he had quickly discovered, when using the instrument of the law too bluntly could prove politically embarrassing. Those knuckleheads would actually have booked Felicia Marden, Dan Parker's stepdaughter, when they stopped her and found a couple of joints in the glove compartment of her car. Luckily Lou knew all about Young Life and was able to believe her when she said somebody planted the stuff to discredit her group. Anyway, he was smart enough to take her home himself and tell Dan the whole story, which was probably one reason Dan wanted to support him for first selectman.

"What did she say, Grimes?" Lou asked.

"Well, something like, 'Help, I need help . . .' And then there was a sort of noise, and the phone went dead.

I tried calling back but all I got was a busy signal, and the operator couldn't get through either so I come right over here for you."

"Okay, let's go."

On the way over, Lou got to wondering where the hell Horner and that other kid of his were. It was Saturday afternoon, and one of them should have been around. Funny, the Horner kid was supposed to be so sweet on Ben Adams, and he hadn't even seen her at the funeral. They couldn't be out sailing, because Lou knew that Horner had had to sell his boat. The man had to be running short of dough—everybody knew that little outfit he was mixed up with down in Stamford wasn't bringing in peanuts. Nobody could see how Horner could go on living in that glass house of his unless the judge left it to him in his will, but that wasn't even probated yet. The last time Lou talked with Dan Parker, Dan had told him he was holding his fire against Horner in the *Record* because he figured the fellow would be out of town before snow fell. He wouldn't say why exactly, but it had something to do with what the judge had told Dan just before he went off on that race. When Lou said in that case there wasn't much reason for him to run for first selectman, Dan argued, "If the doc gets back in, they could appoint someone even worse than Horner in that job— that Mrs. Church, for instance. Listen, Lou, when it comes to politics, I'm the kind of guy who wears a belt with suspenders."

Thinking about Horner's being on the skids was about the only revenge Lou was likely to get for what had happened to Ron. When that crazy Polchick let him down, he knew that the time had come to give up looking for Betsy Horner and the Avery kid. He still didn't know whether Polchick was lying about not finding them, but it wouldn't make sense for him to do that since he was the guy who had double-crossed the Horner kid in the first place. More likely, Lou had just let Polchick play hippy a little bit too long and he'd gone and turned into some kind of a beach bum himself. What did he say? He'd found a new "life style," whatever the hell *that* was.

Maybe he was a fairy in disguise, and he and that Hartwell Brooke . . . Anyway, Lou had finally closed the books on the case because the only other person in town who was at all interested, George Avery, had sold his place and was moving back to Houston.

When they pulled up in front of the Horner house, Lou could see the trouble before he got out of the car. Golden October sunshine lit up that glass living room like a showcase, and the brightest spot fell right across a body lying in the middle of the floor. Dressed only in a nightgown and a flimsy housecoat, she was curled up like a fetus, and one hand still held onto the receiver of the phone. A big red setter, dancing nervously around the body, began to bark its head off as they approached.

"Oh, Christ," Grimes said.

"Listen, as soon as we get in, get that phone going and call Doc Shepherd," Lou ordered.

The door was locked, Lou told Grimes to shoot it open. As they entered the living room and headed toward the body, the dog, twitching and growling, stood over its mistress. "Good boy, good boy," Lou kept saying, but just as he was about to crouch and have a closer look at Susan Horner, the dog leapt. Lou put up a protecting arm, and the dog buried its teeth in his wrist. "Shoot the son of a bitch! Shoot!" he yelled.

Grimes' first shot missed, ricocheting off the stone floor and making a fuzzed star in the pane of one of the great glass panels facing the sparkling Sound. His second sent the dog into a spinning, howling mess; the third brought silence. Sucking his wound, Lou reached down with his other hand for Susan's wrist. "She's dead all right," he said, "but call the doc anyway, and don't touch the body."

Grimes pried the receiver loose from Susan's grip. While he was waiting for the call to go through, he noticed an empty whiskey bottle and a spill of pills on the table by the phone. The label on the overturned pill box marked "Worton Drugs" said "Valium. As needed. Dr. Bruno." There was also what appeared to be a long letter. Although it had no salutation, it was written on light blue paper with the printed heading: "Mrs. James Gilbert

Horner, Soundview Road, Worton, Connecticut." Grimes picked it up and handed it to Lou. "Here, maybe we'd better read this while we're waiting."

"You left me alone, all of you, left me alone just when I needed you most," the letter began. "I woke up crying —I don't know why—and called and called and nobody came. Nobody came but Rusty. She licked me and licked me as if she were trying to tell me something. And then I knew what it was. I really was alone. All alone. How could you all do that? I had this dream. I saw Betsy coming down a long aisle in this white white dress and she was smiling and holding onto her father's arm and Jim was looking so serious and proud, and then it just vanished and I was awake and alone and knew it would never happen and I started to cry. I tried to make myself feel better thinking it might happen for Julie and then I remembered it was the day of Ben Adams' funeral and I guessed Julie might be outside somewhere walking around and thinking about it and I got up to find her. I decided I would go to the funeral with her. Then I found the note. It was wicked wicked of you to put it there Julie. You know how hard it has been for me to get through the days. I was just going to get something to calm myself and get over my crying so I could be with you and help you. The pills Dr. Bruno gave me hardly help at all. And when I saw that note there and realized how you must have been thinking about me when you put it there and when I knew you weren't even going to the funeral of the boy you pretended to love I was sure that you have a heart as hard as your father's and I began thinking there was no use for me to go on living at all.

"When I started thinking about it I was scared at first —not of dying but of dying alone, so I started trying to reach Jim. I couldn't remember where he was staying so I called his partner at home and he couldn't remember either but gave me the number of the convention. I got some sugary little girl who said Mr. Horner wasn't at the meeting she thought he was back at his hotel with *me,* and then I *knew*. Just to make sure I called that Church woman and when her husband answered and said she was out of town I started crying again and I knew what was happening because he hasn't even tried to touch me for so long I can hardly remember what it's like. Everybody says I don't understand, even Dr. Bruno, but I think nobody understands me only Rusty who's sitting here with her head in my lap and whimpering a little.

"I am not exactly sure what's happening I am sitting here and writing this and sipping just a little whiskey and taking some of Dr. Bruno's little pills with it and feeling much much better much much much calmer I am not frightened anymore and I am glad to be alone I can even appreciate how beautiful it is outside with all the trees turning red and gold and the Sound looking like a field of diamonds maybe it is better to leave a beautiful world than an ugly one maybe when I get finished with this I'll get dressed and go out there and just lie in the sun and . . . But it would make it harder for the people who will find me, I wonder who they will be. Wouldn't it be funny if it was that Chief Dominick? I wonder how he would feel then about arresting Betsy I wonder if she really did have his grandchild the way Jim thinks . . . I guess I'll never know, I guess I never will understand.

"I don't know why I am even writing this I might just as well talk to Rusty. It is getting harder and harder to write I feel too calm now, like I'm sinking like I'm going to sleep maybe I will just go to sleep but then I would wake up alone again in the dark I couldn't stand that I have to stop writing and take some more pills to be sure . . ."

The words that had been flowing into an ever larger and more uncertain scrawl just trailed off. When Lou finished reading, he said to Grimes, "Jesus, what a mess! That stuff in there about me, forget it—the woman was obviously nuts but who can blame her? I wonder where that other kid is. Can you find the note she talked about?"

They did, and it enraged Lou. "Can you imagine—the little bitch down there in Washington while Ben's being buried? And that Horner off with that whore! God, no wonder the woman killed herself."

Lou could hardly wait to show the notes to Dr. Shepherd, but the doctor insisted on examining the body first. He pronounced Susan Horner dead of an overdose of drugs and alcohol and signed the necessary papers. Then he read quickly through the notes, took them over to the fireplace and struck a match. "I'm going to burn these," he said.

"Hey, you can't, doc, they're evidence," Lou said.

"Evidence of what? I've already testified to the fact that she was a probable suicide. All this can do is hurt a lot of people more. And do you want everybody to know your boy and Betsy . . . ?"

"Come on, doc, the woman's crazy—"

"Not about that, Lou. It's the God's truth. I don't know what happened to the child, but I do know she was carrying it. So, shall we burn this?"

Lou nodded. The goddamned little slut—doing that to his boy, lying there helpless in the hospital. None of these rich pricks were any good, and all this proved it. Like Maria said, Dr. Shepherd was as bad as the rest of them. Here he knew about what that little twat was doing to Ron all along and never said a word, and now he was trying to protect them. Damn right he'd run—he'd tell Rocco as soon as he got back to the club. It was the only way to make sure that this town got back a little respect for morals, some law and order. If only the Horner woman hadn't mentioned him in that note it could have been useful with that stuff about her husband and the Church woman. But maybe now that he knew, he'd figure out how to use it anyway.

Chapter XV

As much as he hated funerals, the Rev. Dr. W. Anderson Wolfe usually loved baptisms. Being pastor to a suburban congregation through all those years when America's young women considered motherhood the highest form of fulfillment, he had more than his share, but he never tired of the ceremony. For one thing, the young mothers were invariably at their prettiest, flushed with pride and full of the special kind of vitality the Lord seemed to provide for their nurture of the helpless young. Andy Wolfe always felt a not unpleasant glow in the presence of so much warm and yielding feminine flesh. He often envied the babies and felt a faint regret for them that the ceremony itself was a kind of symbol of their separateness, of the fact that too soon they would have to leave the comfort of those willing arms and breasts. Viewed in this light, their wriggles and howls as he sprinkled cold water on their frequently bald little heads and blessed them "in the name of the Father, and of the Son, and of the Holy Ghost" were perfectly human and appropriate responses. But all these somewhat muddled feelings were peripheral to the core of Andy Wolfe's joy in baptisms: they celebrated the one thing in which he could believe without benefit of theology, the constant renewal of life.

Although the brief baptismal ceremony was usually part of a normal Sunday morning service, parents would from time to time come seeking special services to accommodate illness, or relatives visiting from out of town, or, as in the case of Charlie Church, embarrassment. You'd thing a man with Charlie's proclivities would be proud to display to the world the fact that on the verge of seventy he had finally become a father, but Andy would appreciate the probability that Charlie's skin had been licked a little thin over the years by all the tongues wagging about his sexual life. The chances were great that people would be more amused than admiring about the late arrival of a little Church. Then, of course, there was the fact that Charlie, like all of the Churches before him, was nominally an Episcopalian. He had given up the church entirely when Father Funston, despite their comradeship in the Tuesday Club, had acted as stuffy as the Archbishop of Canterbury and refused to marry him after one of his many divorces. (It was an amicable enough exchange . . . "You know, Charlie, that I hold the canons of the faith above the changing perversities of people," Father Funston had said. "And you know, Arch, that I think you are full of shit." But, as Charlie explained to Andy, he didn't want to put his friend on the spot again.) He wouldn't bother having the child baptized at all, he said, if it weren't for Pauline and her thing about that Church family Bible.

For once Andy Wolfe wasn't happy about performing a baptism. He knew too much, and he wondered whether he could go through the ceremony with a straight face, let alone a quiet heart. In the end, though, he felt obliged to be guided by his conviction that he had no right to deny the offices of the church to anybody for any reason and particularly to a child who, despite all talk of original sin, simply had to be innocent if God was good. But when he saw the baby, Andy was grateful for the privacy of the event. The only witnesses in the echoing sanctuary were Pauline's parents, who had understandably been reconciled with their daughter by the arrival of a grandchild and had flown in from Detroit for the occasion. Studying the little group in the light of a knowledge only Pauline could share, Andy could see at once that the baby did not resemble any of them. Like an x-ray, his vision discerned beneath the rolling fat of the baby's cheeks the sharp outline of the real father's jaw. He was glad that Charlie Church, proudly bouncing the child, was, for all his artist's eye, quite obviously blinded by pride of fatherhood, confirmation of manhood. Fortunately long practice in the pulpit had made Andy a good actor, and neither his face nor his voice betrayed him as, laying a damp hand on the little forehead, he intoned, "Charles Church IV, I baptize thee . . ."

Never comfortable in the role of confessor, Andy Wolfe was apprehensive when Jim Horner asked for a private talk after the first full session meeting of the fall. The Lord knew Horner had to have plenty on his mind. The only time Andy had seen the man since that terrible night aboard the *Helena* was under the equally terrible circumstances of his wife's funeral. Horner had kept himself under the same kind of rigid control as he had shown on the boat, and Andy had been grateful for that. But every man can reach a breaking point, and Andy would just as soon have Horner come apart somewhere else than in his study at nearly eleven in the evening.

Horner came to the point quickly. "Under the circumstances, Andy, I think I should offer my resignation from the session."

"Now, Jim, don't do anything hasty. I don't know what kind of Christians you think we all are if you feel that we hold you responsible in any way for Mrs. Horner's tragic death."

"I'm not only talking about that, Andy. I'm talking about everything. All of you believe I killed the judge—I can feel it. And I guess you have a right since I accepted responsibility—"

"Now, Jim—"

"Oh, don't try to put me off. How do you think I feel sitting across the table from that son of a bitch Kevin White, looking pious when I know he's been going around the club showing a chart on which he cleverly demonstrates how I screwed up on the tide? You've seen it, damn right you have. And not one of you has lifted a hand to help me around here in the work you supposedly assigned me—in fact, Marguerite Hilsman damn near sabotaged it. If we're all marching to Onward Christian Soldiers, somebody's way out of step—me."

Anger could be therapeutic, Andy thought. Besides, no use making things worse by arguing; and Jim's resignation would open up a place for Dan Parker, who probably wanted to be an elder to help his Congressional campaign but who would put the church on the map if he won. "Well, I can't stop you, Jim, if you feel that way . . ."

"Yes, I do. And there's another thing, Andy—a more personal matter I'd like to talk about if you don't mind."

Andy glanced at his watch but tried to sound receptive. "Well, certainly, Jim, anything."

Jim took out a pack of cigarettes and lit one. "I don't know whether you're supposed to smoke in confessional or not," he said, "but all this is new to me."

"Jim, don't feel you have to—"

"I know I don't *have* to. I want to. You see, besides my disastrous social blunders, I've been knowingly committing a real fourteen-carat sin. It's called adultery. I think Susan knew about it, and I think that's why she . . . did what she did. It's a hard thought to carry, Andy. Even for a hardened sinner like me."

Andy's immediate thought was that the rumors about Jim Horner and Pauline Church were true. If he was surprised it was only because he found it hard to visualize Jim Horner, of all people, in such a situation. As for himself, he preferred his personal relationships to be, like his religion, essentially passionless and structured, and found it difficult to understand why intelligent people persisted in messing up their lives with something so disrupting as sex. Yet there were at least a dozen examples he knew of right in his own congregation . . .

"From what I knew of Mrs. Horner, she had many troubles, Jim, and I don't think you should blame yourself—"

"Why not? Isn't this what's meant by the wages of sin? Shouldn't I be roasting away in hell?"

"If there's anything important in our doctrine," Andy said as soothingly as possible, "it's forgiveness of sin. Look at David . . ."

Andy was surprised when Horner began to laugh . . . was the man losing his mind?

Horner quickly checked himself and said, "Andy, I'm sorry. It's just that somebody else used the same line. David, the King—the kingly sin."

A bit puzzled, Andy said, "Well, I only brought that up because you know that good did come out of that sin—the birth of a child who became an even greater king. Solomon."

"There'll be a child coming here too . . ."

This time Andy was really stunned. He thought people knew how to take care of things like that these days. "Oh, my Lord . . ."

"Yes, a bit messy, isn't it?" Jim said, getting up and pacing in front of Andy's desk while he puffed on his cigarette. "You see, without that I could just walk away and neatly repent of my sin. Isn't that what you have to do to be forgiven? But this way I've got obligations that can bring on another sin, or at least a scandal—and divorce, since the lady is married too. Anyway, I think you can now understand why I must resign."

Andy could indeed. Most of the people out there in the pews in front of him were paying with their time and money for respectability, or the appearance of it. They could forgive Jim Horner for losing his daughter to the bewildering youth revolution in which so many of their own children were involved; they could also forgive him for losing his wife to alcohol, an affliction so respectable that the church itself sponsored a chapter of Alcoholics Anonymous. But the idea of an elder of the church cuckolding a neighbor so publicly would be intolerable.

"As to that, Jim, there's no problem. Just send me a letter, and I'll offer it to the session. You can say something about the press of business making it impossible to fulfill your duties. I really must thank you for coming to me like this. You're right, a scandal could hurt the church, and there I have to draw the line. I really wish you the best . . ."

Jim stopped pacing, ground out his cigarette and said in a voice now barely under control, "Couldn't you do a little more, Andy? Couldn't you tell me how to live with myself? I didn't mean to hurt Susan, you know . . . I really wanted her to get well . . ." He looked at Andy with an intensity that made him squirm. "I'm really not too experienced, Andy, at being the world's champion sinning son of a bitch . . ."

This was the moment Andy had dreaded. He had so little to offer. "I can only repeat, Jim, that your sin is, well . . . not so uncommon. There must be more than a few others right here in this church, and they are somehow going on. The best way, as I see it, that you can make amends to the dead, if you feel you must, is to serve the living, do what you think you have to do for the woman you feel you love, and for your children. I don't know whether that helps but—"

"It does, Andy, it does," Jim said, and a kind of excitement had come into his voice. "I guess I have been taking myself too seriously, but I'm afraid I was brought up that way—to think that Jim Horner could run the world if he was only good enough and kept at it. Pretty arrogant, isn't it? Well, thanks, Andy, thanks for your help . . ."

Andy Wolfe didn't see Jim Horner after that, so he never knew what solution he had arrived at, until the baptism of what Pauline Church was claiming as her husband's child. But he was aware of him. Anybody in Worton would have had to be deaf and blind not to be aware of Jim Horner in those last weeks before the election when Dan Parker took the wraps off the *Record* to get Lou Dominick elected by a write-in vote. He attacked the Youth Commission and its hot line in a series of front-page editorials that made Andy increasingly grateful that they had Dan on the session instead of Jim Horner. The worst of it read:

Do You Know Where Your Children Are?

There's a New York television station that every night asks this pertinent question, and the people of Worton should take heed. Your children may be down at Adams Point in a facility sponsored by the town itself. Far better that they be in a saloon in Port Chester. Consider these facts:

336

—At the very moment that the town of Worton was sorrowfully but proudly burying its latest hero, Benjamin Adams III, the director of this facility and an eighteen-year-old Worton girl were in Washington parading against the war in which young Adams, an outstanding example to all of our youth, gave his life.

—The town's Youth Commissioner, who bears ultimate responsibility for the facility at Adams Point, was, on the day of days when we were honoring our war hero, "out of town" as was, by coincidence, a young female member of the commission whose idea it was to establish the facility at Adams Point.

Is it any wonder that we ask: what goes on at Adams Point? What would your children hear should they be so ill-advised as to call that number? What would they see should they go there in person? Dr. Shepherd assures us blandly, as doctors are wont to do, that he is giving the town the right prescription. But Dr. Shepherd has no children of his own to suffer if the medicine doesn't work. We say enough of Dr. Shepherd's perilous pill.

Regrettably, Mr. Anthony Francetti, the Republican nominee, must share responsibility for the shoddy operation at Adams Point. As a member of the Youth Commission, he failed to sound an alarm loud enough for all of us to hear.

There is only one man in Worton who understands how to deal with the situation—Captain Lou Dominick. Father of seven, founder of Little League, a war hero himself, Captain Dominick knows from experience that in sparing the rod we do indeed spoil the child. This town has overwhelming evidence of it.

By writing in Captain Dominick's name for First Selectman, we can do far more than demonstrate that Worton Cares About Kids; we can make sure that Worton is *Safe* for Kids. *Then* you won't have to wonder where your children are.

Whether as a result of attacks such as this, or, as Dan Parker preferred to think, the beginning of a major response to law and order, Lou Dominick was elected First Selectman of the Town of Worton, the first Italian ever to hold the post. There was general rejoicing in a packed Hill Club on election night. Only one important member, Tony Francetti, was missing, and it was said that Tony no longer spoke to his son-in-law and that Lou was seen buying his liquor in another store. But Lou showed what a good fellow he was at heart by bringing Nick Santori back from exile in New Jersey and installing him as Acting Chief for a couple of years so that Nick could get his pension and, cynics said, keep the spot open in case Lou lost the next time around. As one of its first official acts, the newly balanced Board of Selectmen by a three to two vote abolished the town's Youth Commission, putting all such matters under an expanded Department of Parks and Recreation, which was instructed to find ways of keeping the schools open at night so that kids could play basketball and enlarging the Little League field.

But that wasn't quite the end of it. "It's like trying to kill a snake with a stick," Rocco Finch complained to his fellow selectmen when it was discovered that the hot line was funded through the fiscal year and intended to stay in business. To everyone's surprise, instead of gratefully going back to his golf, Dr. Floyd Shepherd joined a new committee to raise private funds for the Adams Point project. Jim Horner, the chairman, issued a statement in which he said, "Through the next months we will be giving the people of Worton an opportunity to say with their money, instead of their vote, that Worton *Still* Cares About Kids."

Thinking about this statement after the baptism that had reminded him so forcefully of Horner, the Rev. Dr. W. Anderson Wolfe suddenly began to laugh aloud, shattering the silence of his study. It was, he realized, the first good laugh he had had in a long time, and he suddenly had a feeling that everything might be all right. Like Horner himself, he had fallen recently into the sin of taking life seriously when so much of it was clearly absurd. Well, from now on he was going to repent through laughter. He could hardly wait to get home and tell Audrey the joke . . . she had never much liked Charlie Church anyway.

"Why do you think he dropped out, Loren? Was it the Tet offensive or was it a noble gesture to push the peace talks?" Fielding Small asked.

"Neither. It was the McCarthy offensive."

"Another children's crusade. You were the first to use that expression, weren't you, Floyd?"

"Well, actually it was Jim Horner. But in the end it probably won't work. I think what happened to me right here was the first straw in the wind. We'll have a conservative next time around."

"Right," Loren Johnson agreed. "You know the slogan they're using in Indiana—'Feel Safer with Nixon.' They say the fellow's packing them in out there."

"Dreadful thought," Father Funston said, "but I really don't think it is very delicate of us to talk politics in front of our new member, do you? After all, we invited him to join us not as a failed politician but as a man of science."

Ever since the death of Dr. Benjamin Adams, the Tuesday Club had, indeed, felt a lack of balance in its discussions. The name of Dr. Floyd Shepherd had naturally come up because of his political views, but inviting him seemed out of the question while he was busy nearly every evening in Town Hall. When the doctor was ousted by Lou Dominick in the election, Loren Johnson, who had come to respect him as a fellow selectman, began pressing for an invitation. Although they were willing to concede that the doctor was a fine fellow, they expressed strong doubts as to his genuine seriousness about anything but golf. "Well, just tell me who else you can think of in this place," Johnson had said. That unanswerable question had settled it.

"All right then, what's the subject for tonight?" Small asked.

The good father wiped the beer foam from the mustache he was trying out at the insistence of his daughters, who wanted him to look more "with it," and suggested, "How about faith healing?"

It was a natural. The long battle that Helen Brooke was waging against death had provoked more discussion around town than almost anything since her own granddaughter's shocking accident. Hearing about it, the hopeful ailing began coming from the Episcopal and Congregational and, some said, even the Catholic churches into the Presbyterian fold to be stroked by the Rev. John Peters' magic hands. Instead of taking pride in this swelling of numbers, the Rev. Dr. W. Anderson Wolfe viewed it as a threat to the peaceable kingdom in which the pastors of Worton had long refrained from raiding each other's flocks. Moreover, he was certain that Helen Brooke could, and would, pass away any day, affirming his own doubts and creating an embarrassment for the ministry of the church. If only he had let Amos Brooke turn that boat around! He was sure that Amos would have taken Helen down there to Memorial where the onus of her death would have properly fallen upon the heads of the doctors. Andy Wolfe was not alone in his doubts. Without actually violating the rules of their union, Dr. Shepherd's medical colleagues let it be known around the cocktail circuit that they thought his failure to spirit his patient out of the hands of that spook and into a hospital verged on malpractice. Agreeing, some of the more practical members of the church session like Al Cranshaw, the Cadillac-Oldsmobile dealer, began agitating for Peters' resignation.

But the will to believe prevailed over the strength to doubt. Even as sensible a woman as Marguerite Hilsman rose in defense of Peters, who, as she liked to remind people, proved himself a real Christian by the way he had handled that business about the nigra children. But the clincher was Marion Stanton. Possibly unbalanced by the shock of her father's death, Marion had not only gone about telling people that Peters was curing her mother but actually started going back to church. Not only that but her impossible son Amos was said to be so impressed that he was planning to study for the ministry. To those who knew the Brooke family well, no greater miracle could be wrought.

The case became a matter for public discussion when *News,* which forever seemed to have a watchful eye on Worton, printed a couple of paragraphs of the Rev. John Peters' healing sessions. For a while it seemed the once sinful suburb would become a kind of shrine; a keen-eyed railroad public relations man went so far as to have several thousand brochures on Sunday service between New York and Worton run off. He had a difficult time explaining the cost to his boss when Helen Brooke's demise suddenly sobered everybody. By the time the question was raised at the Tuesday Club, the participants were well aware that John Peters' days in Worton were numbered. A golfing buddy of Dr. Shepherd, an IBM executive, told him that he had seen Peters wandering the halls at Armonk, trying to sell somebody on a new way of bringing religion and business together by hiring him to sell computers to large churches and religious organizations. Actually the IBM man didn't think it was a bad idea, especially since Peters was such a hell of a golfer, and planned to put in a good word for him.

"You don't pull your punches, do you?" Dr. Shepherd said, looking around at his fellow members in this most exclusive club in town.

"Rule of the club," Charlie Church explained. "A while back we voted three to one that God was dead, but Arch here keeps plugging away at the business anyway. I should think, Arch, you'd be unhappy that Peters didn't find any help up there after all. Looks bad for your profession."

"No worse than for the doctor's," Father Funston said. "Tell me, Floyd, did anything actually happpen there—medically speaking, I mean?"

"Just the usual remission. I gave her six months, and she took about eight. No miracle in that."

"I got the distinct impression aboard that boat that, if Amos had lived, he would have had her down in Memorial. What then?" Small asked.

"Well," Dr. Shepherd said, "she might still be breathing, plugged into all sorts of tubes and machines."

"Isn't that the glory of your profession—making it hard for people to die? Puts us on opposite sides, because I'm supposed to make it easier," Funston said.

"Ah, I detect a statement forming on the subject of the evening. Maybe I should take notes," Fielding Small said. "What you're saying, Arch, is that it isn't the job of religion to heal but to comfort. Isn't that it?"

"Something like that. But I don't like the word 'comfort.' Let's try acceptance. I don't think the church is in the business of trying to alter the will of God, but to give its members rites and rules by which they can learn to accept it. You'll remember that Christ, despite all temptation, didn't try to work a miracle to save himself . . ."

"Of course he knew he was going to get up in a couple of days. Makes a difference," Dr. Shepherd said.

Small howled. "Atta boy, Floyd, you're really getting the idea. Hey, Tony, another pitcher over here!"

Unruffled, Father Funston went on, "Seriously, the thing that bothers me about science, not only medicine but all science, is the belief it has spread abroad that man can somehow remake the universe in his own image. It's the real heresy of our century. Go ahead and use up all the world's oil; we'll make more somehow. Forget about heaven and hell; you won't have to go to either place when we cure the last disease. And so on. Why, people even think economics is a science that will get rid of poverty. Isn't that right, Loren?"

"I'm afraid so. But if economics is a science, then, speaking as a scientist, I suffer from no such delusions."

"Now, wait a minute, Loren. As a doctor, I know medicine has more questions than answers. But social planning has certainly proved itself. Look what Roosevelt did with the New Deal, despite all the confusion."

"There, you see, even we who pride ourselves on being intellectuals like to think the other fellow knows what he is doing," Johnson said. "You've got to admit, Floyd, it was the war and not the planning that pulled us out. Ironically, it's a war that's taking us down the drain now."

"Hey, we're getting off the point," Small interrupted. "I take it that you don't believe in faith healing either, Floyd, which is probably the first time you've ever agreed with a man of the cloth."

"I'm not so sure. Like I said, I know the limits of medicine, but I have seen strange things happen. You remember the Dominick boy . . . For a while there I was sure he was going to pull out of it—live, at least. It wasn't faith in your sense that was keeping him going, father, but a dosage of illicit love and drugs. What do you make of *that*?"

"I think you're a bit soft in the head about those kids, Floyd," Church said. "Weren't you the one who told me once that there's nothing wrong with a kid that a good dose of age won't cure?"

Dr. Shepherd laughed. "I guess so, but—who was it, Emerson?—who said a foolish consistency is the hobgoblin of little minds? What I really need from you gentlemen is contributions to the cause."

"Do you think you're going to make it? I think Pauline really dropped out because she figured the town wasn't behind you," Church said.

"She's probably right. The town isn't scared the way it was when they elected me—or rather it is scared about different things. Then they were worried about Worton's reputation wrecking real estate values and such. Now they're scared to death of their own kids, and they think Dominick's the man to put them in their place."

"Isn't it sad?" Loren Johnson said. "When you're afraid of your children, you're really afraid of the future . . ."

"Amen," said Father Funston, lifting his glass. "Here's to feeling safer with Nixon!"

Nobody drank.

If there was anything that might be called a sign of the times in Worton, it was the one posted on one of the crumbling brick pillars beside the entrance to Brookehaven. It read: "ACREAGE FOR SALE, Inquire at Sound Realty, Post Road." Marion Brooke Stanton hated the thing. All sorts of people from New Jersey or Long Island, some of them with their kids and dogs, wandered in any time of the night or day. They were nearly driving the judge's old spaniel mad and scaring her half to death. She complained to Howard Hilsman who, as her parents' acknowledged attorney, more or less managed things. But nothing was done about it. At times Marion felt that she had lost control over her life a few hours after her mother's body was lowered into the ground, and the men with the papers in their hands came to see her.

They'd all gathered in the judge's study. Marion was the only family member present; on the phone, Hartwell had refused to come up to see his mother before she died—"I couldn't stand it, I want to remember her the way she was." And for the judge's funeral he'd flatly said, "I don't think he would want me." Hilsman, flanked by John Baxter from the bank and Henry Ogilvy from Sound Realty, seemed nervous, or embarrassed, or both. "Couldn't we have a drink before we . . . get down to business?"

Marion nodded, and Hilsman passed whiskeys around, saying when he handed her one, "You may need this."

Until that moment Marion hadn't given a thought to the practical matters involved in her parents' deaths. For years everyone had supposed that the judge, being both lawyer and banker, had arranged for his fortune and estate to pass smoothly into the hands of the only descendants he acknowledged, Marion and her children. Though it was somewhat of a surprise when it turned out that the judge in the manner of too many lawyers, had simply failed to "get around to" making a new will, the document he had drawn up at the time of his marriage sufficed to transfer "all worldly goods of which I am possessed" to "my dear wife, Helen Jennings Brooke." Several times Howard Hilsman tried delicately to get the ailing Helen Brooke to make her own intentions clear in a new will, but Marion kept him away when she saw how nervous it made her mother to think of death in the midst of praying for life. "I'll take care of all that when

I'm better," Helen would say, and Marion, convincing herself that her mother would indeed be better, agreed.

Now Hilsman, making a show of putting on his glasses and ruffling papers in his briefcase, was saying, "As you must have guessed, Marion, your mother died intestate . . ."

"What does that mean?"

"She left no will, and, as a result, the estate is, as they say, up for grabs. But it isn't as bad as it might sound. Unless your mother has some other relatives who might have some claim, we can probably work it out to divide it between you and Hartwell . . ."

"But I thought Daddy said he had taken care of Hartwell."

"He thought so too. He talked to me a couple of times about it, and I told him he ought to get it in writing. But you know your father—he'd say, 'I'm not about to die yet, Howard, I'll get around to it.' Luckily he did one thing, though, before he went off on the *Helena*. He came to see John here and arranged to call that loan on your old place."

"I thought Jim Horner had bought that."

"Well, let's say he was trying to buy it. You see, the deal your father made with him was a year-to-year agreement that Horner would only have to pay interest and whatever principal he could afford. Horner hasn't paid a dime of principal, so your father dictated a new agreement, calling for regular payments. We'll have to offer it to Horner, of course; he has an option. But I'm very doubtful he can afford to exercise it, so the property should come back into the estate—and a good thing too."

Marion shuddered. "I don't want it. I never want to see that house again. All the terrible things that have happened there . . ."

"Well, Hartwell may want it," Hilsman said. "If not, you're going to need all the money it will bring, and as Mr. Ogilvy here can tell you, it's gone up a third or more over Horner's option price. The way things were left with no provision at all to get around them, the estate taxes are going to be murderous. Unless Hartwell settles for some property, you may even have to sell Brookehaven."

Marion understood then why Hilsman had provided her with a drink. The cushion for the shocks of too many deaths too fast had been Brookehaven. It was days before Marion could bring herself to believe that her father was not coming back, that she wouldn't look out one day to see the *Helena* standing in from the Sound to salute the house, as she so often did, before rounding the point to her mooring. Marion would wander through empty rooms, the bewildered dog at her heels, looking at pictures of the *Helena* and the yachts before her, fondling the pipes polished by her father's hand, inhaling the aromatic compound of tobacco, whiskey and old leather he had left behind. When at last the funeral ceremonies certified the fact of his passing, she still had a sense of his living presence in the house, and she anticipated the same for her mother. In any tolerable and meaningful future, she would go on living there at Brookehaven, leaving in time some of herself behind for her children.

But when despite all entreaties Hartwell refused to accept ownership of any land in a place where he felt he was not wanted, the accountants sharpened their pencils, plugged in their calculators and finally informed Marion that, in order to retain the house and a couple of surrounding acres plus enough capital to provide the style of living to which she was accustomed, and still pay the taxes and give Hartwell his share in cash, she would have to sell not only her old home but the remaining acreage of Brookehaven. Hence, the sign. Since the house and its outbuildings sprawled over nearly an acre, she would lose most of the waterfront, the tidal pond and the buffering woods to the north. While zoning would limit the number of houses that could be built and economics would guarantee that their owners be among the wealthiest persons in the land, it was nevertheless certain that Brookehaven would be transformed into an anachronism like an ancient Victorian lady who, surviving beyond her time, still wears the fashions of her youth. Instead of admiration, Brookehaven would doubtless provoke in future generations an amused curiosity about the eccentricity of anyone who would choose to live in such a monstrosity.

However much it annoyed and hurt her, selling off the land was in Marion's mind the only acceptable one of the possible solutions presented to her. Her children, to whom the austere Judge Brooke and retiring Helen were something less than real, urged her to move back into the glass house where their own childhoods had been passed, for the most part in merciful oblivion to the deterioration of their late father. So did the men of affairs like Howard Hilsman. By living in her old house she could sell the whole Brookehaven estate, quite possibly for top dollar, to one of the corporations seeking to escape taxes and turmoil in New York. Now that Lou Dominick and his Hill Club group were in control of the town, there was talk that they would open the doors to the kind of development that would not only keep taxes down but provide employment for their relatives and children. To the new generation like Lou, the estates where their fathers and uncles and grandfathers had bent their backs in labor were a distinct eyesore.

But Marion stubbornly resisted all such advice. She'd had her fill of houses. For all its apparent promise of the good life, hers had hardly fulfilled it. Bad enough the memories of Bill, staggering through so many scenes of recrimination. What would haunt the place even more was something that shame would forever keep her from revealing to a living soul: her last experience with Susan Horner. . . .

When Marion had gotten a call from Susan on that awful Saturday, she'd been thoroughly annoyed. The woman was obviously out-of-her-head drunk and it wasn't yet noon. Although Marion had not seen her, or even spoken to her, since the day she'd reluctantly taken her to Dr. Bruno's office, Susan acted as if they were the greatest of friends. Her words were slurred, but her voice had an unmistakably crazy lilt to it . . . "Oh, Marion, isn't it just the most divine day you ever saw? You remember how the maples here are . . . they look like they're all on fire. Wouldn't you like to take one of your walks and come over to see them, and maybe we could gather the leaves and make an arrangement and have lunch on the terrace in the sun. Wouldn't it be fun? My whole family's away and—"

Marion was curt. "You know my mother's ill. I can't leave her."

"Oh, Marion, please, please . . . just for an hour . . . I'm so lonely and it's so lovely . . ."

"Sorry, Susan, I'm afraid it's just impossible. Another time."

After she'd hung up, Marion did begin to relent. There was an alarming note of hysteria in Susan's voice, and perhaps a short visit—she wouldn't stay for lunch or anything like that—would calm her down. Anyway, a walk was a good idea on such a day if only for the sake of the spaniel, who was missing his customary rambles with the judge. Marion took the waterfront path which brought her out by the sliding glass panels of the living room. She could see Susan quite clearly sitting head down by the telephone. The panels were locked, so she knocked. Susan's setter, Rusty, began barking, and then she and the spaniel whined and clawed at each other through the glass. Susan looked up, started to rise and fell to the floor. She began crawling toward Marion on all fours. Her eyes, or what Marion could see of them through a mop of uncombed hair, looked wild. She wasn't dressed, and the loose neck of her nightgown revealed what to Marion's eye was an awful detail—pendulous breasts swinging as she crawled. Marion had fled in panic.

Later when she heard what had happened, Marion told herself she should have called somebody for help. But, as she also kept arguing with herself, she really had no way of knowing then that Susan was anything more than just plain drunk. Even so, Marion's shame persisted in her acknowledgment that, deep down, she hadn't really cared. Back in the fastness of Brookehaven that afternoon she had, in fact, taken a kind of secret pleasure in knowing that she would never be like that sniveling woman . . . she was a Brooke. Knowing from bitter personal experience that there wasn't, after all, much you could do for weaklings, she resolved never again to become involved with Susan Horner. Then came the awful fact of deliberate death that altered the drama Marion had witnessed to real tragedy. It was what might have happened to Bill if he hadn't been killed in a careless accident, as she still firmly believed despite all whispers to the contrary, and for Marion it forever put a curse on that house of glass in which a person could not even hide from the world the indignity of death.

When Howard Hilsman had called and invited Marion to a meeting with Jim Horner in John Baxter's office at the bank she'd tried to get out of it, but Howard insisted that they might need her to make a decision as to disposition of the property. She hadn't seen Horner since her father's funeral, and she didn't want to now. She not only blamed him for the judge's death but felt he must also have some responsibility for reducing Susan to the shambles that stayed vivid in her memory. He had become a kind of devil in her mind, and she was surprised to find that, despite all that had happened, Horner looked somehow younger and better than she remembered. It was almost indecent. Her own hair had started graying right after Bill's death, and she'd let it go as a sign that she was, after all, a woman of sensibility. Fortunately from her point of view the atmosphere in the banker's office was conducive to nothing more than the coolest civilities in greeting.

John Baxter handed Jim Horner the paper the judge had dictated. It didn't take long for Jim to get the message. "So that's what he had in mind," he said when he'd finished reading. "He knew that I could never come up with such payments as this. A thing like this could wipe me out, and he knew it."

"Oh, I wouldn't look at it that way, Jim," Howard Hilsman said. "It's just that the judge began to worry about having so much money out at such low interest . . ."

"Except it was *his* idea," Jim said. "I'm sure you remember, Mr. Baxter, how we sat here and he argued me into it? He promised there would never be any time limit so long as I met the interest payments. You heard him. Now it's obvious from this paper that if I don't pick up the option I lose everything, even the money I put in from Bramble Road, and I happen not to have another cent in the world."

"But you did sign the agreement," Hilsman said.

"I thought I was dealing with a gentleman . . . you are all gentlemen, aren't you. . . ?"

"Please, Jim," Hilsman said, ignoring the sarcasm, "You're forgetting Mrs. Stanton here. It's just possible, if she agrees, that we could return some of your investment once we get the settlement worked out. As her attorney, however, I must advise her that she's under no obligation to do so, and with taxes and the division of the estate, Mrs. Stanton is in no position to be gratuitously generous. She has no other source of income and does have three children to educate. She's even going to have to sell off some of Brookehaven—"

"You can have your damned house," Jim said, rising. "I can't stand the sight of it—and your money too."

"Now wait a minute, Jim, you haven't given Mrs. Stanton a chance—"

"A chance to what—to give me something if there's enough left over? I think you've made it clear, Howard, that I would be robbing a poor widow and her children down to their last million. I don't think I could stand having that on my conscience too."

When Jim had slammed out the door, Howard Hilsman sighed and said, "Well, there goes a fairly expensive load of pride, but it does make it easier for us."

"Isn't it a little harsh?" Marion asked. "Lord knows I don't have any use for the man but—"

"Neither did your father," Hilsman said. "Baxter here'll bear me out that it was your father's intent, as Horner suspected, to make it hard enough for him so that he'd have to move on. The judge felt that the fellow had lost his head over that youth business and was going to prove an embarrassment to Dan Parker's campaign for Congress. I know you're your father's daughter, Marion, and

I doubt you'd want to go against his last expression of his will. The Horners of this world come and go . . . the important thing is to save as much of Brookehaven as possible. In any case, I suspect you won't see him around here much longer. If he was telling the truth about his finances—and I think he was—he won't be able to afford a dog kennel here. And you know, people like Horner can't stand the public embarrassment of moving down from waterfront. Oh, no, he'll be gone. What's to keep him? His wife's dead, one of his daughters is gone, the other is living over there at Adams Point with that Schine. They'll be gone soon enough too, because from what I hear nobody's giving them any money and Benjy Adams is so angry about the way they behaved at the time of his boy's funeral that he won't renew the lease. So you see it's going to work out just about the way your father planned."

Hearing Howard Hilsman talk made Marion feel considerably better. He sounded so much like her father, making everything seem reasonable and right. And she *was* her father's daughter. Saving as much of Brookehaven as possible was more important in the long run than what happened to people like the Horners, and seeing Horner around would always remind her of so much she wanted to forget. She could remember once discussing Bill with the judge. "You have to learn, Marion, that there are a lot of weak and foolish people in the world you can't do anything about. Just don't let them drag *you* down," he'd told her, and, by God, she wouldn't.

"All right, Howard, you men do what you think best," she said, "but please get somebody to take that sign down at Brookehaven. It looks as if we were giving up, and you know that nobody coming off the street can afford the land. Oh, and while they're at it, have them paint over that BR OKE on the mailbox."

Chapter XVI

"Go ahead, spit it out. I'm practically shock proof by now," Jim was saying to his partner Paul Richards. They were having a drink in a back corner booth at the Chinese restaurant below their offices. Since Paul Richards was the sort of fellow who scooted home to his wife and children in Darien on the dot of five, the invitation to a drink in itself signaled something unusual.

"Yes, I guess you are, and I know I'm going to sound like an ungrateful son of a bitch, Jim, since this whole idea was yours, but you haven't been around the office too much lately and . . ."

"Jesus! You are a certified son of a bitch . . ."

"Now wait just a minute, you don't know the piss poor state of the books, Jim. There isn't enough money coming in for both of us. Right now, I don't even know how we're going to pay Angie on Friday. I guess we could get another loan for a few months but—"

"One of us has to go, is that it?"

"That's about it. I thought you might be interested in this letter . . ."

Under the heading identifying it as from Alexander P. Thompson, vice-president of public relations for a General Motors division and addressed to Job Hunters Anonymous, it read:

I am on a scouting expedition for just the right person to fill an important opening in my office. I am coming to you first because of your reputation for discretion in these matters since knowledge that I am going outside the organization in my search would cause serious personnel problems at the moment.

What the position calls for is a mature man with both a general news background and significant experience in industry. Although the starting salary is only $25,000, the opportunity is almost unlimited. Whomever we hire will, in effect, be my assistant, and my own retirement is compulsory within five years.

The fringe benefits are as fine as can be found anywhere. Because of the importance of this position, I have been able to persuade personnel to offer an accelerated pension program to accommodate an older man as well as the usual stock options. As you are probably aware, there are many pleasant places to live in the Detroit area, and, indeed, I am sure I could locate a suitable home in my own suburb of Grosse Point, one of the best known residential communities in the nation.

It may be asking too much, but, since you are located along the eastern seaboard, you might know of a man with the professional qualifications who also has sailing as a hobby. While this is in no sense a requirement for the job, I would find it personally persuasive since I have recently acquired a yacht which I plan to enter in the long-distance lake races. Being aware of this might also prove enticing to anyone considering a relocation.

Naturally I am anxious to fill the position as soon as possible. While I can give you a few months to look for the right person, I must absolutely have someone in place before the end of the year.

Even before Jim had finished reading, Paul said, "How about that? Right on the nose."

Jim shoved the letter across the table. "Don't you really know who this Thompson is? He's Pauline Church's father . . ."

"Oh, well, listen, Jim, if I were sitting where you are I'd figure she'd done me a real favor. I'd take it myself if I had the qualifications. But I thought since you have nothing to hold you here—"

"I still have a daughter, you know."

"But I thought she was—"

354

"Don't try to be delicate, Paul. Yes, she's shacked up, as they call it, with Arnold Schine. Matter of fact since I got evicted I've been bunking in with them at Adams Point myself. I want to tell you I'm damn proud of what they're doing for other kids and I'm not going to leave Worton until I see their program funded . . ."

"That's another thing I've got to be honest about, Jim. Oh, I know you're trying to do the right thing and I admire you for it but your community activities are one reason the business is in trouble."

"What do you mean?"

"Well, you know a hell of a lot of the guys we have to go to for jobs for our clients live in Worton. Some of them have told me quite frankly that they think you're some kind of an agitator and they don't want to do business with us. Be realistic. Sooner or later these kids are going to grow up somehow or get lost, but where does that leave you? You've got to eat, and you're still young enough so that you're going to meet another woman one of these days. God, Jim, you of all people have to know how hard it is to find something at your age, and this could be your last chance. . . . Well, listen, I've got to run—Helen's got some kind of an outdoor bash going. Think it over, okay?"

Jim watched Paul head out into the sunshine. Easy for him to talk about being realistic, and where had he heard that talk before? . . . Truly, Pauline was a damn witch. She not only wanted him out of her bed but clear out of town, as if he would ever lay claim to the child. And she was trying to do it in a way that would let her tell herself for the rest of her life how wonderfully she'd treated him.

Jim signaled for another drink. His life had definitely fallen apart, and damned if he could make sense of it. Except for Pauline, he'd played strictly by the rules . . . and maybe that was much of the trouble. Other people thought nothing of changing them to their own advantage. It reminded him of a time in a race when he was leading the fleet to where the weather mark was supposed to be only to find that the buoy had gone adrift, giving the sailors behind him the edge; the committee had disallowed his protest—to allow it would be a reflection on the way they'd run the race. As Shakespeare put it in one of those aphorisms his mother had beaten into his head, "Nothing can seem foul to those that win." Except what exactly was it to win?

But, square as he was supposed to be, shouldn't he at least be one of the winners? He kept going back in his mind to that sense of dread he'd felt going out into the night of Sissy Stanton's death, that certainty that there was "no hidin' place down here," as the old hymn put it. Maybe God, if there was a God, had just decided to knock the stuffings out of a very stuffy man, and he was certainly succeeding. He was learning the hard way, you'd better learn to take things the way they actually were instead of the way you were told they were supposed to be. He'd gotten himself into the position of being the messenger of the bad news that all was not well in Worton, and he was being treated as all such messengers are by people who wanted to believe that their power had made them secure . . . he was getting killed.

He decided he'd better stop drinking . . . what the hell kind of vainglorious thoughts were these for a guy who had just got himself royally screwed! Which notion brought him back to Pauline, who'd done the best job on him of all. He doubted he'd ever forget the way she broke it to him. . . .

It was after his talk with Andy Wolfe, in his own house where, after Susan died and Julie moved out, they had taken to going because they could be sure of being alone. At the time, before the afterlight of Judge Brooke's power had burned him, he had some wild hopes that a new kind of happiness might redeem the place. Pauline seemed so different from Susan in her pointed disregard of how things would look that in her presence no ghosts were possible. She loved to take advantage of the place's openness and isolation, and often, as on this particular Indian summer day, they would lie naked together in the sun, teasing, investigating, consuming. Afterward, stroking the curve of her belly, Pauline had asked, "How do you like the new me?"

In answer he let his hand join hers in admiration and move on up to cup breasts that were also beginning to swell with the pressure of the new life inside her. In its mysterious way, pregnancy was turning the marbled figure of the Egyptian princess into the warmest of pink flesh. "I love it," he said, "and not just because it's mine."

"Charlie thinks it's his, and he may be right."

"You're a devil."

"A witch. Isn't that more New England?"

Jim had decided that Andy was right—no amount of guilt could bring Susan back from the grave, but at least doing the right thing now might make up for it. Besides, he wanted to. "Listen," he said, "you know it's got to be mine. If Charlie could beget a baby he'd have hundreds by now. So now that . . . well, you know that I love you . . . I think we ought to get married—"

"God, you *are* square—and you still use the wrong words. I thought we weren't going to talk about love."

"What do you call this?"

"I don't *call* it anything. You needed me, I wanted you, period." She laughed. "Or rather, no period."

"Very funny . . . but what about now? Are you trying to tell me you no longer—"

"No—but there will come a time soon . . . I can feel it here inside . . ."

"A baby will only make it better. Believe me. I know . . ."

"Not for me. When I have this baby I'm also going to become *the* Mrs. Charles Church and get into the Good Book and—"

"Pauline, you're not serious. Talk about being square . . ."

"I certainly am serious. I told you in the beginning. There are as many Thompsons as Joneses in the world. When I was little we lived in six different places. I never even saw my grandparents. Now I'll finally be part of a whole family history—three hundred years of it."

"But I thought you hated this place."

"Not the place—the people. But don't you think they could do with a good witch? Once I get my name in that book, I can start looking down my nose even at Marion Stanton. . . . Oh, come on, be realistic, Jim. How long could it go on this way? If I did marry you, wouldn't we be just another couple named Horner, which isn't much better than Thompson, arguing about money and kids and living God knows where."

"We could live here."

"Could we? You know that's not very realistic either. I'll bet you've got a mortgage bigger than all outdoors, and from what you've told me about your business—"

"So it's not for love but money—Church money."

"Well, you are a word man . . . anyway, why not? Maybe money doesn't buy happiness, but happiness sure as hell doesn't go far without it."

Whether it was from the shade inching ahead of a dropping sun or from a pause in his heart, Jim was suddenly chilly. He actually shivered the length of his body. "We've got to get you home," he said. "It wouldn't do for *the* Mrs. Church to catch cold. Hell, it might turn into pneumonia and keep her out of the Good Book . . ."

Jim never tried to see her again, and she, pleading her belly as women once did in ancient courts, resigned from what was left of the Youth Commission. Jim was not surprised to read a small notice in the paper to the effect that Charles Church IV had been baptized in the Worton Presbyterian Church by the Reverend Dr. W. Anderson Wolfe; nor to see later that Mrs. Charles Church III had conducted members of the Worton Audubon Society on a bird walk on the Church property; nor, still later, to note that Mr. and Mrs. Charles Church III celebrated their wedding anniversary with a small dinner party at Golden Hills Country Club for Mrs. William Chesney Stanton, Mr. and Mrs. Howard Morton Hilsman, the Rev. and Mrs. Archibald Funston, Dr. and Mrs. Floyd Shepherd, Mr. and Mrs. Loren Johnson and Mr. and Mrs. Fielding Small. He wondered if they all knew that she was a witch.

Being nearly half a century old, the very walls of the locker room of Golden Hills Country Club seemed to have soaked up a permanent masculine bouquet, essence of sweat, urine, talcum powder, whiskey and tobacco. Just inhaling this aroma as he came in off the course always gave Floyd Shepherd a delicious sense of ease. Muscles a little achy from plodding up and down gentle hills (as a medical man, Dr. Shepherd considered the golf cart an abomination), lungs washed with air, eyes stretched from following the arc of a ball against an open sky, he felt entitled by reason of earned virtue to the small fleshly indulgences of a drink, a steaming shower, a cigar. Golden Hills was one of the last clubs in the country where aging and dignified Negroes, grandsons of men who had stepped off the underground railway in New England, produced silver trays with cut glass decanters, laid out thick fresh towels initialed GHC and dispensed gentle philosophy on demand. It made it possible for a politician like Dan Parker, hailing from the snow white land of Worton, to expound on the thinking of blacks since "some of my best friends are Negroes . . . why George at the club was telling me the other day . . ."

"Yes, sir, Dr. Shepherd, I was very sorry to see him go. First Dr. King and then Bobby. Course there ain't many people but you around here I can tell that to, but I don't know what's coming to this world," George was saying as he poured the doctor's whiskey.

"I swear I don't either, George," Floyd Shepherd agreed.

"And the way they treated you after all you done for this town . . ."

"I was a fluke, George. I don't think they'd even have let me in this club if they'd known I was a Democrat then. You hear the way they talk around here, don't you? Things are just getting back to normal, George—in this town at least. Maybe I'll even get in some golf. You know, I broke ninety again today."

"That's good, Dr. Shepherd . . ."

"Not for me, it isn't. Has the sauna been fixed yet?"

"Oh, yes. Mr. Parker, he's in there now."

Something about sitting together in a sauna, naked and streaming sweat, reduced men to the commonest of denominators, Floyd Shepherd thought, a little like the army. His doctor's eye couldn't help but appraise Dan Parker's hard, lean body a bit enviously. Maybe he was wrong about that business of having it with younger women, but then of course Dan had come off the courts instead of the greens. His own little ball of a stomach attested to a gentler form of exercise and perhaps a gentler philosophy of life. Although he had no desire to talk to the man most responsible for his political defeat, simple courtesy demanded some sort of acknowledgment. "Wouldn't think you'd have time for this sort of thing, Dan."

"Have to keep in shape," Dan said. "When they talk about a political race, believe me, they're using the right word."

"How do you feel about the news from Los Angeles?"

"Terrible, of course, but it just shows what can happen when you get too mixed up in that Israel thing. God, I'm glad I don't have a lot of them in my district. Of course, this means that old war horse Humphrey should be heading your ticket, which ought to make us a shoo-in. Still, I don't believe in taking any chances, and now that we're alone here, Floyd, I'd like to give you some friendly advice . . . get Horner and these kids out of Adams Point before it's too late . . ."

"What do you mean—'too late'?"

"Well, I've been sitting on information that could make things very embarrassing for him and for your friends the Churches . . ."

"Such as?"

"That kid of Pauline Church's is really Horner's."

"Dan, you can't really know a thing like that."

"There were other people beside you who saw that Horner suicide note before you destroyed it—more than one witness, in fact."

"So what? A roll in the hay doesn't necessarily produce a kid. If it did, there'd be standing room only out there. You know you can't publish anything like this . . ."

"There's the oldest form of publishing in the world—the mouth."

"I can't believe even you would spread stuff like that for the sake of politics."

The last thing Dr. Shepherd heard Dan Parker say was, "There's more than politics involved in this . . ."

Back in the locker room, the doctor dressed quickly. The smell of the place had turned sour for him, and he wondered if he shouldn't try after all to find another club somewhere or start playing on the public courses. He was the only one in the Tuesday Club who belonged to Golden Hills except for Arch Funston's honorary ministerial membership. He could remember squirming a little at a recent meeting when the others were smugly taking Richard Nixon apart for staying in some segregated club over in New Jersey. So far he'd been able to quiet the voice of conscience with the argument that a busy doctor owed it to himself and his patients to take advantage of the nearest facility; he could hardly count the times he'd been snatched off the course and carried behind a siren to some emergency. But right now he felt that any place where he was likely to encounter Dan Parker was a place to avoid. Maybe the answer was to vote for the fellow so that he could go down and stink up Washington instead.

When he left the club, Dr. Shepherd decided to go to Adams Point to find Horner. He'd heard the man had holed up there after Marion and the others had taken over his house, and he was in the process of turning over his failing business to his partner. Dr. Shepherd had a grudging admiration for the fact that Horner still thought he could collect enough dollars to keep the hot line open, although there were times when he thought it was more of an act of revenge than anything else. What bothered him most about Dan Parker's nasty rumor was that it could be true. He probably should have hated Dominick for blabbing to Parker, but he really didn't—Lou was just a poor bastard who'd been put through more than he could understand. The thing was that, as Charlie Church's doctor, Floyd Shepherd had long suspected a form of sterility but he could never persuade Charlie to take any tests. "What the hell, doc, it's enough at my age that I can get it up . . ." So having no good reason to disbelieve Charlie's assurances that he was enjoying regular relations with his wife, Dr. Shepherd accepted the pregnancy as authentic. Even if all the rumors about Pauline and Horner were true, a modern girl like that wouldn't allow herself to be impregnated in an affair. Still, it was plausible enough to allow people to indulge their natural tendencies to believe the worst. And, if they did believe it, his friend Charlie Church would be crushed, and the hot line would be out of action.

Despite his efforts on behalf of the facility, Dr. Shepherd usually made it a practice to stay away from Adams Point. His long association with town authority was inhibiting to the sort of young people who used it. More important, they sort of intimidated, even depressed him. Like many good men of liberal philosophy, he realized, he found humanity a sight more lovable in the abstract than in the concrete. When he'd see those kids at the Point, so damned similarly dressed and long-haired he couldn't have told the boys from the girls from the rear if his eye for anatomy hadn't been professionally sharpened, he'd sometimes wonder if they weren't a kind of human graffiti. And the fact that, in one of the most spectacular spots on earth, they spent their time huddled together in the chauffeur's apartment above the garage, turning the air blue with smoke and loud with rock, seemed a deliberate rejection of all they'd been handed on a platter. Arnold Schine's explanation that "it's just their way of saying that they aren't going to take any more crap" was a bit hard to buy.

Still, Dr. Shepherd always went away from the Point feeling more sorry for the kids, and their parents, than angry. Knowing how few patients he—or any doctor— ever cured of anything, it was enough for him that Schine's way, right or wrong, had saved even a couple of human beings from disgrace, or even death.

But it wasn't enough for the Dan Parkers and Lou Dominicks and Rocco Finches and Howard Hilsmans, the power boys in town, and it never would be. "I can't see why the hell that Schine doesn't tell us what he's doing down there," Rocco would argue at meetings. "Listening—that's all he'll say, for Christ's sake. We're spending fifteen thousand dollars a year on that thing, and we don't even know whether he's working with ten kids or fifty, or what, and he doesn't either. We only spend half as much on Little League and there's a hundred kids at least getting something out of it. So they kept some kid from getting busted. Hell, that's worse than nothing if you ask me. That's interfering with the law. And how do we know they talked some kid out of killing himself? People who are going to do that don't sit around talking on phones." No use to explain that that's exactly what they did, but he did try to use Marilyn Monroe as an example. "Who? That dumb broad. She was crazy," was Rocco's reply. "I say let's shut it down." . . .

This time Dr. Shepherd didn't find Jim Horner at the Point, but what he did find made him understand better Dan Parker's fury and his final, somewhat enigmatic statement. Although the changing faces of most young people were a blur to the doctor, he at once recognized one of the girls lounging around the apartment. Felicia Marden, Dan Parker's stepdaughter. Even if she hadn't been a star in the children's crusade that elected him, he would have had her face imprinted on his conscience by the many times it had appeared in her stepfather's *Record*—as a leader of Young Life, as a candy striper, as a prize-winner in school, as member of the Congressional candidate's happy all-American family.

"I didn't know you were working here, Felicia," he said.

"I'm not. I'm *hiding* here."

"What?"

"Hiding. I didn't know where else to go."

"What do you mean—'go'?"

"I mean, when I ran away from home I didn't know where to *go*."

"When did you—"

"A couple of days ago."

"Why?" One of the small profits of being so publicly identified with the hot line was that young people seemed to have few reservations about talking freely with him— a privilege Dr. Shepherd tried to use sparingly since he usually didn't really want to hear what they had to say.

"My stepfather has been keeping me locked up in my room. I have to scream to get out to go to the bathroom. He even drives me back and forth to school himself and has the principal, who's scared to death of his paper, watch me all day."

"But why?"

"Because the cops found a couple of joints in my car."

"From what I heard it was somebody playing a trick on you."

"Oh, that was the first time. This time I couldn't snow them so Daddy Parker said he was going to keep me locked up until after the election—all summer. Can you believe it?"

"What did your mother say?"

"She agrees with him. She wants to go to Washington so bad she can taste it. So, anyway, I bribed one of my kid sisters to steal the key and let me out. She's probably getting hell now too, if they can figure out which one it was."

"I suppose Arnold and Mr. Horner know you're here . . ."

"Oh, sure. They're the the ones who said I could stay until they can find another place."

"Does your father know where you are?"

"I think so. He caught me talking to the hot line once when I got out to go to the bathroom and knocked the phone right out of my hand. But I think he's afraid to come after me. He's afraid somebody will find out, and they sure will. I'll scream."

Driving away, Dr. Shepherd knew that Adams Point was finished. Whatever their motives, Horner and Schine should never have taunted Parker by putting up Felicia. Under any other circumstances Parker undoubtedly would have had the police on them by now, but for the next several months he couldn't—as Felicia was smart enough to know—afford a scandal. So he would use whispered rumor and innuendo, every trick he could think of, to get even. Ironically Parker actually stood in no danger of any kind of exposure himself because it would run counter to the code of Adams Point to use Felicia's problems to embarrass her father; its interest was in protecting her.

Dr. Shepherd decided that he himself would have to make some sort of public gesture to quiet Parker's vicious tongue, which could only hurt Charlie Church, and Horner as well. Since there was no future for the project in any case, better it be laid to rest with the least ugly fallout possible. And to that end he would write a letter to Parker, for publication in the *Record*, in which he, Floyd Shepherd, would put Adams Point out of its misery in rather general terms . . . as a result of his "inside knowledge." As first selectman, kindly physician and so forth—he'd be believed. What it would also do, of course, would be to bring down upon him the misunderstanding, if not hatred, of the people who'd trusted him, including virtually all of the young people, and there would be no way at all of explaining his action without himself starting the very rumor he wanted to silence. Well, was it better actually to be a good guy, or to have people think you were? He guessed at this point in his life he'd opt for the former. Back at his office he scribbled off the letter before he had time for second thoughts and had his nurse deliver it by hand to the *Record*. Charlie Church would retain his pride of fatherhood, Horner would at least not have one more kick in the ass directed at him, Schine & Co. would be out of Worton by July when the town funds ran out, and maybe, just maybe, he would be too.

Julie especially liked to play with Arnold's beard, run her fingers through it or rub it with her cheek. It was stiff and curly and black and smelt faintly of tobacco smoke. He had a lot of hair on his chest, too, and it was long enough so that she could pull it and make him howl when she felt like teasing.

There were times, particularly when she'd hear a hymn on the radio or something that would remind her of all those days in Young Life and Sunday School, when Julie wondered whether it was right to be turned on by a man's body. She once tried to talk about it to Arnold when they were lying together in bed, and one of the things she loved about him was that, instead of being funny or silly or crude, he said, "The trouble with you, Julie, is that you were brought up on the wrong part of the Bible." Then he got out of bed, turned on the light and came back with a book. "Listen to this," he said. " '. . . his locks are wavy, black as raven. His eyes are like doves beside springs of water, bathed in milk, fitly set. His cheek are beds of spices, yielding fragrance. His lips are lilies, distilling liquid myrrh . . . he is altogether desirable. This is my beloved and this is my friend . . .' Now there was a girl who was really turned on, and it's in the Bible, too—'Song of Solomon.' As for you, '. . . your rounded thighs are like jewels, the work of a master hand. Your navel is a rounded bowl that never lacks mixed wine. Your belly is a heap of wheat, encircled with lilies. Your two breasts are like two fawns, twins of a gazelle . . .' "

"That's beautiful," she said, and Arnold closed the book, and together they went to those wells and springs from which they could drink their own wine of desire, and she stopped worrying about loving too much. It was easier to enjoy loving Arnold too, now that she was having such good talks with her father. Either she'd grown up or he'd changed, but these days they seemed more friends than father and daughter.

It was terrible to think that it happened because of what her mother did, but it probably was true. She'd never forget that Sunday when she got back from Washington and found her father just sitting there staring at that jagged hole marring their spectacular view. Somehow that seemed to get to him more than anything else, and he kept telling her again and again about how the police had had to shoot Rusty. She knew, of course, it was a way of avoiding talking about what really mattered, and they both went around being brave for the sake of each other until after the little memorial service at the church. When they got back to the house her father offered to scramble up some eggs for dinner. She agreed, because she thought just doing something might be good for him. She heard him banging around with pots and pans and saying, "Dammit, where the hell do you suppose the egg beater is?"

Thinking she could help, Julie ran into the kitchen and saw right away why her father was making all that noise. He was trying to cover up the sounds of his crying. She went over and put her arms around him and said, "It's all right, Daddy, I feel the same . . ."

He pushed her away and tore the apron he had put on and said, "Let's get out of here. Being in here reminds me too much of her."

At a pizza place on the Post Road, after they'd choked down a little food, he seemed to have himself under control again. "I'm sorry, Julie, it won't happen again . . . Betsy called me yesterday . . ."

"She *did*? Where *is* she? *How* is she?"

"She's in the Virgin Islands, working at Hartwell Brooke's hotel. I've known about it for some time but I promised I wouldn't tell anybody. When she heard about her mother, she wanted to come home but Hart argued her out of it. I think it was just as well. She's still a fugitive, you know, and Lou Dominick almost surely would have had her arrested . . ." He went on to tell Julie about Betsy living with Leo Polchick.

"And you don't mind that?" Julie asked.

"I don't know that I'm in any position to *mind*, Julie," he said and, pushing away his mostly untouched plate, lit a cigarette. She had sense enough to stay quiet until he began again. "Julie, you've been through so much lately that . . . well, there's no sense in my not being honest with you. You've probably heard talk about me and Pauline Church, and I'm afraid your mother knew . . . or guessed. I don't know whether you can understand this, Julie—or, anyway, accept it—but for a while I think I actually loved two women at the same time . . . not the same way, of course, but—"

"Oh, I can, Daddy . . . I can understand . . ."

And she told him all about the wonder and beauty of

her first passion with Ben, and about Arnold, and how different it was but that it never was the same as with Ben . . . different, not better or worse. At first she didn't think it was right, but now she did and felt easy and good about it. Seeing him listening to her, as if he were hearing her for the first time, she was encouraged to go on. "Daddy, I'd like to live with Arnold at Adams Point, I just can't stand that house . . ."

He winced inwardly but managed to keep his voice calm. "I can't blame you, Julie." He smiled briefly. "There's no particular reason that I can see for us to try to be what passes for respectable anymore . . . there doesn't seem to be anybody around to appreciate the effort." . . .

Of course, being alone so much, her father began coming over to visit at Adams Point. When Mrs. Stanton and Mr. Hilsman gave him that raw deal on the house, it was Arnold's idea to invite him to move in for a while, and she loved Arnold for that. "Your old man's okay," Arnold said, "and he seems to be getting the short end of every stick, the latest courtesy of Pauline Church. He talks about how worried he is for you, about my not being able to afford college and the rest, but frankly I think we should be worried about him. He's really been getting it four ways at once."

Later, they asked Jim what *he* was going to do.

"I don't know. I really don't know . . ."

"Why don't you just cut out and do what you want?" Arnold asked him.

"I don't know what I want—not anymore. I've been doing what other people want—and to be fair, what I assumed I wanted—for so long . . . Well, that isn't your problem. It's mine."

There was an ache in Julie's heart when she'd see her father off by himself, but Arnold, as though reading her mind, told her, "I know it's rough, Julie, but maybe leaving him alone is the best we can do for him, and maybe we can learn something from what's happened to him . . ."

She hoped so. God, did she hope so. One night she

awoke frightened. . . . Something was happening, and it took a long while for her sleep-fuzzed mind to realize what it was. The usually silent Point was exploding with sound. Rising seas were shushing in and out of the rocks, a loose door banged and echoed through the cavernous garage below them as a swinging branch scratched like a fingernail on the tiles of the roof. Her eyes, getting accustomed to the dark, saw the window curtains playing and fluttering like ghostly wings. It was a northeaster, rare in summer, and she knew it would soon be lashing them with rain. Through all the other noises, her sensitive ear picked up the rhythm of the breathing that told her Arnold was still sound asleep. She got up to close the window against the storm. Although it muffled the sound from outside, the closed window seemed to enrage the wind—she imagined she could feel its frustrated blasts shaking the whole building. She remembered hearing about the hurricane that had once ravished this coast, and although Adams Point had stood sturdily through it then, she wondered if this could be the coming of another such storm that might blow them all away. In the irrationality of the night, she grew more certain that it was. She didn't want to be alone, and turned to Arnold.

A heavy sleeper, he hated to be awakened suddenly so she pretended to snuggle by accident against his warm, bare back. No response. She ran her fingers through his hair, along the edge of his beard. He slapped at them as if they were giant flies. She toyed with the hair on his chest and along the flat of his belly and on down until she knew he was astir. His voice sounded grumpily pleased. "Hey, what gives?"

"The storm. Can't you hear it, Arnold?"

"Oh, it's just a northeaster. Happens all the time down here. I wish somebody'd fix that goddamned door down there. Now come on, Julie, go back to sleep."

"I can't. The wind's so spooky . . . don't go back to sleep, Arnold."

"You're certainly making it hard for me," he said and laughed.

And then he turned and was kissing her fiercely on the

lips and gently down her neck, his beard tickling her breasts into rigid points, his hands opening her. His love was as overwhelming as the storm, and as it was happening she remembered another storm and what had happened then . . .

"God, oh God, Julie, why don't you wake me up more often?" Arnold was saying.

"It was the storm . . ."

"Well, here's to it."

She hesitated, then: "Arnold, the first time it happened for me was in a storm—God, I nearly drowned," she said, shivering in memory.

He held her even closer. "Well, this is a kind of first time for me, Julie. It's been good but never like this. Funny, isn't it, happening just when we know we have to go . . ."

"Maybe that's why I was feeling so scared. We don't know where we're going—"

"Sure we do. Like I said, back to the city. We'll get part-time jobs, and you'll go to school. We both want to be doctors . . . you fix their bodies, I'll try to put their heads together . . ."

"I'd like that," she said. It was the first time Arnold had ever talked that specifically about the future, which encouraged her beyond the words themselves. A heavy drumbeat of rain was now drowning out the wind's chaotic clamor, and a dry bed in a dry room seemed suddenly the best place in the world to be.

Chapter XVII

First Selectman Lou Dominick was a bit nervous about the community Thanksgiving service. It was to be held in the Worton Presbyterian Church, and it would be the first time he had ever set foot inside a Protestant sanctuary. He had avoided it at the big Ben Adams funeral by assigning himself as police chief to keeping an eye on traffic, but he was a politician now and had to be there. He hadn't really reckoned on the fact that politics would call for fooling around with your religion, but Father Reardon assured him that it would be all right—he'd be right there beside Lou on the platform . . . he was supposed to give the benediction. One thing Lou was happy about was that he didn't have to speak. It had been decided to let Dan Parker do the talking, in honor of his election as the first Worton man in history ever to go to the Congress of the United States. Of course, the selection was no surprise since the idea for a single community-wide service instead of separate ones in all the churches had been brought forth in the *Record* right after the election, and it was appropriate since Dan was an elder of the church, whatever that was.

Lou figured that his family, at least, didn't have to take a chance on hell fire by going with him. But the girls told him not to be silly. They'd already been in Protestant churches lots of times with friends. What else had they been up to behind his back? he started to say, but Maria intervened to tell him that he ought to be glad that his daughters hadn't been in a lot worse places, like that Adams Point. He had to buy that, and one of the things he was going to be thankful for during the service was that they would never have a chance to go there—the whole operation had been blown right out of the water by Dr. Floyd Shepherd's surprising letter. It showed that the doctor was a prettty good guy after all, the way Lou had always thought he was. Too bad he decided to retire and move south, but then why not—doctors stashed away a lot of dough, and like Dr. Shepherd told everybody, he could play golf all winter long in Florida.

The more Lou thought about it, the more he realized that he had a lot to be thankful for, and he would certainly be praying—at least when Father Reardon prayed. His oldest girl was getting her RN the following year, and the next one had just been offered a scholarship at Manhattanville. Joey was still so fat and clumsy that he couldn't hit a slow pitch right over the plate, but he had won the science prize in school and everybody said he should be a doctor. Although he was only dragging down $10,000 as first selectman, the other ten he'd gotten from the money he put away after the Stanton settlement made everything pretty comfortable. And then there was the future. Dan Parker promised to get him something good down there in Washington, probably in the FBI. There was no doubt that Dan could do it. Dan's picture was right there on the front page of the *Record* shaking hands and talking to President-elect Nixon like an old buddy. Not only that, but Dan said he knew John Mitchell pretty well when Mitchell lived up near Worton somewhere. The way Dan put it, Nixon and Mitchell would certainly want a man down there with Lou Dominick's record for being tough with all these hippies and drug addicts. In his own words, Dan wouldn't be doing Lou any special favors either, because Dan was sure that being able to point out that his home town was so clean it didn't need a hot line anymore, unlike so many other towns in the district, was what got him elected.

When Lou finally did get himself into the church and was sitting up there on one of the folding chairs near the pulpit and looking around, he realized that it had been a good idea to pick the Presbyterian church. It was by far the biggest in town, and it was so modern that, except for a little gold cross on a table back of him and the stained-glass wall at the rear, it hardly looked like a church at all. There weren't any saints or candles or prayer stools around, and even the glass was in one of those crazy patterns that looked like a little kid had put it together from bits and pieces. Lou didn't agree with a woman he'd overheard telling a friend as they walked in, "I wish they had used the Congregational church. This just doesn't feel right for a Thanksgiving in New England." If the services couldn't be properly Catholic, he thought it was a lot better that they be held on neutral ground. When Father Reardon came in and sat down beside Lou he nodded in the direction of the stained-glass wall and whispered, "Looks like the juke box up at the Hill Club, doesn't it?" Lou had a hard time to keep from laughing, but he knew right then that it was all right to relax and enjoy the show.

Putting all the thankful people in Worton together turned out to be a good idea. Instead of the scraggly congregations that used to drift into the separate services, a goodly crowd was filling nearly every pew. From his own seat behind the pulpit, the Rev. Dr. W. Anderson Wolfe eyed them with interest. He missed some faces: Amos and Helen Brooke, George Avery, Floyd Shepherd, Bill Stanton. But among the faces he saw were some surprises: way back in the corner was one he never expected to see again, Jim Horner's, and right down in front were Pauline and Charlie Church, probably giving thanks for the unexpected son and heir. Thank God they'd left the baby home—squalling babies in church reminded Andy Wolfe too much of the time and place in which he had grown up when people thought going to church ought to be a family thing and where there was never enough money for baby sitters anyway. Another surprise was Marion Stanton, who had confessed to Andy very frankly that she had lost her faith over the Peters matter. Well, Marion did have something to be thankful for: from the way Andy heard it, she lost only half of Brookehaven when Hal Church and Seth Parker got together and paid her a premium price for the right to use the name in their Brookehaven Estates development of $200,000 homes.

Whether all the people out there were thankful or not, Andy Wolfe had no illusions that they had been drawn to the service either by him or the unusual edifice his ministrations had raised. The main attraction had to be the Honorable Daniel Parker, who had outpolled even Nixon in his district and who was already being talked about in the press as a prospect for the Senate and beyond. The popping flash of a *Record* photographer, whom Andy had permitted to work in the sanctuary since these were not regular services, drew his eye to the Congressman's handsome female family, propped up and grinning like so many china dolls in the front row. The only one missing was Felicia, and it was said that it had cost Dan Parker a pretty penny and a few job promises to seal the lips of the warden at the reform school where they took her after they found her hiding in Father Funston's attic. Dan and Arch Funston hadn't spoken to each other since, and Andy, with his new resolve to savor the humor of life, was rather enjoying watching their discomfort as they sat side by side and tried to ignore each other in front of the whole church.

If Howard Hilsman had had any sense, he would have taken the chair between Father Funston and Dan Parker himself. Howard was up there on the platform too, since he had moved into Judge Brooke's position as Chairman of the Republican Town Committee and would likely manage Parker's campaign if they decided to go for the Senate. The Hilsmans and Parkers were getting very thick these days. That bean pole of a Hilsman boy, young Tim, who was sitting beside his mother down there in the congregation, was going to work for Parker in his Washington office as soon as he got out of Yale. From what Andy understood, it was a near thing with Tim. They almost lost him to that pied piper of a chaplain up at Yale, Bill Coffin, and Howard was so worried about it that he came to Andy for help. Fortunately Andy, who hated getting involved in these family matters, didn't have to do a thing about it. When Howard threatened to cut his son off without a penny, the boy told him that he had just been fooling around down there in Washington. "Jeez, Dad, Julie Horner and that Arnold Schine were down there too, and they were even smoking pot, I saw them," Tim told his father by way of diverting the spotlight.

374

Howard took the information to Parker, who used it as the basis for what people now thought of as one of his finer editorials, and whatever else you might say about Dan Parker, you had to admit he was grateful.

It was almost time now, and Andy got out his glasses and the notes he had scribbled for the opening devotions he had been assigned as host minister. Getting just the right text for the occasion had taken quite a bit of thought. Anything too Christian wouldn't be appropriate for an essentially civic ceremony like this that would draw all sorts of people, from Father Reardon, there on his right, to a well-known atheist like Fielding Small, sitting down there along the left aisle with that little mouse of a wife. While he was thinking along these lines in planning the service, Andy enjoyed once more a rush of relief that Peters had resigned without fuss or scandal. Andy doubted that the fellow would ever have the subtlety to recognize a problem like selecting a text that wouldn't offend non-Christians. A member of the congregation from IBM said Peters was doing very well over there in Armonk, and Andy wasn't surprised to read a note somewhere that Peters would address the church's next national assembly on the subject: "Let's Streamline the Church with Electronics." That would be another thing in life that Andy would be glad to miss. His phlebitis wouldn't stand sitting through all those meetings. And would it be a sin in view of Audrey's feelings to give his own private thanks to God this day that Dr. Hammond had ordered him to give up going to Maine in summer and take the sun in Florida in winter instead? There could be compensations for growing old.

As combined choirs from all the churches flowed in processional down the aisles, singing, ". . . America, America, God shed his grace on thee, and crown thy good with brotherhood, from sea to shining sea," Andy hobbled up into the pulpit. Taking a good grip on the rails, he looked out over the crowd with a feeling of confidence that, by turning to the Old Testament, he would strike just the right note. When the music died he opened the big Bible in front of him and said: "Friends and neighbors of Worton, I have chosen as a text for today's Thanksgiving meditations one that I am sure you will all agree is most appropriate to those of us so fortunate as to live in a community such as this. It is a brief passage from Psalm Sixteen—'The lines have fallen for me in pleasant places; yea, I have a goodly heritage.'" Andy closed the book and let a well-timed silence pass during which he thought he saw people exchanging smiles in recognition of the aptness of his text. "Let us pray," he said. "Almighty God, we thank thee on this special day for our town, for our country, for our state, for our nation. We pray that thou wilt make us worthy of the manifold blessings thou hast bestowed upon us not only as Americans but particularly as dwellers in one of the pleasantest places in thy wide creation. Amen.

"And now it is my pleasure to invite into this pulpit a man who needs no introduction, I'm sure, to any man, woman or child in Worton. It is particularly fitting that the message of the day should be brought to us by our own elder, Congressman Daniel Parker, a native son of Worton whose whole life stands as a symbol of that greater American way of life for which we are here gathered to give thanks. Born in near poverty in a small and rustic New England village, Daniel Parker has risen to sit in the highest councils of this nation. I am sure that all of us will draw inspiration from him today. Congressman Parker."

There was one little bit of awkwardness when Andy's leg almost gave way as he tried to let Parker into the pulpit, but he managed to catch the back of a chair. Dan didn't notice, of course. His face was radiant as a search-light as he stepped up to offer himself to his constituents.

"I can only be humble at this time and in this place," Dan began. "I can only thank God, and ask you all to join me, for the fact that he has seen fit to return the leadership of this great nation of ours to a man of such proven faith as Richard M. Nixon. A Quaker, a friend and confidant of such men of God as Norman Vincent Peale and Billy Graham, Richard M. Nixon will lead this nation back to the godly heritage we celebrate today. I am grateful to be a foot soldier in this crusade which, with all our prayers, is certain to succeed . . ."

There was more along those lines, much more. Andy, who had been so delicate about religion that he had even omitted the name of Christ from his prayer, almost had to admire Parker's free-swinging partisanship, but then, judging from the polls, there were probably more Republicans than Christians in the audience. Unable to get his leg into a comfortable position, Andy got a little restless, but most of the people seemed to enjoy Parker's resounding assurances as to law and order, the rights of people to restrict their own property, higher profits and lower taxes, and the peace with honor which, under God, would arrive with "the dawn of a new Republicanism." Well, Andy could understand how the people of Worton would want things to get back to normal. God knows, he did too. He just wished his old friend Amos Brooke could be here to see how well things seemed to be turning out, after all. It was a shame, since Andy was sure that the judge had more to do with all of this than anyone would ever suspect. Life, Andy thought, was too often like being a laborer in the vineyard—you got to pick the grapes but seldom had a chance to taste the wine. The thought was so Biblical sounding that Andy got a paper out of his pocket and scratched it down. Might do for a sermon some day.

Andy was only conscious that Dan Parker had rolled to a stop when the organ broke into the opening bars of "Prayer of Thanksgiving." This was to be the recessional, and Andy rose rather unsteadily and took Parker's arm as the Congressman came down from the pulpit. They were to follow the choirs down the aisle, and Andy was glad all that tennis and swimming had given Parker adequate muscle for him to lean on. By the time they were moving through the congregation they were on the third verse of the hymn, and everybody warmed up. With four or five hundred people singing in unison and the sopranos shrilling a descant above them, the sound sent a kind of shivering thrill up Andy's spine. It was one of those moments when it was not only possible, but imperative, to believe in the triumph of the good and the right and in the God who would make this come to pass. It was a glory to be in his service. Along with the rest, Andy sang:

"We all do extol thee, thou Leader in battle,
And pray that thou still our Defender wilt be;
Let thy congregation escape tribulation;
Thy name be ever praised—O Lord, make us free."

From where he was standing in the back Jim Horner saw that vision of glory light Andy Wolfe's face like a shaft of sunshine. He was happy then that he hadn't after all been able to duck out of the service as he had planned before the recessional started. For a while there as he watched the old minister squirming in his seat and jotting notes during Dan Parker's interminable litany of Republican righteousness, he wondered if Andy, too, had lost his faith.

There were moments during the service when Jim himself wished mightily that he could have joined in the chorus of thanksgiving. Although most of the faces around him were strange—he could remember hearing when he was on the church board that something like a third of the congregation turned over every year in the mandatory comings and goings of migrant executives—they glowed with the same aura of great expectations that had so attracted Susan and himself so many years ago. And haunting his mind as he looked around was a conversation he'd overheard on the church steps between two casually dressed, leggy young matrons. "Oh, hi there," said one, "I haven't seen you for ages." "Well, you know how it is," the other replied, "between tennis and golf the summer just goes." Wasn't that what it was all about after all? No wonder people smiled and nodded at each other when Andy read his appropriate text. Here in this sanctuary of good living, Jim's doubts and failures seemed unreal, a kind of bad dream that would surely go away.

Except it didn't, and he felt for a while that it had been a mistake to come into the church at all. It was a bit of sentimental tomfoolery, a kind of last salute to what might have been. Actually, he had been planning to drive as far as possible on a holiday in hopes that there would be fewer trucks on the road. Passing the church on the way to the thruway, he saw the crowds and, on impulse, joined them. Until he got inside, he had never imagined that so many people in Worton would go to church on Thanksgiving, and before he knew it he was pinned down in a pew. Climbing out over the women's legs would have caused everybody to look at him, and the last thing he wanted was that sort of attention. He could just hear the whispers. "Oh, there's Jim Horner. I haven't seen him in church since . . . well, you know, what happened to his wife, and . . ."

Along about the middle of Parker's mind-numbing oration, Jim's roving eye picked out a familiar flow of long hair. Though he couldn't see her face for the press of people, he didn't have to. He'd not likely forget the feel and smell of that hair . . . A witch in church. Could the people around her guess, would they believe it if they could? Probably not. Witches, like tragedy, belonged in darker times and drabber places. Well, the sight of her at least gave him a small thing for which to return thanks: although he had pulled out of the business so that Paul Richards could afford to go on cooking hamburgers for the neighbors on his sunny Darien patio, Jim had ignored that preposterous letter from Detroit. He no longer needed, wanted, that kind of money.

When the congregation rose to sing, Jim tried to push out, but a lady offered to share her hymnal with him. And so it happened that Jim saw that reassuring look on Andy Wolfe's face. It made the whole uncomfortable hour worthwhile.

Though he was hoping to get away without speaking to anybody, Jim found himself squeezed at the door into a confrontation with Andy Wolfe. "Ah, Jim, I was surprised and pleased, of course, to see you here . . . I thought you'd left us . . ."

"I'm on my way, Andy."

"Oh . . . well, and where are you off to?"

"I really don't know, Andy. I'll be stopping in the city,

I expect, to see Julie, and then maybe heading on down to Florida for the winter."

"Well, that's nice. The doctor's ordered me to take the sun too, you know," and then his eyes and voice strayed away to the couple behind Jim. Letting go of Jim's hand, Andy gave them his most silvery smile. "Welcome to our church. You're new in Worton, aren't you? . . ."

It wasn't hard to get away after all. Jim was buckled into his car and almost at the ramp to the thruway before he thought of one other stop he still wanted to make. He wheeled around and drove into the cemetery under a bare arch of trees, as dead now in November as the people they sheltered. He stopped and got out beside a simple marble square inscribed: Susan Smith Horner, 1928– 1968. Actually, he felt that it was right to leave her here in Worton, where she so desperately wanted to belong. It was the rest of them who had somehow made it impossible for her, and she would not have wanted to follow them away.

It was only when Jim's car slipped under the big sign reading NEW YORK AND WEST that he finally began to let go. He hadn't decided where he was heading—he'd mentioned Florida on the spur of the moment because Andy had asked him; people his age didn't just wander the roads or have no idea what they were going to do. It suited exactly the way he had been thinking during those long months when he was winding up his affairs and trying to come to some terms with what had happened to him. He doubted he'd ever be able to let go completely, but at least he realized that the old desire for a place that was safe and sure—it had, in fact, seized him again in church—was a dangerous illusion. So far as he could see, life didn't have much to do with getting *any*where. Mostly, it was all process, all change, from season to season, from generation to generation. Man's folly—come on, *his*, Jim Horner's, folly—was to believe that there was some end, some place, some possession, some state of body or mind, some Heaven in which for the fortunate who dwelt there, the natural laws of change would be suspended—and for those who so believed, reaching such an end justified any means . . . Christians could cheerfully watch heretics burn, whites could set dogs on blacks invading their neighborhoods, people in peaceable kingdoms could expend most of their wealth for deadlier and deadlier weapons to guard imaginary borders, a gentleman like Judge Brooke could turn the financial screws to squeeze a troublemaking Jim Horner out of his quiet community, a Pauline Church could forgo love to be at last in the pages of the Good Book, a Jim Horner himself could go from job to job to meet a mortgage that could never be paid off . . . Maybe he was giving them too much credit, but it struck him that the young people were at least glimpsing the nakedness of the Emperor, and that some of their perception might just be rubbing off on him too. The question was, what would they—or he—do about it?

Even in the privacy of his own car, Jim was somewhat embarrassed by these woolly thoughts. It was what came of being alone so much, of having so much time to think. Probably the people out there who saw him as just a hard-luck guy were nearer to the truth. Here he was— children gone "wrong," wife dead by her own hand, out of a job, damn near run out of town. Wasn't he pushing it a little to hope that through all this he'd found some high road to salvation? Wasn't it just wishful thinking? God, wishful thinking of the same order that had once caused him to describe the troubles at Little Rock as a bright star in democracy's crown, much to the delight of Himself Upstairs, instead of as the first black hole in the sky. Time alone, as they said, would tell, and he was by no means sure he had enough of that left either. How much more sense it would make for him to be back there in Worton still, to be among the clear-eyed constituents he'd seen nodding their agreement with Congressman Parker's promise to put God back on the throne in four, or at the most eight, years! But he also knew in his guts— for whatever it was worth—that he was through with that kind of sense. For him it was, literally, non-sense. As Harry Margolis had once advised him, there was no going back.

Jim wondered what his mother would think if she could

see into his head now, and he was grateful that she had not lived to try, that she had insisted that the picture and scrapbook from the piano top be buried with her. Thinking about her now, Jim suddenly recalled with amusement her reaction when he'd once wanted to recite Robert Herrick's "To the Virgins" in front of the class. Though he wasn't by any means sure what a virgin was, he had picked the poem out of *The Standard Book of British and American Verse,* a favorite of his mother's, for very good reasons: it was reasonably short and the sing-song of it made it easy to memorize. "You're too young to know what that means, James, but I won't have a son of mine reciting a thing like that," Emily Horner had said. "Why, do you know that Mr. Herrick was a minister who was once driven out of the church by Puritans for his filthy thoughts?" Naturally, that was enough to make him learn the poem right away, and it was still with him. He hadn't thought about it in years, but he had a feeling that old Herrick had stumbled on a gospel that might just make of Jim Horner a true believer once more.

As the car sped on, Jim recited at full volume:

"Gather ye rosebuds while ye may,
Old Time is still a flying;
And this same flower that smiles today
Tomorrow will be dying . . ."

People passing him on the road no doubt were looking at him as if they thought he was crazy. So be it. It felt wonderful after being so terribly sane for so very, very long. . . .

Historical Romance

Sparkling novels of love and conquest against the colorful background of historical England. Here are books you will savor word by word, page by spellbinding page.

☐ AFTER THE STORM—Williams	23081-3	$1.50
☐ ALTHEA—Robins	23268-9	$1.50
☐ AMETHYST LOVE—Danton	23400-2	$1.50
☐ AN AFFAIR OF THE HEART Smith	23092-9	$1.50
☐ AUNT SOPHIE'S DIAMONDS Smith	23378-2	$1.50
☐ A BANBURY TALE—MacKeever	23174-7	$1.50
☐ CLARISSA—Arnett	22893-2	$1.50
☐ DEVIL'S BRIDE—Edwards	23176-3	$1.50
☐ ESCAPADE—Smith	23232-8	$1.50
☐ A FAMILY AFFAIR—Mellow	22967-X	$1.50
☐ THE FORTUNE SEEKER Greenlea	23301-4	$1.50
☐ THE FINE AND HANDSOME CAPTAIN—Lynch	23269-7	$1.50
☐ FIRE OPALS—Danton	23112-7	$1.50
☐ THE FORTUNATE MARRIAGE Trevor	23137-2	$1.50
☐ THE GLASS PALACE—Gibbs	23063-5	$1.50
☐ GRANBOROUGH'S FILLY Blanshard	23210-7	$1.50
☐ HARRIET—Mellows	23209-3	$1.50
☐ HORATIA—Gibbs	23175-5	$1.50

FREE
Fawcett Books Listing

There is Romance, Mystery, Suspense, and Adventure waiting for you inside the Fawcett Books Order Form. And it's yours to browse through and use to get all the books you've been wanting... but possibly couldn't find in your bookstore.

This easy-to-use order form is divided into categories and contains over 1500 titles by your favorite authors.

So don't delay—take advantage of this special opportunity to increase your reading pleasure.

Just send us your name and address and 25¢ (to help defray postage and handling costs).

FAWCETT BOOKS GROUP
P.O. Box C730, 524 Myrtle Ave., Pratt Station, Brooklyn, N.Y. 11205

Name_____
           (please print)

Address_____
City_____ State_____ Zip_____
Do you know someone who enjoys books? Just give us their names and addresses and we'll send them an order form too!

Name_____
Address_____
City_____ State_____ Zip_____

Name_____
Address_____
City_____ State_____ Zip_____